KNIGHT'S ERRAND

AN ADVENTURE NOIR

BY

JOHNNY CAT

Copyright © 2018 J.E. Harris

All rights reserved.

ISBN-13:978-1-7287-0694-8

Dedicated to the greatest guy in the world
from the greatest guy in the world.

ME

CONTENTS

1. JANUARY 1939 JUNGLE ATTACK…1
2. SIX MONTHS LATER JULY 1939 HOLLYWOOD JUNGLE ATTACK…10
3. FIVE MONTHS EARLIER FEBRUARY 1939 BURMESE JUNGLE…22
4. SIX MONTHS LATER EARLY AUGUST 1939 HOLLYWOOD…25
5. EARLY AUGUST 1939 TIJUANA BOUND…34
6. LATE AUGUST 1939 CANTINA ALLEY…53
7. LATE AUGUST 1939 SWEATY DREAMS…57
8. FOUR MONTHS EARLIER APRIL 1939 SINGAPORE…65
9. LATE AUGUST 1939 ILLEGAL ESCAPE…74
10. LATE AUGUST 1939 THE OLD PLANTATION…85
11. FOUR MONTHS EARLIER APRIL 1939 VENGENCE SOUGHT…96
12. FIVE MONTHS LATER EARLY SEPTEMBER 1939…101
13. ONE MONTH EARLIER EARLY AUGUST 1939 THE TIDE…106
14. ONE MONTH LATER EARLY SEPTEMBER 1939 FLORIDA…113
15. ONE MONTH LATER LATE OCTOBER 1939 MEXICO…117
16. LATE OCTOBER 1939 BRUNO STRIKES…127
17. LATE OCTOBER 1939 A RUDE DAWN…142
18. LATE OCTOBER 1939 THE CALL…146
19. SHANGHAI…151

20. NIGHT STALK…154

21. BLACK CAT…158

22. HUNG CHOW…165

23. SUMMIT MEETING…174

24. RAINY RIDE…187

25. NIGHT FLIGHT…189

26. TRIBE OF THE POTTY PEOPLE…204

27. JUNGLE STOP…227

28. THICKWILLY…238

29. AKBAR FATUI…262

30. TROUBLE AT SEA…279

31. ISLAND REFUGE…301

32. SEASIDE TRYST…316

33. HOSPITAL…332

34. THE NEXT MOVE…359

35. ALPINE SPRING…365

36. DEATH SHIP…389

37. TRAIN TO NOWHERE…403

CHAPTER 1--JANUARY 1939
JUNGLE ATTACK

Mosquitoes loud as Messerschmitts. Stings of their bloodsucking can become almost a pleasant sensation if you try. And I have to try, Bruno thought, as he inched his way through thigh-high mud and wallow thick with writhing bodies, bodies that if the imagination fooled the mind enough, could become soothing, causing a person to not want them to stop.

Only his determination and will tempered the seething sensations around his thighs as he remembered his reason for being where he was, remembered that he was under orders to bring forth the fruits of honor and the honey of glorious expedition for the bosom of the Reich.

Above the sawing sounds of the voracious insects came the growing rhythm of distant native drums. Above that steady sound a low moaning came across the pit of blackened swamp that revealed a beast out for its nightly feeding. "We two are alike perhaps," Bruno thought. "Only I am better." A quick flash of lightning coupled with an apocalyptic crash of thunder caused the night sky to give rent to a sudden torrent of crushing rain. Noticing a slight change in the shade of blackness Bruno realized his companions were where they needed to be to make the strike. The glow and rise and swell of fervent voices grew thicker through the trees. Only an occasional glimpse of not so distant torchlights slowly began to reveal the outline of a huge native hut slightly tilted on stilts over the water in the dark between the moss and rotted fungus of the trees. The circular hut, though it was made from bamboo and palm fronds, stood like a creature, slightly hunched, as if ready to strike. Several native skiffs were tethered to the thick vegetation beneath. Beyond the large hut were several smaller huts, also built over the water and supported by the branches of the thick trees.

    The signal was given. A cobra, slowly eyeing the scene of darkness, its nostrils assailed by the stench of rot and fermenting organisms bloating in the swamp, was unable to notice the signal, imperceptible as it was. The three men moved in quick military precision towards the primal sounds of the hut. The hut, still billowing flickering light from a hundred ceremonial candles, and belching the overpowering stench of pungent incense through its circular thatched roof resembled a smoldering volcano. From inside this potential of doom came the steady rise in volume of the drums, punctuated by weird cries piercing the dark, wholly unaware of the pressing fate from the advance of the three Germans.

    Bruno was only barely cognizant of Hamm's advance, trusting to Schlitz to be in the place that he needed to be. Ducking under water ten yards from the living hut on stilts, Bruno climbed a slime covered pole, grabbed a rim of frail wood, pulled himself up over the edge silently thanking the howling monsoon winds for not only drowning out the sounds of his invasion, but for also wiping clean the bits of flotsam clinging to his skin.

Once on the deck of boards rimming the hut he moved as the shadow of a ghost along the flimsy wooden railings towards the native guard posted on the rim. The guard's whole awareness had been slightly averted towards the primal scene within the hut. Taking his chance, Bruno quickly grabbed the native's windpipe, and neatly slit the brown throat. Bruno eased the body to the floorboards. In the peripheral of his eye he caught one of his partners moving into position on the roof. Another lightning flash and eye contact was all that was needed to make ready for the signal.

Bruno peered inside the draped entrance of the hut. Incense and smoke was so thick within, it trapped even the light of the torches, creating spherical pockets of light among the dark forms writhing to the rhythms of snake skin covered drums. Bruno's eyes moved up to the roof, where a small hole was beginning to appear. Schlitz had made it to the roof and was slowly cutting an entrance with a machete. Below him, unaware, naked savages slathered in ceremonial oils grappled themselves in time to the incessant beating of the drummers on one side of the hut. Those in front fell prostrate on the straw and tar floor in front of an animal skin covered throne, groveling in honors towards a figure on the dais. In the smoke and flickering light, he realized the figure was their queen.

The woman on the throne laid back, eyes rolled into her head, oil so thick on her skin that it dripped from her thighs onto the flimsy bamboo alter that she lay on. She was clad in only a patch of loincloth draped around her hips, while from her neck hung various gems of shapes and sizes. Raven black hair hung past shoulders muscular and tan. Bruno stopped, though only for an instant, surprising himself on his own loss of focus, as he gazed temporarily at the queen. This was like no woman he had ever seen.

Bruno ran his eyes covetously over the sun bronzed figure of the almost naked girl. Her exquisite facial features gave a strong hint of European bone structure, very different from the primal congregation she had enthralled in her spiritual grasp. Her eyes were glazed. Around her neck the series of assorted jewels did little to hide her full heaving breasts. With her back to the maddening chanting of the crowd, her breath came in shorter gasps as she moved slowly towards the large statue before her. As she moved, the soft parchment of animal skin that loosely covered her loins also revealed much of her shapely hips. Bruno noticed her long dark hair was kept in place by an ornately woven headband. Mounted in the center of the headband, just above the queen's hypnotic black eyes was an exquisite greenstone, formed into an unusual natural shape with odd markings. He licked his lips. Even more enticing than the girl was the stone in her golden tiara. This is what he had planned his mission for, this is what the Fuehrer had wanted him to retrieve, and this is what he was going to steal for himself.

The queen's raven hair was now slick with damp passion. Passion for the large stone idol in front of her. She gazed half lidded at the impervious stone face. This was the god of her people.

Whitish green in color, smooth of texture, the idol was of an amazingly fit and virile man, but with a face very reptilian in shape, as if a snake had assumed human form. Six feet in height, though sitting in a lotus position, the stone green god's arms were extended in front of him, as if ready to embrace his human queen. Its face had a youthful but wise look to it, and it wore a slight smile as if it were privy to some unknown great knowledge. In the center of the god's forehead was a receptacle, an opening that resembled a third eye.

As powerful a presence as this Apollo like figure was, it was the queen that commanded all the energy in the room. She swayed erotically, her back arched, slowly thrusting her hips forward towards the statue, spreading her legs farther apart with each movement, her loincloth slowly opening to reveal her nakedness.

The drummers and dancers were reaching ecstatic glory through their chanting as the queen slowly began to mount the pedestal of the strangely smiling god. Slowly and deliberately, she began to caress the smooth hardness of the deity, as if wanting to become one with it.

Moaning louder than her subjects, she leaned forward, and while still coveting the idol, touched the greenstone of her golden headdress to that of the idol's third eye. It was at that time new demons burst into the hut.

Schlitz had been stealthily cutting his way through the thatched roof when a miscalculation of weight on the freshly weakened coverings brought his premature entrance into the middle of the ceremonial hut causing him to fall between the queen's dais and the southern opening. The savages, wrapped in the fury of the ritual bought Schlitz a few seconds of precious recovery time. Bruno, surprised, but ready, leapt into the room from the western doorway, machine gun spitting death. Four natives fell before the ritual was broken and the natives, realizing something was wrong, descended upon the intruders.

Hamm, carrying the third element of surprise, blazed through the east entrance, firing into the room as well. Within seconds the room was crawling with bodies and confusion. Through the fog and the fumes, hot lead cut through the flesh of the disoriented villagers. They still fought the Germans back, armed as they were with ill shaped knives which had been hanging from their hips, and a fury brought on by religious fervor.

A tall crazed chanter pounced on Hamm from the side, slashing a wicked gash into his right thigh. By reflex, Hamm brought his left arm up, and using the momentum of the native's initial thrust, ran the dagger between the brute's own ribs, piercing his savage heart.

Schlitz moved to the south end of the room, simultaneously slashing and shooting brown limbs and torsos. In the thick fumes of gunfire mixed with incense, Bruno saw into the center of the hut. The glow from the torches showed that the queen had not stirred from her pleasuring of the idol. Her head was tilted far back now, greenstone exposed and gleaming, released from the idol's third eye, while her body wracked in throes of ecstasy. Bruno leapt to the center of the hut and grabbed the crown from the unaware queen. He turned and bolted to the southern part of the room, joining the side of Hamm. The two stood back to back, like a loud two headed carnage dealing beast. Slowly moving towards Schlitz, who had by now cleared an exit out of the southern opening, the three joined together as an unstoppable force. Piles of native bodies grew higher as the three Nazis blazed and carved their way through a wall of human flesh. Hamm's ammo ran dry first, and as he stopped to change a clip, a burly headed native broke through the hot lead circle and grabbed Hamm's throat, stabbing the surprised German in the groin. Hamm quickly reacted, pulling nappy locks of the contender and forcing the savage's head and hair into a ceremonial fire. The native screamed as his hair caught fire and his facial flesh peeled back pink from the flames. Hamm struck the native hard, knocking him into his fellows and upsetting several ceremonial torches. The fires began to spread quickly, brought on by the oil and tar that coated the flooring.

As the violence raged within the hut, the visceral fluids of the freshly mutilated natives, mixing with the dirt and soot of the smoldering floor created a sticky paste. The fire, now totally out of control was eating the outer edges of the hut, licking and burning the fallen bodies, filling the air with the sickly sweet smell of burning human agony, their final cries of death creating a crescendo of horror.

Fate conspired with the S.S. Officers as a craggy burning ceiling beam fell between the Nazis and the screaming natives, effectively giving the Germans their much needed open escape route through the south entrance, and blocking further advancement of the brown skinned mongrels.

Bruno was glad to note as he exited the now stench ridden fuming hovel that one of the native skiffs he had noticed before the attack was tethered to supporting poles right beneath his feet under the catwalk. The three, still firing into the hut, backed out of the doorway and dove off the pier and clambered into the skiff.

The north end of the hut was totally consumed with fire, and the entire structure creaked and groaned as it slowly began to collapse into the water. As Bruno, Schlitz and Hamm used the long bamboo poles in the skiff to guide themselves away, they could hear screams of the burning bodies that were dropping and silenced into gurgling sizzles as they slapped the surface of the swamp.

The usually placid surface writhed and splashed with bodies, some burning, some screaming, others scrambling into other skiffs tethered along the other huts. The agitation and unusual commotion caused another disturbance – this one just under the surface of the water - in darkened caves where pockets of air, fed by natural ventilation shafts to the surface of the marsh allowed crocodiles to gather and breed, and to have a place to drag their hapless victims. The stench of burning flesh and movement of potential meat on the surface of the water proved too strong to resist to the dozens of ravenous crocs now surfacing around the commotion of the fleeing humans. To the cacophonous shrieks of the night was now added the sickening crunch of iron muscled jaws on bone.

Bruno and company had worked their skiff several yards away from the tormented natives that were now pursuing them in their own skiffs, and from the few straggling crocs. Up in the trees, natives ran along makeshift arboreal trails created from vines and tree limbs to form sturdy pathways though the interlocking branches of the jungle.

Spears and curses rained down on the three Nazis at first but became fewer with some well placed volleys from the Nazi's weapons. As their skiff sailed away from the fires of disaster and into the inky darkness of the jungle, Bruno asked, "How is everyone feeling?"

"I feel fine."

"I seem to be losing a lot of blood," said Hamm.

"Schlitz, keep pushing while I check his wound."

Bruno could barely make out the wound in the dark, but he could see enough to know it was bad.

"Don't vorry Hamm, I'll get you out."

"Yavol, mein Capitan. Mitt you in charge, I know I vill make it."

"Chus tink," exclaimed Schlitz as he pushed the skiff into open water, "Ve did it! Ve got der sacred stone for Der Fuehrer!"

A wry smile played around Bruno's lips in the dark. "Ya" he thought. "I did it. The sacred stone is mine!"

CHAPTER 2 --SIX MONTHS LATER JULY 1939 HOLLYWOOD JUNGLE ATTACK

The heat from the key lights was stifling. The drums were getting closer and louder. Grimacing, I carefully inched along the trail, remembering my mark, and keeping a firm grasp on the stock of my rifle. My back was killing me. It had been a wild evening of nightclubbing with one of the make up girls from the set, ending up in a late night at Louie's Lounge, and my head felt as if German Messerschmitts had been dive bombing it all night. In front of me, Gumbo, my native guide, casually known as Ernie, made his way around the foam boulder. Gumbo was an impressive black, straight and tall, with a highly starched and creased khaki uniform, a bright red fez cap perched on his clean looking head. The jungle was thick with cigar smoke, accentuated by the light sensual fragrance of my co-star's perfume and perfectly applied scented make-up. My co-star's name was Aqua Velva, and she was one of those starlets who were only in front of the camera because of her talents off camera. She followed close behind me, trying her best to emote fear. Her perfectly manicured nails constantly readjusted the loose curls in her glamour shot blond coiffure. She wore khaki as well; only the buttons on her blouse were fighting a losing battle against the pressure that was all female and fighting to be free. Her riding pants were tight where it is good to be tight. Her designer heels were of the type that cost a lot to have but were of little substance. Just like Aqua herself.

Behind her, carrying empty bundles and dressed in modest nondescript shorts, was a mish mash of jungle savages direct from darkest East Los Angeles. Gipper the Chimp, my faithful primate companion, was off abusing himself behind a palm.

"Shush, Bwana Dick," whispered Gumbo. "We enter forbidden jungle, home of the Mombak tribe."

"These Mombaks fierce?" I asked.

"They cannibal, Bwana Dick. They eat all who enter village."

"That may be, Gumbo, but those natives have the Sacred Stone of Ya-Ha. I promised Little Johnny in the hospital that we would get the stone for the Mombassa Museum in time for his birthday. I can't let the little fellow down. We must go on."

"Oh, but what if we don't make it, darling?" feigned Aqua.

I turned to her with a determined grin, furrowed my eyebrows, and said in a clear bold voice for all the jungle to hear "We shall make it, for I am Dick Hardwing of the Jungle Patrol. I am honor bound to rid the jungle of all that is not right and good. I will protect you my dear! And once I have that sacred stone and brought that evil witch doctor to justice, we will help these poor ignorant natives return to the simple happy life they led before. Right, Gipper?"

"Ook-ook-eek-eek!" Gipper happily danced in circles, his long hairy simian arms waving in the air, and then he proceeded to clamber over to my leg, positioning his groin against my knee for soft undulation. We all gave a hearty laugh. I patted his fuzzy little head. "Not now, Gipper – first the sacred stone." He unengaged himself and stiffly walked to the trees, where he swung up into the branches, molesting himself along the way with joyful glee.

Suddenly the drums stopped. We froze. There was a beat of silence, then a loud sudden THUNK as a spear seemed to appear from nowhere in a tree to our right. Aqua let out a scream. As if on a hidden signal the air burst with high pitched yelps. The Mombaks attacked!

"We have been discovered! Fire at will!" I shouted. Gumbo and I let go with a few dozen shots, each punctuated in between by Aqua's shrieks. Our native bearers immediately dropped their bundles and ran, many making only three or four steps before being struck with a spear. Aqua stood in the center of commotion, blasting her lungs and managing to pop another button on her blouse for her efforts. Spears, thrown clumsily by the attacking natives, clattered uselessly around us.

Aqua gained power for an extra loud scream, as a Mombak warrior grabbed her from behind and lifted her over his shoulder and stole her, stumbling away through the bushes and trees. Then, as if on cue, the warriors were gone, and the jungle was quiet, leaving only Gumbo, me, and a few trembling bearers in shocked silence.

"They've taken Aqua!" Gumbo shouted, barely able to contain his relief.

"We must save her!" I declared grimly. "We can't let those fiends have their way with her. Come Gumbo! Come Gipper!" The three of us charged the four dozen yards and broke through the jungle into the clearing of the Mombak village.

Rubber skulls were perched atop pointed stakes in front of the four huts that comprised the whole of the native village. The huts formed a semicircle around a low fire on which sat a large black pot. Aqua was standing, bound, but unfortunately not gagged, in the center of the misting waist high pot, and she was screaming bloody murder. Mombaks gyrated, some jitterbugging, all had spears raised and pointed towards the pot.

"While they are busy with Aqua, let's get the sacred stone. It must be in that hut over there," I whispered loudly, pointing to a hut we hadn't seen before. This hut was apart from the others, and since it was larger, darker, and had bigger rubber skulls, it had to be the evil witch doctor's lair. Gumbo and I slowly crept around the perimeter of the dancers. Though they were only five feet away, they seemed to be too concerned about the contents of the pot to notice. In seconds we were inside the witch doctor's hut.

Once inside, Gumbo stood just to the side of the entrance and peered out to watch for disturbances whilst I slung my rifle over my shoulder and searched for the sacred stone. It wasn't hard to find. The object that had been causing all this trouble set on a makeshift shrine in the middle of the dirt floor. The shrine was basically a table with fancy zebra skins for place mats, and stood about three feet in height, with peacock feathers pinned to the sides for decoration. Small crudely carved effigies and various bones lay out in circles surrounding the prized icon. The sacred stone itself was six inches in height and just as big around. A well placed key light just behind it gave the green icon an eerie inner glow as it sat impressively on the alter. The incongruity of electricity and indoor lighting among a tribe of half naked savages seemed to go unnoticed by everyone concerned. I grabbed the sacred stone, careful not to disturb the shrine. The stone was not heavy, about the same weight and feel as glass, but it was bulky. Moving swiftly, I took up one of several skins by the side of the altar and wrapped up my prize.

"Here, Gumbo," I commanded. "Take the sacred stone and head back out the way we came. If you can provide a brief distraction when you get back to the trail, I might be able to get to Aqua. We can rendezvous with whatever is left of our porters back in camp." Gumbo took off out the entrance and to the right of where we had come in. He scrambled with the stone tucked in the animal skin and stuffed inside his shirt next to his ebony skin. He headed back around the native huts, darting from one dark entranceway to the other, his form blending with the grotesque shadows of the dancers that the rising flames under the cooking pot were throwing onto the squalid huts. When he got to the beginning of the trail, he stood erect, faced the dancers, and brought out the green glass stone from its hiding place. With both hands he waved it high above his mocking face and laughed in a mighty, hearty tone: "I done did dood it! Da sacred stone beese mine!" The natives stopped their grotesque and uncoordinated dancing and drumming. All eyes were on Gumbo. The witch doctor, ancient, shriveled, with random gray patches of steel wire hair on his wrinkled head, glared with bloodshot eyes as he sat on a small leather pedestal. "Death to the blasphemer!" he spat from his almost toothless mouth and pointed accusingly at Gumbo.

A beat of a second after the command was given, the frothy natives burst into a screaming shouting frenzy, a roiling, broiling sea of hatred and excitement. Aqua's high pitched screech skipped like an aural stone over it all. The gang of natives moved as one towards Gumbo, waving their spears and shields. Gumbo turned to flee, followed by the entire tribe down the narrow jungle trail. The trail proved to be too narrow for some, however, and more than one slipped, stumbled, and outright fell over the other in their unfocused attempt to pursue. Seeing my opportunity, I raced a beeline for Aqua. The old witch doctor tried to disassemble his small cross-legged figure from the leather stool and stumbled stiffly into my path. I stopped long enough to give the wizened form a solid cracking uppercut to his stubble chin that, even though it came to within inches of actually striking him, knocked his body five feet to my right into a pile of vases and water jugs, smashing all, and giving him a much needed dousing. His crumpled head lifted, started to speak, then slumped over, finished. I chuckled heartily out loud, "Ha! Ha! That is for my peace loving jungle friends everywhere!"

"Save me, Dick Hardwing, save me!" Aqua said bravely, her chin held high, as she struggled with her bonds while standing in the pot. I gave an athletic sprint over to where she was, and as I got there, she relaxed and fainted. I quickly undid the knots that held her wrists and picked her up out of the waist high water with both my arms bulging. I tossed her lightly face down over my left shoulder, her head and blond curly hair angling down my back. Using my right arm, I swung my rifle around and out of its shoulder sling, only to fire point blank towards the receding jungle warriors. Though they were several yards down the trail by this time, I managed to fell a good score of them. Another blast took two more. This time I heard another rifle blast from the other end of the shouting natives. I knew that Gumbo, hearing my blast, turned on his pursuers and opened fire. I smiled grimly, knowing that Gumbo and I had played our time honored trick of a trap on the witless natives. No matter how many times we did it, they always fell for it. This particular jungle path was very narrow, with fat boulders, taller than a man on each side, and extremely flat and vertical, no place to grab a proper hold. We had managed to bottleneck the entire tribe on this small path. There was no retreat and no advance, and we were managing to weed out the warriors with each successive blast of our guns. Their puny rubbery ended spears bounced harmlessly around us. Except the one stray well aimed spear that smacked Aqua square in the behind. That was when the show ended.

"SON OF A BITCH!"

I would have had better luck trying to shove butter up a wildcat's ass with a red hot poker than trying to restrain Aqua from squirming and clawing her way off my back.

"I WANT THAT BASTARD'S HEAD!"

Aqua had only one volume level. Bullhorn.

"Cut!" yelled Percy, our short and decidedly sweet director, fluttering his hands and fingers like an out of control sea anemone. He came floating over to where we were. Aqua had regained her steady stance, with a face red as a persimmon. The extras and production crew quickly backed away and braced themselves for the onslaught of Aqua's personality. "Honey, it will never happen again," he sputtered in a high nasal voice.

"Damn right it won't," Aqua hissed. As she and Percy became embroiled in her perceived injustices, the make up girl immediately ran over to me, powdering my face and running her fingers through my hair. "Get away from him, bitch." Aqua's attention was now redirected to the dark haired make up girl that obviously prided herself in her hands on approach to her job on and off the set. The make up girl gave me a knowing grin that brought back the night before in sudden clarity for a split second. I returned her grin, and as she brought her hand down from my face, her other hand slipped a small piece of folded paper in my shirt pocket. She then turned, ignoring Aqua, and slinked away. Percy saw this sudden interruption as an opportunity to get away himself, lisping commands to everyone, clapping his hands, and shouting "Get set for the next shot, c'mon let's make magic, people!"

"I saw that! You'll never change, will you? You were supposed to be with me last night. I worry myself sick when you don't show up, and then I read in the gossip column this morning that you were seen in the company of some cheap little tramp."

Aqua paused only long enough to catch her breath and begin her tirade again, only this time with greater energy, as if she had had an extra bowl of bitch flakes that morning for breakfast. I was preparing to open my mouth and provide some feeble explanation as soon as she took her next breath when the situation turned worse.

CRASH!

Aqua's tirade was squelched by the sudden sound of shattering glass. Aqua and I both turned towards the source of the sound. Ernie, or Gumbo, depending, stood just off the main set, his eyes two round blobs of white set against the midnight hue of his skin, his mouth hanging open, tongue trying to form words, and his hands, big and powerful that once held a sacred green stone, now suddenly and definitely empty. Scattered green glass now lay at his feet in a thousand pieces.

"KEE-RIST!" The director was the one having a hissy fit now. "That's it for the day! That prop cost a fortune! Having it replaced will kill the rest of our budget and delay our wrap!" One thing I realized as I watched this tirade was that I had never noticed a man to spit as much as a part of his natural conversation. "The studio heads are going to roast me alive!"

"Don't worry, the studio heads are too Kosher to go for boiled ham," I smirked. The director glared "bitch" at me and looked as if he wanted to slap me silly. Instead he proceeded to flit over to the scene of the accident, taking care of business in a quick and hasty fashion. Percy may have been a sissy, but he was a talented sissy.

I smiled to myself, thankful for the respite from having to deal with a distraught Aqua. I turned away, walking slowly while cupping my hands to light a Lucky, and wondering which cocktail bar I would treat the little make up girl to. Or maybe I should just go out myself and take a chance on romance. Either way I needed a drink.

I had almost managed to get beyond the main lights when I heard Aqua's razor sharp voice; "Sterling, don't think you can sneak out so easily on me like that!"

She started at me at a hot trot, wagging her finger at my bemused face. "You may think you're hot – SHIT!" She froze in midair, a lovely statue with her foot arched up before her. "I just stepped in monkey shit!"

This outburst of feminine screeching brought Gipper out of his onanistic frenzy. He had climbed to the top of the trees, and this had brought him up to the metal beams that crisscrossed the underside of the studio's ceilings. Here he had braced himself into a comfortable position. Hearing the cry of the female, Gipper moved as fast as his little chimp legs could take him. He was on Aqua's leg in a dry hump frenzy before she had a chance to draw her last breath. As I turned once more to head to the soundstage door, my last vision was of a couple of grim faced production assistants attempting to pry Gipper's groin from around Aqua's khaki covered thighs. Between the screams of Aqua, the lustful grunts of Gipper, and the unnaturally high pitched ravings of Percy, the air became thick enough with cursing and ranting to draw everyone's attention to the epicenter of anarchy, allowing me to finally disappear out of the soundstage. Once outside, I was able to gain exit through the gates of the studio, toss a quick wave to the guard on duty and disappear into the relatively quiet bustle of Gower Boulevard in Hollywood.

The sun was doing its best to fight the reddening sky that was pushing the yellow fireball down behind the rooftops of surrounding studios and palm trees. As shadows leaned, I made the short two block walk towards Santa Monica Boulevard that brought me inside of a small joint affectionately called Louie's Lounge. The place was dark, quiet, and the late lunch crowd was long gone, leaving a lone schizophrenic playing eight ball with himself in the center of the room. The jukebox by the rear in the corner booth cooed a slow swing number. Louie was behind the bar, a staunch imposing figure in a white apron with hair to match, meticulously cleaning the inside of a beer glass with a well used rag. He gave me a quick glance and I winked "the usual" back at him and tossed him a fin. He smiled as he set the drink before me. "Well, well. If it ain't me good friend Mr. Sterling Hanover – or should I say Mr. Dick Hardwing of the Jungle Patrol, live and in person! Good day's shooting?"

"It was for awhile. It was so good I almost started believing that jungle nonsense myself. Then my leading lady decided to pitch a fit, so I decided to play hooky."

"Oh, Percy ain't gonna like that."

"What can he do? So he complains to the studio head, big deal. Those boys owe me anyway, what with all the revenue that comes in from what I do. I'm a popular boy, Louie. King of the jungle movies, idol to adventure starved kids everywhere. That's a lot of Saturday morning popcorn. Besides, Percy has too many problems right now to do any more shooting today."

"Say, ain't you about done with that new adventure serial?"

"Yea, I figure we have about twelve chapters worth – once they stick in the stock footage and all."

"Awe, can't wait to see it. And speakin' of serials – oh, uh, cereal – my kids just got enough boxtops to join the Dick Hardwing Jungle Patrol Breakfast Club."

"Breakfast club?"

"Yea, the one where you gotta save up twenty boxtops of Ranko Oatmeal."

I stared at him in wonder.

"You know, Ranko." Louie stuck his elbows out from his side like he was ready to flap away. Instead, he bellowed above the jukebox, his voice getting higher and louder. "Eat Ranko first thing in the morning, budda-boom-boom-boom, and have that Tiger Fighting Feeling all day looooongggg." This last note Louie hit with a pierce that threatened to crack the barware. Recognizing the jingle, I joined him for the finale; "Ranko, Ranko, Ranko, RAAAAAANNNNKKKOOOOO!"

We both laughed at this point. I slopped back my drink and he poured me another, still laughing.

"Wow, I had forgotten the studio was tying in with that promotion. Your kids really eat twenty boxes worth of that slop?"

"Yea, I made'em – ha, ha! Sure plugged'em up tight though. Oh, hey, I got a hold – or I should say my kids got a hold of your new comic book. Wanna see?"

"Sure. I heard these things were coming out."

Louie handed me a well studied copy of the comic. On the front was a fairly flattering rendition of me under the frantic bright banner "Dick Hardwing Jungle Patrol Comics." I, or rather my artistic rendition, was bulging oversized biceps in a torn khaki shirt. One arm was firing a fist into a face of some devilish looking jungle savage. In the background a woman, semi clad in leopard print and exotic jewelry on her arms and neck stared at me in disbelief. My other arm was raised high into the air, clutching a bright green rock. A rather large word balloon, pointing at my pearly whites proclaimed, "I did it! The sacred stone is mine!"

CHAPTER 3 --FIVE MONTHS EARLIER
FEBRUARY 1939
BURMESE JUNGLE

After a week of arduous traveling, the three Germans arrived at the hut of a native way station on the shore of a major tributary that emptied itself into the Andaman Sea near Rangoon in Burma. One of the Germans resided in a wooden box, as a result of the fatal wounds suffered in the temple attack, while the others readied a communiqué for contact with the German High Command.

"Our time will come Bruno, when this is all over, we will be as rich as foam on top of a good lager."

The two men sat on stools at opposite ends of a bamboo table each sipping a warm potent brew from small cups. A large noodle bowl was placed between them by the owner of the hut.

"It is a shame about Hamm," muttered Bruno.

"Ya, but it could not be helped. He gave his life for the Reich" said Schlitz.

"Tell me, Schlitz, do you feel that there is glory in giving your life to the Reich?"

Bruno placed both his hands under the table and looked contemplatively at Schlitz.

"What a silly question! We are expected to if need be."

Bruno smiled thoughtfully. "What about your family – I mean the honor of your family?"

"Of course, there is always that. Your family was great at one time, Bruno – you had titled land."

"My family is still great. Just because a new regime usurps my family's rightful belongings does not make it just nor does it diminish the family name's proper titles and greatness," Bruno growled, his eyes narrowing at Schlitz.

"I do not want to argue history, Bruno, I want to celebrate our success."

"Of course." Bruno took one hand out from under the table and raised his cup. Schlitz laughed as he raised his cup and stood tall bellowing "To the honor and the glory of the Reich!"

A slight smile crept over Bruno as he quietly spoke. "Yes. To honor and glory."

The bullet ripped through the underside of the bamboo table, spraying shards and rice as it penetrated the supper bowl on the journey to Schlitz's left cheek and brain. Schlitz appeared as a gargoyle momentarily, and, still raising his cup in a toast, fell with a twisting crash on the grimy floor. The owner and sole other occupant of the hut entered, awaiting orders from Bruno.

Bruno stood and stared beyond the lifeless grinning body at his feet, his gun still smoking from its barrel. "Place this body in the casket with the other body. Then fill the box with rats that need a good meal. Take the box on downstream to the port along with the message I handed you earlier. You are to give that message to the German ship captain that will meet you on pier seventeen. As far as you know, I never came out of the jungle. The box was delivered to you by natives from the interior that you had not seen before. By the time my little surprise has been discovered, I will be long gone, and you will have returned to your family in the province."

The native nodded in thanks as Bruno handed him the payment required.

CHAPTER 4--SIX MONTHS LATER
EARLY AUGUST 1939
HOLLYWOOD

"Happy now, Missa Hanover?"

It was one of those boringly beautiful Southern California days of cocktails and sunburns; where the palm trees seem to hold up the sky, and the sun takes its sweet time in heading for the horizon and the gray haze that awaits to meet its fiery embrace like a reluctant lover. The stillness of the day was broken by my sighs as I lay on my stomach with my eyes closed, soaking up the warmth of the plush lounger by the deck of my new kidney shaped pool. I had a fresh icy drink waiting to give me inspiration on a small stand. On that same small stand by my side was a phone. This was my morning to rest and deal business between my writers and my agent. Welcome to my office.

Still wet from my mid-morning dip, I felt almost ethereal as soft feminine hands plied my lower back, gently making their way up to my shoulders. I knew my house girl, Ha-Nee, would smile whenever I sighed. She had a hell of a touch, and knew right where to soothe my aching back.

"Missa Hanover have hard day yessaday. I know, because that when back frare up. You no take you pills. Dokka give pills, but you no take."

"Why take pills, when I can have one of your special cocktails? Besides, my back has been killing me for years, ever since I took that fool fall during the folly of my youth."

"You no have to twirl in air to impless me."

She pressed her palms between my shoulder blades and I let out a slow moan this time. Keeping my eyes closed, I could picture her working as an inspired artist works clay, a master sculptor, pushing and rearranging a work of art. She was quite a work of art herself, and I felt blessed by whatever silly Asian gods she believed in for bringing her to my employ. She did the work of three house servants, not because that was what was required, but because she wanted to. See, she seemed to have a very obvious infatuation with the boss of this not too modest Spanish bungalow in the Hollywood Hills. She was more than happy to cook, clean, launder, play secretary, and generally mother me in order to get me to roll over and let her rub my belly like a overly pampered Labrador retriever. Her long raven hair was pulled up in a bun fastened with what looked like a couple of chopsticks. She definitely dressed for comfort, with my encouragement of course for maximum exposure. Right now she was wearing the cutest little one-piece bathing suit I had given her last Christmas, and somehow it had become her regular uniform. And though she lived in a servant's room just off of the kitchen, she didn't always spend her nights there. Yea, nothing like buying them right off the boat, before they become corrupted into American feminist ways.

Thinking about Ha-Nee also made me realize how happy I was with my lot in life. Here I am, a yokel from little ol' Galveston, Texas, where I spent my earlier life as a gym and track star at the local public high school. Then school was over. When all my buddies went off to college or business, I was left behind with some ribbons and school records and not much else. Not many employers cared for a guy who could climb ropes in record speed or do a two and a half summersault off a high beam. So, I got work in one of the semi-permanent carnivals that frequented the Galveston Bay area, apprenticing myself into a tumbling and acrobat act with their crack hi-wire team. Things were swell, until Marian showed up and I took that tumble - in more ways than one. Just one extra flip in the air, just a half second longer defying gravity eighty feet from the ground, all for her. Knowing she was watching me, showing her how I was a star too. Thank God the net broke my fall without breaking my back. That sweet stunt put me on the injured list for a while though. By the time I was ready again, the carnival had moved on. So I figured it was time for me to do the same. I had been hearing about possible work as a stunt man in Hollywood but didn't want to leave my carnie buddies. They saved me the trouble. They left me, so off to California I went. This was in 1929, and the industry was changing. Boy was it changing. While a lot of people were losing their jobs due to this thing called sound, my work was just beginning. I got a shot at doing stunts for Hollywood kiddy westerns and serials. I did well enough. I got called on a regular basis, which brought me to the attention of my current agent. Things really took off then. I got the opportunity to do more than just stunt double work when the proposition for a job with a twelve chapter adventure serial called Dick Hardwing of the Jungle Patrol turned up. The day I met the writers for my audition and story conference, I fantasized everything I could about myself into the title character, putting in my own little bits about what he should be like. I even got to help pitch the story to the studio boss of Excitement Pictures, my sweet little struggling studio. Guess I did a good job, since the boss hired those writers to work for me, while I got the lead role acting in the story.

Dick Hardwing really broke the ice. Another Jungle Patrol picture, a B-film, some personal appearances, all proved very popular. My beautiful home and life style was dependant on the weekly allowances of America's youth.

Yea, Hollywood had called me, and I had answered; only now it kept calling and calling – an incessant ringing in the file cabinet of my memory marked Try to Forget. I walked across a couple of white fluffy clouds to where the lonely steel gray cabinet stood. I opened the top drawer and there sat the phone, still ringing. I picked up the receiver, and tried to shout hello but nothing came out, and though I held the receiver to my ear, the damn thing continued to ring. Then it stopped and I opened my eyes.

The suddenness of my awareness made Ha-Nee start, and she took a sudden step away from me, the phone still in her hands as she whispered into the mouthpiece. "Missa Hanover Lesidence – Oh, it you. He no talk now, in confelence." I stared quizzically at her and waved for the phone. "Oh, he here now, prease stand by."

I raised my eyebrows to ask who it was, but all I got was a furrowed set of watery eyes and a stifled sob. She thrust the phone at me and took off at a trot, heading round a palm tree for the kitchen entrance door, pausing long enough as she opened it to give me a hurt glance and disappear inside.

I took this in for a second, and gingerly held the phone to my ear. "H-Hello?"

"Sterling – this is Marian."

In those few words my life was humbled.

In the few seconds it takes to formally exchange pleasantries consisting of half-hearted inquiries into each other's health and affairs, my thoughts could only picture her as the way I had last seen her. It had been at an evening pool party for a mutual Hollywood friend. She had been wearing an astounding deep purple cocktail gown, bedecked with a soft glitter in the thread that only served to make her look like a small universe of dreams, right in front of me. The soft white pearl onions in her Gibson complimented the long strands of pearls around her neck. Her raven bobbed hair was as black as her eyes. Not a cold distant black, but a soft inviting darkness like an indigo velvet covered bed an hour before sunrise. I stood there and wrapped myself in the luxury of those eyes before she opened her mouth and snatched that luxury away, leaving me uncomfortable and naked before her gaze.

"I've become engaged to Colonel Goodwin. We marry on the morrow. I am sure you understand. And now, if you'll excuse me, I am to meet my fiancée at Chasen's for dinner."

And with that, she had walked out of my life. Or so I thought.

"Sterling, are you there? Hello?"

"Uh, yea, sure. Guess I'm not used to hearing your voice lately."

"Sterling, I need your help." There was a small waver to her voice that struggled to cover up a great sadness. "Harry has been found dead in Tijuana. The Colonel and I were informed late last night by the police. They are not sure how it happened."

"Do the police have somebody?"

"They tried to question one of his friends, another sailor named Bob, but the sailor fought with the police and got away. Harry's body was discovered in an alleyway. There were no marks they could find. It is as if he just fell down."

"What was he doing in Tijuana?"

"He was on leave from the naval base with three of his friends. They were celebrating. According to them he went outside by himself and that was it. Sterling you've got to do something!" there was a real cry to her voice now.

"Who were the police you talked to?" I said calmly, hoping to ease her growing panic.

"They were military police. All they could tell me was what the investigating officer, a Capitan Gonzalez on the Tijuana police force had told them. The body is in the hands of the Mexican police, and will be shipped back home in two days. Oh Sterling, something just doesn't seem right," she cried softly into the phone. "Look, there is not much I can do here in Virginia.

"Alright", I told her. She had a way of making me do anything she wanted and I regretted it. Anytime and anywhere. Harry was a good kid – too good. Harry got to have all the things I didn't when I was growing up.

Plenty of money, courtesy of his father, the Colonel. In fact he got to have a few things I can't have now, like Marian. Strange thing, Marian's marriage to the Colonel. She provides him with a son like that and yet the Colonel treats him coldly. Sure, a kid's got to have discipline and a firm hand, sure, but not coldness. A parent's discipline and guidance has to be tempered with love, or it's no good. I guess I continued along this line of thought a little too long when Marian's voice pulled me back in.

"Sterling? Did you hear me?"

"Yea, I heard you. Guess I drifted off in thought there for a while. "

"Please don't start."

"Start what, Marian? Don't start the fact that I'll turn cartwheels every time you breathe my name? Don't start because you have the life that I couldn't provide you, so you had to have it with someone else? That cold fish? Because he can make you happy yet I couldn't? I guess I'm still trying to adjust to the realization that I'm still your fool."

The hushed silence on the other end only brought me remorse. "Oh, hell, look I'm sorry. The more I try to figure out why we didn't make it, the more I realize why we didn't. You know how I feel about Harry. He's like a son to me."

A slow muffled sob was the response on the other end. "Please, Sterling. I know you cared for him."

She didn't know the half of it. I have always been concerned about Harry. He was so much like the kid I would have wanted with Marian. Only I wouldn't have provided the cold coddling he had received. I would have shown him what it takes to be a man. Instead, he had to go out to try to find out himself. He had joined the Navy as an enlistee just to upset his old man, which was fine with me. I was proud of him that day. The Colonel only gave scorn. So he goes out on his own and gets killed. And now I get the job of errand boy to claim the body for shipment back home.

"OK, I'll leave on the next flight and call you when I'm done." She gave me the details on where Harry's body was being held, and I jotted them down on the small notepad on the end table next to my folding cot. I told her goodbye and hung up. I sat up, threw the towel that I had been using as a pillow around my neck and stood up. I grabbed the phone again and dialed my agent.

The sultry but chilly voice on the other end answered "Lou Finkel Agency."

"Hi, doll, tell Lou his favorite boy is on the line."

"Hello Sterling. He is all wrapped up in a meeting. Are you sure you want to talk to him right now? He is still a little steamed at you for walking off the set yesterday. Not to worry, he did his usual quick talking and calmed everyone down."

"Good old Lou. Look, I just need to let him know that I have to leave town for a day."

"Going anywhere you can take me?" I could feel her eyebrows arch clear over the phone.

"Not this time. I have to make a run to Tijuana as a special favor for a friend. And it is not what you are thinking." A small giggle came through the line.

"This is Friday, if I can catch an evening flight, I'll be back by Sunday to get some rest by Monday."

"Good, that is when the call time is set for. That jungle epic is just about wrapped, supposedly. Just some close ups and stray shots left."

"Great. See you later, doll"

The smile I was wearing left as soon as I hung up the phone. I stood there staring at the shimmering water in the pool. Some special favor I was pulling.

CHAPTER 5--EARLY AUGUST 1939
TIJUANA BOUND

After a fairly uneventful flight, and a rather eventful dialogue with the stewardess, wherein I gained her private number, I stepped from the airport into the loud and boisterous late afternoon streets of Tijuana, that hot little border town where the gringo military go to take their libidos and sobriety for a fantasy ride before going out to fight for Mom and apple pie. The heat was like a large woolen blanket laying over the town. I was wearing my white cotton pinstripe suit that seemed to provide adequate ventilation for a while, anyway. I did a quick feel for my wallet in my coat pocket, noting to myself that the few pesos mixed with American dough ought to buy me what I want without too much trouble, or too many questions. I took an eyeball through that same wallet as I strolled down the tarmac to the exit and caught the image of a photo. It was the photo I had of Harry the one and only time he came to visit me in Hollywood. It was just six months ago. He had decided to stay with me (if it was alright – hell yes it was) the night before he was due to go into boot camp in San Diego. We had a great time that night – or I did, anyway. He was naturally nervous and a little squeamish about the whole affair. My only reassurance was to let him know that he should approach this new part of his life like Dick Hardwing approached the unexplored parts of the Congo. Ready for danger, welcoming action. Remember which pocket you put your knife in, and always wear a rubber.

We went to the Brown Derby that evening for a good meal. I smiled and proudly introduced Harry to the local crowd of friends and strangers. They all smiled accordingly and I had the resident photographer snap a pic of us hoisting our highballs. A honk as I sauntered to the curb caused me to break my thoughts for a moment and realize why I was here. I took one last look at that picture before I shelved it away. A quick cab ride and quicker haggle brought me to the local constabulary – a one Capitan Gonzalez, the man in charge of this particular crime in this particular part of town. The police station was a peach colored stucco affair, with only a small faded sign modestly announcing what was housed within. The building almost seemed shy next the other buildings lining the streets and alleyways of the area, all loudly proclaiming, some in two languages, what possible pleasures lurked within. I left the hectic taxi honking and general sidewalk mayhem of vendors and hustlers for a different kind of hustle within the police station. It was a quieter hustle, granted, but a hustle was still in the air. The outer foyer of the station housed a large and high booking desk, mounted by a frazzled officer, while on either side were two desks each piled with paperwork and the flashing and ringing of phone lines. The officers manning these stations moved at a quieter pace than the booking officer at the high desk, and as a result, wore less harried grimaces. An exchange in broken English with the officer of the high desk brought me to a large office in the back, and the lair of Capitan Pedro Amarillo Francisco Jesus Gonzalez.

    Capitan Gonzalez' office was a claustrophobic affair, though it was relatively large. Gonzalez himself was large enough to give the room a false perspective of closeness. There were no windows, and no natural light, except the faint trickle that was able to find its way in through a skylight directly above the good capitan's desk. A small electric fan on a side table hummed and did a slow nod "yes" up and down to Gonzalez, scattering a small bevy of belligerent flies in its efforts to please the rotund officer. His desk was a riot of papers in search of a filing system and weighing them down from the slight rustling of the subservient fan was something that at first resembled a shaved and gutsplit china pig, but a longer glance proved it to be a large flour tortilla stuffed with beans, chilies, and something resembling pork. A small bottle of tequila with a pickled worm residing there in complimented this unique plate. Gonzalez was chewing lazily and reading Hollywood Confidential when he looked up and stood to greet me, loosening his gourmand grip on his mex-feed and extending a waving hand in welcome. That hand not only had the odd resemblance of a cow teat with its five bloated udders waving in the country air at me, but it seemed slick and slightly dripping, a result of probing the mutilated beast masquerading as a meal on the desktop. The slight light of the room coupled with the upturned shade perched atop a small lamp teetering precariously on the edge of his desk served to illuminate the shadows on his puffy pockmarked face, a face containing bulbous lips framed by a small drooping moustache, half open eyes (a result of the afternoon mescal no doubt) giving him an uncanny resemblance to Charlie Chan on a three day bender. With all the sweat and grease on him, I felt nervous about lighting my cigarette. Every limb on his body that was conjoined with another seemed to be a constant fount of perspiration, creating ripples within the circular pools already present on his khaki colored police uniform. His cap and top shirt button were nowhere in sight. As he spoke, the flies gathered in the warmth of his breath.

"Well, well, the famous Americano jungle man from Hollywood."

"So you know me, eh? Glad to make your acquaintance."

"Know you, sir, I always see your pictures, even when I am supposed to be on duty. I read all about you, too, in Hollywood Confidential."

Gonzalez waved the copy of the magazine at me with his free paw and loosened his grip on my hand. There I was, a snappy dressed guy on the town, with a cute little script girl on my arm posing candidly on the cover.

"You must be thirsty after your trip." He pulled a small paper cup out of his desk. The cup was the same kind used for fluid samples in doctors' offices. It looked used. "Have a drink, it is wonderful tequila, I tink"

"Didn't know my work made its way over the border," was my grimaced response to his invitation.

"Si, the movies do, but this wonderful periodical doesn't. My cousin, he is a pharmacist with a little shop just over the border. He saves them for me."

"Yea? What's his return on the transaction?"

"Let's just say I can help make sure he gets the medicinal items he needs that can be a bit hard to come by. But I am honored senor. What brings you to my humble precinct? You are here to help me solve a few open cases? Clear up the books of unsolved crimes?"

I poured myself a shot, betting on the potency of the liquor to sanitize the cup. "Hardly. I am looking to solve just one. You read the papers, hell, you probably dictate them. You know why I am here."

"Anything, senor."

"There was a young sailor boy died here two days ago. In an alley outside the Black Cat Cantina. Heart attack was the general description. I am here to identify the body for shipment and find out what I can for the boy's mother. Victim's name is Harry Goodwin. I have a picture of him here."

I started to hand the small photo to him but stopped short when Gonzalez became intrigued by a fly slowly walking across his desk towards his lunch. He slowly rolled up the movie magazine. He continued to stare at the fly while still talking to me. "Natural causes in the alley, huh? Yes I think I have the file here. You will be disappointed, senor. Not much there. People drop dead everyday."

As he finished speaking he brought the magazine down like a sledgehammer, the fly guts leaving a dark green streak across the desk and the magazine with my picture on the cover.

"Were there any marks on the body, bruises, and cuts, any indication of a fight or a struggle?"

"Nada – his body was clean, but later the coroner was only able to find a small puncture wound and bruise on the scalp line behind the left ear. While the bruise and puncture wound were fresh, they don't seem to have any connection with what happened."

"Any idea what he was doing in the alley?"

Gonzalez didn't flinch, but quickly stared directly at me and smiled. "Outside a bar full with our city's beautiful women? A young healthy boy can find many ways to entertain himself in an alley with a warm senorita."

"I am sure. Had he been robbed?"

"Robbery? We found a thin wallet with his ID and some dinero." He opened the top left drawer on his desk and pulled out a small bag. "Minus shipping and investigative expenses of course."

"Of course." I stiffened in my seat as my lower back began to throb slightly.

"Have another drink senor." He poured another round as he lectured. "Sir, I pride myself on not incurring expenses on the citizens I am sworn to protect. Simple items such as stamps, paper, all cost my people. They are but poor hardworking people senor. They depend on my efficiency to keep expenses down. When expenses are low, there is no need for talk of taxes to pay for city services. And my people do not like the talk of taxes. When taxes are talked of, there is also talk of a new capitan of the police as well."

"So you collect your own private taxes, huh?"

"Taxes pay the salaries, senor. It is only fair that those who desire our services the most should pay the most. We only take from those who can afford it, senor. And the dead. They have to pay taxes too. Death tax, senor."

I didn't hide my scowl at this point. "Sure, I got you. How much was on the body, after taxes, of course"

"A minimum of cash, senor, ten pesos tops. Not even enough to pay for his drinks he ordered at the bar for him and his friends."

"Any jewelry or rings?"

"No, senor."

"Anybody at the bar say anything?"

"The fellows he was with were busy with the local nightlife. The one called Big Job Bob; he was sick - big strong man like that with a weak stomach. When we confronted him outside he became belligerent. He attacked one of my officers and ran. Naturally my man had to fire at him."

I raised an eyebrow, curious at this bit of trivia. "Did you hit him?"

"Si, he went down, but before we could reach him he was up and gone again. We looked, but he disappeared. Don't worry, a big gringo like that with a bullet in him, he will not get far."

"What about the people in the bar?"

"No one saw him except the bartender. Oh, and the doorman saw him leave. Alone. As I say, not much here. A boy has a heart attack out of the sky and drops dead. These things happen all the time, even to the healthy ones. A toast to the hope it doesn't happen to either one of us, eh senor? Say I have a couple of other cases here, you and me, we work together; make a pretty good team, eh senor? I give you a split of the - what was that you say? Private tax? Hahahahaha!" Gonzalez heartily poured another for himself, while I shifted uneasily in my wooden chair.

"No thanks. I better go ahead with the identification now, but I might want to visit you later."

Gonzalez glared suddenly at me. "I must warn you sir, that there are things called investigative taxes as well. Anything else you need, will take up my time. And time as you know is money…"

"Save it."

"Senor before we go down to the morgue, one more thing."

"What is it?"

"Will you autograph this magazine for me please? Gracias, senor!" I glared back, stood up, and waited for him to lead me to the viewing. He continued to smile and tossed the magazine back into the open top drawer, but not before I noticed a curious green stone among the jumble of other contents inside the drawer. Slamming the drawer shut, he growled "Follow me." Standing up, Gonzalez scooped up his tortilla wrapped grease soaked lunch in his left hand.

We left his office and crossed the short hallway in back of the front desk and opened a door. This door didn't lead to a room but to a set of steps descending down into what I could only imagine someone's definition of Hell would be like. It was a black pit in front of me beginning at about the fourth step.

"Perdone me, senor, we must go down before I turn on the light. Allow me to go first." He walked on ahead and down the steps and I was reminded of that strange boatman you hear of in mythology, the guide that leads you across the dark river Styx to the hereafter but is yet immune. As I held the rail, I reached bottom, afraid to move lest I disturb what I feared. A short grunt from my companion and a white light evaporated the ink that filled my eyes. As the light glared my vision, he said "come closer to the light. That's it, move closer to the light." I moved towards the sound of his voice, and the light. Slowly my vision straightened and the colors and echoing shapes focused. The dull pounding in my back sharpened and I realized I hadn't brought my medicine.

"I always close my eyes in the darkness before I turn on the light. It is not such a shock that way."

I assented "hmmm" and saw where I was. A dirt floor surrounded by dried mud augmented by the same dried mud formed in the shape of bricks here and there, while bits of white natural marble ran in thick veins as it would in a natural quarry. There was a cool dryness here, not unlike a natural fruit cellar. Only there was a strange fruit being stored here, in metal file drawers, with numbers and names. The air contained a hint of an ancient air as one would smell when finding a perfectly preserved old book in an attic. I was motioned to a closed shelf on the bottom towards the far wall. The naked white bulb of light cast distorted shadows here in this corner as the bulb did a slow circular dance at the end of a long wire suspended from the ceiling. "You will now please identify the body?"

He slid the drawer open, and there he was. A small, untanned naked boy, so fragile and now so very alone. A kid that meant so much to me, yet I never did anything about it. There in that low shelf in a low room of a sad and sorry cluster of blocks, far from home was the repository of all my guilt, my emotional procrastinations, my unsown good intentions. An avalanche of broken glass images, wishes, fantasies, and regrets came at me so fast I didn't have the time or courage to sort them out. Then the shards quickly buried themselves back in my subconscious again, but not without ripping open a hole in my thoughts. The pain of the ripping made me choke, close my eyes that were quickly flooding to the point where I felt I was drowning in salt water. The pain in my back decided to take a trip to my brain, causing me to weave slightly on my feet. A disembodied voice that I realized a second later was mine groaned "Yes, that is Harold Goodwin."

"Bueno." Gonzalez bent down, his left hand never releasing its stranglehold on his bulging lunch. "As you see, senor, there are no marks except for this." He turned Harry's head to reveal the small wound. It looked no worse than a pin scratch.

"When can this be ended?" I choked. "When can he be shipped home?"

"The coroner will have him boxed and ready to go later today." Gonzalez stood up, shoved the rest of his lunch in his mouth, but not before a large trickle of grease ran down his elbow, dangled ponderously, as if wondering what to do next, and then fell onto what used to be Harry Goodwin's smiling face. Gonzalez used his left foot to slam the drawer shut. "We will handle everything according to instructions."

I exploded internally, and the room grew warmer with the heat of my anger. "Wipe it off."

"Que?"

"Wipe your filth off the boy's face."

"It is time to leave. I have many pressing matters."

"Wipe the boy, pig."

Gonzalez laughed. I wondered why he continued to smile as my fists balled up and I started to swing, wanting to do my best to push his fat face into his skull. The reason was explained in an explosion of suns that came from the back of my head through my eye sockets.

My body's momentum carried me forward as I collapsed into flabby arms. Someone had tripped my off switch.

Two voices were talking in Spanish. The lower voice was coming from the mound of flesh that was holding me captive and thanking the other. The owners of the voices carried me, lifting me by my armpits, and dragged me upstairs, banging my shins every step of the way. Warm air made the million suns evaporate into the streaming light of a much larger sun forcing its way into the main room of the police station.

"Coming around, senor? Bueno! Do not blame Deputy Gomez for doing his duty. You are lucky he came down to investigate. You were about to break the law."

I focused hazily on Gonzalez. "Clean up my boy."

"It is not uncommon to be upset at a time like this. This is nothing special. We have this all the time. Now do you go?" His face suddenly changed to a scowl: "Or do you stay in one of our clean jails as a permanent guest, Mr. Jungle Man?"

Our eyes locked in contempt. "I'll go. But I'll be back." Turning slowly I rubbed the back of my head and made for the door. A rumble of laughter erupted behind me. "Sure, Jungle Man, you come back any time!" the rest of the cops in the place joined in the laughter, making noises like animals in a jungle.

Stopping as I opened the door, I wheeled and addressed the room, "Yea, I'll be back. You bet I'll back. Especially you, Gonzalez," I shouted. The taunting in the room died down. "You can bet your life on it!"

A salty taste was in my mouth as I boiled out of the police station and back into the setting sun soaked streets of Tijuana. My boy. That is what he always seemed like, what he had always been to me. Marian's damned colonel sure didn't feel that way towards him. I always felt like I should have been his dad. What a laugh on me, though. I would have made a lousy dad. Too much scotch and dames and make believe. I stormed down the streets past the vendors, taco hawkers, and kids begging for change until I was able to coax a burning smoke exhaust perfumed taxi and its driver away from the curb for a quick ride over to the Black Cat Cantina.

The sun seemed unable to find the rim of the Pacific horizon, as its once solid and firm push of sunlight slowly broke away into uneasy tentacles of yellow orange rays, stealing into the city streets, some fighting through open doorways, others bouncing off the glass panes crusted with smoke and mud. I stood in front of the cantina, with its fancy neon scrawl across the arched doorway, giving a low hum. In that doorway was not a door but swinging doors and the occasional fly buzzing lazily in and out. Beyond was darkness, and maybe in that darkness an answer. The street around me was not busy, only a few couples or a lone passerby. This was that odd twilight time, when the day shoppers and tourists were disappearing back over the border because it was getting late, yet it was still too early for the night revelers to emerge and begin their bacchanalian rituals. A sharp pain in my lumbar made me stiffen and stretch my shoulders back. My hands reflexively went to the source of the pain and gently massaged my lower spine. I hadn't hurt like this in quite a while. My frustration of the day's proceedings seemed to manifest itself in physical pain. Not to mention I felt as if I was growing a second head in back of my scalp where that Mexican cop blackjacked me. My throbbing nerves seemed to be pulsing out a steady meter to a Latin beat I was hearing. Coming out of the darkness of the Black Cat's doorway was a trebly mambo coupled with low whispers punctuated with loutish laughs. Bracing myself I sauntered in to face some answers.

Pushing my way through the swinging doors into the unknown I was submerged into an inky sea of black. Feeling my nose curl against the stench of old tobacco and beer, I headed for what looked like the bar, straight ahead of me. I almost made it. The only light left of the day was sneaking under the doors and heading for the bar. It almost made it. Both of us stopped about halfway way to our destination. The light just plain gave up. I needed time for my eyes to adjust, though I could feel eyes on me. There was a big formless lump behind the bar, with two smaller lumps propped up on the bar to my right. The lump in front of me quickly dissolved into what some might call a face. Below that face were two huge hands swabbing the inside of a beer mug. The face spoke. "What do you want?" I stepped closer to the bar. My vision seemed to have shifted to an infra-red wavelength. I could see my surroundings in a dull dark red glow once I stepped out of the last comforting rays of the sun. The two lumps on my right evolved from featureless clay into a U.S. sailor, and on the other side of him, head tilted in earnest conversation, was a young girl with more cleavage than clothing above her small waist, and skin tight skirt with a slit up the side just to keep her conversation interesting. She was dark like a Mexican Senorita, but with an Asian flair in her eyes that tagged her as Pilipino. As long as my eyes were getting accustomed to my surroundings, they might as well get accustomed with her.

Just as my eyes were really getting their focus back, the primary former lump behind the bar belted "Hey, amigo! Pay attention! What do you want? What is your business?" I turned my head towards him. He looked like a veteran of too many bar fights, and probable instigator of most. He was giving me a look that would neuter a bulldog.

"What's my business? Don't you know? You're a bartender." The second head on the back of my scalp was growing larger and starting to give the orders now.

"So I'm a bartender, bright boy. What are you? I don't know you, and this is a private club." This guy was more American than Mexican, but more gangster than gringo. More East Coast than West Coast. How the hell did he end up in this joint?

"So, you know everyone that walks in the door?"

"Yea, most everyone. Like I said, this cantina is private, so we have our regulars. So unless you are willing to ante up an initiation fee, beat it. I'm only asking one more time."

"I don't know how could I resist such a tempting invitation, but you see I am only seeking some information. Information on a death that occurred in your alleyway last night."

"You working for the police?"

"In a way," I lied. "I am willing to pay you personally more than what the initiation fee probably is for this place."

"American dollars?"

"Si, amigo." I pulled out my wallet and opened it. One last greedy ray of light from the window by a table of now suddenly quiet sailors played against the greenish tint of Andrew Jackson beaming up at me from beside his fraternity of brothers encased in the leather wallet in my hands.

The bartender rolled the stump of the cigar in his mouth from one spittle dolloped side to the other in thought. "Sure, amigo." He took the bill from my hand as I placed the wallet back in my coat pocket. "Whiskey?"

"Gracias."

He placed the bottle and shot glass next to me.

I had to mentally push the other throbbing head from my own and talk straight. I did a quick reach into my pocket and pulled out the bent up picture. "I want to know if you know this kid in the picture. Was he a regular?"

"Gringo sailor, huh? They all look alike to me. And they all order the same basic drink – beer and tequila shots. If they are getting ready to ship out in the morning, a lot of them will have whiskey. I didn't get a look at anything when the police came. I was too busy working in here."

"This kid was in here last night with some buddies all wearing Hawaiian shirts."

"Not original – look, it is a sad thing but what I'm telling you I already told to the cops last night."

"Well maybe this will help," pulling out the picture from my wallet and placing it between two fingers of my right hand. He furrowed his two eyebrows into one while looking at the photo. "Yea, I saw him here, right where you are now."

Glass tapping on the bar made us turn our heads. It was the bargirl and her dozing sailor friend on the next stool down.

"Hey Perez. Gimme a drink for the admiral here."

"Sure, Juanita."

"C'mon, admiral wake up."

"I don't need no help, I'm OK." The redheaded little squirt tried to shove the gal on her shoulder as she blocked his hand, sending his arm into the top of the bar, which made him temporarily lose his balance. He tried reflexively to fix his position on his stool by leaning back and bumping into me, slightly sloshing his glass of beer onto the bar and banging against me in the process.

I sneered at his tilted profile and let forth a slow growl. "Watch it."

"Thorry, pallie. My apothegees. As he turned around to spray his courtesies at me, he noticed the picture in my hand. "Thay, that guy looks familiar."

I raised an eyebrow. "What can you tell me about him?"

"You a cop?"

Everyone seemed to be worried if I was one of the honorable constables in this area. "No, a family friend."

"Good. I hate cops. Cops around here don't do nothin, unless you pay'em for it. Cops were sure in here last night asking questions, though. Seems some squid got hammered in the alley."

"Yea, I heard. So you were here last night?"

"Yea, I was here." He poured some beer in his mouth, spilling some from his mouth as he talked. "And so was your pal in the picture, for a while, anyway."

"This is the kid that was murdered in the alley"

"Gee, that ish too bad."

"Take a closer look, will you?" I handed him the picture.

The way he twisted his face and screwed his eyes up, he looked as though he were trying to squeeze a thousand swirling images into one "Yea, I seen him around a few times. Hung out with a tall dumb guy. Crazy." He shook his head.

"What's crazy?"

"The way the big dumb guy would follow this kid around. Mutt and Jeff. Even tried to dress like him, right down to that green rock."

"Green rock?"

"Yea, he and his buddies all had'em, said it was like a fraternity or something. That rock seemed to mean a lot to the big guy."

"How so?"

"He kept staring at it while it was hangin' around his neck, and playing with it real reverent like."

The sugar doll swinging her crossed legs pulled his arm. "Baby, you talk too much. Be with me." He still attempted to stare at the picture in his hand.

I continued the conversation. "Can you tell me anything about what went on last night?"

The bartender pushed a jowly arm and a glass his way. "Here's your drink, sailor."

"C'mon, baby; talk to me, not him." The girl was squeezing his thigh now.

The sailor continued, unswayed. "Usual wild night. That kid was a nice swabby. Bought drinks for all his buddies, and me too."

"Yea? Then what?"

"Then what? He goes outside and disappears, that's what! I had to pay for my next drink!"

"You're breaking my heart. See anybody with him?"

A soft hand tilted the sailor's head away. "Drink with me, lover!" The girl's lips were insistent.

The bartender growled "Your lady's getting anxious."

All he got was a puzzled look as the sailor turned his head back to me, screwing his eyes to focus.

My eyes forced his to clear. "I asked you a question."

"Hang on, yea, now I remember. A real vamp – she was here with some new girls working the bar that I hadn't seen before."

"Baby let's go upstairs." The girl was swinging her legs back and forth quickly enough at us to not only offer a hide and peep show of her basement office, but to let me know what was on the stove in the back of the kitchen. I wasn't interested in what was on the menu.

"I don't need your static, sister."

"Hey, don't talk to her like that," the sailor half lidded exclaimed.

At that point the pain that I had been fighting against earlier came out of nowhere and squeezed my spine. My nerves took the load and passed it onto my fingers. My fingers found the sailor's neck and passed the pain on once more. I lifted him up by his neck with both hands. I breathed into his face. "Look, I need info, and I need it bad. You can tell me nice, or I'll shake it out of you."

"Get your hands off the customer," came a wet tobacco rush of air from behind the bar. I dropped the kid back on his stool. This time it was the sailor's turn. "It's OK Perez," he gasped. "You don't have to be so rough. I'll tell you what I know. Look, the guy was a nice kid, I don't mind."

"I mind." Tobacco talked again.

I leveled a stare at the bartender. "I'm not talking to you."

He stared back. "I'm talking to you, and I'm telling you to beat it, or get beaten." Somehow a blackjack had mysteriously appeared in his left hand. His arms were spread out on the bar, coiling like two fat snakes. I put away the picture. "Sure, sure. I'll go."

As I got halfway across the now quiet bar, I heard a voice. "Hey mister."

I didn't need to turn around to know it was the sailor, but I stopped momentarily in my tracks. "What?"

"I'm…I'm sorry mister."

I turned my head long enough to give a quick survey of the bar before heading out the door.

"Yea…you're real sorry …all of you"

CHAPTER 6--LATE AUGUST 1939
CANTINA ALLEY

I stepped out into the somewhat uncertain evening. The sun was long gone from the streets, but still layered the top of some of the taller buildings like golden cream on a glass of Kahlua. The raucous sounds that had been coming through the door before I went into the cantina started backup, echoing as I left. My jaw was clenched. Big help I was. All I had done was upset the cops and some goon sailors that might have offered a better explanation than what I had been initially given. Lighting a Lucky and loosening my tie, I turned right and headed for the alley where my boy died. Shadows were covering the area in purple velvet. A streetlamp at the corner broke the velvet with a slice of sickly yellow light. The alley stretched to the next street beyond, cars and the evening's pedestrians wandering back and forth. The street where I stood looking into the alley wasn't as busy yet. The alley itself probably looked like a lot of other alleys in a lot of other towns on both sides of the border. Some garbage cans on the left side against the building. According to the fat capitan, the cans were where Harry was found. It looked like it was going to be the same kind of evening as it was the night Harry died. Probably just another night. Nothing too much out of the ordinary. The pictures that the good capitan showed me taken at the scene at the time of the crime flared up in my memory as if branded. I consciously transposed the pictures in my memory over what I saw in the alley. Laughter and loud music were starting to grow all around me. Just another night. The alley is just like any in any other city now. It all has a blanket of uselessness of life laying over it, like discarded waste, used and glistening in the glare of the streetlight. Yesterday's happiness bringing tomorrow's headaches. No memorial for what took place, nothing to suggest that anyone had died on that spot. As I journeyed partway down the alley to the trash cans I curled my mouth into a slight hint of a grin. I couldn't understand the reason. Events in life, though not turning out the way I wanted all the time, at least had a sort of sense, a screenwriter's logic, a regular three act drama formality. This didn't have it.

There was a loud raucous peel of laughter ending in a gurgle ringing out behind me. A sailor bumped into me from behind, as I was staring down the alley, and the impact jostled me aside. The sailor fell to his knees and retched into the same mud hole where Harry had lain two nights before. Down on his hands and knees, backside up, he turned his head to me, mouth wide open in a grin, with ringlets of vomit trailing from his toothy grin. "Shit, I feel better. I thought I was gonna die!" I recognized him as one of the loud sailors at the corner table in the bar. Frozen momentarily, I sprung out my right foot and kicked the sailor square in the ass, knocking him face first into his own bilge. "Maybe I ought to finish the job." I snarled as I leapt on the sailor, kicking and beating, watching his eyes start to close in half-conscious. As I grabbed the boy by his collar with both hands, I pulled him up out of the grime and shoved him into the brick wall of the building next to the cans. I stared into the pock-marked green face.

"I'm sorry I bumped into you sir, I'm really sick." mumbled the sailor, pleadingly.

"You're just a kid. You got no business here." I sneered. "Get out."

I let go of the kid. He fell to one knee, wavered a second then ran stumbling down the end of the alley where he had come from, turning back towards the bar.

I turned to look back down the alley, trying to figure out why – the reason. What did Harry do to deserve this? I needed to talk to his buddies – that Big Job Bob fellow especially. He knows something that just might make a sort of half-assed sense to this, if it could be made at all. I didn't have much time to contemplate how the pieces might even begin to fit before I heard a sound behind me and a voice give out "Hey, creep." I did a slow turn to face the group of rowdy sailors from the bar. Only they weren't laughing this time. In fact, they seemed downright deadly. The group leader, a second class petty officer with no discernible forehead under his sailor cap stood in front and spoke.

"So you think just because you play a big tough jungle man in the flickers that you can come down here and kick around one of our shipmates?" The sailor speaking looked like he learned to walk upright only last week. He was huge and was grinding one hairy mitt into his other paw. I just shut up and let him run his mouth. "I got a feeling like you ain't being patriotic like you should be in these troubled times. I got a feeling like maybe we should help you to have a little more respect for the armed forces. Right boys?" Various grunts emerged from beside him.

"Look, I'm glad you boys recognize me from my films. Any other time and I'd be glad to sign some autographs for you, but right now I'm a little busy."

"Eh heh! He's busy, he says. Didja hear that?" The group slowly circled around me, cutting off any exit. I didn't need this.

But I got it anyway – a clip against my right ear from a fist I didn't see hazed my hearing against the fist I did see, square and true, straight against my left eyebrow, courtesy of the big swabby in front of me, and my eyebrow opened up to rain blood and sweat into my vision. I thrust a few jabs at the air as a rain of blows fell around my head, but it was a kick to the small of my back that brought me down. The pain of the kick flared up and covered any other pain I was being dealt. The sailor's catcalls faded in my ear as I as I did a slow collapse into the same puddle in the same alley that seemed so very popular.

CHAPTER 7--LATE AUGUST 1939
SWEATY DREAMS

I was floating on a yellow cloud. Sounds of cherubim seemed just out of range, with an occasional trumpet call. Occasionally the cherubim would sing in Spanish instead of Latin. It was kind of pleasant, floating in the faint darkness. I didn't want to open my eyes completely just yet. All I felt like doing was drifting. A golden light rained down on me from above. My eyes fought to focus slightly. The light was beckoning and I wanted to get closer. I made a sound that was certainly not speech, but it caused a reaction. I began to hear someone calling my name. I didn't want to leave my cloud but I was being pulled toward the light and the voice. Suddenly there was an eclipse outlined against the light. The eclipse took the form of a gently floating angel. The surrounding light cascaded around her gown, giving it a shimmering quality. The voice spoke again, and it was the angel beckoning. The gown the angel was wearing was taking on a greater form, like the kind of gown you see pretty young girls wear to a nightclub. Maybe there is a bar in Heaven. A bar filled with beautiful little angels, and the drinks are on the house.

The cherubim in the distance let out an awkward bleat on some trumpets, and I distinctly heard them begin to play mariachi music. I didn't realize that Heaven would have such odd smells. Somehow I figured roses and lilacs, or a slight Chanel scent. Instead there was a faint aroma of Bar-B-Q, piss and exhaust. The angel in front of me had a face now. It was the girl from the bar. She was standing blocking the light from the yellow bulb of the streetlamp. I was lying in mud with some paper trash brushing my cheek from the slight breeze in the alley. So much for Heaven. I always figured the place was overrated anyway.

"Senor, please come with me. I can help you." She helped me to my feet as I braced myself against a wall.

"Why?"

"I know the young nino you talk about."

"Why didn't you say something and save me all this trouble?"

"I tell you later. I take you to a hotel near. You rest there." I gave in to her will and let her hobble me down the back end of the alley away from the light until we came out on the next street over. A clutch of rundown three and four story rat traps offering rooms for the night or hour were greeting us with garish neon. Girls hard at work doing nothing were hanging around the front of these joints like flies around a group of garbage cans. We went in one of these joints with the girl barely giving a nod to the rummy behind the metal grate at the front desk, and climbed the stairs up three stories and turned left, walking down past a couple of doors until we reached one on the right at the end of the hall. She pulled out a key from somewhere and put it in the door, pushing it wide open while helping me shift my balance. The door opened to reveal a naked bulb hanging from a slowly turning ceiling fan, an ancient dresser just to the left of the door, a separate bathroom through an open door on the right by the far wall, but most delicious to me was an overstuffed beat up four poster bed jutting out from the middle of the left wall. The bar angel helped me over to the bed. "You rest senor." She made me feel like a little sick kid, undoing my shoes and helping me out of my jacket. I must admit she was a brave sort of girl, helping me with my mud and sweat stained shirt and tie. "Ow- sorry, guess I have some bruises beginning to grow."

"Not to worry, there is a shower in el bano. You go clean up, I will send you clothes out to be cleaned next door. They will be back soon."

"Look, I need to know why you are being so good to me. I need to know what you know about the boy."

"You need to rest first. Go take the shower. I will get us comida. Then we talk."

Too tired and sore to argue, I took out my wallet, handed her some bills, said "Thanks, kid," and like a good little boy I went in the bathroom to shower, handing my pants out to her from behind the door. I heard the door slam as I got in the shower. The water was cold at first but quickly warmed up, and my thoughts floated away on the steam. I had only planned on coming down here for a sad simple business that should have had me on a return flight right about now, but instead, here I am black and blue and naked in a strange hotel with a stranger woman taking care of me. There was a slight bubble of panic to my thoughts. What if she doesn't come back? I had to smile at myself on that one. Now there was a story for the tabloids.

After I toweled off, I answered the call of the bed. It wasn't much of a bed, but it was all I had. The sheets looked like the maid came to change the stains once a week. It was soft and I was tired. I dozed off and must have fallen asleep, for the room was entirely dark when I heard the tapping at the door. I got up, grabbed the towel, and wrapped it around myself and made for the door. I heard my angel call out. "I have your ropas senor. And food." I opened the door and let her in. She beamed at me and handed me a box with my clothes inside. In her other hand was a fair sized bag. "I bring us food and drink. Tacos and wine. Was I gone too long? Where is the light?"

"I guess I fell asleep. I feel a lot better now. Sore, but better. Here is the light."

Shifting the box of clothes to my other arm, I reached up and pulled the small chain from the naked bulb hanging from the ceiling by the foot of the bed. The soft glare from the low wattage bulb searched the room for shadows to kill. It got most of them. "Let me get dressed, sweetheart. Be good and get our dinner ready."

I retired to the bathroom and made myself presentable with my pants and shirt. I decided not to opt for the tie and coat. I looked out the window in the bathroom and smiled. Opening it I could hear the traffic. The sounds had picked up, with the occasional whoop of someone thinking they were having a good time. I realized I hadn't today, and went back into the room. Angel had a spread laid out at the foot of the bed that consisted of a towel on which was set a box of tacos that smelled delicious, and a bottle of wine on the table by the bed, already opened and ready to serve. I was impressed. I should have been suspicious, but I was hungry and a bit beaten by the situation. I did manage to ask her one question.

"Why?"

She sat on the edge of the bed by the table with the wine. She looked away as she picked up the bottle of wine, saying "I saw the boy that night."

"This is what I already assumed."

She handed me the wine and bid me to settle on the bed amongst the food with her. Reaching over, she turned on the small lamp on the nightstand by the bed, while I straightened up and turned off the overhead bulb. The room seemed cozier and almost pleasant, in a run down sort of way.

She began to speak, and as she spoke the room grew warmer as her story grew longer. Apparently the boy had entered the Black Cat with some other sailors. They all had civilian khakis on with Hawaiian shirts, and they all were wearing an odd looking greenstone around their necks. Though they weren't in uniform, she could still tell what they were. American sailors all have that look and swagger to them. The boy didn't quite have the swagger right, though. He still seemed so young and very impressed with his surroundings and his friends. She had been working a sailor that was blitzed enough to the point he was more interested in talking to the bottle than to her. Bored, she decided to eavesdrop on this new group while through the smoke and clatter of tongues came the loud hot harsh music of a live hot jazz band, the cornet battling the rest of the instruments for supremacy.

I told her the wide eyed boy's name was Harry Goodwin, and asked if she could tell me about his friends. She could. There was a big bruiser, evidently the oldest in the crowd. A sort of brick wall with arms and legs and looked about as bright as a brick as well, from what she told me. But he seemed gentle, like a bear is gentle if left undisturbed. He acted as a shield for Harry, a protective big brother, rather than a bodyguard.

That must be Big Job Bob, I thought to myself.

She told about the other fellows with them, someone named Red, who only wanted to dance, and another name I recognized from a letter that Harry had written to me from basic training. A Texas boy by the name of Eddie Harris.

"I know of him," I told her. "Harry had written to me and told me about this guy named Eddie. He sent me a picture of his new friends. I was so happy to get a letter from him, I used to get a smile reading it over and over." Maybe the wine was loosening some memories in my head, but I could picture the letter, the handwriting and the photo. "I can still see what that letter said: These guys I'm with are the greatest. Lord knows I would never have met them at the academy or anywhere else but right here. Those Big Spring guys —funny name, the big mouth boys from Big Spring is what they should be called. Always ready for fun or trouble, doesn't matter. Good guys especially that Eddie Harris. He'll get somewhere someday, no matter how much he mouths off. Guess I don't mind that they give me a hard time or call me names. They wouldn't hang around with me if they didn't like me. And hell, I like them. Hope to see you soon, signed Harry" I smiled a crooked smile and lowered my eyes towards hers. "I used to keep that letter in my dressing room."

She moved what wine, food and papers that were on the bed over to the nightstand. The sounds outside played a sweet tune, sad but sweet, but they weren't quite in the same key yet. "You still haven't given me an answer."

"To what?'

"Why?"

"He reminded me of my brother who was killed by banditos when he was a boy. My family is very poor, senor. I work doing what I do because I support my young sister and grandmother a small village in the mountains. My brother was killed trying to keep the robbers from stealing a money box from our home. I knew what I had to do for them to survive. I also help you because you are different. You make me feel like a good girl again. Do you not like me anymore?" she whispered, her lips pouting at me as her eyes grew soft.

"Sure, you've been the only one that has been of any use." I sensed her hurt. I reached my hand over to her chin and touched her gently with the tips of my fingers. "I don't mean to sound as cold as I do. Circumstances have not been the best for my situation right now. I need someone to help me." A second's glance between us and I was crushed with her warm pillow lips against my cheek, while I held a grip on her that I didn't need to explain. Our mouths met, there was a rustle of linen, and for once I wasn't the one angling to turn off the light. An emotional release swept over me, as it seemed to do for her, and the rustling of linen became indistinguishable between the rustlings of clothes. Holding her ripe smooth body with passion while her experienced hands explored me, our low moans became in sync, keeping the same rhythm, until soon we were playing the same song. It seemed as if the sounds outside all joined in on our one great chorus, and this time, everything was in the same key.

After a while the sounds outside played out and became muted under the slow whirling overhead fan cooling us in the dark. The soft purple light from the neon outside danced on the walls and ceiling, stopping occasionally to reach down and give a solid outline to her figure nestled amongst the white linen. Our bodies were occasionally illuminated by the glowing embers of our cigarette that we shared. The heat that was unbearable a few hours ago was comfortably warm and pleasant, lulling me into that Daliesque world of sleep and wakefulness. Her gentle hands soothed me further as they ran over the sore muscles in my back. Her warmth instilled a cool relaxation in me and I began to dream. She became my angel of sweet mercy again as I drifted in her touch. The clouds closed in again and the soft neon colors danced in the distance. I slept.

At some point in the night I realized that the shimmering dancers were gone and I was staring half-lidded at a dark grey ceiling fan turning solemnly against a dull and chipped plaster ceiling. The colors were gone. So was my angel. A slight shadowy movement in the dark by her side of the bed made me start. The shadow spoke "Sorry darling to wake you. Let me go freshen up, I will be right back." I could see her a little clearer now. She had her dress draped about her and she was carrying a small bag as she closed the bathroom door.

"Sure, angel," I smiled. My eyes closed as I said her name, and as I listened to the sound of the running water in the shower, I slept again, turning my head to rest where she had been. The darkness was complete.

CHAPTER 8--FOUR MONTHS EARLIER
APRIL 1939
SINGAPORE

Bruno stood at the end a gilded bar, one hand holding his small colorful layered cocktail, his other hand clutching a box in his coat pocket. He reflected on his good fortune while sipping his pousse café, his good fortune being his great looks and fine taste. That taste was also reflected in the clothes he was wearing. Sitting in the trendy bar surrounded by other fashionable and well to do clients, he felt quite at ease and proud of himself. The people around him were a mix of affluential Asians and occidentals, enjoying each other's company, but all the while looking out for other romantic possibilities outside of the partners they were with.

He felt many eyes upon him with almost a pleasurable burning sensation. With each survey of the room, he met smiling glances his way. Women were sure to note his carefully pressed fancy white slacks, neat belt, gold threaded vest, dashing white summer jacket with folded white kerchief peeking from the breast pocket. Some of the young men surveyed him as well, he noticed. How envious they must be of his high cheekbones, strong angular jaw, and intense blue eyes with a thatch of blond hair neatly topped with a baby blue homburg. What a most dapper figure of an aristocrat and a fine example of Aryan manhood he must present!

Paying for his drink, he left the small but expensive club with a smile. Walking towards his destination a few blocks over he thought back to his earlier days as a child in Germany.

He let himself slip into the past as the city lights of Singapore blinked on one by one behind him. He thought of the thugs of his childhood that used to kick him to the muddy ground. The witless brutes at the military academy that would taunt him because they secretly knew he was better than they. His own father relentlessly pushing him, on and on, to win this competition, or that scholastic achievement. His industrialist father, running his own son like a factory machine for his own suppressed frustrations. Father could be worse than the schoolmates at times. Bruno still winced at the memory of the lashings.

A flash of light and a loud explosion startled Bruno back to the present. Bruno stiffened, quickly clutching at the precious box in his coat pocket. He turned his head and relaxed again as firecrackers in the street exploded in smoky chaos. The Festival of the Hungry Ghost had officially begun. Crowds of Buddhists, Taoists, and tourists were gathering in the bright costumes of celebration. Intimidating paper maché heads scowled fiercely, looking almost like Maori warriors. Foil masks and striking colors of many cloths reflected wildly in the lamps and torches that lined the streets of the square. Red banners with oriental symbols stretched from one sidewalk to another. Bruno smiled.

"Heathens. Amusing heathens." He held his gold capped cane in his white gloved hand and used it to move through the thickening crowd of chanting, laughing people.

Through the heady fumes of the huge burning joss sticks and candles, he could make out the open air café where he was to meet his private guest for the evening. Out in the open, unobtrusive, he and his guest could watch the spectacle of the festival undisturbed and unobserved. The pageantry was filling the streets with revelers, leaving only the outer rim of tables filled with people, all watching away towards the avenue. Seating himself against a far wall of the patio where he could see all, he motioned to the waiter, and promptly ordered champagne. As the waiter left, he noticed a well dressed little man with a black moustache approach his table. Bruno stood, nodded towards the gentleman. The man gave a quick smile and they both sat down. Bruno noticed that the man was fashionable, but not to the quality of Bruno. He was also small and Bruno's nose twitched with the greeting of a faint musky odor. The man spoke with a Dutch accent as he pushed his card across the table with his jeweled fingers. "I hope you a pleasant evening, sir." His card said "Hans Zilver - Agent – Collector Fine Art & Primitives - Amsterdam."

"I know who you are, of course," the little man grinned. "Do you have the box?"

Bruno waited, studying this person. The gaudy but expensive rings on nearly every finger of the little man's hand gave it an effeminate touch. The man had money but not the taste required to handle it properly in matters such as these. Still, this was a business deal. A slight smile played on Bruno's lips as he nodded.

The waiter brought the ice bucket with the champagne and glasses, popped the cork, and served the gentlemen unobtrusively while the two stared at each other and smiled. The little man picked up his glass. "I-I-I do not know which is colder, this glass or your smile. Cheers."

"Apologies, it is part of my habit. Cheers. To a successful deal."

The two drank deeply, one pair of eyes never leaving the other, with only the growing din of the festival providing the soundtrack to their scenario.

"The client who sent me is very excited about our meeting. This is an essential piece. He has had no way of acquiring something of such great hidden legend. He was not sure it even existed. I must admit I had never heard of such an item myself, so I did have reason to doubt the veracity of your claim, but after checking your credentials, well, uh, as you see, here I am."

Bruno lit a cigar as the little man talked, all the while noticing how his own cigar was larger and firmer, more robust, than the little man's small brown cigarette that sat nervously between slightly trembling and dainty fingers.

"Your client did not waste time." Bruno teased, hoping to gain more insight. He noticed that quite a crowd had assembled in front of the café, all backs facing him, except for two dark men who had come to sit a few tables away and sip liqueur quietly, not talking. "I am pleased. Any news from home?"

"Ah, yes." The little man fumbled for a newspaper in his jacket. Bruno truly was pleased with the way he set up his deals for trading collectibles. Hide in plain sight, use prearranged code words. There was something dirty about sneaking around in back alleys making black market deals. Bruno preferred well lit, clean, tasteful proceedings. He picked up the folded paper, felt the thick envelope that supposedly contained the Swiss Francs within, and placed it inside his white jacket. The little man with the black moustache was definitely perspiring now. "What a distasteful affliction," Bruno noted to himself.

"Danke. I have your chocolate." Bruno pulled out the box from his pocket and placed it on the table. On the box was a picture of some pieces of chocolate set against the Bavarian Alps. The little man's eyebrows worked like warring caterpillars on his brow, his black eyes looking wantonly at the box, then his hand quickly picking it up. Looking nervously around, he opened the box slightly to peer inside. Giving a quick smile, he closed the box and hurriedly placed it inside his pocket.

A series of loud firecrackers and hollers of delight sounded above the heads of the crowd, attracting Bruno's attention. Towering fifteen foot figures, constructed of bamboo frames covered in brilliantly colored paper with the bodies bearing broad golden armor plates and roaring tiger heads on their bellies sauntered by, propelled by the natives inside them, and twisted through the throng in the parade, with constant explosions and noisemakers following in their wake. One particularly fantastic demon head was dancing in front of the crowd at the café. "Colorful cacophony," thought Bruno. "Everyone is watching the festival. Everyone but the two dark gentlemen at the other table. They still sit and stare at their drinks"

Bruno's half second of thought was interrupted by the waiter wondering if there was more he could do.

"Yes," replied Bruno, staring at the little man. "You shall tell me how honest my companion is." Bruno reached into his jacket pocket, opened the paper slightly, and without looking, felt into the envelope and pulled out one of the Swiss francs. He stared directly at the little man. "This should settle our tab."

"Yes, sir. I will return with your change."

Bruno's smile stretched across his face. As the smile grew, the little man with the black moustache relaxed more visibly. "The waiter tells me you are an honest man," Bruno told him. "Let us toast to a successful transaction." Waiving his cigar in victory, Bruno poured them both another glass, finishing the bottle. Stuffing it upside down in the bucket of ice, Bruno gleamed. "Now we can relax."

The little man had gulped half his glass as Bruno's gaze drifted over to the table where the two men were now staring back intently, one rolling a large smoking cylinder between the tables towards them. Bruno had started halfway out of his chair when he was hit with a deafening explosion. The next thing he knew he and his companion were surrounded by a deluge of large firecrackers that had instantly parted the crowd. A group of half a dozen black attired masked thugs seemed to appear out of nowhere. Bruno could only defend himself as he called out "You allowed yourself to be followed, idiot!" Bruno managed to hold one assailant against a chair long enough to unscrew the top of his cane and unsheathe the sword contained therein. Spilling over a neighboring table, two of the attackers were on the little man, one holding him while the other swiftly sliced off the ringed fingers with a butterfly knife in order to pry the box from what was becoming a bloody stump. It took the other four to take on Bruno, although with a flash of his sword there were soon three. Over the little man's howls of pain and the screams of the crowd, Bruno's arm pinned a thug to the ground while he ground his thumb deep within an eye socket, feeling the soft tissue give way to warm blood. A swift crack on the back of the neck caused Bruno to loosen his grip.

With the little man left to bleed, all attention was placed on Bruno. They managed to hold him up long to slice open his pockets, emptying them into their hands. The paper fell to the side unnoticed at first till one of the black clad gang spied the envelope with money jutting out. "Aiieeeee!" the assailant shouted as the envelope was grabbed and its contents spilled. Sadly, the attacker stopped long enough to examine the contents. Bruno freed his arm and flashed his slime covered blade across the thug's arm and into an armpit, slicing off a neat bit of muscle, retrieving the rolled newspaper. Bruno took his toll on the arms that held him, slicing one throat in a lucky move while managing to stick the paper in his pants. As his hand came back up, the little finger was ripped from his left hand by the butterfly knife. Bruno was backed against a wall at this point, so he could deal with his aggressors straight in front of him. Another quick slash and the knife wielder was out. Another well placed round of fists and blade flashes managed to give him space to move. Backing quickly away, he retrieved his homburg and was down the sidewall of the café and around the alley, seconds away from his pursuers as a curious but happily distant crowd began to take notice of what had just happened.

Cutting across one alley and back down a forgotten passageway that emptied out into yet another alley,

Bruno could begin to hear faint sirens below the noise of the revelers. Although he himself was hurt, he knew that the others were far more damaged and would be moving somewhat slower. Blind luck coupled with a natural soldier's instinct led him to a darkened street where he could walk along unnoticed by relatively few witnesses. An occasional sharpness of streetlamp light gave him solitude enough to check his wounds. His breathing was intense and forced, a sign of adrenalin working its way through his system. "Nasty bastards. Nasty filthy bastards. My clothes are a disgrace and a ruin. My hands, poor things." He stopped under a lamp to observe his left hand, the strange numbing in it giving surprise to his eyes. "Bastards. They sliced my fifth finger and have ruined my suit with my own blood. They have taken a piece of me and made me dirty in the bargain. Incredible bastards."

Taking his kerchief from his pocket, he wrapped it around his hand in a mild tourniquet to protect his wound. Running his hand down his pants, he found the paper with the lump of payment inside. Fighting the pain that was now beginning to sear his entire hand, he stopped long enough to open the package inside the paper. The slight smile of satisfaction on his face turned swiftly to a sharp line of anger. Opening the paper, he had seen the first few bills on the top and on the bottom. The bulk of the package was filled with newspaper clippings carefully cut to mimic the size and shape of the high denominations of Swiss currency that acted as teasing bookends on the valueless payment. "People are going to die. Oh, yes, most assuredly, quite a few will die for what they have taken from me." The slight smile returned to his face, but this time it was coupled with a distant prophetic gaze, amplified by a red seared hand that brought greater pain that Bruno was no longer aware of.

He sauntered through a gathering fog down the darkened distant, almost empty side streets, the misty blackness acting as his confidant and giving succor to his mental ravings until he was swallowed up, becoming a spirit of the night and a member of the evil things that lurk behind the veil.

CHAPTER 9--LATE AUGUST 1939
ILLEGAL ESCAPE

I am not sure at what time later I noticed the banging or which bang I noticed first. What I was sure of, was that it was the cops. Nobody bangs on doors like cops. I called out "Un momentito" as I sprang out the bed and into my pants in a sudden move and made for the door. I might have made it, too if I hadn't stopped to fasten my belt. The big foot that entered by the door jamb was impressive as was the big cop behind it. Two cops standing in my doorway with guns drawn were framed by the amber early morning light streaming into my darkened room. The head of the fruity desk clerk bobbed in and out of sight behind the shoulders of the cops, babbling in some sort of tex-mex mélange about the status of the décor.

"We are here to arrest you for the murder of Capitan Gonzalez," the Big Foot Cop said as the smaller cop put his gun back in his holster and strutted over to flick on the naked light bobbing under the fan.

"Murder – what are you talking about?"

"After you left early this evening, Capitan Gonzalez went back to his office. An hour later he was found dead, his throat slit, his head down on his desk. You were the last one he had any dealings with. You are suspect numero uno."

"You people's power of deduction is amazing. I had been gone for over an hour, yet I killed him."

"You have the motive. We were told to bring someone in now. You win the prize, gringo."

"Wait – how…?"

The smaller cop lunged to my side to grab me. Then the blur began. Reflex obtained from doing my own stunts in all those jungle flicks took over. I side stepped the smaller cop's lunge, bringing my elbow down hard between his shoulder blades as he went by, tripping over my outstretched foot. As he went down, he fell heavily against the closed bathroom door, banging it open to reveal an empty shower stall with the water still running. The window by the stall was wide open. I could only take this for what it meant in a second of time, for the Big Foot Cop was in my face with his pistol muzzle shoved against my cheek and his hand gripping my throat and shoving me towards the wall. The smaller cop was already back on his feet, grabbing me from behind in a full nelson grip. Big Foot straightened up with a smile and shoved a hammy fist into my gut.

"Murder. Assault on an officer. Theft," he heaved.

I could hear the desperate desk clerk's whinny of "Mos Dios!" as he ran away down the hall.

"I tell you I don't know what you are talking about!"

Big Foot caught his breath. "There was the greenstone missing from Gonzalez' desk."

"A missing greenstone?"

"Si. You thought you could come back and steal that greenstone that used to belong to that dead boy. Do you deny knowledge of this?"

"I don't know what – wait, I do remember seeing a greenstone in Gonzalez' drawer, but he quickly closed it. I didn't think it was the boy's. If it was, then Gonzalez was the thief, not me!"

Big Foot slapped me hard across my face, opening the skin above my right cheekbone. I could taste blood and sweat at the corner of my mouth. I had to get out of there fast, before the frame could stick. "Look, Big Foot, I want a phone call to my studio. I want a lawyer."

"Ha!" Hot breath and spittle flew in my face. "You don't get nothing but a busted gut I think. There is nothing you can do."

I tried to relax, so that the cop holding me might relax his grip. "I have an alibi. I have been with a girl all night."

"Is this so? Where is this girl?"

"She was in the bathroom taking a shower; she said she had to freshen up."

Big Foot turned to the direction of the bathroom, where only the water was running. "She is not there now, Senor. Maybe she wash down the drain, huh?"

All I could look at through the door was that open window. The curtain fluttered uselessly against the stagnant breeze that blew inward. A slight hint of dawn sneaking in seemed to be sealing the reality of my fate. "I guess she left by the fire escape."

"Si, not only did she leave by the escape, but she come to us with a tale of how much you hate Gonzalez and how you come to steal the greenstone. Your alibi is not an alibi, she is an honest citizen, doing her duty to keep Tijuana clean, gringo. Now you will give us the greenstone so we can convict you quickly."

I hesitated. I never took my acting much more seriously than an easy way to get dames. Now I had to act because my life depended on it. "Alright. If you look in the nightstand by the bed, you'll find it." I held my head down while I said this, not trusting my eyes for the lie. "Ah, good for you. Now maybe you will not die as slow. Put the cuffs on him"

Smiling, he walked around the foot of the bed, headed for the nightstand drawer. My vision became sharper as my muscles relaxed under the other cop's restraint. The overhead bulb had been disturbed during the initial struggle and was looping light and shadow lazily against the objects in the room, creating crazy distortions of the shadows in the room. The smaller cop was fumbling for the bracelets as Big Foot began to open the nightstand drawer, his eyes turned away from me for the first time. One snap of one of the cuffs behind my back was the signal I needed. Before he had a chance to click the second, I wheeled and grabbed the smaller cop unawares, my knee colliding with his groin as I swung the loose bracelet dangling from my wrist as a weapon and slammed the open end of the other wrist lock into his eye. With both his hands reaching for his wound, I tried to grab his gun, but Big Foot was quicker and grabbed me, barreling the small cop over into the dresser head first where he lay quite still while we struggled on the floor. Big Foot was on me pinning me down, grunting in my ear. This time I was on my side and managed to get both hands on his throat, squeezing hard enough to cut off the air from his lungs. I slowly pushed him up and away from me, his face growing pinker. His hulking frame had my body pinned against the floor, crushing my knee caps together. He struggled to keep me pinned with one arm, his other reaching for the holster at his side. Slowly and desperately trying to maintain the stifling grip on his throat with one hand, I moved the other to grab his wrist that was already in possession of his gun. A deadly reverse tug of war that seemed to last indefinitely, but was only seconds, saw the strains of my hand against his wrist, my hand moving slightly up to his palm that held death; death that was moving pointedly towards my gut. The black gun still managed to cock as my hand mashed the fingers that were on the trigger. Unable to breathe, Big Foot tried to shift his head for release from my left hand. At that moment I was able to twist his wrist backwards, while his fingers completed their job. A loud bang followed by a scream and Big Foot pulled away, writhing, and grabbing his leg, already a fountain of red. I slipped away from him like a crab until I could brace myself against the bathroom door. Already a large crowd could be heard making their way towards the still open front door of the room. The shadowplay of the fan and the dancing bulb made it look as if I were in a badly edited silent flicker and the final reel was about to run out. Big Foot let go of one paw from his wound long enough to find his gun beside him and started shooting wildly at me. My only escape was the bathroom window, still very wide open. My angel had escaped this way. Now to find out if she had wings.

  I threw myself out the window in a small panic. A fire escape was there, right where I hoped one would be. The two final shots from Big Foot's gun reverberated in the room above. I could have taught a spider monkey a thing or two by the way I swung down the escape and into the quiet stench of the dark confines below.

I was in an open grassy area that fed into an alley a few yards away. Shirtless, shoeless, wanted by the police, I was glad that I at least had my pants on. I really kicked over the ant's nest this time.

The sun was lancing shafts of light down the alleyway that I headed for. That alley in turn angled off to the left, where a pick-up truck piled with empty lettuce crates was parked to the side. I hid behind the truck and peered beyond. The alley opened onto a huge open courtyard, surrounded with cafes and shops all around. In the middle were stalls after stalls of all sorts of fresh produce. This maze of a mercado was swarming with early morning farmers and merchants, Indians, short-haired dogs of all kinds, but no two alike, occasional turistas, fat women with little ones swarming like flies around their robin red skirts, all of them babbling and haggling, and the smell of food – food cooking every few feet, the clanging of cookware drowning out the constant chaos of oompah accordions all playing the same basic song on a hundred different phonographs and radios. I was intrigued by this festival of the senses when a hand touched my arm, making me realize my somewhat embarrassing condition. "Senor – peso? Cambie para pobresito?" spoke a peasant beggar whose wizened face was made more gruesome by a cavernous and toothless empty mouth. I began to sneer, and then I saw he was better dressed than I. At least he had a shirt and some shoes. Not wasting time I smiled, pulled out a wad of green and motioned him around to the back of the truck, trying to explain in broken Tex-Mex and sign language that I wanted to buy his clothes. At first he was insulted by my gestures, and thought I was a fag, but I soon convinced him with another dollar that I only wanted to switch clothes, and he could buy new ones with the money I was giving him. Already the yowling of the police sirens was converging on the mercado. In seconds they stopped and I knew they were on foot in stalls and shops. I thanked the old beggar, and a happier gummy grin I've never seen. The old beggar's clothes were simple but dirty, with the air of grease and stale booze. The simple peasant farmer shirt and loose but sturdy pants held up by a sash looked like they used to be white once, but right now they were as good as tailor made.

   Taking his mangled sombrero and placing it on my down turned head; I tried to pass my way into the crowd away from the cops. The sandals were a clumsy fit, but they worked. If I kept my collar up and didn't look at anyone, I might make it to – to where? Across the border. Yea right, here I am, penniless now, wanted by the cops, unable to look anyone in the face to plead my case to. No phone calls, no easy cab ride. The border patrol would catch me if I tried to walk it across the bridge. I walked evenly but surely about five stalls when the busy sounds around me went sour. A commotion was taking place behind me. I stood behind a couple of giant piñatas and had a peek. The old beggar was being given the treatment by a couple of cops as he was trying to buy some clothes at a stall. I could tell they were wondering what he was doing in my pants with no shirt or shoes. One cop argued while another gave the old man a patdown. The patdown cop shouted with delight as he pulled an object out of the pants' pocket over the old man's objections. My wallet! Damn! I had instinctively put my wallet back in my pants after I paid the old man but before we switched. No time to worry now, the other cop was blowing a whistle, signaling others to the search, no doubt showing them the picture on my driver's license. The old man was crying now as the cops roughed him into pointing a shaky finger right at me. I took off at a clip, not waiting to see if they followed the old beggar's direction and not looking back.

Whistles blew, cries cried loudly, dogs barked and joined in the chase, one looking at me, tongue lolling, thinking this a great game. I passed a stall of chorizo sausage on my left, grabbing a handful and slinging a heap on the ground, where the dogs considered this their treat for a fine run. I glanced at a cop trying to make it through the middle, but getting attacked by some of the hungrier hounds for his intrusion. A fast right, a quick left, more items bumped over, I managed to give a quick slap on the ass of a docile burrow and brought it to life, its kicking, thrashing hooves busting the support of the stand it was tethered to. The burrow spread its anger around the crowd, twisting, kicking, and causing the crowd to run in panic and providing an effective barrier against the cops as I ran down one open aisle and twisted down another.

As I turned down a third aisle, a crowd of fat mamacitas arguing over dead goats hanging in a butcher stall was blocking my way towards a building arch and the exit of the courtyard. I quietly ducked under the tent flap of a closed up stall next to what looked like a small warehouse on the edge of the market, leaned up against a pole in the semi-darkness, and caught my breath, the sounds of confusion still ringing in my ears. After a few seconds I realized I wasn't the only one breathing.

"Silencio" a muffled voice pleaded in the shadows. As my eyes adjusted I could see that I had snuck under a flap that covered a large entrance to small warehouse. I could make out light from an opposite large opening on the other side of the building. Framed by the light was the silhouette of a good sized produce truck. Nervous breathing was all around me. As my eyes adjusted I could see men standing or shuffling anxiously from one foot to the other. A large man in khaki began herding the men into a low compartment on the truck. Confused, I would have turned to leave, but a police whistle in the distance changed my mind. Seeing that the men around were dressed in the same basic peasant worker outfit as mine, I decided the best idea now was to dummy up and play along.

    I could see that the tent stall was backed up directly to the building, hiding the building's low loading dock. The men herded like sheep, silently obeying the Khaki Man's silent signals. I held my head down and blended into the crowd heading for the truck. I saw that we were being crowded into a very tight area, with way too many of us to have any comfort. I balked for a second, only to be pushed headlong against the port side of the compartment. Small holes covered with mesh a foot apart or so had been drilled near the base of the floorboard. Nervous, sweaty, anxious men were squeezed in all around me until we were practically in each other's laps. I could just lower myself to look through the peephole to see Khaki Man make another signal to a couple of dockworkers.

    Crates of lettuce, along with mangoes and plantains were being stored above us. A few seconds later a hand reached down and pulled up a metal door effectively sealing us into the belly of the truck. I could hear some slight shuffling of wooden crates against the sealed door of our compartment and I knew those crates were there for camouflage. The truck engine made a slight growl, and we were moving, out of the warehouse and onto the street.

The heat and the darkness were relieved only by the small mesh opening at my side I closed my eyes to the claustrophobia that made me want to scream and lash out against my silent comrades in the gloom. Time meant nothing as the truck turned, stopped, started, finally stopping for a small eternity. At least when the truck moved, some air came in through the hole. A hand grabbed my shoulder in the darkness, urging me silently not to move, not to breathe. Another hand came out of the darkness to place a covering over the hole. Cut off from everything except heat and no air, I could hear officious voices speaking Spanish, then the truck rumbled to life again and we were gone, only to stop and repeat the process, only this time there were officious English and Spanish voices conversing, another acceleration of the engine, and we were going once more. Going once more? To where? It didn't take me long to figure out. The barriers were removed from the tiny plugs to the outside world and all I could make out was asphalt. Like those heads of lettuce I was being transported to a market, but the lettuce was lucky. I wasn't headed to the local grocery when it was all over. No sir, I was headed straight to a different market.

Cramped, uncomfortable and sore, I closed my eyes to rest. Maybe I could get some sleep before I arrived wherever I was going. In the darkness, the picture that Harry had sent me of his buddies loomed into my mind's view. That picture always made me smile. He and his buddies dressed in the same civvies, Hawaiian shirts and khakis, looking as if someone had just told a good joke. Hanging out in some store front in San Diego, they looked like four of the three musketeers. As I started to drift with the rumble of the engine into sleep, the picture started to fade. Funny picture. All laughing. All dressed alike right down to the pendants hanging around their necks.

 Greenstone pendants.

 I was awake for the rest of the ride.

CHAPTER 10--LATE AUGUST 1939
THE OLD PLANTATION

The bag of oranges rested easy against my hip as the cab pulled up to the estate gates of Mr. and Mrs. Colonel Goodwin.

"Stop here, driver. I'll walk up." I paid the driver and bailed out of the somewhat comforting cab into the humid heat of a late Virginia afternoon. I hadn't taken two steps toward the open driveway gate of the old plantation and already I could feel the beads of sweat wanting to drip between my shoulder blades. I couldn't see the house from the drive as it seemed the ancient oaks had taken command of any view I might have, their moss hanging as beards from old men, making them appear wise. A squirrel announced my coming and ran somewhere ahead. As oppressing as the light and heat were, I still managed a sly spring to my step. Only a couple of weeks ago I had literally been farmed out as a half-assed slave illegal laborer on an orange grove north of San Diego. Keeping my mouth quiet and pleading ignorance, which was readily believed by all concerned, contributed to the further demolition of my ego, but I held steady until a decent unobtrusive escape could be made. Making to the nearest highway, English returned to my tongue and I thumbed my way to Los Angeles and my former existence that was beginning to reach a state of chaos. Still, it beat sitting in a Mexican jail for assault and possible murder. Hell of a career move.

My latest Dick Hardwing serial was finished, the studio's attorneys were dealing with the Mexican government for extradition while playing the hush-hush publicity game, my agent no longer talked to me, but his secretary still had the hots for me, so the information got through. I was free for the next few weeks while the film went into release, so now I could take care of personal business. And this was personal. I approached the imposing house, where a great Bentley was parked to the side. A fastidiously tailored chauffer polished and preened on the car, shining its gleaming sides daintily while still managing to grant me a nod and sneer of disapproval as I meandered to the huge front door.

A quick couple of raps with the knocker brought a sound of approaching footsteps. The door opened and my heart was sucked in to that exquisite face before me. I felt like a bee drawn to her pink rose petal skin. Black hair framed her face against the cool dark of the interior, her lips pursed slightly as a gentle breeze ruffled through the folds of her diaphanous summer dress. The moment shifted and I finally felt my lips move. "Hello sweetie. I got here as soon as I could."

"Sterling!" She started to take a step forward then caught herself. "Please come in. Our servant Jessie has the day off. You look hot, like you could use a drink."

"Thanks."

"How is your back?"

"Could be better. Actually I hadn't thought about it till you mentioned it just now. See, I've been busy."

"Yes...I know. Let me take you up to Harry's room. You don't mind if we talk there, do you?"

"I suppose not. Why? What do you want to show me in Harry's room?"

"Nothing in particular, it is just that I spend all my time in there now and ... I thought that maybe you might get a better feel for what Harry was like if you saw his room."

"Yea, I suppose I would. Look, Marian, I need to tell you that what I said the last time we were together back at my place in Hollywood was…" I never noticed the large figure standing off to one side.

"Humph..." it said.

"Oh, Sterling, you haven't met my husband, the Colonel, have you?"

"No I haven't. Pleased to meet you sir." Marian took the bag of oranges from me and left as I shook his hand.

"Wish I could say the same for you. I don't like this business. It is an embarrassment, and I still think it is basically a foolish idea to bring someone like you, especially you, in to the situation. There is something shameless about it. However, I do like that you appreciate action. You portray a man of action, now is a chance for you to see if you know what you are doing. I have a chance for you to prove yourself on something other than a Hollywood set or the front of a microphone. A chance to see if you can back up what the public thinks you are about." He paused, eyeing me. "Cocktail? You must be thirsty after walking up from the main gate."

"Thanks. I almost expected to be greeted by some dogs as I came up. Usually these large estates have porch dogs of some kind running around."

"Sir, I do not keep animals as pets. I hunt and kill them."

He turned his back and moved off to a room to the side of the main door as he talked, as if expecting me to follow him. I did. We entered a large oaken room filled with the fragrance of brandy, tobacco, and death.

Scowling at me from all sides of the high walls were mounted animal heads, frozen in one last grimace, their glass eyes passing judgment on me as much as the Colonel. One side of the room had a full length glass cabinet filled with a small arsenal of guns and weapons from various eras, while the other side had more curios than I had seen outside of any museum. Everything else in the room seemed to be made from animal skin and bone. Furniture, rugs, even the large oval frame over the fireplace that held a picture of the good Colonel holding an elephant gun proudly next to a very dead elephant, all of it used to be very much alive. All of it was all made of remnants of various animal parts. Feeling as if I were on trial, I pleaded. "Sir, all I've done is to gather some not very pleasant information and get myself in dutch along with it. I might want to lay low and leave this job for the authorities."

He grumbled as he shook the tumbler of liquor from behind a small plush leather bar. "Authorities. Slow moving dim-witted bureaucrats with no personal involvement in this situation other than saving their own paycheck and making sure they don't have to sweat too much or they might miss their coffee break. They won't do. There is too much at stake here. The death of our child will be dealt with my way and my way only."

He handed me my drink as he came around the other side of the bar. I was a little kid looking up at an oversized bully. "Maybe you're moving too fast for me, but I am just an actor. Okay, maybe a bit of a hack actor but…"

"You're also forgetting that you are a prize ham as well."

"Alright, look. I've delivered the information for you quickly and efficiently like I promised. You are forgetting that I loved the boy as well, but this is all I can do. Now if you'll forgive me, I think I will be on my way." I started to nod and turn, but something about his demeanor kept me in place.

"Not so fast." He was more intense now, determined, moving closer to me. "I am glad you are exactly who you are. You have a passion and a personal stake in this. I know how you felt about the boy, and I know you would like to get your hands around the throat of the killer just as much as I would. I am preparing to offer you triple your present salary of what the studio pays you, plus expenses for what I want done. What I want you to do is track down this killer. The easiest way to do that is to find those boys that were with him and follow the trail of that greenstone that was around his neck in his pictures. I believe that if you find the greenstone, you will have the killer.

The greenstone again. "Look, I don't know much about this greenstone.

What if I say no?"

"You won't say no. Your ego won't let you. Your greed won't let you. I won't let you. I have money Mr.

Hanover, and this money gives me power. I happen to have a strong influence over the broadcasting and newspaper industries not only in this here state, but across the country. A few well placed phone calls from me, and a certain Saturday matinee idol of boys and girls everywhere will suddenly find themselves without a hero because of a certain casual liaison a few years ago. A liaison that almost ruined a young girl's life. Do you understand my meaning, Mr. Hanover?"

"Yeah, I get you. I get you all the way from China, loud and clear. How long do I get to think about it?"

"Take as long as you want, Hanover. Only give me a decision before you leave this house, in say, twenty minutes?"

His bushy eyebrows formed one long hairy rain gutter across the top of his face as I felt myself being pushed by the force of his will to exit the room. I turned against the chill of his gaze and left, turning back into the passageway, walking between rows of smaller artifacts and symbols of lost philosophies lining the hallway towards the marbled staircase where Marian stood waiting for me. I motioned for her to lead the way, after the fashion of a true southern gentleman. A sad smile was my gift as she ascended. As she walked up the stairs, there was no way I could not help but watch the gentle sway of her hips. She was beautiful and I desired her. I wanted to take her, right then and there on the stairs and let her know what I felt for her. Instead, I swallowed and continued. Reaching the top, she turned, catching my eyes catching her. She was smiling, "Sterling, I've missed you. Especially now. Our boy.." she let out a quick sob as I reached for her. Holding her to me I was struck with how our emotions pooled together, blending, touching, a physical thing, emotional, our hands remembering. She pulled back from the embrace, panting, "The room." Walking a few steps down the hall, she opened a door into a lost life.

Harry's room was large, spacious and opened up onto a balcony. Beyond that a green forested valley reached out to the distance and held my view. I turned away and saw that the room itself was an organized clutter of shelves, stacks of magazines, maps hastily tacked on the wall, Romanesque paintings, and photographs. A small stack of letters set next to a chess set at a table by the balcony doors. Recent cigarette butts filled a small stand next to the table.

"I sit there all morning while I have my breakfast." She stood in the doorway with some uneasiness as I moved slowly towards the window next to the balcony doors. I must have stood there, silently staring out the window at that green valley as Harry must have done, for an entire minute or more when I heard her clear her throat. "I'll bring you another cocktail."

"Sure, kid." The door closed softly behind me and as it did I could feel my shoulders droop

On the wall to the right of me were pictures of a family. One was of Harry as a child, playing with Marian while the Colonel read a paper in the background. All the other pictures were of Marian and Harry enjoying things that a typical family does. The Colonel was absent, not surprisingly. Marian and Harry made a nice family, a family that could have been my family if I had played my cards right. Only I would have been in all of the pictures with them. "Sure, that would have been a great family," I thought out loud. "A child I barely knew and a woman that I..." I caught myself before I could go any further.

Looking farther down the wall next to a mirror I saw my publicity still, framed and autographed "To My Little Pal." Not a bad looking guy I thought to myself. I caught myself in the mirror. Eyes hollow, face tanned but ragged, I was looking a bit like hell now because of the last few days. My shoulders seemed as if a great weight has been placed on them. This is a look the great jungle adventurer Dick Hardwing, idol of popcorn gorged boys everywhere could never show anyone else. Dick Hardwing, inspiration for a thousand Saturday afternoon backyard safaris, as coolly portrayed by that fine actor Sterling Hanover. As I walked over and touched the picture frame, the slow rot of my deteriorating thoughts seemed to enter my bloodstream, coursing their bile through out my entire frame. Watching myself in the mirror, the tailor-made clothes I wore that used to fit me handsomely now seemed to be oversized and slack, as if representing the physical shrivel of my body. I had to turn away and straighten myself. If I kept this up, I'd end up blowing away like so many dust balls in a summer breeze. As I continued to walk around the room, I couldn't help but to touch Harry's objects gingerly as if they were fine crystals. I wandered to the table by the balcony doors and looked at the stack of letters next to the chess set. I could see a game half played on the mahogany board. I wondered which side Harry was. As I studied the chess set, I could see that the white knight was in trouble and in danger of being taken by a pawn. I picked up the knight and studied the situation, wondering where to place it on the board.

  A sudden soft metallic squeal of a brass doorknob and Marian appeared with a cold cocktail and a soft greeting. Startled, I furtively placed the chess piece in my pocket, trying to hide the effect of what the past few minutes worth of reflections had just done to me. My smile hopefully hid feelings of guilt for not knowing the boy as I felt I should have, and for the fact that Marian might not want me touching or prying into what has evidently become a shrine for her.

I turned away from the table and took in the fastidiousness of the room. "I haven't touched it since the day I got the news." She was almost whispering. "The maid dusts it once a week." She walked to the table and picked up the letters, handing them to me. "These are from Harry," she sighed. The letters looked well read, and were filled with descriptions of his new friends. "He wrote about his friends a lot. They all seemed to be very close. You may have the letters if you like. They could be of some help."

"Did you volunteer these to the police?"

"Only the information that was in them. You can see how well the police did with it."

She turned towards the balcony as I gave a cursory glance at the letters. His buddies' names were all there. Big Job Bob seemed to dominate the letters. References were made to Bob's background as a former professional wrestler in Mexico. Then I saw it. One of the letters that made a few short references to a greenstone caught my eye. I must have made a slight sound when I saw it because before I could read it I felt Marian's warm stare and put the letters in my pocket without reading further. "He was artistic."

"What?" I was temporarily jolted away from my thoughts.

"Creative." She crossed the room over to Harry's bedside. Next to it was a large stack of well thumbed

National Geographics and Detective Monthly Stories. "He was quite a photographer. He always wanted to be published in a magazine. Seems like he thought it might be some sort of reconciliation with his father. His father never appreciated him." She turned to me with moist eyes. "When Harry announced he wanted to shoot wildlife, the Colonel was overjoyed. That is, until the Colonel found out that Harry wanted to use a camera instead of a gun." A slow intake of air produced a softer exhale of sweet breath from her red lips. I nervously finished my drink, feeling I needed something to do with my hands that didn't involve crushing her soft form to me and stroking her dark hair with gentle "It's OK's" and "I knows." I didn't have to wait long before she obviously read my thoughts and decided to offer her arms and her lips. She grabbed me harder than I had hoped, a desperate clench that made me hunt for air between wet kisses. She made my mind up for me, without me even being aware of it.

Just as suddenly, she pulled away and faced the wall. "I can't do this." She walked over to the bedside, fingering a half unwrapped rather large painting. "The Colonel gave him this picture to put over his bed. He couldn't stand the one that is there."

I saw the one that was there. It was a rather good rendition of an idyllic Greek setting, all robes and ponds and doves and antiquity. Boy, they sure knew how to live in those days, according to the painting. What I saw half opened on the floor by the bed was another rendition, only this was of Napoleon riding a white horse into battle. Bodies and armaments lay in disarray around him. "Me, I like the pond, myself," I smirked. She flashed those dark eyes at me, joining me in my smirk. "I know," was all I got out of her.

She soaked in the room again for what must have been her thousandth time. "Sterling, I need you." My heart made a reflexive flutter. "You know why." Her gaze bore a hole straight through me. I found myself saying "Yes, I know," when I wasn't even sure what I was saying. I knew, sure, but it wasn't anything I could tell her, or even explain logically myself.

Before I could shake the feeling she put me through, I found myself going down the stairs, back into the entranceway to the Colonel's den towards the front door. Marian and I smiled warmly at each other until I passed the den, when the man himself pounced on us as a lion pounces on a couple of gazelles.

"What is your answer?" was the roar. I stopped, did a slow turn with a slight smile leftover from being with Marian.

"Yea. I'll do it. But not for your reasons." I could feel Marian's warmth against my back as I opened the front door and went outside, back into the stifling humidity. The glare of the sun off the polished Bentley left me dazzled a bit. Constantly polishing, and still in the same position I had seen him in an hour ago was the chauffer. Like an attendant gargoyle on some French chapel, he repeated his original nod and scowl at me as I made my way back down the driveway to the main gate.

My train back to Los Angeles was filled with dreams, nightmares and soft thoughts.

CHAPTER 11--FOUR MONTHS EARLIER
APRIL 1939
VENGENCE SOUGHT

"I will not let this stop me. The more others try, the more they will suffer defeat, not I." Bruno wandered west, lost in thought, bandaged hand in pocket of the new grey suit he had picked up earlier in the day. The Singapore sun was wandering with Bruno to the west as well, to set, and as it did Bruno was telling his troubles to it. "You and I are similar" Bruno thought with a smile. "We may look as if we are going down, yet we always rise again and continue anew."

The contents of the box that had cost much obsessed in Bruno's thoughts. "I will get what I want. The stone will be mine. It wants me as I want it. It grows closer to me."

The Singapore street Bruno was walking emptied out on to a large busy pier. Ships of different nations were there, all with different tongues, yelling, giving commands, all in an overlapping babble. Bruno strolled casually to the end of the pier, away from the docked ships and towards the clutch of grimy bars and shops. He wrinkled his nose.

"This odor, how can these pigs live with it?" The sweet smell of fish and musty spices were almost overwhelming. Bruno entered a mildly crowded pub towards the end of the pier. Taking a table near the back, he motioned the bartender for a beer.

As he sat sipping his pint, he thought again why he was here. That stone. That precious item. He had defied the Reich for it. "I went in," he smiled to himself. "Snuck up on that ceremony in the middle of a pouring monsoon, that horrible torch lit bamboo hut, interrupting the ceremony where that amazing woman was slathering herself with scented oils in front of my goal. Killing who knows how many unfeeling savages. What do I get for my troubles? What do I get for continuing the traditional hobby of my fine respected industrialist father and family?"

Bruno's eyes became harder and more distant. "Idiots!" Banging the table hard, he caught himself, and, smiling towards the bartender, again ordered another drink, only this time whiskey. When the glass and bottle were brought, and he poured himself a healthy shot, a story emerging among the murky vapors of his glass. Curling his fist around the now quivering drink, he recalled to himself the previous evening, and how the botched deal and subsequent robbery had cost him his finger.

Last night after the battle, he had been bleeding badly, and had wandered without seeing where he was going, when out of the gloom he saw a sign that read "Pharmacy" in half a dozen languages. Luckily it was still open. Once inside, he was surrounded by bottle after bottle of herbs and mysterious eastern potions. He had asked the small bespectacled man behind the counter for a doctor. The wiry man smiled and disappeared into a back room. A few seconds later, an even smaller ancient man appeared, white pointed beard trailing down the front of his white shirt. He fixed Bruno's chopped finger with a mortar full of odd pastes and compounds, and as he did, he and Bruno talked. They talked of thieves and rings of thieves. The old doctor revealed that he was not above doctoring and healing people with mysterious "accidents", and not reporting them to the police. After Bruno's description of his assailants, the old doctor just smiled slightly and told him which ring it was. This ring operated in the smuggling and black market operations on the main pier.

"I must set my trap carefully," he thought, snapping himself back to the present. Suddenly straightening up, he took the bottle and glass with one hand, and strolled to the bar confidently. Whispering to the bartender, Bruno smiled and slipped him some coin. The bartender grinned back, whispered "The Character," and went to the end of the bar where the rough Character was nursing a glass of rum. Eyebrows rose between the bartender and the rough Character. The Character shot Bruno a glance and walked unevenly over to where Bruno was. Bruno did his best to not let the Character's foul breath break his own easing smile. "'Keep sez ya lookin' fer somethin' to buy," the Character sprayed.

"Oh, yes. Quite so," Bruno replied smugly. Bruno then described an item he knew about that would be most coveted in a place like this. The Character's rummy eyes widened. They tested each other verbally to see if the other was bluffing. Finally, the Character became slightly more confident, admitting that he knew of someone that dealt in Asian trinkets. An hour or so passed with Bruno feeding the Character more and more rum, while his own glass remained half full. And then Bruno got the info he needed to continue his journey.

The Character brought up the name of Old Salt, a smuggler that dealt in Asian trinkets, though these trinkets could be quite expensive. Old Salt was a friend of the Character, and earlier that day the Old Salt had shown the Character an item that matched what Bruno was looking for. Bruno got enough details to realize that this trinket was the object he sought. After a few more minutes of conversation, the Character asked about the price of what Bruno would be willing to pay, and what the Character's cut would be to connect him to Old Salt. Bruno tried to assure him that he had money now to satisfy all concerned, but the Character wanted proof up front. Bruno smiled, said he would show him, but not here at the bar. He told the Character to go to the restroom and he would be in there in a few minutes, so as not to arouse suspicion among anyone in the bar. The Character agreed to this proposal, stating that the object was indeed of the quality that Bruno wanted, and that the deal and the transfer would take place at a better location.

The Character left. Bruno could hardly contain his eagerness, his bandaged hand throbbing stronger as the seconds ticked into minutes. At the right time, Bruno went to the back toilet of the bar following his nose with disgust towards the steadily growing stench of bodily odors emanating from a tiny room. Once inside he could see the room itself was situated over open slats and boards with holes cut in them for evacuation straight into the harbor. The Character had his back to the door and was employing one of the spaces in the slats when Bruno struck.

The Character never had a chance. Ignoring the pain in his hand, Bruno had the Character's windpipe closed with a grip from behind, while his stiletto was pushed up hard under the Character's ribs. "Where is Old Salt?" Bruno breathed in his ear.

"He ain't around, I sez."

Bruno could feel warm blood running onto his hand from the blade of the stiletto. He liked it. "Speak or I dig deeper." He felt the Character begin to give in.

With tears starting to stream from his eyes, the Character managed to choke out that Old Salt had already left the country that evening on a steamer bound for San Diego. Bruno knew he had to move quickly.

Bruno pushed the knife in, twisting it as he did. He kicked open a part of the slats and shoved the Character's body through. He closed his eyes and shook with pleasure, waiting to hear the body hit the water below.

Five hours later Bruno was comfortably tucked away in a private room on larger, more professional ship bound for southern California. He was carefully smoothing the pleats on his slacks and enjoying a cocktail. He should arrive not long after Old Salt.

CHAPTER 12--FIVE MONTHS LATER EARLY SEPTEMBER 1939

Something funny about the light in the Hollywood Hills. The rays seem to curve and bend around corners. Dancing among the hills against the rising steam of the cool morning, one pesky ray managed to sneak its way through the heavy draped curtains and latch on to my left eye, causing me to glance that same eye towards the clock at the side of the bed for sympathy. I didn't feel like getting up yet. "Doesn't matter" was the message I received from the clock and the ray of light. The light seemed sympathetic for awhile, since it eased my pain by shining sweetly on Ha-Knee's bare beautiful ass next to me. I lay there with a smile, admiring the ways her soft skin plummeted and rose with the curving form that was her gentle sensual nakedness. Slightly hypnotized and continuing to smile, time felt frozen as my gaze fondled her beauty. The bed was an ocean of blankets and covers that were all kicked back from the playfulness of the night before. Damn, I don't remember to sleep in enough I made a note to myself.

The rays were now starting to slide towards the oaken furniture beside the bed, losing themselves in wooden darkness. Ah, the furniture was indeed a black hole of coolness dotting the room, a resting place for the eyes to follow. Those eyes of mine seemed to have their own will, drawing themselves back to Ha-Nee's subtle beauty.

Paradise was being disturbed. It was under attack. Somewhere in the black pits of the furniture, there was an air raid siren. Calling louder and louder, and canceling my fantasies. Damn phone.

Ha-Nee moaned slightly. I struggled my sleeping arm over her warm body to the receiver, slipped it out of my hands once, caught it on the rebound, and banged my temple as I tried to pull it towards my ear. "Yello," I mumbled.

It was Sharlene Dahl, the go between from my agent and the studio. For some reason my agent dealt directly with the studio, and bargained me like so much pork belly stock, as if I didn't have any sense or control. OK, maybe that was true. As long as the money and the girls and recognition were coming in, I was taken care of like a golden goose, and reacted accordingly. Those movie eggs were golden alright. I was made rich off of saved up lunch money and pop bottles in vacant fields of trash. I didn't mind.

Baby Dahl, as I liked to call her, was my own inside conspirator. That one night on the town six months ago proved to make her a confidant ally. I could trust her sweet phone calls of honey over the pile of manure my agent filled my ears with.

"Hello, Baby Dahl," I smirked into the phone. Ha-Nee stirred quickly beside me, easing catlike out of the bed, mentioning something about getting me breakfast and left the room.

"I won't ask if you are alone," Baby asked.

"I would hate to start the day with a lie," the smirk etching itself deeper in my face.

A slight north breeze blew through the phone, and then the sun came out of the receiver.

"Sterling sweetheart, I have a new script for you, even though you have managed to sour almost everyone with your latest antics."

"So I took a Mexican holiday."

"It was the death that provided the sympathy towards your situation."

My smirk did a small turn down.

"What else could I do?"

"You do what you can, lover. Listen, this script is solid. The last of the Saturday serials might be over. That adult script you wanted? It is right in front of me."

I sat up on this. "Really?"

"Yes, I have already given it a glance, and this is serious stuff. Nice budget, too. Sterling, I think this will put you over as a serious actor. Right now, even with the recent publicity, which, by the way has actually helped your image, you are some strong business. Your agent is bargaining you like the front page item you have become, playing one studio against another for the spoils"

With what I had been through lately, I became euphoric. "Baby, you are a sweetheart. Let me know when you want to get married."

A cup clinked noisily as Ha-Nee sniffed and settled the breakfast tray. She had a smirk now, but not a happy one. Sensitive kid.

I noticed she had placed a telegram on the breakfast tray. I opened it while discussing script details and Ha-Nee set the bed like a fine table.

"Yeah, babe, go ahead…yea…mhmm…OK, well send the script on over" I mumbled as I glanced at the message, not quite as excited as I was earlier.

She went on, talking about how the script approval was a done deal, and the budget wasn't skimpy, and locations were already scouted with Florida jungles winning. I should have been euphoric, but I studied the telegram some more. It was from the Colonel.

The Colonel was getting serious with me. Money had been wired to a Swiss bank account for me to withdraw from anytime. Quite a sum, it was. Too much to turn down. With a mix of emotions and motives, I chewed on the piece of toast Ha-Nee fed me between large gulps of coffee. I gave her a smile and a kiss and returned to my conversation with Baby Dahl. "Sweet, I need you to dig up some info for me on the side about a fellow named Big Job Bob. He used to do some pro wrestling down in Mexico, so I am sure he has left a trail of clippings and agents somewhere."

"Sure, Sterling. Mind if I ask why?"

"Oh, just doing a little research for an idea I have."

"Sounds interesting, but you might want to finish this project first. This is quite good."

"I am sure it is, and so are you. Thanks, sweetheart."

Later that afternoon, the script arrived with notes covering the details, a contract, and a plane ticket to Florida leaving the next morning. I wired the Colonel my agreement that I would begin as soon as possible, film schedule permitting.

As I packed that evening, I showered, shaved, whistled, chatted with Ha-Nee. She had my wallet and toiletries laid out for me on top of my dresser. As I finished packing, I noticed that also on top of my dresser was the knight that I had put in my pocket when I visited the boy's room. I smiled at it and put it in my pocket again, not sure why. As I stood there thinking, from behind me a pair of silky hands went under my shirt and down the front of my pants. "You want Ha-Nee give you more than goodbye kiss?"

    Boy, I was hot alright.

CHAPTER 13--ONE MONTH EARLIER
EARLY AUGUST 1939
THE SALTY TIDE

"I am getting warmer"

Bruno mused to himself. Old Salt was easy. He had a loud mouth and too many friends. "I am sure they will all mourn his passing." He had to laugh out loud at this thought. The sun's rays entering his cabana slowly baked their calm heat into his skin. His eyes opened slightly and focused on some young boys playing on the beach, building sandcastles as the waves rolled steadily closer and closer with the approaching tide.

"You will fall. You will wash to the cleansing sea and be gone."

Riesling from a frosty ice bucket poured cool down his throat. Bruno began to doze and dream. In his dream he remembered seeing himself catching a rather besotted Old Salt stumbling out of his "usual rounds", as the local bartenders had said, and stumbling almost head long into a lamppost. Bruno reached out of the shadows to help.

"Whew," a noxious wave of fumes blew in to the air from the rummy breath of Old Salt. "That woulda hurt!" Old Salt lost balance again as Bruno helped him back to his feet.

"Thanx again, pal."

"Sure, what are friends for, Old Salt?"

Old Salt's eyes screwed together. "Do I know you?"

"Sure, we met in Singapore last time out."

Old Salt cocked his head unscrewed his eyes and let out a bray of spittle. "Hell yea, I remember now. You were the one with the chink that had her hair dyed blonde."

"Yea, that was me," Bruno smiled at this fib.

Old Salt stopped, mouth opened, and a layer of hell spilled out of his throat. "Shay, I had a pip, didn't I? Shay, how bout you and me have a drink for old times sake. Oooooo-I gotsa bottle in my room."

"No, my friend, let's go to my room, I have a bottle of the good stuff."

"Well, you do look kinda fancy. You ain't a fag ner nothin is ya?"

"No, in fact I have some girls showing up in a half an hour. Join me; it might get lonely for one of the girls."

"Shore, whaz a pal for?"

"Let me get a cab."

Bruno did his best to keep Old Salt awake back to the hotel. Without much prodding, Bruno got him to talk about his business of trading and dealing black market objects and trinkets. He talked about one particular sailor boy but couldn't quite remember the situation. They both laughed at their supposed lack of memory as Bruno helped Old Salt into Bruno's beach front room. Still laughing, he plopped Old Salt in a chair at the table as Bruno placed high grade Jamaican rum in front of him.

"You ain't kiddin', is you!" Old Salt bellowed.

"Naw, I don't kid. Hey, what about that business of the strange tiki greenstone that dopey sailor was interested in, that must have been a strange ordeal. Who would be involved in a crazy deal like that? Do you just pass it on to another black marketer, or do you deal with, let's say, real people?"

"Oh, the kid wanted copies made for his buddies, so they could be kind of a fraternity. Five or six of them, I don't remember. Kid had some money, seemed, OK, so I did the deal for him. "

"What were his buddies like?"

"Well I don't remember much, but one of them was a wrestler. Used to be professional down in Mexico. Big Job Bob, yea that was his name. I remember, see, cuz I used to follow that stuff. Wiped a guy out in the ring and disappeared. Well, imagine my surprise, when there he was, sitting right in front of me."

"Mexican?"

"Naw – German actually. Got a big family down there, though. Touchy, too, boy! Any cracks about Nazis and Germans, and he gets real red in the face. Aw, hell, anyway, I know this Flip engraver and carver runs a curio shop here in San Diego. The guy is amazing. Could make more money if he wasn't wanted for everything under the sun."

"Like perhaps being a master counterfeiter," Bruno casually babbled, while watching Old Salt's reaction. "I have a beautiful stone bust of my mother's head – just a small one, four inches long – do you suppose he could replicate it, in case my original gets lost? I move around so much, and I do love my mother."

Old Salt pursed his lips at Bruno for a moment as his red rimmed eyes swelled with moisture. "Sure he would. Who wouldn't want to do that for a guy what loves his mum?" He stared down at the table for a bit, lost in remembrance. He slowly told Bruno the Filipino's name and location of the store without moving his eyes from the spot on the table where he had transfixed them. A loud sniff and a snort erupted from his tilted head.

Bruno placed a large shot glass in front of Old Salt. He grinned as he grabbed it and sloshed it unceremoniously down his throat. Bruno walked slowly, grinning and laughing to himself as he reached on a high shelf behind him for some rope. Turning sharply, he swung the rope over Old Salt's chest, pinning down his arms in the process. Old Salt started to get confused and struggled, wanting to break free from his bonds. Bruno quickly grabbed Old Salt's head with both hands and shoved his skull done hard on the table. "Arerthsv" was all that emerged from Old Salt's spittle filled throat. Bruno grabbed Old Salt's hair and yanked his head back roughly, Old Salt's eyes went cock-eyed and he produced a weird snore that enveloped the room. Bruno turned around and while still holding the mass of greasy hair with one hand, reached under a counter, producing a large bag of salt and set it on the table. Bruno then yanked Old Salt's jaw down swiftly from his upturned head breaking Old Salt's jaw with a loud crunch. Grabbing a swizzle stick from the table, Bruno placed it in the bloody gaping maw of Old Salt's mouth, propping it open. Releasing his grip on the half conscious unmoving sailor, Bruno quickly bound him to the chair with the rest of the rope. Taking the Kosher salt, and grinning at the irony of it, emptied the bag down the stink hole of Old Salt's gaping mouth until the salt overflowed and slid down his cheek to the floor. Old Salt started to choke and cough as the suffocating salt burned and sank down his throat. Noticing his return to consciousness over his increasing agony, Bruno felt compassionate.

Taking a bottle of 151 rum off the shelf, Bruno upended the contents into the salt pile in Old Salt's mouth. The powerful rum drained a hole in the center of it as Bruno poured. Old Salt's body began to shift and pulsate, eyes trying to focus on the fact he was being killed by suffocation. Old Salt indeed.

Thrashing, fighting his bonds, the chair flipped sideways, and he rode the floor on that chair like a snake on an electric rail. His eyes became focused, then bugged, then empty of light. Blood, mucus, stray bits of bile managed to make its way up through the salt spreading a dark lake on the floor. He quivered like that for a half hour or so while Bruno made a drink and watched. Bruno enjoyed the sailor's death, his torture. As he watched and sipped he envisioned faces from his past. The older kids that bullied him as a child in that damned school became mixed with visions of his father. All the while he felt himself becoming stronger.

He was so strong he grabbed the Flip counterfeiter on his way to open his shop the next morning. Bruno had some old piano wire he had happily found in the trash bin of the music shop next door to the Flip's and wrapped it around small man's neck. The little man tried some silly Asian defense moves, but he was out of shape and obviously not Bruno's better. Before his throat spilled blood and bile, the Flip pleaded for his life and told Bruno everything he needed to know about the sailor boy, the trinket, and all the others involved, including some names he had written on the receipts. Bruno felt thankful for this knowledge, and so Bruno killed him quickly. Bruno took his victim's keys and went in the shop. He fumbled around in the small office and found the receipt book and took it away. In it were the names of a couple of the boys. That was all he needed.

He phoned a number in the book the next day. The kid named Red didn't know who Bruno was, but he knew who Bruno mentioned. Bruno told him he was Big Job Bob's German uncle from Mexico. Red was nervous enough but made a date anyway.

After picking up Red in front of the base, they rode in a cab to a nearby upscale Mexican restaurant. Initially anxious, Red warmed up after a couple of drinks and some enchiladas. Bruno asked Red if he had the greenstone. He did. It was around his neck, very convenient. Not wanting to push, Bruno instead relaxed and relied on small talk. He wined and dined Red to the point where he was comfortable, with Bruno gathering information as he went. Red was becoming very relaxed. Bruno asked to see this greenstone that this nephew had written about. Red showed it. It was obviously one of the fakes. Bruno smirked and handed it back to Red as he handed more info than Bruno needed about Harry and his famous father's relationship.

Bruno directed the conversation back to Big Job Bob, explaining how he was worried, since Bruno hadn't heard from him in a while, and the family was becoming concerned.

Red was unsure at first, and then remembered a small place in the Yucatan. A hide-a-way as Big Job had described it. Big Job had mentioned more than once that all the fellows should take some R&R down there. Red gave some idea where this place was, along with the local village that was close. That was all Bruno needed.

After dinner and much more conversation, Red was half lidded and fumbling slightly. Bruno took Red outside, got him in a cab, and thanked him for the information. Bruno paused for a minute, reflecting on his next move, and then headed towards the hotel at the end of the block. On the way he noticed a newsstand and stopped to pick up a pack of cigarettes. He lingered long enough to rest his gaze on the local paper. One small item caught his eye and kept it. Something about a murder in Tijuana of a navy boy, a Capitan Gonzalez, a stolen greenstone crucial to the crime, and an account of an escaped suspect. The escaped suspect's description proved of considerable interest. More than his curiosity was aroused at this point. He smiled as he took a long, slow walk to his hotel.

There was a chirping in his head that shook him gently back to the present. Night dissolved into a warm glow of dawn as he stirred from his remembrances and smelled the salt of the sea. There were gulls moving in on a stranded crab on the beach, showing no mercy. Watching them, he planned his next move.

The sand castle had descended into the tide.

CHAPTER 14--ONE MONTH LATER
EARLY SEPTEMBER 1939
FLORIDA

Hot. Sticky. That might work in some situations, but not now. My shirt was clinging to the back of my shoulder blades, and I had to adjust my clothing as I stepped from the plane on to the tarmac. The relative comfort of the plane and sweet attentions of the stewardess didn't brace me adequately for the smack in face I got from the humid winds that swept from everywhere at once.

I was blind.

Someone one grabbed my hand and helped me grope my way to a waiting darkened interior of a car. Once inside I felt like a blind beggar receiving a miracle as my eyesight slowly returned. A quick "Jesus" helped expedite the situation.

Voices pierced this new light.

"Yassuh, Massuh Hanover, she sho am hot today. Yall's ain't used to dis mess is ya?" The driver continued to prattle as my vision finally cleared and I fell in and out of consciousness until we disembarked on the set.

The set was in one of those many swampy areas of the Florida everglades that had been used in previous films involving jungle hero types. As I emerged onto the set, I was impressed at the efficiency around me. People setting up shots while other were striking old previous scenes, moving with an efficiency that seemed to thwart the sweltering heat.

I was approached by the people from the hair and wardrobe departments, wearing big smiles, having much humor, extremely jokey, and an all round good nature. So different was this atmosphere than the usual Hollywood studio process that I began to lose my initial aggressiveness and actually began to melt and enjoy myself despite the heat.

The second unit was filming all the heavy action scenes that day and every time someone yelled "Cut! Print!", the sounds of splashing and laughing emerged as everyone who was not in make up or costume jumped in the deep pond next to the set in order to cool off.

Later that evening over cocktails I finally met my co-star. A knock-out to be sure. Tall, blonde, and looked great in her jungle queen outfit. Oddly, the story we were shooting was not all that different from the serials I had done so many times before. This time, though, the budget was actually adequate, the sets were real, and the dialogue was seemingly realistic. Nice change.

Everyone on the set was in a great mood. I knew this was a sign that the film was going to be a good one. My costar, Sugar Kayne, helped to assure me. She was hot property, and the head of the studio was helping to develop her, but he was too late. She was plenty developed all by herself.

One late night over dips in the pond with her proved that I hadn't had happier times in a long while. The balmy days and blissful nights with Sugar blended together in a frothy cocktail of pleasure. Regretfully I knew I had to break this spell.

The next morning before the first shoot of the day I approached some of the Mexican workers at the service craft to grab some breakfast and inquired if they had ever heard of Big Job Bob the wrestler. I could have kicked over a hornets' nest. They became very excited and the air flew with exclamations of "Ayiiiiiiiiie!", "Chingao!", and other excitations. Turns out a couple of the boys were big wrestling fans that had followed the sport for years. One had even kept a scrapbook. I asked, and he was proud to lend it to me.

That evening, when the shooting had wrapped, I stayed up most of the night looking at the scrapbook full of old photos and clippings in Mexican lingo that my fair mustering of the language could take me through. I slowly managed to discover that Big Job Bob had a small place in the Yucatan Peninsula, his family was proudly German, and they had lived in that area for several generations while keeping ties with the rest of the kin in the Old Country. The German transplants had become quite well established as a powerful presence in the area. With that and the rest of the history I now had, I made a couple of phone calls to Baby Dahl in LA. I also contacted the Colonel, and he was surprisingly languid, offering some needed information on what to look out for. He happily said he would have money waiting for me in the bank of Merida in the Yucatan. The last few days of shooting gave me the chance I needed to gather even more info from Baby Dahl about Big Job's exploits in the wrestling game. Some loose directions and I was good to go when shooting wrapped, and we were granted a couple of weeks to take off.

I had a beautiful evening with my costar the next night.

CHAPTER 15--ONE MONTH LATER
LATE OCTOBER 1939
MEXICO

    I sat having myself a semi-cool beer in one of the most pleasant spots I believe I had ever been to. The small quiet Yucatan village coastal town I had retreated to was beautifully warm with the locals the same. Everything, the simple but tasty food and drink were all on the cheap. This would make a great investment for a vacation resort someday. Too bad my reason for being here was too dark and bitter to really enjoy the place.

    Still, I reflected happily over the film's wrap a couple of days ago. This one was the pip, without a doubt. This one film will put me over the top into absolute stardom. I couldn't have been happier, but I wasn't. The pit of sadness in my stomach as a result of my mission wouldn't let me.

    The Mexican cooks running the service craft on the set had been an amazing help. With their information I knew Big Job Bob was around here somewhere. Just as I had that thought, I noticed a poster on the wall by the bar. It was an advertisement for a wrestling match in a nearby city dated three years ago. El Gigante VS. Big Job

Bob. There was his picture, sure enough, the same as the cooks had showed me. I asked the bartender about it, but there was too much misunderstanding to grasp what he could tell me.

A young boy driving a burro pulling a cart loaded with fresh fruit halted directly outside of the cantina. He was a smart clean looking lad, very busy, running fruit to a stand in the town square just across the street. I admired the kid's ability to hustle, grabbing baskets of fruit and running them to other businesses in the square. I watched him work his way around the square. Eventually he came in the cantina.

He babbled some business to the smiling bartender, did a neat transaction, and then turned to me. "Senor gringo! My fruit, she is fresh and bueno para tu! Please buy my fruit – my grandmother is sick in the country and needs the dinero muy mucho."

"Sure, kid, I'll take some of those papayas." I grinned as I gave him the peso. "Where'd you learn your English?"

"Oh, I get around, you bet,"

"Like wrestling?" I baited.

"oh, si. Big Job Bob, he is my amigo."

"Know him personally, do you?"

"Si, I make deliveries to him, and bring from town the things he needs. Things to live on, groceries, whatever he asks for that I can get."

"Give me a ride out there? I will pay well if you do."

"I will be very happy, senor!"

I soon found myself on a bouncy buggy ride with a happy lively burro pulling us across a high bright landscape. The sky beamed its blue beauty until it almost turned black if you looked at it long enough. A slight cloud of dust kicked up behind us as we trekked down a well travelled road, then turned down one less travelled. The boy and I continued to talk.

He told me had learned his capable control of the English language from hanging around Big Job Bob's family. His family and Big Job Bob's were great friends, and the kid obviously enjoyed being around the well known wrestler. He admitted to knowing some reasonable German as well. Smart kid. I was lucky.

I found out that Big Job's family had been living in Mexico for several generations, part of the migrant group of Germans that moved to Mexico in the 1800's and established communities. Big Job Bob's family was pretty much gone to unknown quarters these days, with only Big Job secluding himself on the family's property in a small, rustic, but capable beach house. The kid winked and told me that Big Job made his own brand of tequila that he sells in the local bars.

"How is he about having visitors?" I wanted to be sure I was not welcomed with a shotgun in my face.

"He has visitors, but they always seem to come up from the beach." An odd thing the boy said, I thought. This got my curiosity.

"Why the beach? Why not the road?"

"I do not know senor."

As we ambled down the dusty trail, I could see the ocean and the beach house come in to view. A slight gust of cool wind made me notice some clouds coming in from the ocean. They looked fairly dark and brooding. "Looks like a potboiler about to blow in off the Gulf."

"Si, senior."

We pulled up about fifty yards from Big Job's porch. The boy waited while I climbed down from the cart and walked toward the cabin. Big Job Bob had seen us coming for a while, glancing our way as we had been pulling up. He was cleaning some fish while a small fire was devouring a stack of mesquite logs. His hands were quick with a rather viscous looking knife. He was dressed in worn shorts, with a sleeveless shirt, sandy and dark from working the fire. Around his neck was an odd shaped greenstone. A big guy, alright, and he looked like a wrestler. He also looked like he could be mean.

"Hello," I spoke first. "Big Job Bob? I'm-"

"I know who you are." A faint smile played across his lips as he spoke. "Your son told me a lot about you."

I let that remark slide.

"C'mon inside. The wind out here keeps shifting and blowing smoke in my eyes" he exclaimed, tossing a towel over the fish. "Having some grilled fish tonight – want some?"

"Not right now."

As we walked up the steps and crossed the porch, a large ancient dog stumbled over, wagging its tail. I petted him as Big Job opened the door. I waited for him to play his hand. He did. "I expected you sooner or later. I am just glad you don't work for the police."

"So am I."

The squeaky screen door on the front of the house announced my entrance. A gust blew the screen door shut loudly behind me. The sound startled Big Job. He turned swiftly. "What do you want from me?"

"Information. I want to know what happened that night. Don't worry, I'll keep it confidential," I lied.

"Drink?"

"Sure."

"I have been wanting to tell someone. I guess you are the only one I can tell. Do you see this?" He pointed to the greenstone carving hanging around his neck.

"Sure, I couldn't miss it"

"This is what started it. This is why I had to do it."

"Want to start from the beginning?"

"Let me get us a drink."

As he moved about the cabin my thoughts rambled through the scant scenery around me. I had been given odd pieces of information about Bob. If he was a trader, what did he trade? No one really comes from town, they come by water, but he obviously had no pier. Sure he had some odd curios in his shack, plenty in fact.

While Bob disappeared in the back room, I peered around the shack. Artifacts, trinkets, some genuine antiques of Mexican, Spanish, and German design were inside the shop. A good half of the shop was devoted to religious imagery. Catholic Mary symbols, Jesus crucifixion pieces and many native Indian objects, knives, machetes, pottery were on long tables and hanging along the wall. Through an open door I could see that Bob had small living quarters in back of shop. Old beat up books in English and German lined a large shelf in the back with a view of the counter of the shop. A large book with a title of Conversational German – a Refresher Course was setting beside an ancient cash register and a pile of paper receipts. A lock box was under the counter. Two large benches filled the main room. One large bench in the middle of the room had various tools and metal shop parts. The other bench was against the wall, filled with fishing tools and equipment. A small but well stocked bookshelf sat above the fishing tool bench. It was filled with metal working books, fishing manuals and magazines, some comic books, some books in German, and an odd assortment of philosophy, science, and metaphysics books. Sure, he has some curios, but hardly enough to run a business, even with his tequila sales on the side. And where was the family these days? Big Job Bob was a curio himself.

A shortwave radio standing in the corner began to sputter and crackle, its red bulb blinking. Through the window the sky was getting darker as the storm was coming in. It looked like no rain, just clouds and wind at this point. Bob came back in with some of his precious tequila for us to share, quickly turning down the radio, its light continuing to blink.

We went outside on the porch to talk.

Bob cleaned some fish while we talked. A smoker beside him leaked the occasional plume. Bob's knife work and cleaning became emotional as he talked about Harry. "He was like my little brother. I mean, my real little brother. The one that died because I wasn't there to save him."

"What happened to your brother?"

"He went swimming in the ocean. I went inside for only a moment. I came back he was gone. I don't know what happened. I do know that if I was there I could have done something," his voice cracked.

"He was smart too. Harry, I mean. Everyone kidded me behind my back because I'm not smart as most people. They didn't dare kid me when I was looking, boy, or I'd woulda whumped'em!" His hand clanged the knife against the side of the smoker. Bob continued through the sparks set off by the clang and the wind. "Harry made me smart, he didn't laugh. He took time to explain things to me, so I wanted to protect the little guy."

"I noticed the book inside on philosophy, science and such. Did Harry get those for you?"

"Yea. As I said he explained a lot of them to me. I try to be more careful in my thinking now. Like where I have the greenstones." He kept on at his work.

I raised my eyebrows on that one. "Bob – did you kill that cop?"

Bob looked straight through me. "I had to so I could protect the oath of the Fearless Four." He put the cleaned fish on the smoker to dry, walked over, and motioned me inside the shack. "Come on in, have another drink."

Once inside, he told me to sit down at the table. "I want to show you something." He went to a shelf and brought back a bottle of tequila, some more glasses, and a cigar box. He opened the box to show me pictures.

There was Harry, Big Job Bob, and two others, all standing outside a jeweler's shop in San Diego. There were several pictures of the same guys, in groups twos, threes, or fours in various locales, with or without grinning girls accompanying them. In all the pictures, they were wearing greenstones around their necks.

I recognized Eddie Harris and Red in the picture. "You know, Harry wrote to me about your gang," I said as I continued to study the pictures.

"Not a gang. We were a fraternity." Then Bob picked up an object that was at the bottom of the cigar box. Bob put the object in my hand. I shifted in my chair when I saw that it was another greenstone. I placed it back on the table.

Bob began to tell me the background on the greenstone and the Fearless Four. This fraternity was a friendship pact between the four guys, there was what sounded like a silly initiation between them, but Bob, the big dumb guy, took it all to heart.

"The Fearless Four made a pact," Bob, went on. He told me that the others kidded and played it as a joke. It seemed Harry, though, was a little concerned about doing the mock ceremony to Big Job Bob, since Bob took everything so seriously. "Harry respected me. Told the other guys to knock it off."

"I broke a guy's neck in the ring," Bob blurted out. The broken neck was why Bob quit wrestling and decided to go into the Navy to escape from everything. Bob talked about headaches he gets, says he thinks they are from trying to teach himself. It would be so much easier if Harry were there to teach him. "Maybe I wouldn't get the headaches. Sometimes I get the headaches so bad I don't know what I am doing. I guess I get kinda crazy and violent. All came from those years of wrestling I guess."

Bob told me he killed Gonzalez alright. He knew Gonzalez had Harry's greenstone, had seen Gonzalez look at it and pocket it as he was interviewing Bob in the alley after all the commotion happened. Bob fled so he could come back later to get the greenstone. He said he broke into Gonzalez' office through the skylight. Dropped a wire noose down through the skylight around Gonzalez' neck, tightening it and slitting his throat before he could cry out. Gonzalez had a radio going loudly while reading Detective magazines and drinking. He had been singing along with the radio with his door closed.

By the time Bob had finished telling me all this, I had a pretty clear picture of why he did what he did. We had a couple of tequilas more while I studied the greenstone and asked him about what happened next. He gathered up the pictures and put them back in the box. He started to talk as he put the cigar box back up on a shelf.

He said he had managed to escape across the border and return to his family. His family had migrated to Mexico generations ago, although he was lucky enough to have been born in Arizona. His family still has close relatives in Germany, and maintains a love of the Fatherland and their family origins. Though his family was all loyal Germans, he grew up and became close with the local Indians. A few more shots led Bob to brag about what he learned from the locals. Growing up they taught him to become an expert tracker, hunter, survivalist, and animal expert. As Bob finished telling me his story, I laid the greenstone on the table and his eyes glazed over in thought for a moment. He placed his hand on the greenstone, holding it tightly. I kept quiet and let him think while I absorbed all the information he had just handed me.

"Thank you," he said quietly.

"One more thing," I said after a moment passed. "What happened to the other guys in the picture?"

He looked up at me from his bowed head. "Last I heard was Eddie Harris jumped ship somewhere in China. The others, I don't know."

A gust of heavy wet wind blew itself through the screen. "Look, it is getting pretty dark and lively out there. I need to get back to town before the boy and I get washed into a ditch." Just as I said this, the red eye on the short wave receiver started blinking again.

Bob saw the blinking eye. "Can you pick up some supplies for me from town and come back out in the morning? There is more I want to tell you. I would go myself, but I have some private business to take care of about an hour later tonight."

"Sure thing."

"Thanks." Bob scribbled a quick list and handed it to me.

We got up, shook hands, and went outside. I said goodbye to him as he stood on the porch and I walked over to the cart. I woke the boy, who was piled under a blanket. The storm covered most of the eastern part of the sky, but there was no rain yet. Luckily the moon was shining bright in the west.

The boy sleepily prompted the burro along at a fair steady pace. I reflected on Bob's talks, and what I knew about him so far. German family still loyal. Large unknown shareholdings on eastern coast of Yucatan peninsula. Questionable income for Bob. Radio sputtering with incoming messages. Private meeting later? Then we should pass someone on the road before long.

We passed no one on the road back to town. That indeed affirmed my suspicions. Bob's family was in the smuggling business, with Bob and his little shack a point of contact.

CHAPTER 16--LATE OCTOBER 1939
BRUNO STRIKES

"I feel clean and covered from harm", Bruno thought. The wetsuit he wore made him feel insulated and safe from the ravages of the sea. He clasped his seafaring knife and pistol. He loved the feel of them and kept them close, and in turn they gave him comfort, keeping him guarded against damage. He saw the coast of the Yucatan Peninsula in front of his small boat. As beautiful as the coast was, with its fountain of colors splashing against the sky, he still kept a third eye against those who might see him here. He watched the shadow of darkness caused by the threatening storm descend with him towards the beach.

"My new Nazi friends – how easy to deceive." Bruno smiled and mumbled to himself as he reflected on his new companions that had procured this boat for him. "A child could have had these lazy operatives taken care of. I wander in as a visiting German citizen on vacation, and a few easily dropped words in a cantina against those that were obviously not tourists or natives, and I find the source I need. I raise my glass to toast the glorious Reich. They tell me to be quiet, and immediately the conversation occurs. I let them know of my supposed covert operations, flash some papers too fast for them to scrutinize completely, and push some names and information only someone in the German Information Exchange would know. They have business, I have business. GEI points of contact exchanged; cumbersome checks against my fake credentials and a quick series of interrogations are made. Big Job Bob was the one I wanted. They know what he is and have dealt with him before. Locations are specified by my new idiot friends, and now here I am in the dark of night approaching a small shack on a beautiful beach"

      Bruno sat offshore, anchored in the small craft, supplied by his new friends, wondering about the fore coming events. He realized he loved the Swiss. He cracked a sly smile as he continued to mumble. "They are such pacifists, the lying bastards," he pondered. "Especially the ones I pay so sweetly to keep my accounts straight. Like referees in a game or street fight. They will hold your money and stay equal until the conflict is over. Then, meanwhile, they collect their interest and come out the winner without question or harm in the long run, no matter who wins. Neutrality equals profit in conflict." He continued, this time speaking internally to himself, though the sounds of the sea would have drowned out any small conversation. He continued his thoughts. "The darling bastards held my money so I could purchase my credentials and fake orders to get where I am now, in a boat supplied by those fellow Nazi officers, stupid idiots. The lazy operatives were lucky to have won what they have already, trading deals for jewels and information from a beachcombing informer, whose family has strong underground connections, but whose only claim to fame is getting his head cracked in the ring." The small craft gently swung in towards the coast approaching its target.

As the boat approached the shore, Bruno's mind focused on what he had to do. His reason became sharp. His mission was different, it was double pronged. He had it in place. Get the greenstone at any price. The Nazi High command wanted this rock for its powers of longevity while Bruno wanted it for its price on the black market. He was robbed and disfigured in a way he would never forget, and neither would anyone else.

His history pushed against him again. The dark starless sky, with its occasional roiling blobs of grey storm clouds sprayed a cleansing mist and the smell of salt, the bouncing of the boat, made him feel alive. He contrasted this freedom clearly against growing up as an only child in an abusive yet protected and influential household. He winced against the wind and wondered if it was the spray from the ocean giving rise to the tears in his eyes, or was it his eyes giving the salt back to the ocean? Steady hands worked independently of thought at this point. His past slapped his cheek as the wind slapped the crashing waves.

Spumes of mist presented themselves to him as scenarios. He mumbled, again quietly to himself, describing the scenes that presented themselves to him in the form of waves and froth. "An only child I was, tormented and teased in all the best schools. They knew my name before I even arrived. I remember after one particularly tough beating, someone told me my father had just died. His death was my balm. The trust fund from the family name was now all mine. I was lucky in my inheritance. My family's industrialist fortunes had hit a peak with the war to end all wars, but, of course, it slumped when it failed to shift to other markets after the Armistice. The old family profits soon fell into decline."

A grim smile touched his lips as his reverie continued into the darkness. "Until the rise of Uncle Adolph. Being left in charge of a somewhat still powerful industry, and being so young as well, meant that I had courage others didn't. The Socialists gave me the means to restore the power to my family. My mother, the whore, was quick to ascertain connections with the best and most virile of the Nazis, and bless her, got me the position in the SS black boot society I now exploit. The old used dishrag that was my mother is long gone now, death by exploitation I assume. My family castle and business holds strong, with the castle empty but for a contingent of servants, and caretakers, overseen by the trust"

Surf splashed against Bruno hard, freeing his awareness against the past. He felt new scars find home against old scars. His broken nose, earned at the rebelling of his younger self towards the school bullies that seemed to constantly taunt him for his fair features. His foot long thigh scar, from an operation when he was a child, thin and sickly. "I am thin and sickly no more. This is my shining time!"

A light from a fire on the shore. A smaller light burning from a window. His small crew pulled in and weighed anchor close enough to the shore to let Bruno finish the meeting with a short swim. Though the wind was surging in gusts from the east, occasional sucking retro winds brought sweet smells coming from the beach. Smoked fish of some sort. "Delicious. I can't wait to meet my host," he said quietly.

Pushing the sea and sand aside, Bruno walked to the shore in his tight black wetsuit, blinking a signal with his flashlight. Frowning, Bruno realized with disgust what a sandy dirty place this was and began to feel very uncomfortable. He was surrounded by water, everywhere, and no place to take a bath. He became angrier and angrier.

His target, Big Job Bob was waiting for him on the beach, surrounded by a halo of white light reflected from the torches of his shack and the smoker spewing a wonderful smell of sizzling fish. Bruno smiled, even as a sand flea found a home on his exposed leg as he pushed his way out of the surf. He emerged, as if from a nautical cocoon to greet his endangered host.

Big Job Bob spoke in German to Bruno, saying "Hello and welcome." Big Job Bob spoke the tongue fluently, impressing Bruno. "Too bad he is a slob," Bruno thought. Bruno hated his unkemptness. He also noticed his goal, draping from Big Job Bob's neck. The greenstone at last.

Big Job continued in German and Bruno replied in kind. "Come inside" Big Job beckoned. Bruno stepped up the rickety steps, crossed the porch and entered the shack. Sand, some fleas, even a spider web in the corner added to the hovel's grotesqueness.

They stood on either side of a wreck of a table, a tequila bottle sitting half empty next to a dirty glass. "I need to see your orders," Big Job demanded. Bruno handed the fake orders to him. "These don't make sense," he said. "Something is not quite right. There was not to be a meeting until later in the morning"

"It is all good," Bruno assured him with a big closed mouth smile. "He begins to question my contacts," Bruno wondered. Big Job asked sordid details about things Bruno knew nothing of. Bruno began to get frustrated, and started to sweat. Big Job continued his interrogation and questions, as Bruno became angrier. Bruno completely fumbled two important questions and didn't care. That was when a glint of light caused Bruno to see another greenstone sitting on the table. He tried to suppress his excitement, but this only made Big Job more nervous. He knew something was not right. "No deal."

"My friend, I understand your hesitation after my faulty memory lapse, but surely you wouldn't think I would come all this way without some compensation. Those greenstones, for instance. The one around your neck and the one on this table. I will pay a small fortune for it right now, no more questions from either of us. Then I will leave as I came." Big Job looked confused, swayed a bit, not sure what was going on. "No…" That was his short reply. Bruno showed him a small packet that he had in his wetsuit. He opened it to show the contents. "Diamonds, my friend, courtesy of some Swiss friends. High grade stones." They faced each other across the table, and both stood resolute.

Big Job frowned and repeated the "No…."

"I am obviously dealing with an idiot," Bruno thought. He had ways of dealing with idiots like this. He will take both stones, keep his diamonds, and sort out which greenstone is the true one later. He slowly put the diamond packet back.

A growling at the screen door that Bruno recognized as coming from some filthy beast. The tension in the hut was thick, and Bruno wanted to go outside. A few seconds later passed and the beast at the door started to bark. "I see that it is better that I leave. I am sorry. We both could have gained what we want."

"Go outside and leave"

"Really, Big Job, tell you what, I will leave, and be back with more proper credentials. You really have done me quite a favor, keeping me on my toes like this."

"Go now!"

As Bruno moved to open the screen door, a nasty beast howled and railed against his ankle. He gave the offending creature a solid kick across and off the porch and into some cacti. Next thing, Big Job was on Bruno's back like an avenging angel. He screamed in Bruno's ear "NO HURT DOG!" as they both went down the steps and on the sand. The howling in the air from the dog caused a sorry soundtrack as Bruno pulled himself away from Big Job, turned and reached for his pistol. He tried to stand and aim as Big Job shoved him hard a distance of several feet towards a tequila still, knocking his pistol bouncing end over end into the fire. Several bottles smashed as Bruno hit the shoddy platform of the still. The alcohol from the surrounding bottles spilled and splashed into the flames of the burning embers from the still and a small fiery outbreak ensued against the lean-to stand. "His strength is surprising," Bruno thought. "He is much more agile and quick than I had expected."

Bits of grass and straw amongst the swill and trash next to the still began to ignite. Bruno pulled his knife as Big Job lunged towards him. Bruno barely had time to swing the knife when Big Job kicked it out of his grasp. "I have underestimated your prowess as a wrestler," Bruno shouted.

Bruno grabbed a half broken bottle of tequila to ward Big Job off, but Big Job kept pushing, taking the vicious slashes of the glass against his skin with no effect, other than to grease the situation. He came at Bruno with a leap and a roll, grabbed him with a neck grip, and they tumbled as one towards the shed and the grill. A set of fish hooks hanging near the grill make an attractive weapon for Big Job. Holding Bruno face first down in the sand Big Job raked the rusty hooks across Bruno's back. Bruno cried out, pain searing him, making him rabid, making him stronger. They reversed positions. Bruno pinned Big Job on his back next to the fire, and grabbing the hand that held the hooks, pushed it slowly towards the flames. Big Job freed his hand for a second and gave the hooks one last deep rake in Bruno's back as Bruno cried out and recovered his grip on Big Job's hand and pushed it in the flames. Big Job Bob dropped the hooks, screamed with pain, grabbed a log of flame from the fire and slammed it to the side of Bruno's head, breaking his grasp.

    A moment's hesitation caused Bruno to be subdued, as Big Job Bob stood and threw him in the nearest cactus brush by the still. Bruno's wetsuit served to stifle most of the quills, and only proceeded to fuel his adrenaline. Bruno's mind raged. How dare he do this to me? Impertinent swine! Big Job Bob lunged for him as Bruno managed to grab his dropped knife from the sand. Big Job averted Bruno's knife thrust but was answered by falling face first into the mound of cacti, as Bruno's knife once again slipped from his bloody sweaty hands. Big Job Bob became berserk, beyond more pain than he could stand. A kick of the sand in Bruno's eyes, and the former wrestling bully knocked him down and proceeded to twist Bruno around so that his head was caught between Big Job's knees. Bruno faced outward, unable to get a grip, as Big Job grabbed his ankles and held him vertically upside down, trapped. Big Job leapt in the air and pile drived Bruno's head in the sand. Bruno couldn't breathe, his inertia was dampened. Piles of heavy fist blows rained down on Bruno as he struggled to regain. Bruno lurched up, catching Big Job Bob off balance, and they both rolled in the fire. Bruno grabbed a flaming faggot with his hand, not minding the pain, and strapped it across Big Job Bob's neck. Bruno pinned Big Job down, enjoying the sound and smell of Big Job's baking flesh sizzling against burning wood. His boozy filthy soaked clothes ignited against his roaring of pain. Big Job Bob grabbed at Bruno, clutching, and finally pushed him away. The burning wood cooked Bruno's flesh as well, and he let go and crawled away. Big Job flinched like a tubby roach on its back as Bruno swaggered to get up. Big Job was literally on fire, his clothes giving a nasty stench against the smell of burning flesh.

  Bruno retreated towards the area where some fish were lined out to be smoked, and in a quick second, saw the machete that was setting there. He grabbed the long knife and looked back just as Big Job Bob rose up, only to see him fall to his knees, his hair catching fire at this point, his screams agonizingly loud and off key. Bruno took the machete and gave a clean but not forceful enough cut across Big Job Bob's bull-like neck. Big Job Bob's head dangled on his neck, his voice strangling off like an alley cat being swung by its tail. He fell with his legs landing in the fire, his clothes and skin giving a soothing crackle like fresh eggs put on a hot griddle. Bruno grinned, as amazingly enough Big Job pulled himself away from the fire, and crawled like a slug towards his shack, and suddenly collapsed. That quaint smell of burning flesh tickled Bruno's nostrils, and relaxed him a bit. "So much for him," he thought. "I am weary."

He sat, barely able to breathe. Rains began to hit in great big greenish drops. Smells of flesh, fish, tequila, salt air washed over him with the rain as he eased down in the sand. The wind had stopped. Big Job Bob's body was five feet from him. He looked at the slickly cut neck holding the necklace containing the greenstone. That was safe for the moment. Slowly, pain crept up on him.

Bruno looked at black flesh on his hands. He felt the pain continue to mount. "I don't have time to feel the other wounds on my back," he grumbled in agony. "Filth," he spat as he looked at the charred body of Big Job twitching slowly. Bruno tried to find some comfort by sitting on the steps leading to the shack. He didn't mind the rain. He didn't mind the pain.

He began pass out and into sleep from the pain. He dreamed of his father's brutishness towards what he called weak and sallow. In his dream he tried to impress his father, but because of Bruno's constant sickness, he continually disappointed him. This disappointment spilled over in his dream to include his classmates, taunting, kicking, calling names. He knew he was a small, weak, sick boy. But not forever.

Something crashed behind him.

Bruno awoke. He must control this pain. The fire was spreading. The lean-to was blazing, it had just shattered to the sand sideways, igniting the shack, now catching as well, held with the leaping licks of the building inferno. The rain tormented him from the sky as the burning blaze carried on its own fight against the clouds. Slowly rising, he made himself move towards the body of Big Job Bob. He bent and grabbed the greenstone from Big Job's former neck, and rising with great pain, moved towards the shack, machete in crisply burned hand.

He swerved inside unsteadily, searching for what he must have. Through the haze he saw the other greenstone on the table, next to the bottle of tequila. His pain mounted against the heat of the shack, already becoming full of flames. Bruno swigged a blast of tequila, pouring more over his burns as he threw the machete on the table. The burn of the tequila evened out the burns of his hands temporarily, so he could get a good look at the greenstone on the table. Lighting a cigarette from a pack on the table, he gingerly released his grasp on the greenstone in his hand and compared the two, while constantly knocking back the tequila to help him focus. "Obvious fake, the one on the table." He smiled and quickly congratulated himself on his acute skills then cried out against the pain of his hand. Bruno again poured the remaining tequila over his wounds, felt a quick stab of pain, then a quick relief. Lighting a cigarette began to give him some calm, just long enough to allow him to stand and grab the greenstone matted with blood and dirt in one hand and grab the machete in the other.

As he stumbled through the tacky screen door, the filthy dog, obviously working with a broken hip at this point, attempted to give Bruno a bite. "Last revenge for your master. This is what I do with masters!" Bruno yelled, swinging the machete, effectively severing its head like he wanted to do its master's, only with much less effort. "Damn thing should have been dead long ago."

He crawled and collapsed on the porch, stood and staggered, rain and wind blowing out of control. He opened his pouch containing his papers and attempted to stuff the greenstone inside. Bruno fell on one knee as he did so, but after a few seconds, actually managed to secure the greenstone. He got up to walk unsteadily towards the water, rain beating him hard as he almost collapsed in the surf, but kept on pushing forward against the unsteady sand, going deeper into the brine. Gulping seawater and air, Bruno become one with the ocean and the air and the rain and the pain. The rhythm of the waves, plus the outgoing tide, provided a tempo he could work with. The salt of the water cleansed his wounds as he moved towards his waiting boat.

"Time has no meaning now when coupled with pain and determination. No past, no present, only the now. The only way the future will happen is by taking care of the now," Bruno thought as he clambered in the boat. He pulled up the anchor and dumped it in the boat. He grabbed a thankful hand on the choke and starter of the engine. The engine gave a quick roar as he thankfully glided back towards where he had come from. There was a sound of an explosion bouncing across the waves. He turned to see the hut of Big Job Bob ablaze. "Fire is winning against all odds of the water from above. How cleansing," he said.

He was bruised, but his feeling of accomplishment gave a salve to his wounds and bruises. He had what he wanted.

The motor and occasional splash of sea water helped keep him alert as he motored his way back the few miles up the coast. His excitement at mission accomplished made him smile despite the pain. Once he has contacted his connection, he will be able to have the monies transferred and he can relax, undetected, happy and free. "My father would be proud of me if he breathed. I would still hate him," he said aloud. Focus, he snapped to himself, as a storm wave hit the side of his small craft. Regaining his thoughts, he continued his reverie. "I will be able to make my contact in the morning, meet him with the greenstone, collect, make the money transfer, and I am done. Sitting out the war in Lisbon is not a bad idea."

Another sock of the boat against a wave made him appreciate what he had.

"Not only the greenstone, but what it means to what is left of my once proud successful family," he mused. "To be able to add what I can to regain financial stability, and with that my family pride as a Durst, I am certain will bring me peace."

Pulling up and docking, He agonized as he changed out of his wetsuit into his dry clothes. All he wanted to do was pay attention to meticulously making sure his comfort was taken care of.

A few questions of peasants, and a doctor was found not long after dawn. No questions, and with a flash of coins the doctor took care of him. He had tried to medicate himself with agave and multiple bandages and shots of tequila in the interim between returning the boat and trying to rest in his hotel room. During that time he realized he would never have made it to the doctor the next morning if not for the pain. Pain is what kept him alive.

Hands completely bandaged, he found himself lying in his hotel room above the cantina. The paint on the ceiling gave him visions. "The paint is nothing unusual, just white paint, with those little dots you see upon close inspection, stare at them long enough and those same dots move to create images," he whispered, trying to give comfort to himself.

The doctor's dope was having an effect. As his pain decreased, his images of the dots increased. "I don't like this," he said. "I need to have control. I am helpless. The dots assume what I think. I see home. I see my mother's death. It is the end of World War One. My father is tougher than before. The family seems to be well off for a while." The dots seemed to be forcing the memories of childhood out of his unwilling head. "I don't like them."

He knew his family's name gave him rights – rights to what he wanted to have. "The world owes me a living, and I want everything the world owes me. I tell it to myself, and I agree," he shouted at the ceiling. He lowered his voice and continued. "I take what I want and sell to the highest bidder. Twice have I used this power of my stature to secure my ability to sell certain items of art and curios, all for the glory of the Reich, but with an understanding of what my fair share should be." He knew that fair share certainly concerned a resource base when the war was over.

He raised himself just enough to view himself in the cracked mirror facing the bed. He continued his thoughts aloud in a conversation between himself and his distorted mirror image.

"This war will end someday, and when it does, my family complex will be in a position to ride the wave of defeat to unimaginable success, with me at the helm," he spoke to his reflection. "And, if this notoriously valuable collectable piece is worth its promotion, I will be able to succeed and enjoy the sum of my endeavors. All at the expense of my miserable father and transient mother, and all those idiot jerks that ever gave me trouble at school."

Then there was the greenstone. "I have taken personal insults to my physical character to retrieve it. The damned SS and Goering will not see it. I will be the one to own it and protect it. My investment, my property. I will hide this thing myself to sell on my terms to my procurer. I have been offended to answer to like a lapdog to acquire what I have sought on my own. Now that I have this artifact, I can sequester it to sell to my buyer. This is my shining stone. This is the one that will enable me to continue to amass even more wealth and power when this war is over!"

Visions came again to Bruno, and he lay back in the bed, only to see in the past when his father talked to people long ago that could make his family rich again, even to the point of enlisting Bruno in the National Socialist Party as a fortunate officer with a future. Bruno envisioned the memory of his father making agreements, he saw himself going through training. It was if he was watching someone else but knowing what they would do next.

He fell back asleep, only to have the dreams chase him in his sleep. He saw his father pay off debts quickly as the family's century old fortune became stable again. He saw his father grow fat and rich. He saw him die of gluttony. One last smile crossed Bruno's lips. He was now in control.

He awoke the next morning, feeling primed. As he gathered his belongings for leaving, he realized he was missing his pouch containing his papers.

And the stone.

Realizing what he had done, Bruno stood in front of the mirror, repeatedly slapping his face hard enough to produce blood. Amongst the grunts of pain he continued until he fell back on the bed and cried softly.

An hour later, his thoughts collected, and a damp towel on his face, he knew what had to be done. The stone he had taken from Big Job was now lost to the sea and sand. He has to continue to Shanghai to confront Tika. "I can only hope that the one I had was just another duplicate. With the tentacles of the cult and the power of Tika, she will surely find the true stone," he thought. "That is if it exists anymore."

His smile broadened.

"I will lie my way into her confidence and use her as a lead to find what I want," he chuckled to himself. "When I have it, I will smash her. Everyone will think one of her priestesses did it for control of the cult."

He went downstairs and wired a certain connection for proper papers and further instruction.

CHAPTER 17--LATE OCTOBER 1939
A RUDE DAWN

My little sombrero friend met as anticipated the next morning. We stopped at the local mercado. I bought us breakfast consisting of pastries and fruit. The smell of the baking was wonderful and I had to knock some docile bees gingerly off of the pastries before eating. I picked up some items I thought Bob needed. We took a quick happy jaunt from the village, with loud birds and pleasant breezes leading our way. The sun was a bit awkward in my eyes, as the tequila I had the night before made its presence known for a bit. O boy. I lit a cigarette and smelled the fresh ocean air. Some bites from the ripe mangoes I picked up brought me right around.

We made the familiar curves and turns and saw something unexpected. A black cloud was pushing its way against a blazingly blue sky. Sadness set in as we pulled closer.

Getting there, I told the boy to halt by the side of what was left of the house. I stepped down and had to hold on to the side of the wagon.

Big Job's shack was burned almost completely, saved only by the previous night's thunderstorms. The lean-to where the still had been was now a pile of slumbering smoke, half burned agave and rubble, lending its dark message of destruction to the sky.

I walked towards the remnants of the porch, only to be greeted by a mass of monstrous flies, seemingly protective of their territory. What looked like a black mass of thorns by the porch quickly erupted into a snarling aggressive armada of avenging horseflies. Attacking, biting, and covering me as they coveted their quarry. I had to step back and ask the boy to lend his sombrero so I could at least cover my face as I reentered the zone of the porch. The flies moved away enough for me to see a headless dog, and a few feet away, a mutilated and smashed remnant of a dog's head.

Sickened, I was about to turn away, when I heard a groan from under the porch. Curious, I left the slowly rotting corpse of the dog, and stuck my head under the porch. "Mmmph..." It was Bob.

He was dying, but still aware. He was burned horribly, his hair gone, his face half melted it seemed. His neck had a most notorious gash, almost slit clean. He only spoke a few words, but those few words changed my life. As he completed what he had to say his breath shifted and his life went with it. I sat with him, and held his burned smoking hand, until I could no longer stand the inane bombardment of flies

"Hey Meester – look what I find!"

I started, losing my focus on Bob. Turning, I was hit with an emotion of severe loss. I had to have a moment to compose myself before turning towards the boy. Swift tears, swift recovery. I had tried to hide it so many times before, always fairly successfully. This time I started to lose myself. A quick lurch to my knees after crawling back from under the porch, and I was alright again.

The boy has found some papers blown against a rock, damp and wet, and somewhat smeared, but still legible, and a partially burned pouch.

I told him to hold on to that, as I worked my way carefully into what remained of the shack. Amazingly, the table still stood, with a tumpled bottle of tequila residing next to a small box. What I saw in the box made me kill what was left in the tequila bottle.

A greenstone figure. Those few words that Bob had told me were enough to know that this was a replica and that the real one was grabbed by a German agent on a singular mission of deception and thievery.

I reached to touch it and dropped it quickly, realizing it was too hot to handle. I spat what was left of the tequila in my mouth along with my own gummy mucus swizzle on it and it shattered. Had to be fake.

I went over to where my young friend was waiting.

"Senor, theese looks muy importante"

I released my thoughts to look at what the boy had found He sniffed as he handed the items to me. I saw some singed papers with German writing and printing. None of it made much sense until I saw the ID.

I looked at the picture of the agent, Bruno Durst. His ID was probably fake, but yet, I felt it should be real enough to lend some information I could gather. He looked clean, a non-arrogant German face, appealing, almost like a headshot submitted to my Hollywood agents. Handsome, slick, no element of danger or intimidation. Aquiline face with soft features, almost feminine. This man looked a guy you would share a glass of sherry with, not whatever danger he might present. A pretty boy that might make you want to use the stall alone if you both need to go to men's room at the same time.

The handwritten notes in the pouch were in German but included Shanghai. What the hell? What was the connection? Feeling lost and defeated, I consoled the boy, who was quietly weeping while he sat in the cart. I took over the reins while his tears collected sand and dust from the road as we ascended back towards the coastal village.

Back in the cantina, I asked the boy to read what German he could understand as a result of being under Big Job's tutelage. He informed me that it looked like Bruno was heading to Shanghai, along with a note about a buyer with a name of Black Cat – gato negro. I thanked the boy, bought him a meal, and gave him a hefty duty fee.

I left for the states the next day, only to contact my studio and the Colonel. This was getting out of control. I have a film release coming up, and I don't need this distraction, but still there was something in this that was pushing me forward in another direction. I couldn't seem to think long enough to make a solid decision. Then I remembered Big Job Bob's final words.

CHAPTER 18--LATE OCTOBER 1939
THE CALL

Ha-Nee presented me with a ticket for Shanghai that was wired to me by the Colonel. I had telegrammed the basics of my Mexican adventure to him the day of my departure from the Yucatan. Now I am back, and I find myself a busy boy. Ha-Nee had taken several messages from the studio during my departure, announcing delays on the final bit of filming. I called the studio to check in. I was told there were problems involving the second unit film crew, including sickness and injury. Nothing too serious, but it will delay the release at least two more months. "Good," I thought. "I am free at least that long."

I decided to call the Colonel. Ha-Nee brought me a beer, the phone, and some lunch out by the pool. I watched her walk away, her ass swaying sweetly as the Colonel's phone rang through the line. A gruff "Yea?" resounded in my ear. "It's me, sweetheart. I wanted to thank you for the ticket. Nice of you to want to give me a vacation for Christmas and all, but this just won't do."

"What is your problem, joker? If it is more funds needed, I can arrange that. There are things that I can do to make that happen. Sadly enough, I have to say I need you for this job."

"..and the job in particular is…"

"You have unfinished business, and I have the information and means to get you to finish that business."

I backed off on my cockiness for a moment. I'd felt as if I'd hit a dead end

"What information do you have?"

"My boy was murdered because of a certain item he was wearing. A greenstone. As we both know, find the greenstone, find the murderer."

"I'm listening."

"I think you know what we both want. The police are useless."

"Why Shanghai?" I led him on with this question. I had told him about Shanghai, but I wanted his reaction.

"Pay attention! I have it on good knowledge that there is a woman in Shanghai. An important woman. One that has strong connections with this gang that wants this greenstone. There have been phonies made, and there are people, deadly people, that will kill to obtain the original and return it to where it needs to be."

"And that would be where?"

"Never mind. All you need to know is that the one that holds the original and is the murderer of the boy will be in Shanghai at the Black Cat Club."

"Black Cat Club? I thought The Black Cat was a woman of sorts."

"Of sorts. She has many interests, many powerful connections, and is quite dangerous.

"Is this the woman that killed the boy in TJ? What is she doing in Shanghai?"

"All part of ritual cult that has worldwide connections, dealing with white slavery, drugs, and other hideous activities. She is a leader of sorts. And though she took the young man's life in exchange for what she thought was this sacred greenstone that this cult is so excited about, she is not to be blamed."

"Not to be blamed? She murdered him!" I couldn't believe what I was hearing at this point.

"Calm down, son. She may be powerful in her way, but she is just a shill working for that German fellow that seems to be responsible for the death of your friend in the Yucatan."

This was getting to be too much to take in. "Where are you getting your information?"

"You think you are the only one I have hired to take this job on? Just listen and believe what I tell you. Look, when you find her, don't do anything. She is the one that can lead you to this Bruno character. He is the one you want. Once you find him, you can do what you want with him."

"Including murder?" I was starting to feel as if I were in a cheap detective novel written by a first time author.

"I feel that will give us both satisfaction. I do ask one thing. That you bring me the greenstone that is responsible for this whole affair. That will be proof to me that you have done your job."

"Sure, you can have it. Think I might just lay up in some opium den and collect the money from you, huh?"

"Perhaps."

Thievery and assassination? I stepped back from myself at the thought. It is one thing to take someone out in the movies, play acting, a director yelling "CUT!", another to see the blood dripping. Can I remove myself from the deed and stick with my motive? Yeah, I could do it. Not just me killing another human being. Me killing someone, another animal that claimed the life of my son. Yes my son. About time I admitted it. I don't need to be halfway around the world or in an alley behind my house. If I were there at the moment I wouldn't have hesitated to pull the trigger. Does time and distance make a difference? If I was in the alley that night, there would have been no question; it would have been a reflex. Why should time and distance be any different? This was not a reflex – or is there a thing as a delayed reflex, a planned reflex? Is the pay I am getting the cream in my coffee?

"You still there, my boy?" The voice on the line asked. I jolted to.

"Uh, yea. You can count on me." Another reflex. He talked as I thought. He explained that he had an account in Switzerland that will provide me with what monies I need to keep me going. All I have to do is ask, and the cash will be wired to me.

"Let's do this for Harry," he said, and hung up.

"I need to pack, and it may be for a while," I said to Ha-Nee

She looked at me, a slight downward smile on her face, as she started to get my things together. I hit the shower, changed into my travelling suit and jacket, and double checked my belongings, but while reaching for my wallet I saw the white knight I had absentmindedly taken from Harry's room sitting on the dresser. Without knowing why, I took the knight and put it in the pocket of my jacket. I noticed a tear in the pocket and made a mental note to myself to get it fixed first chance.

I turned to grab my items and saw Ha-Nee, a pleading look in her dark eyes, her pouting lips moist. Without a word I took my jacket back off.

The next day I was on the China Clipper to the Philippines, then after a brief layover, I was winging on in to Shanghai.

CHAPTER 19--SHANGHAI

Arriving in Shanghai in the early light of dawn, I was a bit surprised how easily I got through customs. The Japanese had been in charge of Shanghai since the Battle of Songhu a couple of years earlier. The Jap officials were stoic but reasonable enough to visiting Europeans and Americans, so it was not long before I arrived at the Longdong Hotel in the harbor area. I was still feeling reasonably anxious as I approached the hotel desk. It was a little breezy outside, with a light mist, so I was glad to be out of the weather. I proceeded to check in. "Good looking place," I thought to myself.

"Ah! Missa Hanover! We expect you. You have wire from Amelica. Money all good. Room set," gushed the hotel clerk, grinning widely. He turned quickly, clapped his hands, and rang a bell. "Chop chop!" A young bell hop sprinted over, bowed graciously, and grabbed my bag. "This way, sir!" The Colonel's bank contacts were treating me right, I had to admit.

Once in the room, I showered, cleaned up, and shaved, all the while rethinking my plan of approach. I wrote what I thought I needed on the hotel stationary and headed down to the lobby to have a talk with a fruity looking concierge. The boy smiled at me with a certain twinkle in his eye that I ignored.

"Look, I need a letter delivered. Some joint called the Black Cat. Not far. Much tip."

The smile descended with the twinkle. "You familiar with this place, sir?"

"Not really, but it doesn't matter."

"This prace is not what you Amelicans say....uppy uppy?"

I slipped him some extra cabbage along with the letter.

His eyes went wide "You right, no matter!"

He scuttled off on his business as I retired to the bar and a meal. After a decent bowl of chop suey, followed by a couple of martinis with cigarettes as accompaniment, I realized I was very tired. Couldn't be the martinis and supper, must be the time shift. I paid my bill, smiled cockily to the rather indifferent cute little Chinese waitress, and stumbled upstairs to my room. Once there, I stuck a Do Not Disturb sign on the outside of the door, sprawled across the bed and watched the overhead fan spin lazily as it hypnotized me to sleep. In my dreams, there were giants.

Sometime later I was awakened by the chatter of babbling Chinese voices coming through my open window from the market in the alley behind the hotel. Unknown, but extremely appetizing fragrances also found their way through my window. I rose, cleaned up and went for the door, when I noticed a message that had apparently been pushed under it. The concierge had made contact. I glanced at the clock. Two PM! I had been tired alright. I looked at the message. The name Tika stared up at me. I stuck the note in my pocket. My stomach commanded me to go down to the alley to eat. After gorging on some street food that had no name, my stomach commanded me to go back up to my room to rest again. This evening I will descend on the Black Cat for the next step of my plan. I was asleep before my head hit the pillow. Once again, there were giants.

CHAPTER 20--NIGHT STALK

A pleasant happy hour liquid dinner in the hotel bar belied my actions that evening. I looked over the note from earlier. I was to meet this Tika inside the Black Cat at an exact time much later tonight. Well, that gave me some time to waste. I downed my martini and ate the olive for desert. I left the hotel and wandered aimlessly in the slightly waning sunlight. I rather enjoyed the rough smells and curious sights there were to be seen by day, and wandered shop to shop until I found myself looking at the Black Cat from across the street. Odd place. It seemed dark and hibernating in daylight, only waiting for the return of night to breathe alive again. I felt a cold wind blow over me on an otherwise balmy evening. I returned to the hotel. I tried to rest, tried to push time forward with sleep, another cocktail from the bar then sleeping in my room again, and so on, until I finally went into a coma. I felt myself moving, walking, but not moving my feet, towards a golden dawn of understanding. I had a vision of a man with the head of a crow ushering me down a temple step towards a river. He turned to speak, but I could not understand. As I raised my hand towards him he cawed loudly and kept cawing until I opened my eyes.

I hit my alarm and heard it tumble behind the bed. I pushed myself out and into the shower. Cleaning up, I looked at myself in the mirror. I have to do this. For the boy – but that sounded hollow.

A thorough check in the mirror and I was out the door.

The smells had changed. They were almost fragrant in an odd way, not like the somewhat sour smells of the day. The sounds of the night were different as well – more vibrant, with noises I couldn't define from directions I couldn't fathom. I instinctively pulled myself inward, stiffening my shoulders, putting my hands in my pockets, and keeping my eyes and ears wide open.

Among the various sounds, I picked two pairs of shoes that echoed mine. I slowed my steps, and they slowed. I sped up a bit, and they sped up. I began to sweat. I turned to study something in a shop window, hoping to use the glass reflection to trigger my followers. Nothing. "I must be getting batty," I thought to myself. Still, I was getting more paranoid by the second. Twitching my fingers in my coat pocket nervously, I discovered the white knight I had taken from my dresser. I felt reassured somewhat, and I regained my focus. Find the greenstone, find the murderer, and this Tika may be the one. The Colonel, Marian, and I will at least be satisfied somewhat.

But what then? How will that avenge the boy's death? I started walking again, thinking about what would happen when I do find this person. I am just a little bit out of the country, so what do I do? How to exact my revenge? I was approaching a lot of loose ends fast.

Shanghai has an interesting layout. Streets wind in and out, with alleys intersecting crisscross style. A map would look like someone threw a bucket of noodles on a piece of paper.

I felt a movement from a wandering noodle of an alley. Suddenly I was looking up at the biggest Yellow Peril I had ever seen. You hear about starving people in China? He wasn't one of them. Dressed in black with a bowler hat perched on his oversized head, he yanked me in the alley. My lights went out as well as my legs. I felt four hands move me sideways, while two gruff voices went on in Chinese gibberish. I was laid out and tossed and beat like a piñata. Hands rifled through my pockets, my clothes were ripped. "Great," I thought between my gasping for air. A kick to the groin kept me still while the search continued. I saw tiny cartoon stars of yellow and red in the pit of my conscience. A boxing ring appeared with two little yellow devils in spotted trunks and gloves, boxing it out to faceless cheers. A naked cherub floated above the ring shouting through a hand held microphone to the crowd. I didn't understand what the cherub said, only that it sounded like Chinese. Each time a devil would hit the other devil, I would feel a stab of pain.

The scene became brighter, as two angels with wings of fire descended and shot bolts of light at the devils, who quickly cowered and retreated into the darkness while the cherub described the match, its voice getting dimmer along with the image. The entire scene faded to black as the cherub finally disappeared. The angels smiled and left quickly.

Street sounds slowly returned. God, I was sore. My old back pain flared up like a blow torch up my spine as I tried to prop myself against the brick wall behind me.

The pain brought up the memory of trying to impress Marian back in Galveston when I was showing off with the carnival and almost broke my back. I hadn't felt my back hurt this badly in a long time.

I checked my rumpled pockets and found my wallet. It was all there. Why had I been rolled? What the hell was going on with that? I could find nothing missing – except the pocket where the white knight had been. It was gone now. This made no sense. Why was I robbed of that? It meant nothing to anyone, except for me, and I wasn't even sure or aware of what it meant to me.

I stumbled back into the street, of one mind and purpose. Trying to bury the pain in my lower back, I stumbled rather achingly towards the Black Cat. People chuckled at my disheveled look and staggering gait. Bet they thought I was just a dumb drunk Yank round eye. Yea, well maybe I was. But I was a dumb drunk Yank round eye on a mission. And I was pissed.

CHAPTER 21--BLACK CAT

After much painful effort, I found myself finally standing in front of the Black Cat, oblivious to the gentle bumping of passersby jostling off to some heathen den for their putrid enjoyment. The place was pulsing like a dark heart. Music was throbbing its way outside, where a sign on the wall said "Tonight – Miss Mazola and her D-Cups" in English and what I assumed was the chicken scratch of Chinese writing. The lights were doing double duty between illuminating the sidewalk and being a homing death beacon for rather large moths. I hoped I wasn't one of the moths.

Seemingly, out of nowhere stood the giant Yellow Peril, his expression blank as he seemed to stare through me. I showed the invitation I had gotten earlier in the day mentioning Tika. Expressionless, he pushed aside the curtain.

I have never had the experience of walking into a place at night, and having to wait a few seconds for my eyes to adjust from dark to even darker dark. A vampire would love this place. Nothing but candles, but what the candles showed was exquisite, and I mean exquisite in the form of the female figure. Flesh, rounded female flesh, was all that greeted my eyes at first and I smiled out of pure reflex.

    A sweet almost naked beauty approached me and I showed her the note. A smile later, she was leading me across a deep interior pit of the club adorned with large overstuffed pillows crested with more girls in various states of undress enjoying themselves with what looked like well-dressed and well to do Asian businessmen. The main bar was a rounded affair with the floor on the inside of the bar level with the top of the bar itself. Girls clad only in G-strings crawled on hands and knees, mixing drinks from bottles in the axis of the bar, and serving them to the stoic sophisticated Asian customers. I veered my eyes back to the slender derriere of my guide and walked up a few steps, my back starting to scream with pain, and causing me to limp and look gawkish. We went over to the other end of the club to a private roped off curtained area. All the while, Miss Mazola, a huge black woman and her Chinese band were laying down some sweet jazz about a black woman having the yellow man blues. The girl that had led me through this den smiled, bowed, and opened a curtain to a single room drenched in black velvet. The room contained only a small gathering of pillows, a large hookah style pipe of sorts in the middle, and a small table that was already furnished with a decanter of wine with two glasses next to it.

    As I stood feeling like the damned hunchback of Notre Dame, a curtain parted from a corner, and the most amazing woman I have ever seen entered. She shone like a diamond, brightening the room like a new star brightens the heavens. She dripped sex and eye shadow, with a black glistening shear wrap covering her skin like flowing water, leaving little to the imagination, and brother, I got a great imagination. She stared at me as a cobra might stare at a rat, all the while smiling a cute little Mona Lisa smile. I was intoxicated and I had had nothing to drink – yet.

She said nothing as she poured us drinks.

"Tika?"

"I am she."

A moment of awkward silence on my part as I tried not to drool on myself. Her presence intoxicated me as if I had just been given a sip of booze from heaven.

She presented her hand. I instinctively bent to kiss it, never taking my eyes from hers, but all the while feeling like some pimply faced kid at the junior prom, hoping she wouldn't notice how soiled and sweaty my palms were. At the same time the wracking pain continued to make its way known up my spine from the evening's earlier escapades.

Her strong black eyed gaze made me feel ashamed at my own appearance. I felt intimidated at my crumpled state. I wished I had had time to clean up and change clothing. I wished I was meeting her back at a party in LA, where I could be in control of the situation. I sat on a pillow on the floor in the center of the room, while she, standing magnificently, majestically, grasped one end of the bamboo rods that formed the entrance to the room. The candles flickering her presence reminded me of the magazine photographers snapping pictures of some great starlet emerging triumphant from a night at an awards show. She had pinkish high cheekbones, almost meeting her dark velvet eyes, and her ebony hair, straight as a waterfall, was only disturbed by the movement of her breasts before the flow of her hair stopped at her waist.

"You are he I have sent for. There is talk we must have."

"And I have questions." I snapped to for a minute from my daydream.

"I shall ask the questions." She moved closer and sat on satin pillows slightly higher than mine, but close enough for me to feel her fragrance. I self-consciously straightened out my rumpled coat, adjusted my stained pants, and smoothed my ragged hair, feeling very embarrassed, like a kid caught doing something he shouldn't have done with himself.

"I am sorry for my appearance tonight. I ran into a little trouble on the way over here. Seems someone resembling your doorman and a pal of his decided to give me the once over. Seemed as if they were looking for something I might have on me."

"The doorman has been here all night. Maybe someone else? But then, we all look alike."

"Sister, you don't look like anyone else," I blushed, surprising myself for a change with my brashness at the moment.

"I summoned you here about something we are both interested in. A certain stone." She studied my reaction to this statement. I easily showed her somewhat of my relief, hoping this sordid affair would end soon. I took a long breath but stopped it shortly after.

I heard her ask: "I want to know what concern it is of yours."

I looked up and it seemed I caught a quick flicker of doubt in her eye.

"Why do you want to know?" I was slightly suspicious now, and I needed things to make sense fast. I would tell her somewhat of the truth and hope she would give a sliver of reality at the same time.

"I know you have been looking for the true greenstone, and it has not been easy."

"What do you mean by the true greenstone?"

"I know there are duplicates that are very valuable to certain peoples." Tika stared suspiciously at me. "Why are you here? I know I sent for you, but I have it from my associates you have been trying to find me. Here I am, now, again I must ask, why are you here?"

"To find what I think you have. I was directed here by someone to find that stone, and find who owns it."

"The stone belongs to me and my people. I am bound by its sacred powers to return it to those who worship it and bathe in its radiance. You assume I have it. You assume wrong. You have it and you must return it to me now."

"I don't have it, and I wouldn't be here if I did. I am looking for the person connected with that stone. Several people have died for that stone, one of them very close to me. I also want to find who murdered a boy back in Tijuana over it. Right now a certain Nazi seems to be suspect number one. The fact you know I am here and involved with the stone makes me think you are working with this Nazi. Do you know a Bruno Durst?"

"I ask the questions. I do not answer yours, and I do not like your tone. You obviously have someone backing you on this journey you have started. What is their intention?

"The same as yours. To find the stone."

"You don't know what you talk about. You know nothing of its power and its value, but the person that is sending you your money does. You have ended my patience. Who is this person?"

"I can be stubborn too. I am looking for the stone to find out who killed a boy at another Black Cat in Tijuana. Or is the name of this place just another coincidence?

Her expression turned sour. "I find you deceitful and a liar. I know you have the stone, but you refuse to tell me so. For that you will pay. I will get the stone from you one way or another."

"What makes you think I have it?"

"I have my sources in Mexico that tell me so. Yes, Mr. Hanover, I am aware of what has gone on concerning the stone. I know of the theft of the stone, for I was there. I know of Tijuana, for I was there. I know of a certain German beachcomber – and I know you have the stone. You will give it to me."

"You sure get around, sister. Why would I be here if I had it?"

"That is easy. The stone is very valuable and unique. It has a high price. You want money. Well, you will not get anything for it, but you will return it to those that it rightfully belongs to."

A sudden flair of pain in my back made me struggle to my feet and shout "Dammit, I don't have time to play around. If it turns out you DO have the stone that means I am going to put my fingers around your throat and choke the life out of you, and then I will tear this place apart until I find it!"

My sudden outburst brought with it a half dozen female henchmen dressed in diaphanous gowns that appeared out of the curtains it seemed. As they reached for me, I swung out and found myself face first on the floor with a foot against my spine and my neck twisted back so I was forced to grimace beet-faced at Tika.

"You are useless to me", she spat. "Maybe you don't have the stone. Either way, you will not lead me to it. I believe you are trying to use me to get to the greenstone yourself, so you can steal it for your own purposes. You are a threat to me and must be dealt with" The Oriental women were deft and agile for their size, using exotic fighting techniques to make me stand, before giving me the bum's rush out into the back alley where the Yellow Peril was waiting.

The Yellow Peril just smiled, gave me a crack in the back of my neck with the edge of his hand, threw me in a waiting unmanned rickshaw like a rag doll. I felt the sensation of movement as the rickshaw began a good clip, then more pain as the rickshaw hit a pole on the edge of the pier and I plummeted, upended rickshaw and all into the thick murky waters of the harbor.

CHAPTER 22--HUNG CHOW

The fates are laughing at me, and why shouldn't they? I have been banged up, bruised up, messed up, torn up, tossed out, punched out, sold out as a wetback, kicked to the dirt in an alleyway more than once, fooled and fouled up, then tossed in a smelly bit of drink, all the while merrily throwing away my career as a film actor of somewhat dubious talent, all for the want of a happy bank account and peace of mind. Peace of mind? I thought that was what this would give me when I agreed to go along with the Colonel's and Marian's wishes. I can't lie to myself as much as I try. I want peace of mind with my boy's death as well. I can't rest while this is pushing at me. Those voices keep laughing sweet chuckles. Getting louder, making me restless, but with each movement, I feel pain. Finally my pain pushed one eyelid open.

Three faces came into view – smiling, laughing through a squared off hole in the sky. Natural instinct allowed me to smile back at three giggling girls looking at me from an overhead porthole. Cute. I like cute. Still smiling, I looked around and saw that I was in a cabin, a cabin of sorts anyway. Pretty decent size. Nice cured wood. Solid. My back actually felt good for a change. Soft, yet supportive pillows. A warm wave of smells overtook me at this point, wonderful teas, frying fish, and other spices I couldn't identify. I smiled steadily as I took the chance on turning my head.

A large piece of yellow flesh sat before me. Something soothing and kindly about it made me smile "Hello."

"Herrow!" A large wrinkled face perched on a larger body that seemed broken in to segments like a centipede was directly at my feet. He was stirring a large wok that had the most wonderful fragrances emanating from it. I could almost taste the colors that seemed to sparkle against the dots of moisture and the oil dancing from the kettle to the steam above. I was envious of the steam and colored flavors that formed a column from the coals to the carefully placed vent that led upwards out of the cabin. I eased myself into a semi sitting position.

"I am dry. OK, I give. What goes?" The large chinaman gave a cryptic smile and let loose a high almost annoying laugh. "Oooooooo! You in the plesence of Hung Chow. I am he who plesents himself to you." He gave a quick start and looked up at the three faces that had been staring down at me through the hatch on the deck above. "You girls go now!" He then proceeded to rant in gibberish at the girls that had been staring down at me. "They rike you. Think you velly cute." Hung smiled at me. The girls gave a slight collective squeal and disappeared.

"Where am I?" My idea of heaven wasn't quite like this.

"You no die. You netted, rike fish flom water. We crean you up, change you croths." For the first time I noticed I was wearing something different. "Yea, thanks," I mumbled.

"I fix you croths, and creany, washy-ilonee. We forrow you from Hotel, tly to make sure you safe."

"You forrow - uh, excuse me – followed me? Why? Why save me, not that I don't appreciate it."

A voice from the back of me chimed in "I'm why! Any friend of Harry's is a friend of mine, sport!" I turned to face an apple cheeked young fresh faced guy I seemed to recognize. "We found you clinging to piece of driftwood. Boy, when we pulled you in, what a wreck you were. Your pants were ripped, shirt all stained up. The girls and I had been following you since you left the hotel. Oh, by the way, I'm Eddie Harris," he grinned, pearlies just a-twinkling.

As he approached me with outstretched hand of greeting it hit me who he was. "I know you, Eddie! Harry sent me pictures of you." A smile let loose on my face as I told him, "Damn nice to meet someone with a familiar face around here. By the way, where is here, anyway?"

"Well, here is where I have been for quite a while. Meet Mister Hung Chow," he said, gesturing to the large compound of flesh across from me. "He has been my protector. He seems large but boy he stays small so he can be large."

"OK, well, alright I guess that makes no sense."

"Oh, but it does. Mr. Chow has quite a bit of control in this harbor. There across from you sits the man who knows all that goes on along the harbor and the pier. See, this junk is tied up with other junks with little ropes, and they got these little rope walkways that interconnect all through the harbor, like a power grid of information. Now there are some pretty serious people running messages back and forth between various places. The junks can shove off and move at any time, breaking up the information and connections due to security problems, then they just tie up and reconnect somewhere else to reestablish that chain of information.

I glanced at Hung Chow. He sat over his wok, smiling as if he already knew the future. "Japanese run Shanghai now, but we Chinee show them. They not lest at easy at night. We clawl in their room under door, under window, thlue vent, anyway we can and srit their thloat, then srit their mouth from cheek to cheek on both sides. They have permanent sirry grin for all time."

I took a second to take his last remark in. Hung and his compatriots were like an underground nest of army ants in the Jap's garden of rule. Stomp a few out here and there, but they never all go away, and the Japs still get bit from time to time

"So you are welcoming me to your colony, huh Queen Ant?" Hung just gave a sweet wink at me as he busied himself dishing up bowls of spicy fish from the wok. "Why?"

"I told him about you and Harry and the greenstones," Eddie said, grabbing a couple of bowls and handing me one. "He knows all about that greenstone cult and how they operate."

"Well that is more than what I know."

"Oh, man, Hung Chow knows a lot of things. And what Hung Chow knows, goes. This man is the master seamster, weaving threads of information amongst the junks, then breaking it up and moving that information elsewhere. He has his own couriers doing what he tells them, and we all stay under the radar of the Japs that control the government or anyone else this way. It was one of his couriers that sent you the note yesterday"

"Alright, but I still don't understand what I'm doing here, and what the hell happened to you? This can't be some assignment of yours to spy on the Jap occupiers is it?"

"Ha! That's a good one. I wish it was, my life would sure be easier. Right now, this old West Texas boy is in a hell of a fix."

I tried to sit up a bit more, but a sharp pain in my lumbar made me groan.

"Oh…"

"You just take it easy, boy. You still need to heal a bit. Let me shift the pillows around for you while I tell you what has been going on. It ain't been pretty, I'll tell you for sure."

I took Eddie's advice and took it easy while he told his tale in that easy drawl of his. Seems that Eddie had been out on the town with some buddies while his ship had been in port, and being sailors on shore leave, they did the obvious. They got stinking slobbering commode hugging drunk.

"Back in Diego I got transferred and shipped in one day after the murder. Boy, was I upset, when I heard the news. When my ship hit Shanghai, guess I went nuts at the bar. Months without release, without letting go of how upset I was over what happened to Harry. I went out and did what is a sailor's right. I got plastered first night in port. Beer, whiskey, strange sort of smoke." He gave a good natured chuckle. "You know, they don't have regular Lucky Strikes over here, ya gotta roll your own, and this place is full of crazy tobakky. Ain't knockin' it, but it sure dulled my sense of time. Wasn't sure where, or even when I was. Guess I flashed a little too much change, cause all I remember is not much. I do remember waking up in vomit and beer in a banana bin in an alleyway near the dock. Boy, I guess you could say I had myself a good time, if I could only remember it. Bottles and babes, probably the best time of my life – or the worst - either way I'm sorry I missed it. Nothing to tell my grandkids now."

My senses were momentarily overcome by the spice and freshness of what I had just put in my mouth. This was good! "Wow, this is exceptional."

"Yep, Hung takes care of those he likes. That is what I mean about Hung Chow. See, I was in a bad way that mornin' crawlin' out of that bin, the mornin' sun streamin' down on me, all these crazy women runnin' out'a the back of food joints all yelling; and threatnin' and I mean serious threatnin' with cleavers and soup ladles, wanting me to get out of their trash bins. Well I guess the rats were OK, but a Big Spring boy wasn't. That's OK, no matter. I left on the QT.

"On top of that, I had a monstrous headache caused by a bump on the side of my head that felt like Mount Rushmore, and brother, Lincoln was winkin'. I checked my pockets, I had a major hole in the seat of my pants, and everything was gone, no I.D., no cash, no dignity. I also had the shitty realization that my ship had left without me. Great, now I am a deserter, and my captain will think I jumped ship. My situation really stank. And I really stank. I wanted water, and I wanted a bath quick. Welp, I ran down towards the pier, tripped over a board, went over the side, fell and happily busted my ass off the side of one of the junks and went straight into the drink.

"I pulled myself up and moved among the flotilla of junks along the harbor's edge, getting' jabbered at by everybody, until I saw this here junk. There were some clothes strung up topside, and just as I was helping myself into them, I was ambushed and brought down into the hold. Imagine my surprise to find my attackers were a bunch of young gals!

"Welp, they strong-armed me, and dragged me to meet Hung Chow. He questioned me, wanted to know how I was going to pay for the clothes see? All I had was the greenstone. But that was when things changed. We talked through the day. By nightfall, everything was good, he trusted me, and I trusted him. He also needed someone that spoke English fluently for his trade"

"What goes with all these girls?" I asked, admiring one that was stooping over in a corner handling the cleaning of cookware.

"Welp, Big ol' Hung Chow, see, he loves his gals. Oh they are not his girls, you understand, he doesn't really go for women. But he loves his girls, and loves having them around. Street urchins, well I guess that's what they are, and they love him. Chow is a good guy. He also runs one of the most successful tailor trades in the harbor"

Eddie took a couple of slurping bites and continued;

"Welp, luckily Hung got me a fake credential as a missionary and got me a job here in Shanghai at an orphanage. Can you top that!"

I might not be able to top it, but I could figure it out. Hung needed someone he could control to be his liaison in English, and Hung definitely had the goods on Eddie, and was able to protect him from getting busted for jumping ship. I also know from Harry's letters that Eddie is a fast talker and a mercenary at heart that wouldn't mind making some money from Hung's underground activities. Eddie as a parson? Great cover for someone to move about the city fairly undetected.

I shook off the thoughts. "Back to the greenstone. That thing seems to be causing a lot of fuss. Why was Hung so concerned with yours? There are fakes around, what makes yours so special? What does he know about it?"

"Ooooo I know rots!" Hung chirped up. "I have his gleenstone now as corratelal for his services in my emproy. Whether tlue gleenstone or not, that cult velly bad. Some of girls of mine drugged and kidnapped into cult. Never saw again. This why I help you. You rook for cult. You found Tika. She is high uppy-uppy. Run much. Is queen of cult. Velly dangerous. I fight them for taking girls."

"Hung also makes his money running black market operations supplying revolutionaries against the Japs," Eddie chimed in. Hung gave a cautionary glance at Eddie. "Sorry Hung, but Sterling is OK." Hung just smiled warmly. "Yes. He OK."

Some young girls made their entrance with baskets on their shoulders. "You crothes ready now." I checked my clothes that were part of the other laundry items in the basket. Gee, they looked swell. I got my suit back, not only clean, but pressed, mended and looking rather spiffy. The girls handed the basket of clothes over to Hung. He smiled, took a small bag out and placed it in my hand after observing the contents. "This you?"

I took out the bag. Inside was the white knight that I thought lost.

CHAPTER 23--SUMMIT MEETING

Next morning after a damn well needed night's rest and a full belly thanks to Hung and his bevy of sweet young cherubim, I was feeling rather dapper again. My suit was not only retailored, but was given a facelift that Max Factor would have been proud of. A swell suit gives a guy confidence he wouldn't have otherwise. Even better was the white knight I kept in my pocket. The little trinket brought the focus I needed right back to me. I was centered on my mission now, more than ever before. This is my personal crusade at this point, the Colonel being my patrician, and Miriam a side player. Funny, her memory doesn't jar me as it usually does. I feel I have been freed from some heavy emotional chains. I actually hobble with a lighter feel to my step towards one of the many small food stalls next to Hung Chow's junk, accompanied by a trio of his squealing giggle of girls and Eddie.

Finishing up some odd seafood that I wasn't sure of, but that tasted delightful, Eddie summed up the next step with me.

"Looky here boy. You say you got cash money comin' at you with that Colonel feller?"

"Yes." Anything I said was met with subdued mirth by the young smiling girls that only got cuter as the seconds went on.

"Yea, the Colonel has this Swiss bank account set up, and wires funds into it on a regular basis. All I have to do is ask, and the Colonel or the bank will shoot it out to wherever I happen to be. Except the middle of the jungle of course!"

"Dang, you are a lucky cuss."

"Look," I said, wiping essence of squid from the side of my mouth, "What happens to these girls that are kidnapped?"

"Not much. They just get fed some jungle drug that turns them into willing slaves to the Tika cult. They usually get shipped out to different places and points on the globe. They end up in slavery rings, bars and clubs, all associated with the Tika cult."

"Like Tijuana?

Eddie gave me a hard stare. "Like Tijuana. That club, the Black Cat. That is associated with the Tika cult."

"This Tika – same as the woman I ran into?"

"That was her, and this is her operation. She travels a lot, dropping in unannounced on her servants, the drugged up women and the business people that run her organization. Very undercover, very wealthy, and very deadly. You were lucky you just got beat up and tossed out. She must like you."

Lucky me, I thought.

My legs gave out as if someone had whacked me across the back of the knees and hit me in the stomach. I kissed the sticky curb of the alley.

"Whoa, Jackson," Eddie exclaimed. "You are still pretty weak. Let's go back."

Back at Hung's I was told by both him and Eddie that by the looks of my pain I needed more rest. "Father" Harris, as he was going by, said he was going to transport me to his orphanage on the edge of the city. I tried to protest several times, but each one brought laughter to them and agony to me. Hung gave me a sedative that turned me in to a jellyfish. I floated and smiled my way in a rickshaw to Eddie's orphanage. Once there, I welcomed the happy soothing treatment by a couple of Hung's girls, who made sure I was comfortable. When it comes time for me to go to heaven, I'm gonna tell the angels I would rather go back to Eddie's orphanage.

Eddie managed to visit me at the beginning of the day to bring me breakfast and a bourbon "heart-starter" as he put it. I lay on the cot with my head propped up and we talked.

"So what goes with the girls here?" I asked.

Eddie pulled up a chair, sat next to me and explained, a somewhat serious look on his face. "Hung and I have gotten fairly close. I asked him the same questions you ask me. Apparently some of his girls were kidnapped and seduced into the cult. Now ol' Hung does not take this lightly. He was glad to see me when I appeared, and took me in right away since I talk English so dang good and all."

I nodded with a smirk.

"Now-now-now see, the nearest I can figure," he continued, getting somewhat fired up, "this here Tika queenie takes all these drugged up gals and they all end up working for the cult." I chewed on this with the rest of the information I had accrued. "While the girls work for, and protect her, they also hold her responsible for this magic greenstone she is entrusted with. Since that greenstone is missing, she only has a certain amount of time to find it, or one of her slaves can kill her, find the true greenstone on her own, and become the new queen."

"How long does Tika have?"

"Don't know that one, pal."

"Looks like Tika is in trouble," I said with a slight empathy to my voice. I don't know why I felt a bit sorry for her. It didn't make sense, concerning the circumstances. Eddie bid me rest, and slipped out the door to go take care of business matters at the orphanage.

A couple of blissful days accompanied by some happy ending massages at the orphanage gave me much needed rest and peace until I was good again.

Eddie showed up the third day I was there and helped me move about the open area next to a small airfield. I didn't have to lean on him that much, and we discussed the situation while we walked. Eddie was a fountain of knowledge for me, some things he told me I already knew, some I didn't.

As Eddie had told me days before, Hung is very knowledgeable of this cult. Tika's cult has all female consorts that protect her and will help in her quest to find the stone. The consorts are slave girls that are controlled by some highly addictive jungle drug. She has a limited amount of time to find the stone however, or she will be killed by her own consorts, a sacrifice to the spirit of the stone as punishment. This stone has some power as yet to be determined by those outside the cult.

Back in my room after the evening meal, and feeling much better, I lit a Lucky and thought while the wisps of smoke congealed around me, and sipped some of the good Father Eddie's wine. After a couple of hours of feeling fidgety I went outside and walked around the tarmac on the airstrip next to the orphanage. The night sky was refreshing and coated with winking diamonds. I looked up at them and they told me what to do.

    I tracked down my two angels that had been so good to me during my stay and told them what I wanted. Didn't take much for the eager little beavers to help me out, though it did take a bit of convincing and some tenderness on my part.

    The girls admitted that Eddie had assigned the two of them to me. How sweet. The little China dolls agreed to help me in my new inspiration, to "borrow" Eddie's stone for me to use as bait the following night. I had been thinking steadily about what I would do for days. With the greenstone for bait I could track down the one responsible for my boy's death, or at least gain another lead. The money from the Colonel was needed greatly, but this whole job had risen from a duty to a calling. I have to settle this, or I won't be settled until it is.

    The little sugar darlings led me through tangled streets the next night that ran to the back alley behind the Black Cat. If my hunch was right, I had a feeling that Eddie's stone might be the one that is the true stone, and if it is, then I have a chance for this craziness to stop.

    I still couldn't get my mind off of Tika. If the craziness stopped, then that would be the last I would see of her. I could leave all this, go back to Hollywood and continue as before. For some reason, I couldn't settle for that. I also was beginning to believe that at this point there would never be a way to find the murderer, or end this lunacy. But in the meantime I will continue to follow the Colonel's instructions to follow the trail of the greenstone. This Tika is the key somehow, and I have to get her to open up, and the only way will be with Eddie's stone.

There she was in my mind again, Tika. Her vision haunted me. If ever there was a puzzle, she was the one. She had become a compulsion in my thoughts ever since my time in the orphanage. Maybe if I can reason with her, just talk to her, find out what she knows, and let her know I am not a threat, I can make an appeal to her civilized side.

Meanwhile, the girls led me back to the Black Cat, only this time I am not going through the front where the henchmen would be waiting for me. I had the girls lead me to the alley behind the Black Cat where hopefully I can get in and confront Tika one on one. The girls took me down the alley where I needed to be, then disappeared in the darkness. A series of wooden crates were stacked next to the alley wall. The crates reached up to a small window that was open slightly. Light fought its way through the small slit. Creeping silently up the boxes to just under the window, I heard voices from within.

What I heard next gave me an education I hadn't expected.

I recognized Tika's voice, but there was another, a decidedly male voice with a decidedly German accent. Tika spoke crisp English with a slight British hint.

#

"Verdamnt English gutter tongue," Bruno thought to himself. "I am forced to speak this mongrel muttering in order to get my meaning across. Is it not enough I have to deal with a beast woman to get what I am after? I want the stone, which is what I must have. I have come too far to not have what I want.

"She stares at me now, like a cobra at a mouse. I am not a mouse, but a mongoose, as she will soon learn. She does not trust me. Fine, I do not trust her."

Bruno spoke. "I know you need your stone. I am well versed on your culture." It hurt his mouth to speak this dialect. "I also know that if you don't retrieve this stone, your cohorts will sacrifice you. This is why I am here. I can help you."

"I have to wonder how you know so much about my organization," Tika scowled. "We are very secret, but you acquired some knowledge of us."

"I am a collector and a trader." Bruno did not lie when he said this. "I can get you what you want, and you can get me what I want. While researching your…um..organization, I gained valuable information that you will find most useful. Information concerning that fateful night in the jungle."

She paused and eyed him suspiciously. Bruno thought that there was no way for her to recognize him. Not this fine looking dapper gentleman in front of her, instead of the filthy warrior that destroyed her temple.

Tika looked at him, but with a faraway look in her eyes, as if seeing Bruno and having a vision of the raid on her village ceremony. Still, she did not recognize him. Bruno smiled internally. "These lesser races are so easy to deceive," he thought.

"I was in such a trance that night," she spoke to him in a voice that seemed so far away. "I did not know what was happening until too late. But back to business." She snapped to clarity and bore her eyes into Bruno. "You have knowledge of the whereabouts of that which was taken from me?"

"That is correct, madam. A thief by the name of Sterling Hanover approached me awhile back. He knew I was a collector and might be interested in such things. At first I doubted him about its authenticity, but when he showed it to me…well, there was no doubt. The carving was as I had heard."

"Why did you not take it for yourself?"

"I would be a liar if I said I was not tempted," Bruno lied, laughing to himself. "But I have no use for such an item, except to trade it for something more valuable to my interests. I have told you already of my family's business, and how the war interests need to be played properly so my family continues to flourish, no matter which side wins the war. As it is, my family's factories are always in need of diamonds for industrial use. Right now, all resources are running very scarce."

"Yes you have. As you know something of me, I know something of you. I know of you and your factory's needs. You may have the diamonds you need and more."

"Good, then we have a deal. Diamonds for information on the whereabouts of this Sterling Hanover."

"I know he may still be in the vicinity of Shanghai, since he did indeed visit me several nights ago. He has since disappeared into the underground of the city. No matter. With both our resources, we shall find this thief and recover the stone. I have my series of clubs and dealers scattered around the globe. Members of my organization will be tracking your efforts."

"Of course," Bruno smiled as he thought "She has bought in to it."

Drinks entered the room on a cart brought by a charming Asiatic female specimen.

"We shall toast," Bruno proclaimed and poured the wine from a crystal decanter, filling both goblets, and handing her one.

As they both sipped, all Bruno could do was think of how he was luring her on to track Sterling. Once that happened, then what Bruno had to do was to follow her and her kind to find him. Bruno smiled at the ease of the thought that his connections would simply follow her connections.

#

Standing on the crates outside the window listening to all this, my ears burned bright red, and I couldn't help but feel a shiver run up my spine. I was genuinely scared.

I raised my head a bit, just a bit more, to see in the window. All I could see was the back of Tika's head and the torso of an expensive suit of clothes worn by a rather foppish looking fellow. One hand was extended, grasping a cigarette holder, while a jewel encrusted cuff link dangled from an open sleeve. I noticed a missing finger on his hand.

An amazing looking oriental girl, not more than seventeen, brought a decanter of dark fluid. The gentleman smiled as he and Tika proposed a toast.

All I could make out was something about my death and the securing of the stone. That was plenty to give more shivers. To hell with this. Colonel or not, money or not, I am getting off of this train right now. I am going back to the hotel and get the hell out of here, back to the sanctuary of my Hollywood home and Ha-

Nee, where the scariest thing that might happen to me is making a suicide dive bombing mission into a martini.

Slipping gingerly from the boxes, I landed softly in the alleyway, only to turn and face a female form barely visible all dressed in black from head to toe with only slits cut in her mask to reveal her eyes, nose, and mouth. The ebony material of her costume caressed her obviously female form and exposed her femininity. My first reaction was pure reflex. "Hey, baby, buy you a drink?"

POW – little red Christmas tree lights danced in my eyes.

"I - I guess that's a raincheck," I goofily blubbered, slobber running down my chin as I weaved back and forth like a bobble-headed hula girl. My forehead was beginning to warm from the open handed smack that had been placed against it. I heard a window opening and Tika shouting.

Next thing I knew, I was standing in the room I had been spying on. My guide from the alley tripped me up onto the floor. A few seconds later found me tied to a straight back wooden chair in the middle of the room.

"Vell, vell, vell, vat do ve hof here?" The man with the missing finger glared menacingly at me. Tika remained stoic.

"Well from what I heard, I guess you got me where you want me."

"Oh, yes, danke, very convenient of you to drop in."

"We want what you have." Said Tika directly.

"I don't know what you are talking about," I hesitated. "Well actually that is not true. I know exactly what you are talking about, the green rock."

Mr. Dapper approached me. As he did, I recognized him from Big Job Bob's description involving the missing finger. Things got a little clearer now.

The dirty little Hun took a clean white handkerchief from his jacket and slapped me across the face.

"Oh, ouch." I sneered in to his eyes. "I've been slapped better than that by forty year old floozies at the Brown Derby at closing time."

Boy, what a prissy face smirked right back at me. Handsome soft featured cuss he was, with a hint of someone that had been bullied a bit too much as a kid, and now it was his turn.

THWAK! That was the sound his palm made across my cheekbone as the force of the slap knocked me on my back, the ribs of the high-backed chair causing tomorrow's bruises.

While on my back, my fingers crushed against the knots holding me in place. I could feel the pressure of my weight and the odd position I was in to start to cause stress in the knots, slightly loosening them.

With the fall, however, I blurted out "I know you. I know you from that missing finger. You are Bruno and you are a Nazi." The stinking Nazi flinched and shoved his hand into his pocket. "Yea, Big Job Bob told me all about you. Remember him? You tried to grab what you thought was the stone right before you were sure you had killed him. Well, he didn't die right away, see? At least not before he talked to me about you. You don't want diamonds, you want the stone for yourself!" Tika turned her fiery gaze towards Bruno.

I could sense the moment's mistrust from Tika before Bruno's foot cracked the seat of my upturned chair and his boot slammed into my crotch.

All of a sudden I was squeaking like a new castrati recruit in the Vienna Boys Choir. "OK, OK!" I hit a high strained C on that last OK. "I have the greenstone!" A smug look came over Pretty Boy's face.

"You see? It doesn't take much," he said.

Tika had a mysterious smile on her face as she glared at Bruno. "No it doesn't," she said heatedly.

"My pocket," I moaned in between short breaths. "That is where you will find it."

As Bruno put his hand in my pants pocket, my breath returned to normal along with my wits. "Easy, boy, I've been pick pocketed by better crooks than you." He shuffled his hand a bit more in my pocket. "You sure you don't want to give me a little kiss while you are down there?" He stopped, smacked my already bruising face, and produced Eddie's greenstone.

"Well I must say, you are efficient. In less than an hour of our meeting you have produced results. Results at the expense of lies," Tika snarled.

As Tika and Bruno locked eyes, I was able to reach the uppermost piece of the now broken chair in my right hand, unseen. Tika sneered at Bruno. "Maybe our intruder has a point, Mister Industrialist. Is there something more to you that I should know?"

"You already know of me. You know my family," he said.

"Yes, your family and your industry. Not of you."

The two of them were so wrapped up in their mistrust of each other that I was able to grab a grip with my other hand on the chair leg that had loosened as well.

Bruno was turning beet red as I saw my chance. Thank God all that action training I had making all those Saturday morning serials was about to pay off, only this time, no pulling punches! I was acting on pure instinct as I gripped hard on the loosened limbs of my chair, sprang up, carrying the remains of whatever was left of the chair still strapped to my body, and brought a crushing blow down on Bruno's clavicle with both pieces.

A painful whine was given as he tried to counter with a kick that only hit what was left of the chair still tied to me. My hand brought the crystal decanter from the drink cart across the top of Bruno's head, which hastened the skirmish to a quick conclusion, and opened up a crimson gash on his forehead.

The whole time Tika sat poised, like a praying mantis, waiting for the two males of her species to finish battling each other so she could have the relish of eating the victor.

"Tika, we can work something out," I shouted, not knowing why. I ducked as she leapt for me, and I rolled and grabbed the greenstone that had fallen out of Bruno's hand. She turned, hissed like a wildcat, and sprang again, only this time Bruno was up off the floor. Crashing in to a lumbering Bruno, both went back to the floor as the door burst open and the black clad female from the alley again entered the room. Thinking Bruno was attacking Tika, the female guard was distracted long enough to allow me to leap from the open window and down to the alley below, making my get away, bits of chair dangling from me.

CHAPTER 24--RAINY RIDE

Beaten till pulpy, bruises starting their pounding rise all over my flesh, I ran with the speed of thought through the night, hoping that any chance to make my escape would rise before me. Mercury, with the wings on his feet would have stalled at my speed. The darkness of the night slowed my vision, the air becoming thick with droplets that seemed to dangle in front of me, only giving me anguish as they sought to frustrate my sight beyond slippery pavement and stone walls. Surprisingly my movement exposed no other humans, the alleys winding into open areas where the rain pounded harder and harder, with drain spout gashing gushers in the night on the fuzzy streets below. My feet held steady against the slim slime of the slick avenues. A yellow light of a cab stand beckoned me with its lure. I grabbed the handle of the slow moving cab and thrust myself inside. By chance it was the cab that had brought me to this place from the airstrip and the orphanage. The rain began to pound as the faceless driver muttered "Home?"

"Yes." The cab pushed on, waves of rainwater splashed against the windows from clogged gutters. I lit up a Lucky, dazed in thought and let the smoke surround me with a hypnotic swirl. I took deeper and deeper drags, losing myself in my own personal smog. I can relax for a bit now. I can't even think what might be next. Right now all I wanted was a cool head of tobacco and the chance to sit back and listen to the rain. I drifted off to sleep about the same time I realized that the bits of chair were washed away from me. Good, wash me away. The tobacco smoke soothed me. I slept.

"We heah, boss, quicky quicky!"

I snuffed out the cigarette that had already started to burn my fingers, paid the cabbie and emerged into the now drenching rains that were being whipped by heavy winds. Of course I had lost my hat at some point. Nice.

CHAPTER 25--NIGHT FLIGHT

Disembarking from the cab in the steady downpour, I went running up towards the orphanage and the small air control building at the edge of the runway. In the darkness I could make out the meager lights coming from the inside of the orphanage. It looked dank and defeated. Bright yellow lights hummed at the control building, so I made for them, like a June bug on a burning mission.

Hitting the door, I got a big "HOWDY!" from Eddie. Noticing a large pile of towels on the counter by the door, I grabbed a couple. "Help yourself. Mate!" said a voice from someone I didn't recognize. "The name is Monty Doyle, pilot for hire, and all around swell guy." The voice was attached to a large impressive fellow wearing khakis and a hat with the side brim turned up Australian style, and with an accent to match. He thrust a hand masquerading as a ham hock with fingers at me and shook my hand like he was going to break it.

"Good to meet you," I stammered. "Look fellas, I gotta get out of here and get out fast. There some people on my tail that don't like the game I have been playing."

"No worries, mate. Got to run a shipment for our buddy Hung in twenty. Got room if you are in need."

"In need indeed!"

A big laugh emerged from deep in Monty. "Like I say, Monty is the name, fussing and flying is me game." Monty looked like a picture postcard of a World War One flying ace as he put on his leather flight jacket, removed his hat to replace it with a leather flying cap. His broad grin was framed on top by a pencil thin moustache.

"Say, you don't happen to fly open cockpit, do you?" I had to ask.

"Naw, mate, that's just for show." His eyes gave a twinkle. "Always did admire those fellows though. Now that's what I call real flying!"

"Well, real flying is what I need."

"Look, I've got the only plane out there and I am almost ready to leave. You ready?"

"I'm ready now."

"Ha ha! Good on ya! Let me get the cargo loaded into me Gooney Bird out there, and we'll start straight away."

Monty swiftly moved a flat of boxes by the outside door across the tarmac towards the cargo hold of his twin engine C-47. "Where ya goin' Sterling?" asked Eddie, with a slight nervousness to his voice.

"Somewhere, anywhere, just away from here."

"Great, Monty is heading towards southern India, with a few choice stops along the way."

"India, huh. I guess that is as far away as someone can get."

"Hey look, you wouldn't happen to have seen my greenstone have you?"

"Nope," lying through my teeth.

"Damn." Eddie seemed distant, not quite believing me.

"What is up with Monty?" I quickly changed the subject.

"Aw, the crazy Aussie delivers supplies to certain folks who aren't happy with the current state of affairs around here."

"Well, I am going out to help him speed things up."

I left in a quick hurry from the control building and ran over to where Monty was loading the cargo in the rain. As I helped load, all I could think of was how I had to get away and let things calm down until I could expose Bruno to Tika's cult somehow. That was the only way to keep the cult from killing me.

"Thanks, mate," was what I got in return.

When we finished loading, a flash of lightning illuminated Monty on the tarmac and brawling thunder obliterated what he said as he signaled the control building he was ready.

Another brilliant blast of lightning illuminated treacherous movements to the side somewhere, but my haste made me ignore it. All I wanted was to get the hell out of there.

Just as we were getting in the aircraft a gunshot report cut through the rain from the control building to our ears. We both bailed and ran back to the building.

Bursting in the door, we were confronted with Bruno, smiling, pointing a gun, the fresh crimson wound he had acquired earlier almost glowing on his forehead. He seemed illuminated by the lazy haze of cigarette smoke and the smell of gunpowder filling the air like an old gym sock. His perfectly tailored brown double breasted suit crested with a dark green bow tie against an almost lemon colored pin striped shirt. His head was fit with a matching and slightly tilted Homburg that contrasted against the crumpled lump of flesh and silk piled in a heap in the corner. Two tiny whimpering voices sobbed behind the counter where Bruno stood.

Eddie, looking defeated but defiant burst out "Hung found out there was trouble, and came here to try to stop this man."

"Yes, quite right, you. It seems that as I was persuading Mr. Harris here to let me board the plane. Mr. Chow demanded that he already had a seat booked, and there was no more room. Well I just persuaded him to give up his seat," he said, gesturing towards the pile in the corner.

"Now, if everyone will be kind," Bruno said quietly yet forcibly, as he put on a black raincoat, switching hands with his gun while keeping steady aim. "I have a date with a certain queen that is heading back to the jungle for her health. Seems she has something I need very dearly," and as he said these words, he grabbed the whimpering voices from behind the counter, revealing them to be two small orphans with soaked tear stained faces.

"Hey, give the kids a break, they just wandered in to see what all the commotion was about."

"How the children will be taken care of is up to you. We will walk quietly to the plane and get in, or this missionary Eddie here and these two adorable children will get it, as they say in the amerikanisch movies."

We all walked through the rain outside to the plane, Eddie and the two children accompanying us, only to be left behind the last few yards. "Smile, children, wave goodbye," Bruno proclaimed. "There are your guardian women from the orphanage watching. Make nice."

Eddie and the children waved goodbye, while Bruno's gun, hidden under his black coat, never lost its sight.

Once all aboard, with Bruno's luger directing us the entire time like an overzealous flight attendant, Monty fired up the engine. Bruno sat in the co-pilot's seat, gun trained at Monty, occasionally waving it in my direction in the seat behind the pilot.

The lightning and the thunder became indistinguishable from each other, as we hammered our lurching way up into the sky.

The noise was tumultuous with the roar of engines, grumblings of thunder, stroboscopic lightning, air pocket confusions, and water slathering on the body of the aircraft. Bruno, holding steady his twin aim on us both, began to make slight whimpering noises, sometimes overpowering the surrounding effects. Seemingly afraid to watch the carnage of weather and machine outside, he stared at us unrelentingly. The red crimson wound on his forehead seemed to throb and glow in the light of the control panels in the otherwise dark cabin of the plane.

Bruno suddenly shouted "Why is this verdammt plane so sluggish?"

"It's called the weather, mate. I have been having some trouble with me baby lately, but once the weather smooths out, we'll be right skippy."

"Let's hope so for all our sakes"

A flash of lightning, a sudden air pocket, and shifting of cargo against a black form movement in the hold stole my attention for a second, then I was trained back to the barrel of Bruno's gun. I could tell he was nervous and afraid. He was sweating, a small series of drips forming on his chin, his bow tie bobbing up and down against his throat each time he swallowed hard.

As we flew into the night, Bruno, in his nervousness began to talk to us. I felt as if he was talking to us in order to relieve his stress and mounting fear, as the plane continued to relentlessly lurch in the stormy skies.

"Where ya goin' then mate?" Monty asked.

"I am hardly your mate. A bit of respect, please. I am Bruno Durst, former captain under Goering's command."

"SS, eh?"

"Former special assignment." Thunder rang out like the voice of the Lord.

They talked for the next few hours. Bruno talked mainly, and with each air drop and thunder toll, his palms seemed sweatier, as small damp concentric circles formed under his armpits.

"A bit overdressed for pirating a plane, ain't ya?"

"Please, sir. The obvious fact is that I have style and care enough about my appearance to show it in a sartorial fashion that far succeeds your…well, let's just say lesser but functional attire."

The two bantered for a bit, exchanging personal information, all the while Bruno was keeping steady attention. I dozed for a bit off and on through some of their exchanges. Monty's stories were mundane next to what Bruno had to offer. Only an occasional "seriously, mate?" would emerge from Monty, sounding very smooth. I could tell Monty was not worried in the least as he fought for constant control against the elements. Monty's continuing retorts only encouraged Bruno's soliloquy, while he never abandoned his trained aim on us both.

"Are you clean?" Bruno asked, causing Monty to raise an eyebrow.

"I take me a shower once in a while."

"I mean really clean." Bruno continued a bit dreamily, not paying attention to Monty's remark. "That is what I loved about my uniform. Of all the militaries in all the world, Germany has the best dressed. And within the German military, none are better dressed than the SS. Spit and polish, the yanks like to say. Of course, I would make a few adjustments to the uniform for style's sake, and to add a touch of individuality. Otherwise, it is a beautiful uniform. I was almost sorry to let it go."

"Ain't yer former Nazi pals looking for you?"

"Of course, my dear chap. Dear Chap, isn't that what you say, or is it just the Limey brigade? No matter. Do you happen to have clippers? For the nails, that is. Mine are starting to get uncomfortable." He gave a quick glance at his fingers.

"Sorry, mate, wish I could oblige you. Maybe you would slip and cut yer throat with'em."

"Shame, really." Bruno paid no attention. "My shoes could stand some new polish and a bit of buffing."

Monty shook his head with a sigh.

"Do you like exercise, my friend?" Bruno looking ahead and absorbed in thought.

"I do me morning jumps and press ups."

"I love staying in shape. If there is one habit I wouldn't change, it is exercise. As a member of the

Germanic race, it is my duty to stay in top shape, as an example of my superiority."

"Always been in top shape have you?"

"Actually, I was unlucky enough to be quite sick as a child. My father was disgusted with me and blamed me for the death of his wife as well. With all the family money, and all the success of his industrial holdings, he couldn't stomach the fact that he had lost the love of his life to an unhealthy son and an only child"

Monty spoke up. "Yep, growing up can be tough on a kid alright, I remember…" Bruno cut Monty short. "Doctors," Bruno exclaimed to himself. "I remember all the doctors saying I wouldn't live very long. I remember my father actually being glad about it. No more embarrassment for him. Too bad for him I pulled through. After a few surgeries and with a permanent scar up my side, I decided I had had enough. I pulled myself up through determination, and the knowledge that I was somehow better than my fellows at the school I attended"

At this point Monty interrupted. "Sorry, old Bruno, but I have to drop these here supplies to some folks down below in the jungle. See, they wouldn't mind starting a little revolution against their Japanese friends. Just some gunpowder dropped here and there, along with medical supplies. This is a bit of a supply run after all, and I have me job to do, right? I mean after all is said and done…" Bruno cut him off with a quick "Nein! You will continue under my direction." Monty made a face of resignation and carried on as before.

A few minutes later Bruno mumbled, "Bullies."
"What?"
"My nose was damaged in a fight. The bullies at my schooling seemed to be everywhere. I was constantly

getting into fights I did not start. I made sure I finished them though. No care for my own personal safety or injury, I taught myself to fight with no fear at an early age. My hook nose is my badge of honor."

"Right, right, right, right, right." Monty agreed, glancing at Bruno's nose, which, now that he had mentioned it, did have a bit of a beak like curve to it.

Bruno continued to babble through the night, his gun never leaving its stare. Only on a fuel stop in a countryside air strip did he quit talking and even then his gun stayed on duty.

Finally as we winged our way onward, the storm broke, and gave birth to full moonlight shining down on jungle. Bruno had been quiet for a while, but his aim never wavered.

Then he began to talk about the greenstone.

"Disgusting filth," Bruno muttered

"Anyone I know?" quipped Monty.

"Nein, I am talking about this disgusting filthy jungle we are heading towards. If you only knew what I had to do last time I was here."

"Tell me about it. Plenty of bugs and bogs down there. Never went on foot much though. Cleaner to fly, mate." Monty gave a big smile at Bruno. Bruno returned the smile, then his expression went dark.

"I was in my jungle fatigues, grease smeared all over me, knee high leather boots, and still the filth covered my skin. In a certain way the grime gave me purpose. It made me rage with a single minded machine-like focus on my mission. It made me a barbarian animal brute."

"So what was that all about – if you don't mind saying, that is. Might do you a bit of good to talk about it."

A sly grin came from Bruno. "Not at all. Maybe confession is good for the soul as I have heard. I like you Monty. You are a good listener. I feel I can talk to you about this."

Bruno continued as I listened and stayed quiet. "I was given orders direct from der Fuhrer himself one night. I remember him mentioning Asian cults. He has always had a great interest in anything that might be a key to power. Much like my father. Hitler was very aware of my father's fame and fortune, as my father was of him when it came to the knowledge of outside sources of power."

"Outside? You mean supernatural witchy poo spooky bits?"

"Ya, but there are such things. The occult is not all lies. All mythology and superstition has roots in historical reality. The fantastic happens in the retelling sometimes, but the truth still exists."

Another slight bounce in the plane didn't stop Bruno. He continued.

"My father was much older, and Hitler would occasionally call upon him to learn information, as a student calls upon a respected teacher. I was away in the military at this point, but I remember coming home and being told to stay away from the west wing of the home. My father and Hitler were in deep conversation in the library."

The plane did a slight drop in an air pocket. Bruno gripped his gun and his aim became harder.

I was listening intently now, trying to gather what information I could get that might help my situation.

"The reality of what my father and Hitler had been discussing that evening when I was home long before, started the night I landed in the jungle," he continued. "My mission was to go in and secure an object from a bunch of jungle heathens."

"Sounds easy enough, considering your superiority and firepower," Monty butted in.

"You would think so. These are not ordinary heathens, though. They can be quite modern at times. This village in the jungle serves as a retreat for these people, all of whom are cultists in a special spiritual organization. They come in secret from all over the world."

"Kinda like Muslims making the journey to Mecca, huh?"

"In a way. These people come to worship in the glow of their queen and a certain greenstone of curious origin."

"Curious now is it?"

"Quite. This greenstone supposedly has a power to it and is very legendary in certain quiet collector's circles. Our beloved Fuhrer knows of this stone. He is very interested in such things that might give him power. He has a very special interest in the metaphysical side of gaining superiority"

"So what is this supposed power that makes it such a big deal? What makes people come from all over to go native in the jungle, and even gets your leader interested?"

"Of that, even I am not exactly sure. Supposedly the greenstone gives off radiations of some sort that gives whomever is within its range, longer life. How it works, or why it is supposed to work, I have no clue. I do know its value, however. I know that after the war in Europe settles down, no matter which side wins, I will be able to sell it to the highest bidder for quite a fortune." The low glow of the control lights gave Bruno an odd expression of satisfaction.

"Is that so?" Monty seemed a bit concerned. "Most folks care about their country, even Jerries like you, misguided as you are, must have some love of country."

"Oh, quite, of course, I have great pride in the Fatherland for what it has accomplished in a few short years. With that said, do you not plan for the future? What do you plan to do once the war is over? Do you think about that?"

"Carry on, I suppose. Doing what I have always done."

"That is why you are a fool. All I do is think of the future. In order to take care of the future, I must take care of the present. That means striking out on my own, securing and accomplishing what has to be done."

A moment's pause as he chuckled. "I am convinced that once the United States gets into the war in Europe, and it will, my friend, they are just waiting for any excuse. Once they enter, the US and the combined actions of the allies will eventually tear Nazi Germany apart. While I love my homeland, and the glorious accomplishments of the Reich, I love my family legacy and wealth more. Are you a betting man Mr. Doyle?"

"I do alright at the tables," Monty said with a wink.

"I only bet after summing up all odds over time. Do you realize the economic devastation to Germany that losing the war will bring?"

"Can't be good."

"There is already a fraternity of investors that exists. They consist of Nazis and Americans working together, already planning and laying groundwork on who gets what spoils after the war, no matter who wins. These are extremely high stake players that exist behind the industries that supply this war, especially when the US enters it, and they will enter it, with or without provocation from the Germans. Whatever side conquers the other, these investors will win."

"Got this sussed out, have you?"

"Yes. By selling the greenstone undercover now to the highest bidder, the Americans, or possibly others, I could then use that money to build up some international investments. Careful speculation and researched betting on which companies on each side might prosper the best once it was all over is my concern. As I stated before, Mr. Doyle, I love my country, but I love my family legacy and my wealth more."

A quick air pocket jolt made Bruno squeal slightly, and Monty curse.

Bruno continued his reminisces. "We attacked the ceremonial hut that night, and with much glory and bloody slaughter. All the while this queen of theirs was in a state of rapture and seemed not to even know what was going on. Oily smoke, fire, all led to our success in thieving the greenstone."

All the while this conversation was going on, I remained quiet and inconspicuous, not moving. The greenstone in my pocket was starting to itch against my leg.

"So why are you going back?"

"The greenstone was taken from me by the very person I took it from. I had it in Shanghai. There was this fight. I was attacked and knocked out. When I came to, I was in a basement room alone and tied up."

"So you got away?"

"Obviously. She has the greenstone now. I will get it back. I am going to go to her village temple, burn it down with her in it, and take the greenstone that I rightfully stole."

At this point there was another shift in the gear in the open cargo hold, and out came a shrieking figure in black darting towards Bruno through the glow of the lights from the cockpit. Instinctively I jumped in behind it as it lunged for Bruno, who was temporarily stunned by the shock of the attack.

Bruno screamed, shots rang out, metal ping ponged around the inside of the cabin. Monty leaned hard portside as metal slashed through his shoulder, another piece of shard punched its way through the glass of the windshield and into the fuel line. Darkness and oil fumes mixed with smoke filled the cabin while the grunts and shrieks of those within ensured chaos. Gravity left me. Whining of the engines screeched and stopped. Twisting of the aircraft made sure no one was able to get a firm grip, except for one person.

The plane momentarily righted itself as the smoke cleared, the black figure lay slumped on the deck, and the door on the starboard side of the craft blew open. Bruno stood, momentarily silhouetted against the backdrop of moon white clouds in the distance. Grabbing two parachutes, I watched him quickly strap one on, and fumblingly, he let it open as he bailed from the craft.

Monty had recovered and was fighting the wheel of the plane with one hand. "Krikey! Those were our only parachutes!"

I pitched towards the open hatch, only to brace myself and lean out to see a white billowing object twisting from the starboard rudder. It was Bruno, tangled up in his parachute. He bashed against the belly of the aft portion of the plane a few times before finally loosening himself to disappear in the gloom.

"Brace yourself mate!" was the call from the forward cockpit.

The tree tops loomed up as if in contest as to which one would be the lucky one to catch us, like a bride's maid trying to catch a bridal bouquet. The last thing I heard or saw was the whacking of trees against the plane and the man in the moon smiling sarcastically down at me as if to say "now you are getting yours."

CHAPTER 26--TRIBE OF THE POTTY PEOPLE

I first became aware of the sounds. Loud birds and insects seemed to be calling and buzzing everywhere at once. The smells were next. Odd fragrances I couldn't place and wasn't sure I wanted to. Then an underlying stench of old wet dung and matted hair hit me. Bits of light filtering in through a window and open doorway began to make themselves known. I was having a bit of a problem breathing. I slowly realized this was due to something on my chest. The something on my chest moved slightly, its bare feet keeping grip. Fingers were running through my hair, sorting it out bit by bit, as if searching for something or things.

A snort brought me to the realization that there was a monkey on my chest, carefully hunting through my hair, and pulling out bits of matter, only to put them in its mouth to eat. I observed this for a few minutes, being unable to move.

The cause of my paralysis became apparent as I shifted out of my coma. I was tightly bound with rope vines and was laying on a palette on the ground in a dark straw and mud spattered hut. The monkey finally realized I had come to and scampered away with a shriek that rang through my head like a brass gong. God, what a headache I just realized I had. There was a slow burning at the base of my skull that wouldn't quit.

"Water…" was all I could get out of my mouth.

I was able to turn my head slightly. I saw Monty bound in the corner, and a dark figure to his side that was also bound and not moving. Monty smiled that monstrously wide grin at me. "G'Day, mate!" His upper right arm had a slightly bloodied bandage hanging from it.

He was loose enough so that he could scooch over a gourd of water with his free hand. He held it to my lips as I just stared at him and drank deeply.

"How ya feelin', matey?"

"Nothing a bullet to the head wouldn't cure. Monty!" I croaked out. "What the hell happened?"

"Aw, this?" he said, gesturing with his bandage. "Bit of a flesh wound, no big deal. That bugger of an ex-Nazi clipped me on the plane."

The plane? "Where is the plane? What happened to us? Where are we? What the living hell is going on"

"No worries for now, mate. Number one, the plane crashed. Number two, we are lucky to be breathing, number three, I ain't quite sure." His grin fell on that last point.

"You have been asleep for a while," he continued. "We cracked up in that plane pretty badly. The natives in this here village came a-running, scooped us up and brought us here."

"How long ago?"

"Early yesterday morning. I was conscious enough to remember where the plane went down. The natives kindly grabbed some medical supplies I had on board, and with my instructions, they laced us up nicely."

"If they were so kind to us, why are we bound up?"

"Not sure on that one. I got me suspicions, and they are all bad."

An ancient woman wearing a wrap featuring a dark mosaic design with a white headcloth appeared in the doorway and entered the hut.

Monty eyed her as she approached me with a damp rag. "This lady seems to be our caretaker. About all I can say for her is that she is quiet." The old lady did indeed look a bit like a nurse the way her headcloth was shaped. She soothingly wiped my brow with her soft wrinkled hands and damp rag. She had a face like a sphinx. She began to wipe inside my tattered shirt that had been ripped up and used to bandage my head. As she went for my pants, I must have looked uncomfortable, as Monty spoke up. "Now mate, she is just doing her nurse's duty. Just cleaning you up all professional like. Not that you have a choice anyway."

The old lady finished cleaning me up, traded out the rag with some others in a basket by the door and proceeded to work Monty's back over. "Aw, that's more like it. Scrub down a little lower to the left, will ya darlin'? Mate, this woman has a face like a dropped pie, but I admit she knows what she is doin'." He let out a good chuckle on that one.

As she scrubbed, something occurred to me, and as it did, my face went pale. "Where is the greenstone? My pockets feel empty!"

I twisted and arched my hips against my bonds. As I did, I could feel a lump in my left pants pocket. The greenstone was still there! I maneuvered a bit more, pressing the object in my pocket against my skin in order to feel its outline. The object in my pocket was not the greenstone after all. Something else was there that I could feel, something I had forgotten about. The white knight.

There was a rumbling in the corner by Monty. A wild shriek like a tigress brought the attention of all of us. Hissing, spitting like a cat, a woman all in black, with greasepaint covering her face was shrieking at the world, fighting her bonds. The old lady, ever expressionless, ignored her, while Monty grinned a bit, and said "You don't know this bit of work do ya? She was the Sheila that drove that right bastard Bruno out of the plane."

The old lady left the cabin. I stared at this bundle of darkness and rage that was half leaning against a wall of the hut. Then I slowly realized. "Tika!"

A hesitation on her raving brought her out of her madness for a bit. "You have desecrated me and my people by having that greenstone and not returning it! There is judgment to be had. The greenstone is gone from you, it is where it needs to be, to be worshipped and held sacred. Soon you will pay."

I could do nothing but be glad the binds of her ties were holding strong.

The old lady brought in a tray with three bowls of some sort of mystery meat in a slop broth. She loosened the bonds around my hands, as well as Monty's, but kept our feet bound. She ignored Tika's bonds. I was served a bowl of food first, the overpowering stench almost making me sick until she forced a spoonful down my throat. Then I was overcome by an amazing taste, raising my hunger to a ravenous level. Incredible. I devoured all she fed me, Monty did the same. As the old lady approached Tika, she knocked the bowl from the old lady's hand, and Tika let loose with a babbling rage at her.

The old lady, for once, was taken aback, went from a kneeling position, stood full up, and waving a wrinkled finger at Tika, spouted what sounded like absolute gibberish, staring directly at Tika.

Tika replied in the same gibberish in a very commanding tone. The old woman's stoic face broke some more, only this time with a raising of the eyebrows. Tika scowled as the old lady slunk out the door.

"Bloody hell, they speak the same lingo," Monty said to himself as much as me. The afternoon progressed with a staring at me from Tika, and a general silence.

"You think you know me," Tika said at one point, breaking the silence like a pane of glass. "You know nothing of who I am or my heritage."

"You can always enlighten us," I smartly retorted, with my usual arrogance that I was sorry for later on.

The sun sank quickly in the jungle, turning bright light into darkness almost suddenly. The caws and shouts of the beasts of the day slowly turned into the rumblings of the hungry beasts of the night. Campfires were lit, their illumination sending bits of light through the hut to dance like glowing pixies on the walls. Hushed voices mumbled outside by the fires as the old lady entered again. She seemed different this time. She spoke, but only to Tika. Monty and I looked at each other. We didn't understand a word.

As they jabbered, Monty whispered, "Quite some conversation. Just like they was suddenly long lost mates."

After a long conversation and much glaring, the old lady slunk quickly out of the entrance of the hut. Tika just leaned against one side of the hut and stared into the distance. In the darkness she spoke to us, but as if we weren't there.

"The old woman speaks my language." Not a surprise to us, as Monty and I both exchanged a glance. "She was one of my people. From a long time ago, when she was young."

The evening remained fairly quiet inside the little hut, Monty and I saying nothing as I lay lost in thought. Tika talked to us briefly off and on through the evening, as the light from the fires stole into the hut, and the shadows crisscrossed over Tika's admittedly beautiful face. I was becoming a bit bewitched by her beauty as she told a story of fantastic proportions.

"The old woman knows me. She is one of the wives of the chief. She was a young girl in my tribe when she was kidnapped in a raid on my village. She became his slave." Tika's eyes seemed to close but with a half glaze that stared to past visions, and Monty cleared his throat. "She is old enough to be yer nana, or a Tipuna Wahine, as the Kiwis call'em." He said this and threw a glance at me as if making sure I understood.

Tika fell silent, then continued a bit later. "The old chief loves her. She was always his favorite she told me. He loves her still, she says, even in her old age." Tika's English became less pronounced as another dialect took over.

Tika continued sporadically in the half light, sometimes making sense, sometimes making nonsense. With a bit of interpretation from Monty because of Tika's thickening dialect, I was able to figure out that though the

Chief stole the old lady for a slave, he really does care for the "Old Bird", as Monty described her, and the chief has elevated her to his number one wife due to her wisdom. The only reason the old woman did not run off to get back to her tribe was she cares for the chief as well. Tika fell silent for an indeterminate spell, then spoke.

Her bit of news brought me to full awakeness. The Old Bird is preparing them for the feast.

I got nervous at this point. "Feast?" I looked at Monty.

"Ain't got a clue," he replied with a huff.

A bit of welcome wind suddenly blew its way through the hut. Tika whispered to no one in general "She has become the chief's number one for her wisdom. She has much knowledge."

"But she does not know you?"

"She does not believe I am still the queen of my people. She has been gone so long from her tribe that she does not believe the legends anymore."

"Well, I don't blame her. You said you knew her, you remember the raid where she was taken as a young girl. There is no way, that was years ago, before your time," I said incredulously.

"You do not know the power of the stone," was the reply I got. "And I do not need to prove myself to her. She may not believe I am her queen but that is not my problem, it is hers. She is the one that needs to prove her loyalty to me. She will when the time is right."

As the night wore on sounds of rhythmic humming human voices began, and the shining rays from the central fires grew brighter in our hut. The pounding of drums became noticeably louder, softly, then growing in intensity and madness. Voices loosed cries of passion in the night, sometimes matching the outraged cries of distant beasts in the jungle.

I began to sweat. The toil of the past several days mixed with good old common fear were taking their toll. I found myself gritting my teeth uncontrollably, and grimacing, sweat running down my forehead into my mouth. I was scared. I wanted my script telling me when this chapter of Dick Hardwing of the Jungle Patrol was going to end, and what was going to happen to me in the next chapter ten, or twelve, or whatever it was. I closed my eyes against the biting sting of the sweat from my brow, going in and out of consciousness, with visions of flames and tribal beats pounding whatever was left of any dreams I had.

The next morning I was awakened by the quiet. We were all surrounded by fierce painted warriors wearing nothing but white thongs, and tattoos of brightly colored elaborate design. Before I could react, I was bound and gagged like a calf at roping time. The others were bound the same way, though Tika's face was bright red from her outrageous struggles. We were trussed up onto spears and carried to the center of the village. Voices were being raised now, with a continual chanting and shouting, pounding fists and pounding feet, drums and voices, a constant clamor. The Old Woman was in the center of the village as well, cat calling at Tika, making grimacing faces at her, and spitting at her feet.

We were brought before a peacock of an ancient man, ornate plumes and feathers, with so much ceremonial jewelry and bone dripping from him I was surprised he could stand. The stakes we had been carried out on were uprighted and the warriors drove them into the ground, so that we were facing the heat of the fires and the chief. The chief raised his hand skyward. A throne of bamboo and many furs was brought by overly tattooed and plumed bearers. The old man smiled a toothless grin at us and placed himself on the throne.

"Monty, what the hell is going on?" I shouted.

"We are nothing but long pigs to these people," he muttered under his breath. "I recognize their behavior and the markings of their warriors. The chief will inspect us and then they will roast and eat us."

I felt sick with cold shivers as the Old Lady approached, her face dark and evil, looking very different from her earlier visits to the hut.

Tika remained silent, with a defiant look to her countenance, a bit of a sly assuredness curling her lips.

The burly dark natives began their drumming again, the throbbing lewd pulsating rhythms creating a growing crescendo, seemingly drawing the clouds against the setting sun, creating a darkness once more. Rumblings of thunder added even more tension to the hideous scene.

The Old Lady produced a rather wretched looking jagged knife. She approached Monty, ripped his shirt open, and struck a couple of wicked edges of the knife across his chest in an X shape. She then proceeded to rub oils and herbs all over him.

Monty let out a groan,"Oh, don't let this go on ya with ceremony, mate. All she is doin' is preppin' us for cooking like a bunch of ducks, slicin' each breast so's we gets tender. Lets the fat creep into the meat don'cha know. Better flavor. Once they are done with us on the stake, they stick us in the ground with some hot coals and banana leaves to cook all day, only to dig us up at night to feast and have a hell of a party. Meat falls right off the bones."

The Old Lady smiled as she approached me. Nothing but the tribal sounds of the natives' wild beats and rhythms filled my ears now, louder and louder, so loud until I couldn't bear it without yelling, just for a moment, needing release. I closed my eyes as the old Lady reached for my shirt and tore it aside to tatters. My mind screamed as the terror of this moment had enough scenes like this to remind me what I had done under the cover of a studio soundstage, but to taste, to smell, to feel the real thing right now had me terrified beyond pain, grief, and whatever else I was feeling at the moment. As the Old Lady sliced, the pain meant nothing against what my mind held. She cut me. The herbs and oils provided a slight balm to the pain of the cutting.

Moving to Tika, she ripped her blouse violently, conspicuously holding a grudge and a distaste for her victim. Tika's breasts became fully exposed to view, beautiful, taunting, even to my imprisoned state. She was truly arousing, even in the current circumstances,

As her blouse was ripped from her and her breasts were released, so was the stone I wanted, hanging around her neck and buried in her bosom by a thin line of twine. The greenstone that had been mine was now hers around her neck, and out of my reach.

She stared at me while the ceremony was going on. "Yes, I knew you had my stone. Why else would I have done what I had done? I took what is mine from you while you were passed out in the plane, you silly fool."

As Tika said this to me I noticed a slow softening of the mad sounds around me. The Old Lady suddenly dropped to her knees. As she did, her head bowed, and the guttural growls of the natives stopped.

The clouds had now grown so thick the village center was dark as night. Gurgling thunder became the main sound as I struggled against passing out from the pressure of my bonds and my anxiety.

I glanced to the natives slowly dropping to their knees, and to Tika, jaw defiant, face appearing dominant. The Old Lady regained her composure, slunk over to the aged chief, and muttered her mumbo jumbo.

The chief, never losing his composure or bowing his head, had his entourage lift his throne and bring his carriage closer to Tika, the exotic feathers covering the makeshift bamboo contraption lilting in the breeze of the surrounding heat of the camp fires. A slight mist descended.

The Old Lady babbled more to the chief. "Ok, we got us some parley," Monty exclaimed, with barely noticeable relief. "This could go either way."

"She has now realized my power, and the power of the stone," Tika said in the first strong voice I had heard her say in a while.

"She tells the chief that I am what I am. She recognizes that the true stone is on my neck. The power of the stone only shines on those who are chosen to wear it. I have been chosen for a hundred years."

Movement from the chief, the Old Lady, and the other dark tribesmen did not cause fear, only reverence. The mad sounds stilled, the people gathered closer, with a humility.

Tika began to speak in a tongue I couldn't make out. She spoke directly to the chief. "Monty, any idea of what is going on?" I asked.

"Only a bit, mate. These jungle tongues differ vastly from province to province, but some basic rules remain.

It sounds as if Tika here has been reassigned her position."

"Position?"

"Yea, they know her now, thanks to that stone on her neck. The Old Lady has recognized it as the stone of her people, from back in her childhood. Seems this tribe used to be subservient to Miss Queenie Tika's people at one time, and still hold them in reverence and the power that Tika's people have."

The chief, the Old Lady, Tika, they all talked now, Tika being very determined. The Old Lady cut Tika's bonds, and she stood full and tall, and exposed, her dark long hair flowing down her now naked back facing the chief in a defiance that made her even more exciting to me. What the hell was I thinking? I tried to focus.

The old chief stared at Tika, slowly rose, and walked over to her, looking into her eyes, her brown eyes, that reflected the fires that burned higher and higher in the center of the village. I could tell he was looking for truth in her eyes and he found it. She spoke softly to him.

"She has convinced him about who she is," Monty exclaimed with a sigh. "I ain't sayin' any of this makes sense, but it seems to be working."

More babbling, serious babbling between the chief and Tika and the Old Woman. "From what I make out, they seem to be viewing us differently as well," Monty explained.

The chief seemed to be a bit shaken after some serious exchange of dialogue. He bowed reverently towards Tika and backed away to his throne, his eyes never leaving hers. Tika directed her voice towards us, her eyes never leaving the chief's. "He knows who I am. He now believes as I have told him that I have come from the heavens to exact revenge on the kidnapping of one of my followers long ago."

"She means the kidnapping of the Old Woman when she was a little girl, eh?"

"Yes."

The native drums and chanting started up again, but with a different feeling, more benign, more celebratory.

"I have told them who you are," Tika continued. "You two are minor gods that accompany me as sex slaves, your only wish is to satisfy me of my desires. You are lesser gods, only toys that I play with on occasion."

"Thanks for the honor I think," I managed to grunt.

"At least it's keeping us alive for the moment," Monty reassured me.

The chief gave a signal with a wave of his hand, and two natives cut us loose, free to stand and breathe freely again.

Monty shook his head. "Don't get too comfortable, mate. We might have to prove ourselves yet."

The chief quickly exchanged words with the Old Woman. Tika translated as she stared at the chief and the Old Woman as they spoke.

"The Chief is worried and is asking for the Old Woman's advice. The Old Woman is now finally convinced that I am the protector of the greenstone, as she should be. She is asking for mercy, and says not to harm the Chief, because she loves him and is happy with him."

Tika exchanged a few more words with them both. "The chief is Bo the Elder. He has a son by her named Zo the Lesser. Zo is very sick with jungle fever from a wound on his leg"

More waving of hands and facial gestures ensued. Tika spoke. "They saw us come from heaven in the iron bird. They are now both asking us to take Zo up to heaven in the iron bird to be cured."

The Old Woman and the chief and all his clan were now watching and waiting for our response at this suggestion.

Monty joined right in with Aussie diplomacy. "Sure sweet, wouldn't want to be a cockie! I'll give it a burl, hope it's fare dinkum!"

Monty approached the Old Woman and the chief, Tika alongside. "Let me have a look at the boy, see what wot ails'im."

The chief clapped his hands. A moment went as bearers brought a cot with a young lad. The child was obviously hurting. "Watch me, mate," Monty said as he checked over the boy, observing a nasty gash on the boy's thigh. "Why this ain't nothing a shot of penicillin wouldn't take care of. I have the medicine among the supplies I was transporting. Tika, tell the chief I can cure the boy, and to get his cronies to bring me the crates from my plane."

Tika conveyed this information to the Old Lady, who conveyed it to the chief who let loose with another toothless grin. Shouting orders to his subjects, several natives took off at a split to the plane. Several minutes that felt like hours passed in basic silence, except for some inane mumbling amongst the villagers. When the tribesmen reappeared, they carried box after box with them and placed them at our sides. "Bloody hell, the boongers emptied the plane! Aw, well, no worries."

It seemed as if the whole village was crowding around Monty and the boy. "Gimmee some room willya?" The chief only had to raise his hand, and the villagers backed away. Monty opened a small crate and pulled out a syringe. Then he produced a small vial and began to fill the syringe with its contents. "Ooos" and Aaaaas" came from the crowd. Tika explained. "These people are snake worshippers. That needle you just filled reminds them of a snake's fang. You have impressed them favorably." Monty didn't slow down, but kept on preparing the needle. After wiping down the boy's leg with alcohol, he gently plunged the needle into the affected area. He then used the contents of the small crate to properly clean, dress, and bandage the wound. "The little sprog will be top nick in no time," he exclaimed when he was done.

We were all sent back to our hut, except for Tika, who stayed with the chief and his son. The hours went by with a tenseness that tightened our throats and leaving us unable to speak but left us watching the evening sun sink behind the trees. All time seemed lost but at some later point we were brought to the outside of Chief Bo's hut where the chief sat watching his son. The boy was lucid and moving restlessly somewhat.

The Chief Bo looked down at his son, and for the first time, had a warm look to him. After whispering gently to the child, the boy returned his father's smile and whispered back in the ear of old Bo the Elder. Bo spoke warmly to the Old Lady, and the Old Lady spoke softly to Tika. Tika turned towards us, her eyes flashing, her hair playing about her shoulders and breasts in a sudden breeze. "Bo the Elder says that this is the first time Zo the Lesser has smiled or spoken in days. You have saved yourself Monty. They say you are the God of Healing."

"Krikey, that's a new one," he mumbled. "If it keeps me breathing, I'll take it."

The old chief was standing in front of me now, babbling away with a breath coming from his mouth that I swear was going to bleach my hair white.

The Old Lady translated as Tika said something about me proving my godliness to the tribe. Damn, I was stuck for this one. All I knew was a couple of card tricks I learned from a Vegas showgirl. Well, it was worth a try. "Tell them I am the God of Magic!" I shouted, with as much bravado as I could. As Tika and the Old Lady passed on the translation, they all just stared at me. The light mist was glistening in the torchlight while murmuring thunder rolled through the air. I started to sweat. "Monty, you have any playing cards?"

"Naw, mate, and it looks like you're about to get your dunny door kicked down."

"Give me an idea, something fast. Speaking of tricks, are there any tricks in those boxes of yours?"

"Odd and ends, regular supplies to some rebels I was runnin' them to, and …wait a minute. I must have 'roos loose in me top paddock. Them there's guns and ammo in those long boxes. Take'em out. Show off a bit with it. That should shut their holes."

Slowly and very ceremoniously I opened one of the long crates, took out a rifle, loaded it with the ammo next to it, and made my pronouncement. "See what happens with my magic thunder rod! I can call birds to drop out of the air!" I turned to Tika. "Tell the chief's people to shake the limbs on the tree until birds come out."

Tika obeyed, and as she did, the natives began joyously hanging, climbing and generally swinging the branches of the trees, until quite a few birds emerged, cawing, calling, and crackling in loud tones over the village. This was going to be easier than I thought. I let off a couple of rounds, the villagers backed off, hit the dirt with a collective frightened yell. Two fat juicy birds fell in the center of the village.

The chief conferred with a couple of his warriors. After some chatting, Tika said "The chief is amazed that your thunder rod can pull birds out of the air, and that it spits fire and noise like the rain clouds above us." Some natives charged over to where the birds had fallen and began plucking and preparing them for cooking. As if in answer to the chief, the clouds erupted with a jagged bolt of lightning that shattered a tree by the village huts, and was accompanied with a thunder blast that knocked everyone to the ground.

As everyone lay flat on the ground, the old chief was the first to raise himself up. He shook a wrinkled finger at me and spoke. Tika translated. "He says you are a prankster, a demon that has impersonated the cloud gods, and the clouds are angry. The cloud gods bring water to feed plants and his people, but also bring storms that destroy the village. You have upset the cloud gods."

"Uh, Monty, help – you have anything else these savages might be interested in?"

"Nothing, except, aw, wait, mate! I must be looney. I have some neck oil in those small shaped boxes."

"Neck oil?" The natives were turning grim and slowly approaching. "Crap, you have anything besides oil?"

"Booze, you blinkin' dork! That is what I have in them other boxes! Break'em open and introduce yourself as the God of Party, or some such before they go all off on us like a frog in a sock!"

Tika started up speaking to the crowd before I could make a move. Between loud orations she spoke softly to me and told me what she was telling the them.

She told the crowd that I was a prankster, but a happy prankster, only a benign trickster, not causing mischief but laughter and good times. She told them that sometimes the Gods of the Clouds did not have a sense of humor. The people seemed to buy this explanation, jabbering amongst themselves that the Cloud Gods could indeed be without joy. The people, through the chief, asked what god is he then?

"Tell them I am the God of…God of… uh…PARTY! That is it! I am the Party God! All I need is a lampshade on my head."

"They don't have lampshades," Tika offered.

"Doesn't matter. It would help if you had a sense of humor too."

While she commanded the crowd, Monty and I quickly opened several of the remaining boxes. Sure enough, there was enough brandy, wine, and even Everclear for several village parties. "The rebels needed all this?" I enquired.

"Well, they like to call it inspiration for their cause," Monty smiled.

Needing no further explanation, I related to Tika to tell the people that as God of Party, I can turn water into happy juice.

The natives and chief were interested in this point, and many sized pots were brought in from around the village. The people of the village wasted no time in gathering the bottles, breaking them open, and upending them into jugs, each filled with varying amounts of booze mixed with water and special homemade liquids of their own. Tasting proceeded. Exclamations of approval and foolish sounding laughter began to erupt among the villagers.

The villagers seemed to like me as the God of Party as time went on, building larger fires against the stormy mists. Shouting and yelling progressed. Uncontrollable laughter began. I took a couple of slugs myself, felt brave, and stood on a great stump by one of the fires and screamed out "I am the God of Party!"

The villagers picked up on this and started to imitate me, yelling "POTTY! POTTY!" and then some jungle jibberish that sounded like "OO GOTSA POTTY!"

"Calm down a bit mate, keep yer head," Monty's wise advice came at me. I noticed the light of the fires all around were causing so many illuminations and shadows to dance in the tree tops and off of the huts as the natives' gyrations grew wilder by the moment. "These boongers are going crazy all over the place like a mad woman's shit. You don't need to be goin' troppo yerself."

I calmed for a minute, getting my bearings. It was easy to get wrapped up in this.

"Look, I'm having a look at the plane. Might not be so bad I'm hoping. Let these people see you here, helping them to have fun, whiles I sneaks over to check out the old iron bird as they say."

"Good idea."

"Good on ya as well, mate!"

Monty snuck into the shadows as the natives jostled against each other, singing and starting to shout at the tops of their lungs, all cares forgotten, just a mad tribal dance. Some fell, their cups dropped, only to be refilled at the next beat. Tika stood in the background, magnificent in her stature, the pounding beats having no effect on her stoic bearing, only becoming more beautiful as the evening progressed. She truly looked like a queen.

The party went late, the people getting wilder in their joy, men getting more brazen with each other, the women getting more seductive. The occasional fights didn't last long, most of the time the men were trying to connect punches but they usually just fell over each other from the momentum of their swings. Some of the women on the other hand moved from man to man, only because the man they were with before had passed out after a few moments. There was definitely a pattern emerging here.

Soon the chief raised his hand and made a proclamation against the continual disruptions of the crowd. Tika approached me. "They don't want you to leave. You are their main god now. They want to erect a temple to you, for you to live with them always, and supply always with happy juice. Unless you want this, you need to figure a way out and take me with you. These people are untrustworthy and could turn against me as well given time."

"OK, look. There is still enough booze to keep these people going all night, as long as they don't spill it in the mud. Some are already starting to pass out, and it can't be more than midnight at this point. I say we take turns to sneak away to the plane periodically through the night to check on Monty's progress."

"Good, we will start now."

I had to give one last glance at her naked form before she disappeared in the jungle foliage. With only torn black pants and boots covering her, she was an exquisite female, and exited from my sight too soon.

Turning to the crowd, I moved among them, refilling cups, making sure the gourds were good. As the hours crept by, the ones that were still awake weren't going to be awake for long. Soon the clouds broke, and a bright moon shone down on a village full of naked people all in a great big pile. Snores and whinnies floated through the air like the sounds of so many bullfrogs in a pond.

The unattended fire started to dim down when Tika approached me. "Where the hell have you been? I burst. "What happened to my relief?" Her eyes were daggers as she spoke, "I have been helping to make our escape. How dare you talk to me like that! I have a good mind to slap your face!"

"Sorry," was my reply, and I truly was, and luckily she sensed it. "Just overwrought and tired myself, I guess."

"Monty needs both our help to get the plane workable."

"Alright, I guess these folks are done for now."

I followed her into the bush, carrying a small torch. When we got to the plane, Monty was beaming that big smile of his. "Not much left to do now!" Following his directions, Tika and I helped get his iron bird ready. "Less stowage, so we should have a much easier take off," he said.

The morning light was starting to creep through the branches of the trees. "We might want to pick it up, those jungle folks aren't going to be feeling so great about me once they find I've gone." Sure enough, just as I said that statement there was a rumbling of voices in the distance. "Can't we move this along?" I said nervously.

"I got a few last adjustments, just a tic and we'll be off – got this last adjustment and Bob's your uncle." He gave a final grunt, slammed the undercarriage back in shape, climbed in the cockpit and fired up the engine shouting "All in!"

A load metallic thud came from the tail of the plane. Someone had thrown a spear at us. "The tribe is almost on top us! Here they come!"

We clambered up and got situated as the engine started to turn over, then quit. "Bloody hell, we ain't got Buckley's if this crate don't get moving!"

Monty continued to curse as voices now accentuated the clangs of spear and rocks against the side of the plane. "They say they are angry that their God of Party is deserting," Tika explained.

"Well, that stands out like a shag on a rock!" Monty shouted as the engine turned once more then quit amid screams and clanging from the outside.

A round of grand curses from Monty seemed to insult the engine this time, and it finally gave in and started up. Natives were on the wing next to the propellers and banging on the window when the engines started, and the props unceremoniously ripped a couple of the brown skinned savages in dismembered sections all over their fellows.

The rest of the crew on the ground gave out loud shrieks, covering their ears and falling to their knees in mercy. They showed no more advancement, instead they ran from the noise of the plane as we taxied through the open bush onto a large grassy plain.

"HA!" Monty let go a good shout this time as we gained no more resistance. "Those boongers have a larger battle than us. They have to deal with their first hangovers!" Monty let go with another loud laugh, as we all joined in. I turned back to look at what was left of the tribe in their pain, and I could see a small boy leaning on a crutch and standing among the stricken tribe, waving and smiling at us. It was Zo the Lesser, feeling much better and happy. He was the only one in his tribe that was pleased right now.

CHAPTER 27--JUNGLE STOP

As we flew by early morning light over the carpet of vine covered trees, the sun beginning to peak over the lofty ridge in front of us and a clear sky overhead, I felt hopeful, and I must say a bit happy as evidenced by my small grin as I stared out the window from the co-pilot seat.

Tika was quiet. I didn't know what to expect from her. She was the most exotic woman I had ever met. Beautiful, sultry, internal, provocative, dangerous. She lived in two worlds, primitive and civilized, and was comfortable and commanding in both. She was an enigma.

No one talked as the plane lurched and belched its way over the constant uprising of the jungle floor beneath us. Ahead of us was a mountainous range with no way around. Pulling back ever harder on the wheel of the plane as we climbed higher, Monty finally admitted "This was a damn valley we crashed in. We hit some of the tops of the trees before we crossed the ridge and descended down into the pit of it. That was in our favor, allowed us a chance to glide a bit before settling down." The place looked like an ancient overgrown dormant volcano with its high peaks all around. "Bloody hard to get in or get out. Could explain the folks there not having much contact outside of their village. This here air buggy ain't quite operating on all points, but we should make it over that rocky top ahead."

I have to say my stomach was in my throat a few times as we tried to make the lip of the ancient volcano. When we finally made it Monty and I both let out a loud sigh. We were free to fly straight and steady again. I looked back towards Tika. She sat in the passenger seat rigid as a statue, no presence of emotion.

"Our former passenger bailed out before we went over the ridge into that valley. If he survived the beating he took on the underside of the plane, he may be a bit ahead of us to the nearest refueling station."

"How does he know where the refueling station is?"

"You must have been asleep while Bruno and I talked, mate. His knowledge of this area is a bit alright. He knows where we will be making for."

A slight bug of trouble began to bite behind my brain, making me feel uncomfortable enough to shift in my seat.

A soft but strong voice came from behind me. "Take me to my village."

The voice from the back of the plane made me focus. Tika was commanding like the queen she was. Monty jumped in. "Sure enough darlin', if that is what you want. After bailing us out back there, I guess I owe ya one. I figure you have been through enough. We have to dock for petrol first. We will be close to the Burmese coast at that point. Would you know how to get back to your people from there?"

"I would know," Tika said in an assured voice.

"Are there communications of sorts at this stop?" I inquired.

"Telegraph."

I looked back at Tika. She had a slight smile on her face, as if an ending was happening. I just furrowed my brow in thought.

This had been quite an adventure. What originally took me on a mission to find a murderer had become something else. It wasn't as if the boy's killing didn't mean anything anymore, it was just that the whole damned thing seemed so hopeless at this point. I didn't feel any closer to apprehending anyone for the murder than I did back in Tijuana. Find the stone, find the murderer, I had thought. Not that easy. The stone and its copies had floated around a bit. Could Tika be a murderer? She did have a motive, but so did Bruno. I couldn't picture Tika being that evil enough to kill a young innocent boy. Bruno could have, though. He could have hired a girl from the Black Cat to do the job. These thoughts rambled and wrestled in my head as we made our way over swamps, rice paddies and fog shrouded shrines poking their way out of dense overgrowth of jungle. I took my chance while I could and dozed, the soft jostling and steady hum of the aircraft rocking me to sleep.

A good landing was made at a barely discernible airstrip in what looked like a muddy plateau with a few huts surrounding a series of converging rivers. A lurch was felt as the flap on the plane slowed our descent and speed, pulling right up in front of the main shack. Monty bailed out of the plane and met with the men that came out to greet him. Smiles were had all around. He knew these people at the airstrip well.

The place was fairly primitive. An odd juxtaposition of modern fused with tribal. The Chinese influence and support was strongly evidenced by slim but useful modern trappings, but the people were still in traditional jungle garb. Such an odd mix.

Tika and I disembarked, Tika heading for the main building, as I did. After a quick enquiry, I discovered a man in a soiled turban that ran the telegraph. I thankfully acknowledged him and gave him my message. I returned to Monty.

"Bloody hell, this ain't easy." Monty said as he spat on the ground. "My baby is a fair bit wonky. I need a couple of days to work on her. Thank the stars they have what I need to do it. Sorry for the delay though, can't be helped. Supply hut was restocked yesterday, so feel free to enjoy a bit of frothy."

I did just that.

The late afternoon progressed into evening, with native bonfires illuminating the area. The sound of a loud generator behind the refueling station rambled through the darkness. The young native boy behind the telegraph desk in the slight communications shack became excited as my message was being answered. "Bossy boss! Come quick, come quick, telly-glaph talk!"

"What does it say?" I shouted as I high stepped from the waiting room leaving my meager dinner of something fishy with noodles and made my way into the telegraph room.

"It do not say anything but crick-crick-crick!"

Frustratedly I pushed him aside. "What have you got on the paper?" What he handed me was not what I wanted.

I read it several times and I guess the frown was still on my face when Monty broke into the room. "Bloody hell, look at you – someone pee in your Wheaties mate?"

"I did a check in with my studio about the film I just completed awhile back. The film has been shelved, which means I had been shelved. No excuse, no reason. Great. I feel helpless. Here I am, the other side of the world while my star is slowly sinking into obscurity."

"Aw, sorry to hear that. Stick with me to Ceylon. I got a payoff happening there with this Lord bloke I know. He has right communication set up there, better than this pissflap of a place. In the meantime, let's have a drink. They have some Asian beer here, not much better than maiden's water, but it does have a fair lager flavor to it."

I joined him in the outer room of the communications shack. We sat at a small table and drank and watched the insects struggle in their death throes against a large strip of flypaper by the outside light. I felt a bit like they did. What the hell was happening to me? I felt lost, no purpose anymore except to get the hell back and take care of business at home.

Worriedly, I shot another telegram, this time to the Colonel in a desperate move asking for more money and what the hell is my next step. As I waited for a response, Monty let me know that it will take a couple of days to get the plane ship shape and safely make it in the air to our next stop.

"Got to get to Ceylon, don'tcha now mate? You ain't the only one that gets telegraphs," Monty said through his glass as he slurped his beer. "I got to meet with the man what hired me," Monty said through a resounding belch that hurt my ears. "Lord Thickwilly is the bugger's name. I mentioned him before, but what I didn't tell you is that he owns interests all over creation. Got a nice plot of land and a good home. He is as round as he is tall and pompous but no matter, he pays me well."

Tika entered, clean, shiny and bright like a new penny. This woman absolutely glowed with her beauty. "I will be leaving in the morning."

"Are you sure it is safe? How will you protect yourself?

She stared at me. "I have already talked to some young strong men in the village that will help me." Was that jealousy I just felt on my part? Monty broke in. "Well, luv, seems you do alright for yourself. Whatever I can do."

Not much was said by me as everyone wandered off to get some rest. I sat in the chair most of the evening looking at the stars peeking in through the tattered screen of the wooden door.

The beer and the occasional buzz of an insect lulled me in to a land of dancing bottles on a bubbling sea of booze. As I floated on this liquor lake, I noticed each bottle had a picture of one of my female trysts on the label. The bottles clinked and paraded by me, each picture smiling at me, only to be twisted and turned by the pungent sea and drift away lazily. One bottle, larger than the others, pushed its way through, clanging so as to almost break the others in its wake. As it turned to face me and reveal its label, I saw what looked like Tika staring at me. No matter which way the bottle turned in the liquid, Tika's eyes remained on mine. A vicious scream shattered the bottles and I started to drown. The scream came again, followed by gunshots.

I fell out of my dream and out of my chair and on to the floor. I burst out the screen door, almost taking it off of its hinges and made for a small building to the side of the station that was the dormitory where Tika had been resting.

Monty and a couple of the men from the nearby village were already there. It was a sight that terrified me at first. By torchlight I could see two bodies in the doorway. The bodies were those of a couple of native guards that had been planted there by Tika and were the two that were supposed to accompany her through the jungle. They seemed bruised, but unhurt. Running through the open door to the dormitory, I could see by candlelight the body of Tika. She was moaning slightly, bloodied, but still alive. I instantly took her in my arms. Big mistake.

With a cry of pain coupled with rage, she attacked me, was instantly on top of me, legs straddling, squeezing the air out of me, and lashing at my face with her hands and nails. A few seconds later her attacks stopped as she composed herself and became rigid, still on top of me, but slumping over unconscious, with blood streaming down her neck on to my face and torn chest. We were both breathing hard on the floor of the cabin as more torchlights appeared in the doorway.

"I have been assaulted," She said softly, as she became aware for a few seconds. "He took the stone from me. I am now in danger." A cry of pain overtook her face as she rolled over from me. Being no longer pinned to the floor by her, I gave a quick glance at the surrounding conditions.

One native approached me. "I looky doctor help."

A gentle looking man, as if he had seen enough things that could not faze him at this point, emerged from the gathering crowd. He wandered over, carefully, bent down and started to examine Tika.

"Hurt. Belly bad. Cut at thloat," he said calmly. He looked the part of a family doctor, as if he would know best in his family, with his older, wise face, and gentle smile. "She has cut at thloat," he repeated. "Several stab wound. Foot clushed."

What I could get from him was that it would take several days before she could walk. Nothing for me to do at this point but to go back to the main cabin's waiting room. I felt so singular in my emotions, so wanting her to get well. I felt like a fly caught in her promiscuous web. This is not going to work.

Monty left the crowd and joined me at the table in the waiting room after grabbing us a couple of beers from a cooler. "I need another day to fix my buggy. Then we can take little queenie to Ceylon. She will get better care there."

"You know who did this."

"Sure enough, mate. Our German friend. Looks like he made it here, alright"

"She said her people will track her down and kill her if she doesn't return the stone."

Monty grabbed my wrist in a friendly squeeze and gave me a reassuring smile. "All the more reason to get her out of here. I will do me best to get going, bugger all."

The next day passed with me drinking more beer while attending to Tika along with the village doctor. The local kids gathered around Monty, while he, working on the plane, regaled them with random curses, but in a smiling way, so they kept coming back. Not sure who understood what, but there was a definite rapport there. Taking a break late in the day to come back to the shack, just as I had paid my most recent visit to Tika, Monty, fairly coated with grease and sweat, sat down with me at the table ready to have another beer.

"Damn sprogs, love'em though. Just to let ya know, mate, I am movin' as quick as I can. Almost done. Should be ready to move by sunrise, if those sticky beak little ankle biters don't get in my way." I smiled as we clinked bottles on that one.

"You've been quiet. What's on yer mind?" Monty asked after a few moments.

I sat and gave a small smile and continued to stare at the table top at my imaginary pool of blood forming there. I said nothing. He was popular here, the native kids all knew him, and he had friends in the village next to the station.

But all I felt was alone, except for taking care of Tika. "Just collecting my thoughts."

"Aw, that can be dangerous. You've only got control of the future, not the past. Wot's done is done, no going back."

"Yea," was all I could muster. After a few more moments I spoke. "It is just so odd that I should even be here. My son was murdered by someone supposedly in Tika's cult. I went searching, following a trail, supplied by the boy's guardian. And what do I get? Beat up, cut up, torn down, almost killed several times, and I am no closer than I was the first day I started out."

"Sounds like you've been all over the place like a mad woman's shit alright."

"Then there is Tika."

"Yea," was all the reaction I got out of him as he swigged and turned his head. "Yea. I see her in your eyes."

"That obvious, huh."

He just nodded his head and belched, "Obvious as a pair of dog's balls." We both sat there wordless. At some point we went to find our respective cots behind the communications shack.

The next morning between the bugs biting my arms, the damned birds making a racket, the boiling gurgles of my stomach from the almost food I had been eating, and the two little imaginary demons pounding my head like an anvil, I finally woke up.

"Bossy bossy! You awake?"

The keeper of the telegraph came rushing in with the latest.

"OK, OK, be right there."

The screen door slammed behind him like a thunderclap, then proceeded to bounce back and forth ringing out like the damned liberty bell.

I had to grab my pants and the door at the same time, take a breath, blow out slowly, then slipping into shoddy sandals, I stepped out into the evil glare of the full sun. I was halfway to the communications shack when some young girls started laughing at me, covering their eyes. That was when I realized I hadn't put my pants on yet. Stumbling, maneuvering my legs and busting my ass twice in the process, I got them halfway on and entered the shack.

"Tellyglaph papa san"

The boy handed me the script. It was from the Colonel. He told me nothing new about my next move. Go to Ceylon, meet a certain Lord Thickwilly, a friend of his. Money and instructions will be waiting. Worth my while in a great way. Everything at home OK. Studio OK.

While I wasn't sure about the last bit, I supposed I had no other choice than to do what seemed everyone said to do. Go to Ceylon.

CHAPTER 28—THICKWILLY

It wasn't much of a coincidental voyage across the Indian Ocean, and it seemed to pass quickly enough, considering. Tika and I both slept. She slept mainly though. I kept checking her condition constantly. I was by her side when she was carried from the hut where the attack had occurred. The two natives that had been rendered incapacitated outside her door were able enough to help her on a cot and place her in the plane. Seems they had been taken under her spell as well considering the look on their faces as we prepared to leave.

Monty had been berating the plane most of that morning. His rantings kept me informed of his progress.

"Bloody hell starter!"

"Goddamned oil!"

"Cunt damned tires!"

Monty's flying over the Indian Ocean from Burmese country to the island of Ceylon proceeded the same with him running a continual soliloquy as to our progress and the state of the engine and of our certain rewards once we got there.

"Bloody bastard Thickwilly owes me for this!"

"C'mob, baby, Daddy loves ya!"

"Sweet chariot to heaven I luv's ya."

"Bleedin' Christ on a crutch get it together ya bastard."

"Jumping Jesus in a side car ya damn prop job."

At one point he banged on the instrument panel. "God's dick, quit stickin' will ya?"

The entire time I attended to Tika. She had been seriously hurt and I kept a constant vigil. Every time our eyes met she seemed a bit closer to me. I certainly was feeling closer to her. Eye contact was made each time I attended to her. She had been loaded aboard with plastic bags attached to her arms that pumped fluids in and out. I had been given instructions by the jungle doctor on what to do to keep her calm. For a jungle doc he was OK and well supplied. He was the only man in untold miles with any supplies and knowledge and he seemed capable. His pharmacy was the jungle and he gave me several muddled herbs and potions to speed Tika's healing.

She would glance at me with a disdain on her face that seemed to lighten over time or maybe that was my imagination. At any rate she seemed to grow sweeter and a bit easier in her state.

The weather was warm and calm as we made our way towards the airstrip at our destination. Monty landed the plane deftly and his curses subsided. We were met with several Brits of the RAF and greetings and smiles were passed all around.

Monty led us to the inside of the air shack while a couple of members of the ground crew loaded the sedated Tika to a small couch. I saw that they couldn't take their eyes off of her. Great, I am getting jealous again.

Looking out of the front entrance window of the air shack, I noticed a large touring car just outside of the front of the building. A swarthy man with a tightly wrapped turban leapt out and offered his services in a demanding way.

Monty just smiled at the man. "Envelope, please."

The envelope was handed over to Monty as a large smile emanated from his face. Tika and I were instructed to make our way to the touring car. The two members of the ground crew happily continued to carry Tika out and place her gingerly in the back seat of the car.

"Inside, most kind sir." Turban man nodded his head and waved his hands towards me.

"No worries, mate, The Colonel will take care of ya."

I got in the back seat with Tika, closed the door, and that was the last I saw of Monty. I was led away in the car through the darkening stormy skies and sweltering damp of the air towards the grand estate of someone I didn't know.

"Where are we going?" I inquired.

"Just outside of Negombo, to Lord Thickwilly's tea plantation, sir."

After traveling through some of the greenest lush countryside I have ever seen, we reached the gates of the plantation. It was a large affair, and the fields were covered neatly with tea plants, and plenty of natives picking the leaves. Young topless women did the picking, placing their gatherings in large woven baskets while the men supervised. That's a nice set up. We pulled up in front of a sprawling split level house that seemed to eat up the small hill it sat on. White stucco, with a red tiled roof, ornate carvings framing the windows typical of the area, almost mosque like, but with a large black and white tiled veranda with rattan furniture scattered about, adorning the front porch of the house. A rather rotund man as wide as he was tall, stood waiting on the steps of the veranda, drink in hand. His face was puffy and large like his belly. His face had the complexion and color of a baboon's ass, pink with mottled blue markings. Dressed in white from his shoes to his wide brim hat, there was no doubt he was in charge. For a moment he reminded me of the Colonel as the car pulled closer and he stepped down to greet us.

Stepping out into the bright afternoon sun, he greeted us with a "Huk, huk, huk," sort of a laugh emanating from his mouth. "Jolly good. Welcome to my estate. Please accommodate yourself. My boys will unpack your goods."

And indeed they did in quick time, jostling and jabbering softly, taking our baggage, what little there was of it, only to whisk away silently to the inside of the house.

I must have looked lost, as the Lord blurted out, "Not to worry, sir. I have been informed about you, not only from my pilot, but from your benefactor the Colonel back in the colonies" Getting a good look at Lord Thickwilly, he appeared congenial enough. A large white moustache drooped over his mouth, looking like it contained uncertain quantities of liquid, food, and tobacco. The tobacco emanated from his large overstuffed bent bulldog of a pipe, glowing red and blasting ember and smoke like a volcano. His belly overflowed from the front of his pants like a mountain of granite. He was big, but solid.

His Punjabi servants moved quickly as the head posh boss in a bright red fez barked some sort of lingo at them. Tika was still passed out in the back seat of the car thank goodness, as the servants transported her to the inside the house and disappeared within.

"Please to come and sit on my porch." I did as I was told, marching up the three steps to the porch. I was greeted with the sight of a round table with a round woman on the opposite side. She was dressed splendidly in all white, including what looked like a large cotton ball in her lap. I noticed an occasional pink tongue jutting out from the ball and wiggling. A lazily turning overhead fan was doing its best in keeping the flies away.

I automatically bowed before this spacious woman. "Ma'am."

Thickwilly stood beside me. "I would like you meet Lady Plushbottom. She is residing as my permanent guest. One might say we are an item, if one were to say such a thing." He gave her a knowing wink.

"Oh my gracious," she blushed, holding the cotton wad tighter. "Dear Thickwilly!"

"However, it must be noted that she abhors anything relating to adventuresome violence and ribald revelry. Fainthearted, don'tcha know. Don't quite know how she stands it here, with the heat and the darkies roaming about loose."

"Oh dearie me," was the soft clipped voice that came from the Lady.

"Not to mention the ones we occasionally lose to a pesky tiger or snake in the jungle."

"Oooooooo……..,"her head swooned to one side , as the cottonball leapt on top of her ample breasts and began licking her face. One of the servants ran over to fan her and offer a drink of water. She continued to moan as Thickwilly and I watched.

"I suppose she cares for me after a fashion, wouldn't stand it otherwise." He snapped his fingers and pointed inside the house, as two more of the darkies appeared as if from air, the tassels from their fez swinging in the breeze from the overhead fan. The servants hustled her gently inside, the cottonball, now on the floor, was weaving its way in and out of their legs.

Thickwilly offered me a mamasan chair at the table, as he took the overtly large papasan. I sat, as he coughed phlegm and spittle into a handkerchief. "I assume you want a drink. Two rum and sodas, and see that the lady inside is taken care of." A small brown boy in white tightly wrapped sheets skittered away

"Thank you sir, this is all rather sudden."

"Not to worry," he interrupted. "All is taken care of."

A dark burly servant came over and nodded a voice in his ear. "Of course," Thickwilly said. "Dinner in half a tick. I have been expecting you for quite a while."

"Really?"

"Monty explained your situation, as did the Colonel. Between the two of them, I am up to date on your journey."

The drinks were brought around and were quite refreshing in the damp heat that seemed to seep up from the ground. We toasted, as I told him "I must say you have me at a bit of a disadvantage."

He turned to a servant standing in the corner. "Let Lady Plushbottom know her dinner will be served in her room per the usual instructions. My guest and I shall have our repast in the library" A silent nod from the dark servant caused him to disappear, tray in hand. "I must warn you that Lady Plushbottom tends to become a bit cow-tongued after her afternoon brandy." To this I raised an eyebrow.

"Oh quite," he exclaimed. "If she were here with us this evening, all she would contribute would be exclamations of 'Oh My' and 'Dear Heavens' all throughout dinner. Dear heart that she is, she can be quite trying at times. After all, she is a woman. And that dog of hers, if you want to call it that without insulting other dogs, is nothing but a ball of belligerence that defecates and yaps at breezes. Evil little bastard."

His gaze turned into a stare at me.

"One of my servants will guide you to your room so you may freshen up before dinner." My quick look of concern caused him to admit that "Tika is veddy well taken care of. She is resting with all possible care and consideration"

After realizing I was not to be worried about who was in control here, I wandered off to my bath. My mind stayed on Tika primarily, as the connection between the Colonel and Thickwilly played second in the back of my mind. I relaxed, showered and shaved in my room, which was adequately furnished in white opulence. A reasonably sized window let the setting sun shine through to wander its slowly disappearing light on the bed and floor. I could only wonder what room Tika was in.

After refreshing myself, and feeling pretty good, I sauntered back to the library. Sure enough, Thickwilly was there, standing, and looking overbearing in his demeanor. "Huff huff, cheers" was his response as he handed a large snifter of brandy over to me.

The library was a bit dark, with rich leather smells, even the images in the room had flavor for the eyes as the light of the burning wood danced around the room. Books, seemingly unlimited shelves, and a large, much handled globe was prominent by the side of an enormous and almost glossy mahogany desk. Piled with care on top of the desk were different shades and sizes of papers topped with intricately carved ivory curios. One rather impressive ivory carved pipe holder was on display on the corner of the desk, its shell brown from years of wandering tobacco smoke infusing its sides.

In front of this impressive desk were two over stuffed pompous leather couches, much like Thickwilly and his woman. They were as long as they were round, and facing each other. A long high coffee table displaced the space between the two couches. Upon it were two rather shiny serving trays with silver coverings spewing flavorful steam through tiny openings in the top of the metal lids. Delicate white plates with full serving utensils and cloth napkins were laid to the side of the trays. A large goblet filled with a musky smelling deep red wine was placed where I was obviously supposed to sit. I did, on one couch. Thickwilly continued to stand, just off of one side of his desk.

"With what I have heard," said Thickwilly,"you have had quite an adventure so far."

I squirmed in my seat a bit. He was very overpowering, like the Colonel. I almost felt as if I had been doing something naughty. I looked at him, then returned my gaze to my empty dish and fiddled with my fork and knife.

"Smells delicious," I said, hoping to incite a response.

"Of course it should," was the only response I got. Some Punjab appeared as if out of nowhere and uncovered the silver settings and proceeded to serve us on the gleaming plates. "I didn't see your manservant by the bookshelf. They seem to just come out of the ether."

"Huff, huff, they do blend in well with the woodwork here. Almost invisible don'cha know." Thickwilly approached and sat opposite me at the table. Grabbing his fork and knife he began to devour his meal with audible relish, various popping sounds emanating from different parts of his form.

I had to admit with the first taste of the meal that this was exquisite. "The flavor of this is outstanding, if a bit strong. What is it called?" I asked as I slugged back a large gulp of the potent wine.

"Quite. As naturally as it should," he mumbled through mouthfuls. "Behja Frey is a standard dish here."

"Well it is damn good. What is it?"

"Brains with spices," was his response.

Don't ask too many questions, that is what I need to learn. After slowing down on my intake of the main course and just relying on the rice, chutney, and vegetables, I attempted to get down to business.

"Sir, this all very impressive, but I must ask…"

"You must ask why I am taking such an interest in you." He stuffed his mouth and garbled his way through his next statement. "You are indeed a courier for the Colonel, are you not?"

"Well, I hadn't thought of it that way, but I suppose if…"

"Of course you are," he interrupted," I know all about you because I know about the Colonel. Don't mistake that he and I are friends," he warned with a smile, juice running down the side of his chin. "We are not friends, but we are acquaintances with similar concerns. Right now, our main concern is you and what you plan to do about retrieving a certain valuable stone."

I took this in with some confusion, as if I wasn't already confused.

"I know you were originally on the trail to find out the murderer of the son of the Colonel."

I winced a bit on that one.

"Your journey has changed, hasn't it?" He stared at me between bites.

I had to admit he was right. What had started as a somber but necessary duty had become an unexpected journey that put my life and career in jeopardy. Jeopardy, hell, try the dumper with the handle down, and the water swirling round. I have been constantly sore, my back has become such a steady source of pain I don't even notice it anymore, and that is the most positive thing I can say about all of this.

With a wave of his hand, the dining plates and silverware were whisked away by barely perceptible servants.

Thickwilly stood up and approached me, paper in his hand. His demeanor was not so inviting now.

"I received a forwarded telegram from your studio, perhaps you would like to read it." His expression turned suddenly sour.

He stood before me as he tossed me the telegram. As I read it, the room was not inviting anymore. The leather trappings turned in to a fence, holding me, waiting for a response before the oppressive leather would give quarter. The more I read of the telegram the more the mounted bison and antelope in the study seemed to leer at me, almost mocking, laughing at me with their disembodied heads. The rhino sneered as the gazelle smirked. I had just about enough of this.

"From what I have been given from this telegram, this is no longer about a boy's death but a stone," I stared back at Thickwilly.

"Not just any stone. A stone beyond value." He said this, and standing, leaned over to me, his cigar laced breath covering my face.

"The boy and his death mean nothing to the Colonel now?" I forced the question.

"The boy's death was a means of locating the stone."

"You are a cold bastard you are." Both our eyebrows furrowed in anger.

"Not any colder than you, my son. You have been chasing the almighty dollar since you were born. Taking film offers when you knew there was no prestige or honor, just so you would at least get paid. You are no more of a bastard than I am." He paused, then said "Shall I read the message to make it clearer?"

From what he read, he might as well have hit me with a rock.

I looked at the telegram. It was from the Colonel advising me that he had received a hurried communication from my studio. I was out. The picture had not only been shelved because of my unavailability, but I was also being sued for breach of contract. I was hereby barred from the studio with the caveat "You will never work for this or any other studio again." I juggled the telegram between my fingers while staring into nothing in the distance.

Lord Thickwilly delivered the next stab wound. "Another wire for you relayed via the Colonel. It concerns your belongings in the States."

I read this with much defeat. Damn. My housekeeper quit for non-payment, the bank is foreclosing on my home for non-payment. Ha-Nee was supposed to take care of that, dammit! She obviously has walked out. With her gone, the bills have piled up with no one to pay, so everything is shut down and locked up. Great, I have nowhere to go. Bills collectors looking for me at this point. I am pushed into a corner. What can I do except say OK to whomever hands me money. God knows I need it now.

My appetite disappeared as quickly as my thirst grew.

"I'd like a little more of that brandy please," I managed to whisper out.

"I have much better than that. 112 year old Scotch will provide a better salve, my boy."

I held out my glass rather lazily and a bit unfocussed as he poured the ancient hooch over fresh rocks provided by his ready tongs and waiting ice bucket. The booze ran down my throat like sweet balm. My appetite for solid food was long gone.

He just stared at me as I guzzled the waiting drink, constantly refilling itself with the help of Thickwilly's hands. I couldn't help but smile as the flickering of the flames from the fire danced against the sides of his head like devil horns. I even began to see other shadows move in time with the flames, some from outside accenting the lone window on the far right of the study. Something that looked like shadows illuminated, not by the fire, but by the blazing full moon outside. Shadows furtively moving as wrinkles in the wind.

"OK, you and the Colonel win. I might as well pursue the stone. Everything else is lost to me, so nothing matters."

"Fine, my boy, just fine. You shall see yourself well rewarded. Whatever the Colonel offers you for the collection of that stone, I shall offer larger. Of course, your job shall be easier once the woman leads you to it. You shall need to tame her, so to speak. Lead her around to your way of thinking. Entice her. Offer her love, women like that, doncha'know."

Tika had slipped my mind until now. With my fifth glass filled with scotch, I sloshed my head in Thickwilly's direction. "Sho where is she?"

"Where?"

"Yea, where? I mean right now," I slobbered some spittle down my lip as I crossed my eyebrows in sudden concern.

"My somewhat sloshed friend, She is resting in a room upstairs under much care." He turned away, clasping his hands behind his back, seemingly overly concerned with certain titles on his bookshelf, and the puffing of his cigar. He turned suddenly to me. "I mean what I say in that I will pay over what the Colonel pays you for the return of the original stone. This woman Tika is very important. She has a mental connection, an almost spiritual, psychic connection with this stone. With her, you should be able to track the item down with efficiency."

So I was to use her to find the stone of her people and collect. I was supposed to betray her trust. I am a hell of a nice guy. "I need to check on her."

"She is in the same hallway as your room, she has been sedated and is most probably sleeping. I have had her dinner sent up to her."

I half rose, half stumbled from my chair with the glare of the fire towards the closed door of the den illuminating my way. "I shall return."

"Of course you shall," said Thickwilly with a wink.

Navigating the stairs rather preciously – why have they gotten wider and steeper? – I emerged on the hallway towards my room. A sudden shrieking and banging hit my ears as I made my way to some poor Punjab servant with egg on his face. Real egg. Over easy.

He was standing in front of a door at the far end of the hall, where the loud shrieks were coming from. The door was closed and had only a small window about eye level with the rim of it covered in slop. I approached the dark servant, who was obviously in a state of distress.

"What goes?"

"Most honorable sir, I am to be giving her dinner, but she is giving it back to me in a rather undignified manner. In American, she is food fighting at me."

"Well why should she do a thing like that?" I said as I approached the chaos.

"She says she cannot get out and wants to leave. Most kind sir, may I leave?"

"Yea, sure, I'll take over."

The towel headed darkie bounced away down the hall.

"Tika? Talk to me. Whasha matter." I guess the scotch was really kicking in.

A loud screech of frustration was what I heard. "Do you think I like this?" was her reply through the closed door. I took a somewhat hazy look through the small window in the door. What I saw was one angry queen bee. "Now lishen babe, I am here, everything is OK."

She yelled so loud I almost fell over from the vocal assault.

"The hell it is! I have been seduced by drugs and locked up a prisoner!"

"You are no prisoner," I started to try to explain, not having any real answer.

"Then why am I not permitted to leave my room?"

"I will talk to Lord Thickwilly about this. You have had a hard deal, you need rest. What happened when you were brought in?"

"I have been furtively stabbed with needles since I arrived. " Her eyes looked dark and beautiful through the small window of her door. "They have injected me, abused me by their hornet stings, but I am stronger than they. I may have been unconscious for a while, but not as long as they desired. You see, I am already powerful once more."

No doubt about that. I did notice that she quieted down as she stared at me. In an instant we felt compassion for each other. Then as quickly as it had appeared, the feeling vanished. "Why do you have this done to me?" Her temper flared as she seemed to glow hotter than she already was.

"I am here to help you recover the stone of your peoples," I somewhat stumbled out. "No fooling," I burped.

"You are an idiot infused with liquor. I am not impressed. I have a good mind to slap your face! Let me out now. I won't stand for this indignity!"

I stood and stared and got mad. This woman had me in her spell. "You will not be held here long. But I need to help you help us both. Together we will find the stone. I have discovered some connections that you don't have."

"I also have connections. They track my every move. It doesn't take them long to find me. Remember, I am the one that must retrieve the stone myself, elsewise, after a number of my moontimes I become weaker, others may slay me and grab the power of the stone for themselves, becoming queen."

"What I have is not what you have, but I do have the means to track the one that has the stone. We will find the stone. You may have it back, and I may have the money I need to go back home. Look, this is not about me anymore. I am pretty much wrecked. I want to help you." I couldn't help but cut a resounding muffled bit of gas loose.

"You are detestable," but her heart wasn't in it. It was just an instinct, a reflex.

"Lishen, I am going down right now, to demand you are shet free!" I threw my fist up in the air for some reason. She stared at me. God, she was beautiful.

"I am going right now! This is unreashonable!"

I took off at a leap until one foot went in front of the other and I found myself banging my head against the wall of the stairwell and continuing unfortunately down the stairwell at a quick rate headfirst all the way to the ground floor only to end up in a heap staring at the ceiling. Blackness washed over me.

As I came to, I was aware of animal heads staring at me and cherry wood tobacco invading my nostrils. I gave a good snort. The heads were stuffed and so was mine. I realized I was back in the study in a plush leather chair while an overly ripe elderly woman peered over me only to say ""O my!" and "Deary me!" Her sincere concern was squashed by the order of Lord Thickwilly's command.

"Please escort Lady Plushbottom to her room. This is more stress that she can handle." A quick shuffling of sandals and a turning of my head brought Thickwilly into view.

"Sir, you will be glad to know that I have received a bit of news via a cablegram newspaper from Tripoli. My cablegram service is complete and provides pictures as well as print, just as a normal newspaper you would buy on a common street corner."

"I am sure it does, but why should that interest me?" Two little demons were pounding my temples with jackhammers.

"This concerns you deeply. It concerns your new mission."

"And that is…"

A big harrumph as he adjusted his overstuffed behind in an overstuffed leather chair, hiking up his pants and straightening his seams as he did so.

"As I said, it may interest you."

He began to read from the paper in his hand.

"As reported by the Tripoli news affiliates, an unknown German soldier, Nazi, if you will, Nazi officer has been murdered in Tripoli – jaw and face mutilated with uniform shredded to the point that identification is impossible. Only enough information is that it was a German uniform"

"Some idiot goosestepper gets shredded, so what."

"You may read the rest. I am not accustomed to telling bedtime stories."

I read what Thickwilly handed me. The article was about newly appointed SS Nazi officers attending a big diplomatic shindig on a German cruise line in the Mediterranean. A candid picture was in the paper. One of the officers had his face turned away and was missing a finger. I started, remembered I had been passed out for a bit, and sat up with a jolt.

"Why is Tika locked up?" I yelled at Thickwilly.

He chuckled. "She is not locked up as you say. You over exaggerate the situation. I am keeping her under observation. I know her sole mission is to recover the stone at all costs, including her life."

"How do you know?"

"I am well aware of her cult and its sacred objects, including the mysteries behind those objects. She is being held for her own good, the same as a doctor would hold a patient for quiet observation."

A shriek rang from the stairwell. Indian babbling rang throughout the house. A fast shuffling of feet and sounds distracted Thickwilly to the point where he started for the closed door of the library, but before he could reach it, it burst open, with several Punjabi types, headwrappings loose and draping to tawny shoulders covered in cat like scratchings crying "She is gone!"

The next few moments were rapid in Thickwilley's orders. I tried to follow, but my head was still having a rough tumble over my thoughts as the liquor was fighting with my clarity. I managed to tremble upright, and turned towards the double doors that provided entrance to the study.

I saw natives running back and forth, some bowing with the occasional groveling gestures, then Lady Plushbottom entered the room. The jabbering of the servants, directed by the firm directives of Thickwilly in a guttural tone gave order to the initial chaos, which quit with a resounding slam of the double doors as the servants left.

It was just Thickwilly, Plushbottom and me in the room at this point, and it didn't look pretty.

"Bloody hell, woman, what gives?"

"I was trying to be kind," she bubbled forth, collapsing in the nearest chair, her head down, slowly sobbing. "I felt pity for the poor barbarian trollop and decided to visit her with pleasantness and the morning news service. She seemed very interested in one of the articles about Tripoli. Or some such horrid place. As I left to go down the hall back here, there was this sudden commotion and screaming and I must have fainted from the heat and excitement. I really don't recall what transpired. I only showed her the daily to soothe the poor thing, visit with her a bit don'cha know. Try to educate her to more social standards, you know. That is, of course, the burden of the upper classes, is it not? To elevate the lower classes to understand how things are supposed to be?"

"That does not explain how she is gone."

Plushbottom squirmed, and she obviously had a lot to squirm with. The tears started. Why is it, when women are confronted with accusations, the tears start to fall? Guys can't do that, no sympathy there. Women do it, and everyone is on their side. Even cops.

"The poor dear seemed so thankful. The servant woman that accompanied me was very sweet as well, and stayed with your Tika after I left, I suppose to sympathize with her, Oh, I don't know, I just don't know," she shook as she cried in to her handkerchief. Thickwilly seemed genuinely concerned and kneeled to put his arm around her. I guess the old fart really loved the innocent blathering woman. "My dear, we shall weather on," he said as he patted her shoulder lovingly.

"So, she is gone." He stood up and directed a severe stare at me. "How she could have escaped is secondary to the fact that she must be followed. And followed to her final destination, which is to find the stone."

I was already able to figure out how she might have escaped. "How well do you know the background of your servants?"

"I rely on none but the best of my long term advisors. I shall relinquish no efforts to find out what any might know." His concern was less than gratifying. Lady Plushbottom rose and began to lean into him, to weep into his large countenance as they both stood together.

A rapping on the door brought a quick retort of "Come" from Thickwilly. A large impressive rather tall muscular Punjab entered and bowed, then straightened. "I have questioned the rest of the servants," he grumbled in a low tone, his eyes a fiery brown, and his goatee pointed like a dagger. "My assistants will ring the truth out as to why the priestess escaped."

"Thank you, Vishanti, I trust you to succeed."

A large pop in the fireplace sprang everyone in to action. Howling and yelling in the adjoining back quarters shook us all. "I say, what is the meaning of this outburst?" Thickwilly shouted as he dropped the arms of his lady and started into the side room where a slobbering woman was prostrate on the floor, with two darkies standing over her, her arms grappled and bound, while her captors smiled and dragged her forcibly across the floor. Other servants wielding small cracking whips circled her, containing her in their self-made ring of captivity.

"Who is this woman?" spat Thickwilly, lurching forward into the adjoining room.

Vishanti smiled a smile of recognition. "Her name is Velveeta. She was a servant assigned to the womanly needs of our guest."

Velveeta raised her head just long enough to spit syllabic fire at us all. Lady Plushbottom descended into the nearest couch, thankfully passed out again. Just as well.

As the beautiful young servant woman was held to the floor by her handlers, her garments were coming loose by the grappling of her arms from her captors. Her long black hair soaked in sweat and tears, her arms were continuously twisted behind her back, causing severe pain, and making her cry out curses. Slowly, she began to calm and struggled to her knees, still bound, but began to explain in her native tongue, messages that only Vishanti understood, but translated for us.

"She knows who our guest was," Vishanti said. "She knew that a great reward would await her if she helped Queen Tika on her journey, for she is of the same hidden cult that calls Tika queen. She acted as a loyal servant."

Velveeta stood up now, immersed in tears and anger, but no longer defiant. One breast had come loose and was exposed, quivering as she trembled. I couldn't help be feel a bit sorry for her, but I also couldn't help staring at her tit. Boy I'm a hell of a nice guy.

"Take her away and deal with her, getting what information you can, however you can, and by any means you can."

Vishanti's eyes narrowed, his goatee twisted with his smile in anticipation of what he was going to do. "It shall be done, most excellent Sahib." He turned and exited the room, leaving me, Thickwilly, and the unconscious form of Plushbottom alone in the study. A quick hand movement, and servants closed the doors to the study, and left us standing and staring at each other.

Thickwilly cleared his throat. "Sir, I must persuade you to see my way." And he did.

He talked. I reflected. The stone caused the death of my son. A son by a woman a half a world away that I had thought was mine, even while dismissing her as a lost cause while I pursued my film career, no, wait, that isn't right. I never dismissed Marian. I had only put her aside for the moment. She would never be tossed from my life like an old dishrag. She would always be a clean bedspread, candlelight, good red wine, shimmering shadows. She hurt me. She left me, I will never forgive her for that. Maybe she left me, but I guess I really never left her. I felt weakened and sat down.

"...that stone...," was what I heard next, that damn stone. When I find it, I will crush it. I will render it to sand and spread it in the farthest depths of the ocean. My career is crap, my home life, what there was of it with Ha-Nee, is gone. My career is shot. I have nowhere to go.

As much as I hated this fat blob standing in front of me, as much as I was confused at this point, he made me listen.

"Stand with me, son." He started to babble as I continued to sit on the couch and rub my sore temples.

He told me what I needed to do next, and as I continued to massage my aching head, my pain left, only to be replaced with his instructions. I kept thinking and repeating what he told me as he breathed smoke and brandy in my face. Yea, go to Triploli. That damned renegade Nazi is impersonating someone else and he has the stone. That means Tika will be there as well, looking for her opportunity to strike. That also means I need to be there to retrieve the stone before she does so I can get paid the rest of my stipend from Thickwilly. The rest? What rest? My headache began to clear quickly as he mentioned money up front.

"...and this is just the first part," he continued. "There will be far more for you. All you have to do is get the stone and return it to me. The only way that will happen, and this is the easy part, my boy, is to follow the girl. Vishanti's exploration of Velveeta's induced confessions prove this point. Tika will lead you to what we both want. When you succeed the rest of the five million United States currency will be relinquished into a Swiss bank account to you with my pleasure. Any funds you need for present will be given to you happily. All you need do is send a wire requesting such." His lower neck chins bobbed over each other as he chuckled with excitement.

"I am certain that this Bruno that you speak of in your drunken ramblings is the person in the photo. The details of the mutilated officer would give no evidence, eh? Once the officer was killed, this Bruno character could assume the dead officer's identity easily enough, with Tripoli's black market identity counterfeiters. This man comes from an important German industrialist family, and connections and favors are not a problem for him. Remember, all they found of this dead mutilated Nazi was his naked body, except for German issue socks and underwear. All identity labeling had been removed and the skin was peeled from his face like a banana. His lower jaw was hacked off, the tips of his fingers neatly sliced. Identification became impossible at that point. The dead officer in question was supposedly a new recruit from a far province, rather nondescript, and not well known."

Ok, what the hell, my scruples aren't worth crap. I have to finish this. I have nothing else left. "When do I leave," I said, defeatedly.

"Fine my boy! First thing in the morning. I shall have you at the Grand Hotel in Tripoli in a quick time! Toast, to a successful mission!" He raised his omnipresent glass of hootch, while gurgling the bottle to finish filling a large glass he presented before me. I shakily lifted and drained my glass in his general direction, then sought the solace of the pillow on the couch I was on.

CHAPTER 29--AKBAR FATUI

I arrived in Tripoli not the same way I had arrived in Ceylon. Thickwilly had provided me first class accommodations, even a willing stewardess to ease my pain between layovers. I had a new suit, tailor made. In fact, I had all new shirts and an extra pair of trousers snug in my suitcase, thanks to Thickwilly. I was wearing my new suit, tasty but casual, and I even had a new wallet with appropriate currency and plenty of it. He was nice enough to place my "lucky charm," the white knight, in a special compartment in it. A letter of guarantee and credit sped up the process. I was supposed to meet a close connection of Thickwilly's at the Hotel Tripoli. This connection had been gathering information for me and would relate what he knew when I checked in.

I felt more than chipper than I had in a while when I stepped off the plane on to the tarmac. I imagined myself like Caesar, landing at Alexandria only to view Pompey's head in a barrel like a cranium pickle.

Expected to be overwhelmed by history and culture, I was overwhelmed by chaos.

Making my way off the plane and out of the airport, I was immediately aware of the high rising needles of the mosques, the insect like loud babbling of the locals swarming me outside the airport like angry bees, and of ancient air and dust and sand. The noise of camels belching, farting, the vendors shouting, and I must say, the godawful stench of sweat and dung immediately erased any glamorous intrigue of where I was.

These people, dressed in ornate rags, sauntered about with their never ending chatter and never ending cigarettes, constantly vying for my attention for some rug or trinket that would insure great reward.

What the hell did these people do for tobacco until Columbus?

Grabbing my valise tightly, for that was all I had or needed at this point, I headed for the Hotel Tripoli. An occasional hand slap and tug against my case caused me to hold my grip even more. If I had been casual in my belongings, my suitcase would have been gone for sure.

The market place in front of the airport was in full swing, with snake handlers, cheap statues, priceless amulets of glass, and swarthy bearded natives in white robes galore. I managed to grab a cab out of this chaos and surprisingly enough, the nimble driver managed to avoid the loose pedestrians and animals clogging the streets.

Dumping me out with barely recognizable English across the street from the front of my hotel, I grabbed my valise and went the one block toward the front doors. I tried to argue the cabbie why he could not have gotten me closer, but all he jabbered was there was too much human and camel interference. I got out, checked in, had my bag delivered to my room. I sat and rested for a moment, regaining my strength. I had a small carafe of bourbon delivered to my room for a price. I guess I fell asleep for a while, but when I woke up, the sun was still blazing like it had when I arrived, no change obvious. Does the damned sun never set in this land? The clock continues to tick, but the sun never moves.

I sat up, cleaned up, got dressed and went down to the street to get acquainted with my surroundings, try to meet my contact and figure my next move.

Exactly one half block from the hotel, a street performer was on a small public platform giving a grand performance attempting miracles of magic, or so his placard said. There was a small crowd and from what I could perceive of the jeering and catcalls, the fellow was doing a serous nosedive. His continual failure however kept the crowd involved if only to see what he would screw up next. I actually found myself laughing for the first time in weeks. The more the crowd laughed, the more the guy messed up his act. As I stood in the back, I was struck. I couldn't take my eyes off of his lousy act which was so bad it was good. The rest of the crowd couldn't either. Each goofy trick drew me closer to the front where I found myself actually having a good time at the poor fellow's expense.

The fellow was not the best looking guy on Earth, with his half unwound turban, ragged robes, scroungy black beard surrounding his yellow teeth that seemed permanently fixed in a broad smile. His body never stopped moving from the stage to the crowd and back to the stage.

Roars of gaiety and laughter rang as rabbits never appeared in his hat. His next trick involved two pigeons, only to have them fly away as soon as he introduced them. He then stumbled into the crowd to ask them to offer gifts to Allah for the successful return of the two pigeons back to his cage. His assistant, some sort of midget, dressed in a pale pink turban that ran from her head to her toe, just smiled and beat a green tambourine.

He soon returned to his little makeshift stage to do card tricks. His first trick worked in a clumsy fashion, but his next trick involved some fancy shuffling. He almost made it, his voice stuttering foolishly in some sort of Arabic-English-German hybrid crossover. All of a sudden, in the midst of his telling some horrible joke, his playing cards flew all over the crowd. He immediately started bowing, exclaiming "Most apologies" over and over, and then moved once more among the crowd, retrieving his mischievous cards.

The sun was finally starting to set at this point. The performer was making his way to me, gathering his cards, as the crowd, quieting their boos and laughter became as bored as the sun and began moving away to the shadows. He looked at me and smiled as he bumped into me and reached for a card on the ground. Getting up, he lowered his head, said "So sorry kind sir," and quickly left. I gave one last slight smile and turned to wander down the avenue to admire some of the other vendors' wares. I reflected and thought on the white knight. I don't know why I held on to it so. Souvenir of another time I guess. I reached in my pocket to place my hand on my wallet where the knight was. The wallet along with the knight were gone!

With a determined anger I turned and made my way back to the place where the street performer had been, only to catch his midget assistant turning a far corner. I caught up quickly with her and punted her in an alley corner. "Where is he?" She jabbered as if she didn't know. I started bouncing her like a damned little pink clothed basketball. One final punt into a large wide mouthed urn of rainwater opened her up.

"Most kind sir, Akbar has retired to the Casbah Boyer. Now you leave, yes?"

"Yea, but for one thing. Where is this Casbah Boyer?"

She told me and I moved fast, leaving the little human onion bobbing in the jar.

A couple of quick turns, a few slips in camel dung and I was there, bursting in the swinging doors. This Akbar fellow was easy to spot. He was the one that saw me and started for the back door. I managed to follow and grab him in the alley, inadvertently knocking over a few wooden crates of trash. I was on him with him on the ground and my hand on his throat, my knee to his groin, my other hand a fist raised to give him a solid knock on the forehead. He waved his arms in protest.

"No no no!"

"Where is it you crummy thief? Where is my wallet? Give it to me NOW!"

His frightened eyes stared at mine and for a second there was no resistance from him, only a smile. It was a smile of recognition. "You, sir! You are he!"

"Yea, I am he…him...he…me…or he." I still held my fist raised against his prone figure, ready to belt his temple in.

He waved his hands in surrender. "Do not to be bashing my delicate head, sir. I give what I take. I am most embarrassed. If I had knew who you are, I would not have done what I done did." I eased off on my grip, letting him sit up a bit.

"You jungle man!" Akbar excitedly shouted, gathering his feet beneath him, wanting to stand. His jovial smile made me relax my grip. I let him up.

"Sir, I watch all your movies, you hero to me! You are Dick Hardwing of Jungle Patrol! You best there is! Here, take back all I take!" He handed me back my wallet, contents intact.

"Here, take this, and this, and this." He handed not only my stuff back, but other trinkets and cash he had wrested from the onlookers to his performance. For a crappy magician, he was a hell of a pickpocket.

"OK, enough is enough," I told him, as he calmed down a bit.

"Please to be allowing me to introduce myself. I am Akbar Fatui, master of illusion, controller of dreams, regulator of cosmic forces, conductor of ethereal presences…" I cut him off.

"Quit the crap. You are lucky I don't bash your head."

"Yes, I am most blessed to be assaulted by your most formidable presence. May a thousand beetles infest my grandmother's paisley shawl at disturbing you on your latest adventure, that of which I look forward to seeing at my local theater next week!"

We both stood up and dusted ourselves off. "Look, I am not filming an adventure here. I am looking to find two people."

"They must be the ones that have the lost diamond of Ashir!"

"No, that was last year – I mean that was a couple of serials ago. Look, listen up, will ya?" Akbar shook his head like an overexcited Labrador waiting for a treat. "This is for real, not a made up Hollywood story."

Akbar broke up into uncontrollable laughter. "Made up? Hahahahaha! Is all real! You can't tell me your movies made up. I see with my eyes wide open what happen. You play Akbar for fool. No matter, Akbar love you anyway! You my hero! You come with me to the Casbah. We smoke and talk."

Oh great. Just what I need, another nutty fan at a time like this. "Yea, sure, thanks." Anything to shut him up. The sun was finally tiring of itself and doing a slow nod to the west. Akbar and I entered a dimly lit doorway and I was immediately hit with the stench of amazingly strong tobacco and what I suspected was hashish. Hookahs were surrounded by grizzled men smoking and jabbering on pillows of various colors that contrasted their drab robes. Candles offset the darkness of the interior. Not a woman was in sight in this camel scented men's club.

We squatted ourselves in a corner and Akbar ordered from a man with a face like a rotted turnip root. They smiled and jabbered noises at each other. The server left with his tray. "What poison did you order?"

"Ha! You are my new friend, always to make the jokes with Western tongue that dances in heaven with the humorous ghosts of the Nephilim."

"Yea…sure."

Turnip Head brought our order. Akbar tossed some coins on Turnip's tray and he left. "This is a most wondrous tea, sir,"

We toasted each other with our cups and took sips. The tea was astonishingly powerful, but really good. "What is this?"

"Iron Maiden tea from the Orient. My favorite. Be careful, it is very strong. I drank too much the other night, and I wanted to bang my head to the ground while listening to musicians."

"Well, thanks. You seem to know people around here. If you like sneaking in their pockets, how do you keep from being arrested, or worse?"

"Oh my goodness, I only steal from travelers, hoping my magic will last as long as it takes for them to leave the city. I would never steal from people that live here. As the teachings of Allah tell us, 'Do Not Shit in Thine Own Backyard. Ye Might Step in it and Bring it Back into Thine Own Dwelling.'"

This was certainly wise logic I could not argue with. I was feeling that this fellow was sincere in his ovations. "Listen, pal."

No sooner had I said this than he leaned in my face, breathing whatever digestive juices were lingering in his mouth. "Since you seem to know a lot of people," I continued.

"They are not people, they are family! We protect each other!" He got a little over excited at that statement, but that was alright, that was what I needed.

"How would you like to be in my next picture?"

"Oh, sir, I would befriend my mother in law's best goat for the chance!"

"I am looking for certain people here in the city. I have to find them, otherwise the Evil Planktons from Neptune will surely steal The Lost Ancient Secrets of Ur."

"Oh my, a new adventure for you." He said, laughing at my sarcasm.

"And a new adventure for you, if you have the connections," I reassured him.

"I place my presence as a doormat to your expectations."

Just as he said that, the door burst open with the intimidating glare of the setting sun illuminating the figures of two uniformed Nazi soldiers and an Italian sergeant.

"What are those jaspers here for? The conflict exists in Europe, not here."

"Here is next. They are just pushing their presence, so we are used to it later." Akbar suddenly got serious on me.

A moment of silence ensued, as the entire place, once a squabbling babble of old men grew suddenly surly. Sudden violence floated in the air among the smoke that blew from the hookahs. The place became as silent as a library. Somehow, some way, I wanted to knock those rats to the ground. I don't know how the Muslim types do it with no booze. Maybe that is why most of them are so all fired mean all the time. I wished I had some joy juice right now to ease my tensions against starting a scene. I stared and grimaced, never leaving my gaze from the creeps. They walked silently over and took up residence at a table near the rear. Soon the café returned to its former noisy and smoky normalcy.

I returned the conversation to Akbar. "Seen a lot of these characters lately?"

"They are more and more and everywhere. They make us used to them, so we don't mind later when they are in charge."

I shook my head and asked Akbar about the people I was looking for. I told him about Bruno, what descriptions I had from the last time I saw him. I told him about the connection I was supposed to meet at the hotel, and I overindulged a bit when describing Tika.

"I do not know about the German, I don't know about this Tika or her cult, but I do know who would, if it is possible to know such things. I have many people, many family that work here in hotels, including Hotel Tripoli. I have large family."

A quick conversation revealed he did indeed have family all over Tripoli, working in servant positions in all the major hotels, working as housekeeping, bartenders, bell hops, clerks, and servers in the cafes. All of them working as those subservient menial types that drift in and out of top secret board meetings, or back room crime boss scenarios where everyone needs plenty of ice and booze, where diplomatic hush hush deals happen in closed off penthouse apartments. Maybe with him wanting to follow me around like a lost hound I could get a better break. I could use a good hound to sniff for me right now.

Everywhere someone might talk it seemed he had a relative that was nearby. Again, I described Bruno as much as I could, even to the missing finger, and let him know Bruno might be impersonating a German officer with ease, since Bruno had been one for years. Tika, I could only describe again, to my surprise, with a somewhat glowing bit of desire, to my own red faced embarrassment. "I shall watch, with most anticipation of strange woman with no escort with her," Akbar offered.

I then realized that one of the soldiers kept glancing my way. I smiled and looked back, offering a toast of my tea. All I got in response was a half-smile. He then turned back to his friends

"Watch! I shall show you how I get information so easily from infidel outsiders. But before I do anything you ask, you must promise me."

"Promise what?"

"You take me to America."

"Yea, sure thing." Whatever to get this ordeal over with I thought to myself.

He beamed like the man in the Muslim moon.

I watched as he got up and wormed his way to the men sitting in the back. He was all stooping and bowing, seemingly very subservient and joyful at their presence. They were bothered and bottled up at first, then lightened up at his gesticulations. Two of them even smiled and spoke to him, hopefully offering information. Within less than two minutes, well, maybe more, considering the bowing and exclamations of kindness involving most likely goats, camels, grandmothers, or young girls or boys, he returned to me.

"They ask questions about you at first before they give me information. They wonder what you are. I say you are American archeologist studying great conquerors, and that you admire what they do in their own country. They liked that."

"They would."

"I also ask why they bestow their most wondrous presence in our unacceptable town. They mention a gathering of sorts. That is all they would say."

"Good job! With your connections, we should easily figure out what that gathering may be."

We both smiled, while he told me a stale joke. He directed me to my hotel, although I didn't need him. Turns out I did need him however.

I checked in at the hotel, and thanked Akbar. I asked him where he stayed. He gave me no address to find him. He knew where I was. I laughed at another stale joke of his and said goodnight. Before heading to the lounge, I wired the Colonel where I was, and also wired Thickwilly that I had made it to the hotel with no worries. Sitting in the bar sipping a Manhattan, I figured I might be able play my two benefactors against each other, and come out with a fatter wallet than when I went in to this adventure. A couple more Manhattans, and I grew much more confident. I could feel myself getting smarter as the juice kicked in. I remembered Akbar's stale joke, and couldn't stop laughing. Feeling people staring at me, wondering who this jocular lunatic was, I got up off my stool and stumbled to my room. Still absorbed in laughter, I took off a shoe, undid my trousers, and fell backwards on the bed with a silly grin on my face. And there I stayed for the next couple of hours. Eventually I got up, guzzled a glass of water, and got under the covers, the overhead fan singing me to sleep. I dozed back off thinking about Tika, dreamed about Tika, and woke up thinking about Tika.

The morning sun shattered my fantasies. I lay on the bed staring at nothing and thinking about everything.

A meek but serious "Housekeeping" sounded through my door. I glanced at the clock. Six AM? Mighty early for housekeeping. I grumbled "be right there," that came out "shnark bull vud." I got out of bed, stumbled over a shoe that I swear had moved to the attack position from the night before, did a quick loop de loop backwards dance across the room, only to finish my early morning exercise routine by banging my head against the hotel door. Holding on to the latch on the door, I managed to twist enough from a sitting position to open the door.

A dark skinned skinny maid made a quick entrance, singing a song. Great. Audition time. Once I could focus my eyes and ears, I realized she was giving me information.

"No connection, connection gone, our love connection has died, we will never be the same again, all possible information is lost, lost in our death of love, a spring, once held in our hand, has become a winter out of our grasp" she sang in one of those Count Basie style arrangements Billy Holiday would sing at Birdland. "Akbar." She said as she stared solid at me when saying that last word. I was very awake, but moving upwards and stumbling towards the refreshed towels in the bathroom.

She left the room singing "After You're Gone."

I could only take this as what it was. Akbar proved right. He really did know what he said. His family was really everywhere. And the result of our first meeting? My Thickwilly connection was definitely dead and gone.

After flopping back down on the newly made bed for another hour, I was disturbed enough to go ahead and get cleaned up and go down to the lobby. A couple of nods and glances from the hotel crew as I went outside to a small café stand across from the hotel somehow caused a miraculous appearance from Akbar to appear on the empty stool next to me.

The café stand was one of those stall affairs, easily moved from location to location depending on business. The grilling of onions sucked me in, as customers gabbled their orders and cooks cussed and fussed the food out into eager hands. Akbar smiled and stared at me as I tried to wolf down something with eggs and goat wrapped in a pleasant garlic smelling bread. My somewhat aching head, fresh from its battle with last night's cocktails called a truce with my stomach on this one.

"My partner!" Akbar beamed tobacco stained teeth at me like headlights on a cross country truck driving through heavy bug infested back roads. I had to look away so I could keep eating. "Yea," was my response.

"I have many reports to be telling you," he insisted. "My family loves me and can't wait for me to be big star in Hollywood!"

"Great."

"More soldiers moving around Tripoli. There is to be a large gathering on a ship bound for Italy." Akbar handed me a paper that had a bunch of gibberish chicken scratches but did have a picture of an Italian military officer with a German Officer, shaking hands and smiling for the camera.

He had my attention. "What is this all about?"

"There is to be a big military costume ball tomorrow night on board an Italian liner."

"What the hell is that all about?"

"It says party cruise will show celebration and solidarity in forming an axis against common enemies. It mentions large gathering of Nazi and Italian officials."

"Good information." I thought quickly, though it hurt a bit. Bruno would be impersonating a German officer most likely. He obviously would not want to remain in Tripoli, and would be looking for an quick easy way back to Europe. This party cruise could be his chance. "Will everyone be in costume at this ball?"

Akbar furrowed his ample brows and studied the paper. "No. Only the women accompanying the officers. The officers are to be in full uniform, though they will be allowed to wear masks."

"Any word on finding Tika?"

"Only that a migrant worker was discovered by my great uncle's cousin at another hotel that knew anything about Tika and her cult. They slightly talked, and then the migrant worker got much excited and left."

"Any info on where Tika was or where she went to?"

"My contact did not know. She only leave to not come back."

Was this Tika? Or was it one of her cohorts waiting for the chance to become queen of the cult? I ordered some wine and espresso to think this out. The balance of caffeine and the soft alcohol lift of wine would help balance my judgement. It did.

Tika was tracking Bruno. Bruno was impersonating a dead German officer, there was nothing else that made sense at that point. His missing finger was testament to that. Bruno made that slip when a random photo was made showing a group of Nazi officers. He will surely be wearing gloves next time, and he will surely be wearing gloves at this ball. This ball is his free ride back to the continent under an assumed identity.

Tika is near him. So is her possible associate, though Tika may not know.

"Akbar, any way you can get me onboard that ship tomorrow?"

A big open mouthed laugh ensued from Akbar. "I know you better than I know you."

He gave me a sly wink and nod as he palmed me some papers. "I think way ahead of your head."

I looked at what he had handed me so secretively. It was an official looking work permit translated in three languages, allowing me entrance on board the cruiser tomorrow night as a cabin room attendant, and for that work permit to expire upon conclusion of that cruise.

"Tonight, you check out of hotel, so it looks like you are left. Instead you to be joining me and my families at my home. Big feast for few, but unknown to many, for you to have welcome meal at my small dwelling, with much food and a girl to relieve tension."

"Hey, thanks, but the girl, that is an unknown quantity, and I was never fond of blind dates, and…"

"OH! You prefer young boy?

"No, no, you don't understand."

"Is goat you want? Most happy goats that love men I have plenty of. Sometime goat look better and is preferred over our women after a while."

"I will take my chances with the girl."

The guy beamed so wide, I had to beam with him.

I ended up with my suitcase over at Akbar's that night. I gained some information while the celebration went on, thanks to Akbar's connections. The Nazis were looking for Bruno, while trying to find out who the murdered German was. The body had been so mutilated, the entire jaw and skull under the nose had been removed, so no dental records could be had, and the entire corpse was also unidentifiable from being washed with lime and acid. Bruno could assume an identity like this easily if he had the resources. Where were the resources coming from?

In the meantime, the hookahs were blowing, the wonderful food was flowing, the fifteen people or so were swelling to a much larger crowd, the banging of tambourines with the music was getting louder, the veiled girl that Akbar had for me was glowing. The crickets and crowd noise rose as the strong smoke and gentle laughter of the amazing girl in front of me elevated me to a private nirvana. Later, when things had calmed down, and the party started to wane, the people seemed to disappear in the dark, and my sweet private girl led me to a quiet room where a moon smiled through a window, and she let her veil slip until dawn.

CHAPTER 30--TROUBLE AT SEA

I woke up with the sun, naked as a radish, and was served a fragrant tea by my night's escort, whose face was as glowing as the sun itself. The place we were in was quiet of human voices, only the birds held conversation. We both pleased each other with our wordless smiles.

In quick time I gathered my belongings, gave the girl a tender kiss, dressed and headed back towards the Hotel Tripoli. Of course Akbar appeared out of thin air dressed in glaring white robes and turban, and nipping at my heels.

"Ah, most glorious Dick Hardwing of Jungle Patrol, off on another adventure!"

"Yea, and it's called breakfast. Look, you have been a pretty good guy, and I sure can't complain about last night. Let me buy you a bite to eat."

"Most kind!"

We both trotted quickly, being quite hungry, and stepped in to the lobby of the hotel. I checked in at the desk and they handed me the English version of the morning paper, along with a couple of messages from the wire service.

One was from the Colonel, the other was from Thickwilly. The newspaper headline grabbed my attention first. A quick glance at it and then I led Akbar to the breakfast room. After being seated the waitress took our order. Akbar ordered dates, cheese, honey and bread with Arabic tea. Me, I had hash browns with egg over easy. I was pretty sure that bacon was not kosher around here.

"I have a most amusing and impressionable joke for you effendi!"

"Hmph," I mumbled through my coffee.

"Why did the chicken cross the road?" he snorted bits of fig through his nose as he spoke, barely containing his laughter.

"OK, give."

"To hold his pants up!" He damn near fell out of his chair at this proclamation of high humor. I barely cracked a smile at his absurdity. I did my best to ignore him. I had too much on my mind.

Akbar then babbled something about his prowess with the ladies, and how in the kingdom of Iraq, he was known as the Bagdad Daddy, but I was transfixed at the newspaper.

"Gala Costumed New Year's Eve Celebration of Unity between Germany and Italy" the headlines proclaimed. I glanced at a few of the lines below while Akbar babbled. There was to be a party on board an Italian cruise liner tonight. A New Year's costume ball to celebrate unity. Germany was happy about its invasion of Poland and was wooing Italy into further involvement with something called the Axis, and this party was seen as a way to cement relations with the Italian regime even further. The liner was supposed to leave Tripoli New Year's Eve and make its way to Rome across the spacious night skies of the Mediterranean by New Year's Day.

 Our server brought the food. "Thanks," I said. Akbar babbled again with much fluttering of the fingers, so much so, I half expected an ace of spades or a rabbit to pop out of his hands.

 Akbar continued to flap his lips and dribble food, more of it landing from his fork back onto his plate than made it into his mouth. At the rate that was going, he could eat in perpetuity. I was perplexed. I knew something was up with this oceanic party.

 I looked at the messages. Both had the same information. Both mentioned the picture of the Nazi with a missing single digit. The goal I was to retrieve was on that liner. There was no way to view the face in the picture that I had seen, but there was the best reason to suppose that Bruno had the stone and would be on the voyage, in disguise, this being the perfect opportunity of concealment for him to escape right under the Nazi's noses and that was what both messages reasoned. If Bruno was there then Tika would be there, was what I reasoned. I would be there alright, and this slovenly friend of mine, wearing more of his breakfast on his tunic than what was his what was in his stomach, would be my guide to invading this party heading from Tripoli towards Rome.

 Both messages involved money. The Colonel had wired more money into the Swiss bank account he had set up for me long ago, with proper instructions for whatever bank I needed to draw it from, and Thickwilly had the convenience to wire quite a bit of change directly to my hotel. At this rate, I was feeling a bit flush.

I explained the situation with my directive to Akbar, and he immediately conjured up what I hoped was not a fumbled solution. "I get you where you need to be. I get you onboard. You will be deaf dumb mute. Is best for you. Can you do that?"

"Yea, I can be plenty dumb."

He explained his plan. With his connections, he obviously had relatives that would be serving the party that night, and I was to be in the thick of it.

We left the hotel diner, parted ways knowing where we were going to encounter each other later. I stopped off at the bar on the way out of the hotel and had a stiff bourbon drink straight up, no chaser, bracing myself for the evening.

I wandered down to the docks early in the afternoon to see what was going to hopefully be my showdown.

The ship was an Italian luxury liner I recognized. Italia Flotte Riunite, a beautiful luxurious single stack affair, the smaller of the Neptunia Class. I had often fantasized on boarding this style of ship, though not in the manner as a spy steward.

Late afternoon came, and I found myself swaddled in shipboard servant clothing, a little dark grease slathered over my face and body so I could pass as a native. Akbar joined me onboard as well, as he was in charge of helping to coordinate the work force and division of duties. He went about his work in an orderly fashion among the small throng of us servers and attendants, assigning people in certain capacities. He personally attended to each of our uniforms, adjusting a collar here, straightening a trouser leg there. Each of us had unique uniforms to configure with our specific duties. I was a cabin boy, amusing as that was, garbed in an impeccable white suit with no insignia, straight up collar with two top buttons and just enough room in my neck to feel slightly strangled. Gold styled buttons running down the front of my pure white jacket, covering the top of my equally shining white pants and solid polished black shoes which were way too tight. A tightly woven turban covered my head. When he assigned the maintenance of cabins with housekeeping, he gave only a moment's glance at me with a quick smile and assigned me with the team to take care of the officer's staterooms.

We had discussed earlier what I was supposed to do. Now that I was in, it was up to me to follow through, though I wasn't quite sure what I was going to do.

As the evening drew closer, I was given a set of keys to the state rooms and went about my ordered business, doing housekeeping, getting ice for the Jerry bastards, and following their basic guttural orders, those that I could understand from their hand signals. Those I couldn't, just shouted louder and pantomimed for me, all the while getting a good laugh out of my supposed handicap.

I was also informed from one of the other servants that I was assigned a small locker onboard. I tracked it down below decks. There was little baggage left to my name, which by that time was some shaving gear, a toothbrush and an extra change of clothes that I had carried in a bundle with me from Tripoli. My other belongings I had left onshore in a locker at the Hotel Tripoli. Onboard this ship, I was a new man, a new personality. I don't know when or if I would ever be back, so I suppose my other belongings in the hotel locker will be left alongside the other treasures of antiquity in the region.

Once onboard I was unable to see much of the illuminati boarding the ship, though they made quite a bit of noise. I placed myself near the onboarding section as the guests made their way up the gangplank but was quickly diverted by my coworkers to direct ourselves below decks in order to serve the passengers.

With much hot swing music playing away by a band called Rusty Staples und die Paper Klips, the ship set sail, and my time was spent waiting below decks refusing to communicate to any of the other help. They became insulted and tossed comments my way and then turned away from me altogether. Didn't matter, I couldn't understand their nasty tongue anyway. I couldn't get my mind off of the fact that Tika might be here. I knew she probably was. The German we both wanted was here as well.

The ship let go of the pier and steamed away with a few well-wishers waving handkerchiefs at our departure. The sun was dipping and looking as if it were cooling itself in the clear waters, and the night was already late, with stars twinkling from the calm darkness. Out of the servants' quarters I stepped onto the deck. The air caught me quickly and gave me strength. I had to clear my thoughts and plan. Here I am, my two adversaries are here, I have two financiers depending on me and paying me, my career is in the dumper, OK, that last bit can be resolved by what I do next as well. A deep breath, a look at the universe of stars above my head, and I knew what to do. I have to get to Tika. I know she is here somewhere, and with her I can get that damned stone from Bruno. I have to get in that party room as a guest and I can only do that in disguise. The costume ball was a brilliant cover.

In the steward room I quickly met with Akbar after he instructed the other servants on their duties. While they busied themselves about, he personally instructed me in a quiet manner. I was to be a mute and display a card to those who spoke to me. I looked at the card. It was written in German. Akbar explained that it said "I am unable to speak. Please indicate what you need. Heil Hitler" I was to present this card to the occupants of the German officer's staterooms and to provide towels. There I would hopefully find what I needed to find, for Bruno had to be there. He was obviously impersonating the unidentified dead Nazi the news had reported earlier.

I wheeled my cart of linens and made my way from stateroom to stateroom, quickly surveying those rooms I was allowed in, going about my business as housekeeping, always mumbling, being insulted and joked with, some Jerries just kidding, some were downright mean to where I wanted to punch them. I kept surprisingly calm, focused on what I was searching for. I kept my reserve by staying contained in my thoughts and purpose.

So, I find Bruno's cabin. Then what? He won't recognize me with this dark smudged make up and diaper on my head. At least I hope he won't. If he does somehow, I have to be ready and I have to find the stone in his belongings. He is not exactly going to leave it on the coffee table. This is what occupied my mind as I went about my mundane and somewhat insulting duties.

As I began to end my rounds with no luck, I was getting agitated. Some of the rooms were empty with nothing I could find as to give clues to who occupied them. I was starting to guess that Bruno was already at the party or on his way. I also came to the conclusion that Bruno would have the greenstone on him at all times. To hell with this, I have to get in that party and I need a disguise. I banged on the next door. I heard a loud voice shout "Eintreten! " Guess that was my cue.

Upon entering, I noticed the bathroom door open with steam billowing out. A jelly donut of a fat kraut came out with a towel wrapped around his bulbous torso, big smile on his sloppy face and helped himself to more towels from my cart while giving me a quick pat on the head like I was a crazy little monkey performing tricks for his enjoyment. He poured himself a large glass of Riesling from a pair of open bottles on the dresser and went back in the shower bellowing some aria from a Germanic sounding opera. I started to leave when I noticed his costume on the bed. It was a cheap full white body costume of some sort with a swastika on the front. Lovely. I had to have the cruddy baggy outfit. I could swipe it but then the kraut would easily know who took it and spot me wearing it. I knew what I had to do.

I took the bottle of Reisling and approached the bathroom. The kraut had his back to me and was still bellowing away, rattling the glass stall of the shower, drink in hand while he was soaping up his expansive behind. I raised the bottle trying to strike a quick and easy blow before he could turn around. I should have guessed this approach wouldn't work.

As I began to stealthily put out my hand to open the stall door, he turned to face me directly just as I began to open it and raise the bottle to strike. I thought it was all over for me but he exclaimed as he stumbled forward „Vos is los? Seife in meinen augen!" I saw his eyes were packed with soap suds and were closed as he went to push for the door that I had already opened, he tripped over a dirty towel on the wet floor and fell flat on gut, his face bouncing against the floor a half second later. Groaning, he started to get up and out of pure fear I let him have it across the back of his fat riddled neck, breaking the bottle. He stammered and spat, wavering as he struggled to get back up, giving me time to place my foot against the dome of his bent head and giving him a firm shove towards the glass stall ass first. A loud crash of glass, a major slap of flabby flesh against tile as his feet went up in the air, landing on his back, his skull cracking the tile in the wall of the stall, and with one last sigh it was the end for the clammy kraut. He lay there in the stall, water still streaming hot steam down on his fat piggish form, his whole body quivering as water mixed with blood around him, jagged glass puncturing his face and giving him the image of a pink thorny cactus with eyes or what was left of them. Two large pieces of glassware emerged from the socket of each eye. Blood was running down his face to mingle in rivulets streaming over his large gut like tributaries coming down a mountainside seeking the delta of his crotch.

    This was a bit more than I had meant to do. I hadn't meant to kill him but I had, and now another problem was on my hands. Quickly draining the bottle of Riesling in convulsive gulps I knew my next step. I grabbed a laundry hamper and tried to fit his rather impressive figure in the sack. I got a fair amount in, but not good enough.

    I spied his Nazi uniform hanging neatly over the end of a chair by the door. I got the fat bastard dressed as best I could. I had trouble getting his pants on, as he had obviously been sucking in his gut for years. I pushed down heavily on his belly, trying to squeeze him in his uniform with his body expelling gas and liquid as I did so. Wonderful.

When I finally had him somewhat in shape, I heaved him up and braced him against me, opened the hatch of the stateroom and walked out on to the deck. No one was around so I began to heft my quarry over to the rail.

Just as I leaned him over slightly I heard a voice behind me.

I turned to face a rather intimidating Nazi in a rather relaxed uniform which also reflected his own state. I smiled as I held the fat dying German on the rail, still spasmodically twitching, and indicated a guzzling pantomime with hand and mouth and sound to great laughter from the observing Nazi.

"HAHAHAHA – BLURP!" He then wavered, threw out an arm in a mock Nazi salute, mumbled what sounded like "Heil Edelweiss!"

He walked away, tripped over a deck chair and turned into another hatch on the deck. I took my chance. Over the side with my fat pal with a heave of my boot. I waited for the sound of the splash, waited for any sounds of alarm of which none sounded, then went back to the cabin. It was there I finished more of the wine from the second bottle, gaining fortitude as I looked at the costume. A label on it said "Pierrot" along with a picture of what it was supposed to look like. Not sure what that was I donned the costume anyway, though what would have been skin tight on him was rather loose on me. I took a look in the mirror. God, I looked silly. I looked like some sort stupid albino clown. Damned cheap ass Nazi and his damned cheap ass costume. I lit a quick cigarette from the Nazi's pack on the dresser, cursed the nasty fumes from it, and wished for another shot of booze.

I went through my clothes, knowing I was going to have to toss them overboard as well. Glad I checked, because besides some cash, there was my knight. The damn thing has been a lucky charm for me so far, and so it shall continue. I took the belt from my former housekeeping uniform and looped it around my waist, fashioning a handkerchief from the Nazi's dresser to make a knot and hold the contents hold it intact.

The damned costume looked like I was wearing a short nightshirt over pajama pants, and it was all white. I had big balls of fuzz that looked like they wanted to be buttons, hanging in formation down the front of my shirt. As I stood in front of the bathroom mirror fairly disgusted with myself, I noticed there was a small round tub of white make up, a whiteface style that matched the silly picture that accompanied the costume. Great, I had to wear this on my face as well. Not too bad really, I would remain in disguise with this on, so that is OK. I still felt goofy.

I wiped the goo all over my face and was a bit disgusted as I did. However as seconds went by, I began to actually enjoy the process, remembering my acting skills, being given five minutes before I had to hit the set fully done up with powder and heavy highlighting. Those makeup girls were great, sweet little bouncy boobies that would hover over me, distracting me as they did their magic. They could make anyone look and feel years younger.

I used to love when they would hover over my eyebrows, dangling their little tangerine titties two inches from my nose. I smiled regretfully as they weren't there to help me right now to help make me look ready for this next big role.

When I felt I was finished I stood before the mirror. What a ghostly image I was. Hopefully this would get me by to what I was hunting tonight. One last swig to kill the bottle, a firm belch, my nostril hairs burning from the backwash of fumes from the sweet German wine, and I headed for the door. I figured I could leave my former clothes thrown in the corner since no one else would be using this stateroom anymore besides me.

Stepping out into the cold frisky gusts of sea breeze air again I headed towards the sounds of the festivities. Hot jazz with an oompah beat was bouncing down the deck and ricocheting out to sea, the occasional gusts of wind throwing the sound back, giving a strange echoing effect to the surreal proceedings.

I was hoping to get to Bruno before Tika. I knew she had to be onboard and waiting to pounce at some point. With her underground connections she could even be among Akbar's crew without anyone realizing what was going on.

Making my way to the ballroom, people laughed and greeted me in Italian and German while I just smiled, shrugged and nodded in the affirmative at all who spoke.

I managed to shiver my way from the starboard side of the deck and up the stair ladder to the main ballroom located forward on the uppermost deck. By the lights glimmering through the windows coupled with the lush music of the live band filtering its sound out of the two pure white doors, I knew I was in the right place. Loud laughter and gaiety greeted me as I made my way in. I must say this was quite a lavish magnificent affair to be sure.

The room was very large and very high, with hanging lights and bulbs of various colors bathing the room in shades and shadows, but still maintaining a fairly bright incandescent glow to the action.

And what action there was. Elaborate and fairly skimpy attire on the women, while the men's costumes seemed to emulate various Roman gods and Italian classic figures along with Germanic mythical heroes. The fat ladies all wore metal brassieres with horned helmets and shrieked with high pitched laughter.

I noticed a small bar to the left of me and headed to it. I am going to need a drink for this business. The round plush stool in front of the bar beckoned. I planted my ass on the first available one, eyeballed the bartender, pointed at a certain bottle of brandy and was promptly served. He didn't ask for payment which was fine by me, since I couldn't have made it anyway. Looks like the affair was open in more ways than one. Diplomacy can be swell sometimes.

I took in more of the scenery from my fairly safe vantage point. The high glass windows of the ballroom offered pristine views of the stars above along with the lights of smaller vessels on the waters surrounding us. Waiters with perfect tuxedos were passing back and forth bearing champagne cocktails on overladen trays that didn't stay overladen long. They glided past as smoothly as if they had roller skates for feet.

The room had a blue and gold tinge to it, thanks to the chairs and tables sporting soft blue table cloths and the surrounding wall and high window dressings radiating a gold pattern. The gold hue mixed with the underlying blue gave a sense of antiquity. I noticed no colors of either the Italian state or the German state were present. This was probably an excellent idea by whomever designed this affair, in order to keep rivalries at bay, and peace in order. After all, diplomacy and union were the main course here.

    I couldn't help but notice the large golden fountain in the center of the room covered in flaked gold. It was in the shape of a rather young woman, bare breasted, hands clasping a long pointed golden spear almost twice her height and with a toga style wrapping covering her torso. Her soft knees and bare feet were uncovered and sprayed with water by the many fountain spigots completing a circle around her. She looked so serene, so sure, yet so fragile. As I stared, mesmerized by the beauty, artistry, and expense of this statue, I realized it was augmented with real bright red roses surrounding the statue's brow, giving it a tender touch. The roses came from a real growth that emerged up from a planting behind the statue, twisting its initial thick branches at the bottom to become thin, wiry, and delicate. Then I noticed the thorns.

    The band on the stage on the far side of the room was loud but in a good way, cutting into conversations amongst the party goers just enough without being overbearing and making people shout. They played and sang indecipherable oompah tunes that satisfied the Pinocchio wine wavering crowd along with the Lederhosen beer sotted idiots. The German songs packed the dancefloor, the Italian ones emptied the sausage chompers and packed the wine-stompers. It all sounded the same to me.

I ordered another drink, this time a double. My nerves were starting to fray a bit after my already busy afternoon and evening. I watched as people moved about the dance floor around the centerpiece of the statue, when all of a sudden the band broke in to a Cole Porter tune. Suddenly the dance floor was packed with everyone pressing their cheeks together like prize hams on the way to slaughter.

I smiled to myself. This band was alright, very smooth, very American sounds in their interpretations. I knew I was waiting for someone to show themselves. Which one would appear first and what would I do when they did? That called for another drink as I sought my equilibrium with the ship's gentle rolling against the champagne cocktails that drifted by like sweet butterflies that fluttering from the waiter's trays.

As my throat and belly continued to tickle with drink, I realized I had to have a strategy.

If Bruno appears, and I can recognize him, what do I do?

If Tika appears, and I can recognize her, what do I do?

I had no idea except to play it my way, whatever way that was. Concentrate on Tika. She had ways of maneuvering that I didn't. She had underlings from all parts of the globe just waiting to either serve or destroy her. All because of what Bruno has in his possession.

An occasional stern exclamation from someone at the bar in my direction would make me snap out of my reverie and I would turn, look them in the eye and smile, offering my drink as a toast. Good. As long as I didn't have to speak, I was fitting in.

I was really beginning to admire the women at this affair. They didn't seem to be required to wear much at all in the way of costuming or clothing. Which they didn't.

Despite my mission at the moment, the cocktails were making me lovingly linger longingly as sweet breasts and tushies paraded before me. My gaze grew hazy and then I focused on someone in the distance. Someone that stood out more than a bit.

Was this Bruno that had captured my gaze? I knew I was looking for a German with a missing finger and possible severe injury or scars of some type from the beating received on the underside of the plane before dropping off into the jungle. I also had it figured that if he had a missing finger, he would probably be wearing a glove of sorts.

This person's costume was a rather garish red with Nazi insignia on the front of his red vest. He was covered in a bright ruby cloth, carrying a long stick with a small replica of a human skull on top. A Ju-Ju stick, is what that style of cane was called. What the hell am I doing thinking of that? Great, I recognized what could be called a Ju-Ju stick because said item was in several of my crappy films flaunted by a dolled up actor from East Los Angeles playing a not very convincing witch doctor.

A quick shake of my head to discourage old memories made me notice more of this person's outfit. On top of this red peacock's head was a rather foppish, almost feminine broad brimmed hat, black, with small feathers all around the edge and upturned on one side. This had to be Bruno, as the costume fit his conceit well as I was beginning to know it. But the ghastliest image was his face.

Whitish hue and with a skull's perpetual mocking smile, the oddly blue eyes were firmly anchored in deep recesses in black open sockets as he paraded forth like the Prince of Death among men.

As he passed through the crowd the participants seemed to part while he seemed to glow with a diffused light as if he were Moses parting the Red Sea.

Thus I knew Bruno's entrance was made. There could be no other.

All may have noticed him, but no pause in reverie was made. There was too much fun and drink to be had. I noticed a slight limp and struggle to maintain a certain ingrained majesty to his general form. This was Bruno.

I followed his direction with my eyes. He stood at a pause, his deep vision staring, looking for something or someone.

I slipped of my stool slightly and jolted back to my memories as an actor. I was an actor once, dammit! I know how to look at people, I know how to take the actions and especially the reactions of people and use them in my skill set.

I know how to read people, dammit!

I was an actor. What the hell has happened to me? I turned my head, shook my glass at the bartender and had another drink.

My reverie quickly vanished as I noticed another entrance. From a far corner a vision appeared. Maybe she had always been there. It didn't matter, she was there now. My instinct was operating fully. She was such an exquisite beauty.

She glowed into my sight. A Valkyrie with a tunic of tight grey mesh cloth resembling chain mail, revealing ample legs, a shiny breastplate emphasizing her round breasts. She strode majestically wearing a gilded plated pointed cylindrical crown adorned with images of crows while carrying a shield that shown a glistening golden hue in the lights of the room.

She stood near the open hatch to the observation deck and she seemed to be doing the same as me, not really interacting, only observing. This was Tika in her predator mode without a doubt. I couldn't help but feel my heart leap as much as I tried to ignore it.

I felt like I was watching a silent film when I noticed Tika and Bruno's eyes locked onto each other. She moved slowly towards him and he moved slightly towards her. It was as if a spotlight was following each of them, the way they stood out in the crowd. She seemed to zero in on him with a solid purpose. How appropriate they seem together I thought, though begrudgingly.

His grimace seemed to widen as she came near. He bowed very graciously, offering her to dance as the band broke into a waltz. She gave a slight nod, accepting. I have to admit they danced together extremely well, Red Death leading gently while Valkyrie followed willfully. For Tika to be so jungle like, yet so knowledgeable of Western customs amazed me. How I would enjoy knowing more about her.

In their own private space on the dancefloor, the two glided around each other silently conversing. All of a sudden Bruno grabbed her and pushed her into him with some force. She pushed back, giving him a cracking slap across the cheek. His reaction was one of barely controlled anger and his red costume seemed to almost glow with hatred. He quickly gained her in a hold to keep her from moving away and causing a disruption.

I downed what was left of my drink and moved quickly across the floor, running on aggressive instinct fueled by alcohol. How dare he touch her like that! I leapt at Bruno as Tika retreated into the rapidly disbursing wake of the crowd. Bruno and I both went down to the floor and rolled tumbling through dancers' and waiters' legs alike with crashing glasses and trays falling to the floor, sharp glass biting at both our arms.

Grasping his throat I brought his head down to the floor with a crack while he brought his knee up to flip me overhead by way of my crotch. Ignoring any pain, I twisted sideways and snapped his neck nearly off his shoulders with my wrist, loosening his grasp on me. This only served to separate us for a second, to regain ourselves vertically, crouching and diving again at each other. He managed to grapple his cane that had been hanging from his belt and jammed it in my gut giving me no way to suction air. At this point I didn't need air to do what I was doing. I grabbed his cane away and brought it full force into his face, breaking the cane with a blunt blow across the bridge of his nose. His head snapped back and showered blood with bone, but his advance did not stop. Striking me with his foot in a powerful leg snap to my neck, I felt my windpipe close down. Staggering, I fell on my back.

I lay on the floor quivering like an upended roach watching Bruno move in. Oddly, his move forward seemed to be in slow motion. Maybe it was the lack of oxygen, but time had shifted. The sounds were altered several keys lower, movement was slow, and I noticed I was as covered in as much blood as Bruno's costume was red.

People were moving in to restrain us and as I grabbed Bruno's head once more I managed to pull off some of his mask. As I did I realized only a portion of his grotesque appearance was a mask. I realized I was touching bone and withered muscle. We both rolled, grappling, as the crowd grew in numbers to stop us. All the while constant alarms and screams kept growing louder.

A massive deck shattering explosion filled my ears along with calls of "LA NAVE E IN FUOCO!" and "DAS SCHIFF IST AUF FEUER!" punctuated the air amidst screams of terror. As Bruno and I reached violently for each other once more, another explosion deafened my hearing and sent me to the far side of the dance floor, which was by now listing to the port side at a forty-five-degree angle and was a tumbling mass of bodies, twisting and turning, shouting and screaming. Furniture flew along with people, heavy pieces of furniture trapping and crushing bodies beneath. The large golden statue that had been the centerpiece of the ballroom was ripped from its mooring and slid mightily headfirst towards an escape hatch, its pointed lance managing to skewer four or five people on its way before the sharp metal point ruptured a gas main against a bulkhead, spewing sparking friction and igniting a powerful whoosh of flame that effectively created a human shish kabob emitting a hideous noise and smell.

With one exit blocked by the statue and its grisly deed, people pushed towards another open hatch to the outer deck and spilled out over that deck only to go over the side of the ship, which was beginning to continue its progress towards capsizing.

I found myself captured by the grip of gravity. Forgetting Bruno, having lost him seconds before amid the chaos, I tumbled towards the outer lip of the deck, but found myself grabbing a brass handrail by pure luck. More explosions occurred, the ship sounded as if were being twisted and ripped apart by some angry sea god.

I could see the length of the deck now, saw the ship breaking in pieces. I pulled myself up a bit to wrap my legs around the handrail to secure a better hold and watched revelers roll off me, bounce off the deck with the furniture and glass and over the side and into the inky cold sea.

I looked back to the ballroom to see Tika holding onto a table that was lodged against some other furniture by the bar several feet away back in the ballroom. I saw the table upend, saw her start to plummet sideways towards me, saw her beautiful costume shred amongst the broken glass that scratched her bleeding arms and legs, saw her outstretched arms pass me on their way to bounce over the side to the sea, saw me instinctively grab her as she let out a cry and then pull her to me with my one free arm to hold her as close as I did my own life.

The ship's creaking became overwhelming in sound and vibrations, resulting in a series of explosions that thrust the ship leeward to port and forward, while Tika gave a soft cry of pain through the loud shrieks and yells of the drowning and dying burning passengers.

One yell was coming at me. Bruno, his head and shoulders literally on fire with what was left of flesh on his upper torso and scalp was barreling at us on the nearly vertical deck. At that same moment the bass drum that had been part of the band's equipment rolled forth towards the sea and pegged Bruno in the groin with a grunt. He reached for me as Tika growled like a panther and grabbed his right arm as half of its flesh came off in her hand. His ragged sleeve showed a hole as he dropped out of sight and set off a burst of flame from below as the oil coated water burst alive in the flames from the rim of the ship.

I could do nothing in my shock except to hold Tika against the buffeting of the overturning vessel and against the threatening furniture and bodies pouring past us. I did manage to notice the entire deck of the ballroom floor erupt in engulfing fire and light. One more massive huge sound deafened my ears and I began to lose consciousness. My last vision was of a Red Death floating in the flames of wood and shrapnel, still shrieking, still threatening me. I had no sound now, nor vision, just heat and smoke choking my lungs. The only other sensation I had was holding Tika, and with that, I only held her tighter as my sensations became black.

CHAPTER 31--ISLAND REFUGE

Ouch. Damned ouch. I curled my toes. Goddamn pain shot straight up my spine to the top of my head and curled around my skull to focus back on my eyes.

Eyes? My lids were slight creases that shot the redness of my pain right into my brain. My ears showed more mercy. I heard sounds of waves, birds chattering nonsensically at a loud volume, subdued human voices speaking in a tongue I knew nothing about. Damn, the birds need to shut their fowl beaks.

My brain decided to give me something else to focus on besides what was outside of it. I was given visions. I saw Tika swirling down at me from the ship we had been on, but there was no fire, no explosions, no screaming. Only the sound of quiet waves, a smell of refreshing salt air. The ship was overturned, as Tika slid from the ballroom, quietly, gracefully, no broken glass, no tearing of her costume, just a sensual beautiful glide into my arms. I didn't need to hold on to anything as she landed so delicately against me. We both drifted together, watching the ship turn on its side. We were floating away from harm silently, seemingly elevated from the scene, floating up, up, wrapped in a cocoon of our own making, and turned to each other smiling.

And then she kissed me.

As she kissed me I had a vision of a train going into a long tunnel and emerging on the other side in a brilliantly colored land with giant mushrooms dancing in a thick green creamy broth lake. Little colorful crouton stars popped around the green fields on either side of the dark lake, and tiny fairies waterskied on sliced mushrooms, pulled by tiny broccoli florets driving motorboats, all with a constant sound of water crashing, only to pull back and repeat again and again with a rhythm that lulled me into consciousness.

Shadows at first, becoming clear. I was on a porch, screened in, with dark lumps around me. The lumps began to coalesce into human figures. One of the figures was pushing a warm liquid into my mouth and it was good. The more I had the more I became conscious.

The human pushing the amazing vegetable broth in my mouth was a burly woman with a sweet face like a loving grandmother. I only thought of her as a grandmother because she looked like one. She was garbed in what is typical garb for a grannie, peasant dress, huge apron covering her ample front, hair bundled up not too successfully, wrapped in a bandana and with a scent of garlic, onion and tomato. She was cooing and sweet talking like a mother to a babe in what I guess was Italian, but whatever it was, it was sweet as the food she was placing in my mouth.

I gave a smile and opened my eyes a bit further. The other shapes became clearer. I saw the sweet old woman hovering over me as I lay in a bed in a screened in porch with welcome wonderful sunlight and the sound of waves crashing very near. The sweet sunlight streamed in through the mesh screen of the porch and blanketed the floor around me in a warm glow. I felt good, but I was disturbed. I want to know where I am. Who are these people?

I was soon answered on my next sip of soup. "He'a seemsa to be hokay for now. Justa maka sure he gettsa plenty of rest. I will be backa tomorrow." A funny looking man in a funny little pudgy hat mumbled in what I suppose was Italian and closed what looked like a doctor's black bag and left, leaving an oversized woman sitting by my bedside with a big bowl of what I recognized as a vegetable laced pea soup. If she kept feeding me this pea soup all day, then I was going to pee soup all night. She had a most pleasant smile I couldn't ignore, even with my head feeling like a damaged piece of cauliflower that had been dropped, stamped on, and left on the market floor.

Other shadows became clear. I could tell by the breezes that entered the porch that the screened room I was in was one that faced the sea, with wonderful fragrances of salt, mixed with fresh fish, and flowers filling the room. I immediately felt at ease, with the greatest amount of calm I had felt in months. I had to smile, though I felt someone was holding my head in a vise.

I asked "Where the hell am I Ma'am?"
All that came out of my mouth was "mdfonlbnrl."
"Easy, my little Cucciolo"
I had no idea what that meant, she could have been calling me a pile of hanging dag, but the way she said it was so sweet, so pleasant, I didn't care what she would have called me.

I could have resorted myself to being in heaven at that point, except for the consistent pressure to my skull fighting against the resurrection of my old back pains for dominancy over who can hurt me the most. Maybe these angels were deciding to let me in to heaven or not and had one those pesky grapples attached to my head and backside, like the concession stands they have on Santa Monica pier where you slide in a coin and try to work the little crane to grab the plush toy you want to take home.

The light from the screen window was beginning to open up the room I was in. I could clearly hear the sounds of surf and distance calls of men as they fought against the waves that slapped against piers. I moved my head slightly against the sounds and came to realize that I had landed somehow in a room by the ocean and laid out with nowhere to go.

I wanted to get up but was held back by bandages and pain. I really had to scratch. Really had to scratch. The realization that had brought me up to wakefulness, was that I was wanting to scratch.

Now.

I forced myself against the intense uncomfortable position that my body was in and looked at the woman that had been feeding me. She fussed in what I was realized by now really was Italian, and somehow knew what my poor eyes must have been seeing. She rubbed my shoulder and scratched my back a bit for me. I smiled. She adjusted my pillows and let me sit up to get a better view of what was going on around me.

I could finally focus a bit and I became more aware. The room was comfortable, refreshing in its clean but slightly chilly salt air. The room seemed built of rustic weathered wood, with tall windows that stretched from floor to ceiling covered in screens. The floor itself was made of the same wood, but seemed brushed with a thousand sandy shoes. I happened to be facing east, and the rising Apollo battled my eyelids for wakefulness. I noticed the wall behind me was solid wood, except for a door that I guessed led to the main house. Through my surrounding screens I could see the ocean trying to meld with the sky, azure shades cascading into the other like perfect lovers, melding and becoming one, indistinguishable.

The old woman smiled warmly. "You call-a me Nonna." Her smile belayed the fact that although time had taken its toll on her face and figure, she was still glowing with an inner youthful beauty and a contentment that was contagious.

"Where am I?" I managed to mumble.

"You safe. You home bambino."

Well that cleared things up. When she said home, inwardly I gazed back to the Hollywood hills, Ha-Nee had gained enormous weight, took to wearing printed oversized peasant dresses with colorful bandanas wrapping her hair, smelling like garlic and oregano, eyes were rounded out, and had gained an Italian accent. I started to sit up and move my legs.

A rush of adrenalin and pain. This ain't Hollywood and this ain't home.

I began to stand and realized I was naked. Usual modesty prevailed for me in a rare instance, and I sat back down, gathering my sheets around me like the best of bosom and crotchety friends.

Nonna paid no mind. "You rest, doctor he say so."

I instinctively said "Yes Ma'am."

I got back in bed, looked around and noticed another person on a bed to the right of me by the southern window. She was sitting up and staring at the sea in the background.

It was Tika.

My heart leapt but I wasn't sure why, or which way, up or down. Whichever way it went, I knew I was glad to see her, yet I didn't know exactly what for. She turned slightly so I could see her profile against the outside blue of the sky.

A loud slap of the screen door off to the left side of the porch and I turned from Tika to see a glad figure. Akbar made me smile. His arms were loaded with fresh grapes and small nets of shellfish waiting to be eaten.

"My hero has awakened to sally forth whomever Sally might be! Ah, most glorious morning indeed!" His broad grin, I swear it nearly wrapped around his neck.

"I must reasonably presume you are asking in your head why we are not dead. If we were dead I would not be here, I would be frolicking with my seventy-two virgins down on the beach in most excited nakedness"

This information gave cause to reason we were not dead and to also give thanks we weren't, given the vision Akbar had just planted in my head. There was no exclamation from Tika.

"OK, give, somebody. What the hell happened? Last I know I was grabbing Tika from going over the side of a burning sinking ship." Out of the corner of my eye I expected some reaction from her, but none appeared.

Nonna slipped away with the dishes and went inside of the cabin. Akbar took her chair and came closer, his hands offering the bounty of his beachside endeavors. I took some fruit, leaving the shellfish alone. I wasn't ready for that yet. He set what he had on the bedside table next to a large canter of wine. "Thanks for the grapes. I will take some of the juice if you please."

"Of course, most exclusive one!" He poured a healthy glass of red wine and handed it to my slightly shaky hand. I took a large swig. I felt better.

"By my best favorite goat of my ancestors, I am so blessed to have saved you. The ship, it had some French people on it that do not like the movements of the German and Italian leaders. They bomb the ship hoping to kill everyone.

"Ah, but they not kill me! I, Akbar, am too clever! I help my people where I can, to save lives. As ship lean to turn over, it finally blow.

"I am in water, but surviving, I command large piece of broken wooden siding from ship. Water all around is on fire from the oil escaping from the fuel on tanks. Lots of fire. People dive from ship into water, only to surface into the burning oil, their head and scalps are set afire. Much screaming and horrible burning smells of flesh, and they only sink once again to never come up. Much crying of pain and fear, most horrible visions."

He actually became quiet for once and turned away.

But not for long.

The grin returned, as did his wagging finger emphasizing the best parts of his tale. "I see you, I know my best mission is here!"

I could hear Tika let out an exclamation of exasperation.

"All the light was given by the fires from the ship that had now overturned on its side and was going down. I knew that I had to get you on my piece of wooden siding and get as far away as possible before the ship sank. Bad wave comes back when ship sinks.

"I saved you, you had woman too. You both rested on my long piece of broken wood. You both in not too good shape."

"What the hell, this was the middle of the night, right?" I mumbled.

"Yes, but the stars and moon shone bright. I notice a bronze handle on the piece of large wood we floated on. There was a small treasure beneath."

"What are you talking about? A small treasure?"

"Most yes. We were floating on the main piece of the bar in the ballroom where the expensive liquor was locked up. We were riding our way out to the safe waters supported by the locked expensive wines and booze as you say.

"Came the early sun, a plane comes by, a beautiful red winged angel from Allah! Surely you must remember!"

I tried to think, but it hurt. I paused in my answer. "Vaguely. I seem to remember a red bird that floated on water. Its belly opened and people came out."

"No no my friend – what you saw was a seaplane flown by the master pilot Francesco Agello, very famous, fastest sea pilot in the world. He holds many speed records. He is good man and flew a flying boat to search for shipwreck survivors. He heard of the wreck and came out to do what he could. He and his crew landed on water like roach in bucket of beer. He had a doctor with him, O most fine doctor. We all loaded you and booze and Tika into plane, then flew here to this village where he has many friends. Doctor give you much fine drugs, told me to keep giving them to you."

What a pal. Now that I thought of it, the last thing I was wearing before the ship exploded was that silly damn bizarre outfit. I mentioned this to Akbar.

"Yes, my friend. You were quite to be silly looking in clown outfit when we were taken onboard plane. One of the crew say let you drown at first because you wear swastika on chest, but Agello say no, we are here to save lives, besides, you were to be wearing Pagliacci clothing. Pagliacci most revered clown in Italy."

Great, my life was saved for being a clown. Film critics have called me as much.

"He flew us quick as desert eagle to land here to stay with his very trusted friends Babbo and Nonna."

"Damn nice to do all that for us for free."

"Oh he and the doctor were paid in beautiful bottles from ship's locker. Agello also had clean dry clothes for you to change into." He smirked to himself. "You were looking very silly with clown suit and swastika. We were then graciously deposited by Allah upon this peaceful island shore, along with the wine bar and great piece of wood that had been our saving and taken in by Babbo. He was fishing nearby and saw us land. He and Nonna are a most pleasant couple. Babbo was content to take us for bottles."

"Would you please tell me what island we are on?"

"Sicily, beach village of Pozzallo."

"Why all the way here?"

"With a war bubbling all around, pilot said this was a safe place to hide. There is not a way to tell who all your friends might be."

Another large sound of clomping feet as a small intense scowling rather hairy little man broke into view in the room. He let out something that sounded like a curse as he glared at me and grumbled in Italian.

His gaze was intense and hateful. His English was somewhat better than what I had been hearing. This must be Babbo.

"You are trouble for me."

Well that was direct.

"Nothing but trouble. We have patrols here all the time, people ask us what we see, what we hear. We always say nothing to the point where we say nothing too much. That is when they watch us. What we see we say we don't see but they know nothing must mean something"

I pushed down the urge to ask him to repeat that statement.

Nonna glared at him. "Babbo," she said softly. He grunted and left the porch to the outside, the screen door slamming as he left.

"You not to worry. He bark is worsa than his bite. He actually happy you here. You land with many bottles of vino. Dat is a sign of prosper. You get better, you helpa him with the boats, then you be best friends."

"Sure, and thanks." I meant it too.

Akbar exclaimed, "As I was so kind to be saying, if not for Tika you would not be here."

"You weren't saying it, but go on."

He said that when he found us, Tika was actually holding my head above the water and shielding me from any flames that were still burning from the oily surface of the black sea. She could have let me go to sink, but she didn't. So I saved Tika from plummeting into the water, and she saved me from drowning or being burned to death.

"Not to worry my friend. I kept my dagger on her the whole journey. She seemed to change. Hard to say. She so very crazy, then very soft. She have most severe head bump oozing blood. I still keep dagger on her. Doctor gave her sedative to kill pain."

When Akbar told me this, I sensed Tika turning her head towards me, her head full of bandages. She spoke. "I am not without mercy. You saved me from the sea and doing so you injured your head against some wood when we both hit the water. You were unconscious. I couldn't let you drown after what you did for me." The last sentence had a bit of emotion to it or so I thought anyway. Or I hoped it did.

Nonna explained via translation from Akbar that Tika had been presented to her with a head trauma. That explained the many bandages around her head. Nonna had been giving her sedatives in her soup.

As the afternoon wore on, Nonna left after she made sure I was alright. What a sweet woman. Tika remained silently sleeping. Akbar told some corny jokes that didn't help my condition, then left to go the wharf and make noise down there. The sea and the sounds of low fisherman talk lulled me to sleep once again.

In the night, with a pale moon casting suspicious shadows across the room, a voice woke me.

"It is gone. I am free at last."

I struggled to stay awake as the voice mumbled something else, but my body said no, and I went back to sleep.

Later at some point, at what seemed the early hours, the voice woke me again. Not sure what it said, I groaned and rolled over. Tika was sitting up, wide awake and gazing at the moon shedding its light on her face. "I am free for the first time since I was a child," she said to no one.

I tried to speak and she turned her head, the moonlight glowing behind her, giving her such an angelic effect that my throat swelled almost making it almost impossible to speak. "Tika I hear you. Talk to me."

She turned towards me, and a light came from her eyes that made me instantly awake. With no effort I was upright in my bed, begging to hear what she would say.

Her face turned back to the moonlight. A soft smile crossed her lips and her eyes glazed.

"I need you."

I hoped I had heard right, but I couldn't move without pain. I raised up to a sitting position to look at her. I had to admit it. I was in love with her. This had been building for a while. This was too strange. The strain was too much from moving, but she never left her gaze from the moon. I struggled to stand, only to fall back and pass out.

Next morning I woke with serious anxiety over the previous night. What the hell was I doing? What was I thinking about doing? Why was I even bothering to be so damn puritan at this point? That was a first for me alright.

Shrugging my worries about last night off for a second, I saw Nonna enter with some fresh fruit and a porridge of sort on a tray, and rather excitedly, I saw a small cup and a pitcher of what I hoped was coffee. She served with her sweet smile and set the tray on the nightstand beside my bed.

It was coffee alright, strong enough to tell me to get out of bed and get going. Where I was supposed to be going, I wasn't sure, so after quaffing my breakfast, and with Nonna's direction, I headed for the bathroom to throw up and clean up.

I returned to the porch to see that Nonna had been replaced by Akbar, my faithful sidekick, whether I liked it or not. "My friend, you are most likely to be wondering where Tika has gone. She is walking along the beach by herself. She is feeling much better; the bandages are gone. Akbar can tell she is not same woman that was before."

I was still in my bandages, wrapped loosely around my head, and dressed in a long white nightshirt that I had been wearing since I first woke in this place. I noticed some clothes, tattered but clean, and laying neatly on a table by the door.

"Nonna left some old clothes that belonged to her grown up son for you to wear," Akbar explained.

I immediately had a flash of panic. I guess it showed in my eyes because Akbar burst forth with laughter, tilting his head, his mouth open wide, revealing Stonehenge style dental work. He produced a tattered wallet I recognized as mine, and a small bag containing the object of my distress – the white knight. A bit rough edged, but still a welcome sight.

Nonna appeared from the house and onto the porch carrying a basket of breads and a bottle of wine. "I hear you talk. I am known as Nonna Stregha. I know things no one else-a could know. Doctor he say you stay here few more days."

She opened the wine and broke the bread. Wonderful wine and garlic laden bread slid down my throat and gave me strength.

She continued.

"Nonna, she take care of you alright. I know everyone here, they know me. You needa call home? I know where. There is a cafe in the village. From there you senda wire where you want."

I smiled between chewing and swallowing. Great, just what I needed.

She also told me the place was safe from police and that fascists did not want to stay long here. She knew the pilot that was responsible for the rescue, and I would be safe here.

Perfect, I can heal up, but only for a time. I have to keep moving. It has become a habit, even if I don't know where I am heading.

Just as the cool January wind was starting to kick in, I dragged myself to get up, mentioning there was something I needed to do first before heading to town.

"You take care! You very hurt with shock."

"I will be alright if I have a smoke."

Nonna offered me a cigarette. I took it, and as my fingers trembled, I lit it. Breathing the smoke through my lungs actually revitalized me and cleared my head. "Look, I don't want to be a burden, but is there some wine around here?"

"You silly boy!" From around her round rump, she produced a canter of wine from a shelf behind her.

I took a slug of the wonderful stuff. A long drag from the smoke I had in my hands was stronger that my usual Luckies, but any discomfort was washed away with a generous glug of superb wine. The pain in my back and joints was fighting an old enemy now named cigarettes and booze, and pain was losing.

"Graci, Nonna," I replied, completely expending all of my knowledge of the Italian language.

I told her that I needed to go to the village and send a couple of messages via telegraph., and could she translate what I wanted in order to be able to do it. She worked out some notes for me to give to the lady at the café that was in charge of the wireless.

I quickly changed and headed out the screen door to the docks and the beach. I still limped, but I limped with purpose, almost smiling. This was one thing I wanted to do before I hobbled into the village.

CHAPTER 32--SEASIDE TRYST

I saw her walking about a quarter mile away down the left side of the beach towards a high point that jutted out over the water a bit. Waves crashed against the high rocks from the incoming tide, creating a spray that caught the sun and turned the droplets into prisms of colors. I walked quickly, not knowing if she had seen me or not. She was wearing bits of what was left of her costume, augmented by what I assumed was what Nonna had given her. She looked like the most divine rag doll I had ever seen as she stood on the farthermost point of the rocks, staring into the blue waters of the Mediterranean.

She sensed my approach. I stopped a few steps from her. She slowly turned, the wind giving the shards of garment an enchanted wing like effect as they swirled around her. She spoke and her voice was clear as crystal cutting through the chattering of the birds and the grumbling of the sea.

"I need you." Her eyes beckoned me and I couldn't resist. I took her in my arms. She was tense at first, but only for a moment as we held each other. Then we melted like butter into each other's embrace, her head resting against my shoulder as she held on as if her life depended upon it. Maybe it did. I needed to know more. I needed to know why this attraction I had for her denied everything I had previously felt.

The tension passed between us and we relaxed. She pushed me away softly and said "Let's take a walk."

We walked along the beach away from the docks for close to a mile, neither of us speaking. I certainly didn't know what to say. Her mind seemed half a world away. We came to a small cove, hidden from the surrounding beach and the rest of humanity, or so it seemed. She led me to a hollow place just inside the lip of the cove where water from the sea would rush in and then slowly move back out to the source. Sounds of dripping water echoed inside the cove and we were hidden from the beach altogether. Small frogs sang in happy unison in soothing song. This was a place of peace, peace that was a long time coming for both of us. Small crabs ran happily from one small puddle of sea water to the next, seeming to enjoy themselves as they were constantly upset by the tides. The rocks inside the cove were smooth and slippery, and the entire place offered a calm respite from the warm sun outside.

I glanced at Tika. She was affected by this place as well. She turned to me and took my hand. "I was here yesterday as you slept. I felt this a good place to talk to you."

We both sat together in the cool shade just inside the cove. Her voice echoed slightly as her eyes bore into mine. I was transfixed by her. All I could do was sit and listen as she took my hands.

She proceeded to confess to me in a way I hadn't expected. She talked about how she had been held in a mental grip by her tribe for years, since she was a child. The blow on her head, while almost killing her, loosened that control, and she was finally free and in charge of her actions completely.

I stroked her hair as she told me things I didn't understand at first, but became clearer as time went on, and she began to tell me her fantastic story.

"I was born in the jungles of Burma." Loud cries of the birds seemed to accent her tale as she continued. "My people were not my people." Pleasantly confused and even more intrigued I listened for more as a slight spray from the ocean tide cascaded over our forms, making us cold and instinctively drawing us closer to each other's warmth.

I wanted to hold her so badly, this incredibly attractive but deadly woman. I now know how a male black widow spider feels. My head and life force could be lopped away at any moment but I couldn't stop. I leaned in, but her soft hand stopped my impetuous clumsiness.

"Stop – look into my eyes."

As I did I saw another place, another life inside her eyes. She began more of her story, and as she did, I couldn't pull my gaze away from her, it was as if I was transported to another realm. She leaned closer to me, never breaking her gaze or her hold, squeezing me tighter, running her hands under my clothing. I instinctively did the same to her.

"Place your forehead against mine. I want to join with you." We pressed our foreheads together, still in a locked gaze, and a warmth came over me like I had never felt, as we continued to press flesh against flesh. She said something about joining with her third eye, but I wasn't sure. All I knew was that I was controlled physically and mentally by this woman and was being given a vision and somehow looking through her eyes led me into her past, as if I was there and actually existing in her time and space at a certain point in her life as a disembodied spirit and witness.

At this, we became as one in vision and flesh.

We spent every moment together after that afternoon in the cove as she allowed me to see more visions of her past and I began to understand her. The days turned into long nights as we embraced warmly, such that even the cool, somewhat chilly winter breezes that blew off of the Mediterranean were dulled in their efforts. We didn't stay much at the cottage during this time of her confession, only for the occasional medical checkup and Nonna's wonderful cooking. I swear that woman was feeding the island with all the food she made.

The days and nights dragged on gloriously and the stories Tika shared with me were laid out in bits and pieces, but overall they told a tale like no other.

She talked about her people who were not her people at first. Her true parents were British explorers and doctors who were going on a medical missionary expedition into the depths of the little-known Burmese jungle. They had heard strange rumors amongst the natives of a certain tribe with unusual longevity. This particular tribe was obsessed with a large pure greenstone. Her parents believed this large greenstone and the fact that all who worshipped it seemed to have unusually long life spans were all somehow connected.

By chance and several weeks of searching along with their guide's excellent navigation of the rivers and knowledge of the area, they finally stumbled across the village.

The village consisted of giant Myanmar trees, with an entire village of people living amongst the trees in huts bounded to the enormous limbs, and using connecting rope ladders as paths from limb to limb. The people rarely descended to the ground, as what ground there was consisted of swampy murk, usually full of dark waters, crocodiles and a variety of biting things.

The people were nervous at first, suspicious, distrustful, but non-violent. They posted guards around her parents in one of the huts for a while, but their natural curiosity overwhelmed them, and tribal representatives visited the hut. Her parents' guide served as a makeshift interpreter, translating the gestures and mouthing of the tribal elders.

One particular day, as we lay in each other's arms and watched the sun set, Tika became very open with me. "My parents made the elders of the tribe understand that they had come with medicine and were curious about the tribe as much as the tribe was curious about my parents. Upon understanding that my parents possessed healing medicines and herbs and wanted to be benevolent healers, the tribal elders smiled brightly and bid my parents to follow them up a vine covered walkway to a hut that stood fairly isolated on a large thick branch elevated above the watery murk below."

She told me that upon entering the hut, her parents and guide were unable to see or breathe at first, with pungent fumed clouds of incense thickening the already dense air. The elders that escorted her parents began to light candles and wave large tree fronds to dispel the acrid smoke and fragrant fumes. Once her parent's senses had adjusted to what was within the smoke filled room from the back of the hut through a beaded curtain appeared an ancient naked woman with only a loincloth to cover her, as was worn by all other members of the tribe. She wore many feathers of many colors and was obviously the spiritual priestess of the village. She was short, wrinkled as a raisin, but her glowing energy for life could be felt as a material essence in the room. Around her neck was a greenstone, oddly shaped, that seemed to emit presence, not outwardly, but in an inwardly sense.

"My parents were entranced by this woman," Tika said.

So, her parents stayed.

With the help of their guide and interpreter, they quickly came to understand the basics of the tribe's language.

Over the days, as they pried into the history of the village and the unusual intensity of the stone, the old woman led them to a large main hut that dominated a lone section of the tree tops. The interior of the hut was open and circular, with the exception of a small raised area towards the back of the entrance. Behind that small area was a larger platform with a huge stone, coarsely shaped in an image of a grotesque cross legged human. There was something odd about the face however. There was a large hole in the center of what someone would call a forehead, in a shape that resembled a resting spot for the old woman's amulet. The rest of the figure was misshapen, with appendages resembling arms and legs, but the most amazing thing about the image was its face. There was a smile. Faint, but it was there, along with a closed lidded serenity in the entire countenance.

It was also green.

"My parents knew they were on to something very serious, so they wondered about the origins of this statue. The Old Woman said the stone was a gift from the gods in the sky."

The way Tika went on to explain it, the only way I could interpret this was information was that a rather large meteor had struck the jungle untold years ago, or so the elders of the tribe had transcribed, giving out shards of rock and luminous crystals all around in the swampy land. Once the heat and glow had subsided, the tribe had dug it out, the large remnant of the meteor still glowing with a strange emerald hue.

Since the tribal elders considered this a gift, they carefully pulled it out of the still sizzling waters using bamboo braces and levers. To their amazement, the stone had been buffeted and tossed by the friction of its incoming trajectory so as to form a humanoid shape, resembling a sitting figure. Or at least that was the way they saw it.

"The old Jesus in a tortilla effect," I thought to myself.

When the stone had been moved to its present state in the temple, the natives slowly began to notice peculiarities amongst themselves. Once a child reached adulthood, that child didn't seem to age. Those adults that stayed in the presence of the statue didn't age at all. The women quickly became sterile as well.

Soon the natives realized that by staying within a certain radius of the statue, or basically the limit of the village's boundaries, no one aged past puberty. Of course, this took a few months for the tribe to realize. By then they had also noticed that though the aging process was delayed beyond any measure, they could still die with injury, infection, sickness, animal bites and accidents. They were still mortal after all.

A female priestess was appointed to minister and protect the stone. This only made sense to the natives, as females are the only ones capable of bearing life, and so too, the stone is capable of extending that life.

The tribe did dare to incise a small portion of the stone taken from what was considered the third eye, that point between the eyes and the center of the forehead, for the priestess protector of the stone to bear. What they discovered was that this cutting dimmed the stone's life lengthening powers by a small but noticeable bit, but enough of a bit to worry the natives.

The natives quickly found that by the priestess' act of reinserting the small pendant like stone back in the forehead of the large statue, that this revitalized the entire stone structure back to its original power and the statue would give a tremendous flash of radioactive rays, allowing those present to be gifted with continuing life. Soon an entire ceremonial religion evolved around this reinserting and empowering of life. Dances, drum beats and chanting all evolved around the glorious act.

"My parents enquired when all of this occurred. The Old Woman couldn't say. It had been ages ago. What did shock my parents was when they asked what happened to the original priestess. The Old Woman only gave a wrinkled smile and said that she was the original priestess.

"My parents, surprised by this, judged after talking further with the Old Woman, realized that she must have been several hundred years old."

I must have had a confused look on my face, for Tika gave a funny little smile. "Yes, I was born in the jungle within that tribe."

"But, how, if the women were sterile…?"

"My mother became pregnant before they discovered the tribe. The Old Woman was very concerned about my mother's pregnancy, was very doting. My mother became very sick with fever, and the Old Woman was afraid Mother might die before giving birth. Much ritual and chanting were done and I was born alive and healthy. Unfortunately, my mother was dead at the time."

She said this with a coldness that made me pull my collar up against the breeze blowing in from the sea.

Later after we acquired some cheese and wine from Nonna, we journeyed to a small cliff overlooking the sea. We spread everything out on a red blanket on the grass covered edge and lay back watching the clouds float lazily overhead, enjoying the food and drink and each other's company. After some light talk and smiles I asked about her father. "He was eaten by a tiger." That was her only reply. This prompted several moments of silence that I dared not disturb until she suddenly spoke again and continued her odd tale for me.

"The Old Woman was the only parent I knew as a child. She was very kind and protective of me, raising me in her teachings. She seemed almost telepathic, reading peoples' thoughts and intuitively guessing their intentions. I knew she was raising me as her own and to eventually become her heiress. She showed me the ways of her spirituality, the rituals, the use of certain hidden herbs. Between the jungle medicines and what she had learned from my parents, she became even more respected. All of her knowledge was passed on to me."

The clouds overhead grew slightly darker as she spoke.

"My parents weren't the last to hear about my tribe."

She told me a small handful of explorers followed her parent's trail based on her father's writings that he had dispatched back to London from the final outpost before he descended too far back in the jungle for any messages to make it back out. While his writings got through to the Geographical Society of London weeks later, most didn't believe it. Amongst those explorers that did try to follow her father's path, most of them didn't make it and failed but each time tales of the tribe made their way back by various members of these parties, only to have the legend grow deeper and deeper over the years.

Eventually in the 1880s at some point, a small party looking for the life lengthening powers of the statue and its stone amulet made it to the tribe's village, but by the time they did, Tika was being primed to assume power from the beloved Old Woman. The leader of this party of explorers who did make it was accepted into the secrets and citizenship of the tribe on the promise that he would and could take Tika back to civilization and finance her education in the best Swiss schools. That he did in exchange for being let into the cult.

There was something that was beginning to bother me about this whole story, but before I could interrupt her, she just held her fingers to my lips, silencing me, making me hear the rest of what she had to reveal.

She told me that she left the tribe with her sponsor and attended schools under his influence. She proved very bright, quite so, and became very adept in language acquisition, quickly adapting to the customs of western society. Her mentor had met with his cronies from the Geographical Society and told them of his adventures and his progeny. They indeed were interested and so, following Tika's benefactor's maps, prominent doctors and wealthy Barons and such made their way to the jungle to offer help and devotion to the tribe in exchange for indoctrination.

Astoundingly enough, they were accepted into the teachings on one condition. That the tribe would remain protected from the outside world by this handful of Europeans in exchange for the medicines and care that would benefit the people of the tribe. Rituals of the greenstone and modern medicines meant these European interlopers could live an extremely long time. Greed or sense of betrayal from these new inductees would result in banishment and death from not just the natives, but by their fellow Europeans that were now part of the tribe. Breaking the oath meant death could strike you not only in the jungle, but in Berlin or London by other secret members.

And so the tribe was protected from the outside world by a very small group of influential patrons.

At the time of gathering, none were distinguishable from each other, all appeared the same for ritual. All became equal once naked and coated with grease and tar from the local swamps and trees, and from ornamental trappings and talismans of the animals and vegetation of the region, all ready for ritual. The rituals were held every summer solstice. The tribe continued to remain in solitude from the world by its elite European benefactors.

The sun was beginning to dip in the sky and I had to speak. "Guess I am confused," I quickly blurted out. "I know this is rude, but…"

"I am very old by your terms." She stared at me stone faced. "My parents discovered the tribe in the early 1830s."

I started to do the math but quickly stopped.

Later that evening after we had quietly packed up the picnic and gone back to the house we both left each other to go about our separate ways. Her revelations about her possible age were a lot for me to consider. As I lay back on my rack on the porch, I rolled and lit one of the local tobaccos that Akbar had left behind. The encroaching darkness and sound of the surf and absence of Tika in the cot beside me left me with a solitary aloneness. Soon my head was reeling like an ultimate spinach. I sure missed my Luckies.

The next morning I awoke, oddly refreshed and feeling a bit randy. I noticed Tika down at the beach and the long robes she wore seemed to delight with the wind, as both would conspire and cause her draping cloths to wrap and caress her form, then change, leaving her, the robes carried by the wind, only to wrap other features of her delicate form in seemingly continuous joy.

She didn't notice this, she was staring at the sea as usual, her feet seeming to taste the waves that lapped at her in admiration and honor. I couldn't help but smile as I sprung up, quickly dressed, and having a grab at some dark grapes that were by the door of the porch, I was at her side in quick time.

I stopped beside her, laughing and shaking, still not quite awake and realizing the appearance I must have made, no shirt, stubbly beard, a bit sandy from the previous night, staring at her beauty and wishing I had had a quick shower first. Or at least a good wet washcloth to clean my face. It didn't matter.

She spoke, but not talking to me. She spoke to the sea. The surf rolled her words back to me.

"I have unusual feelings for you. I have never told anyone what I have told you. I feel a seal has been broken. I have begun to empty the chalice. Once begun, I cannot stop."

Being near her for some reason, gave me a somewhat ravenous appetite. I wanted more of her, more of any sensation she could give me.

She led me back to the cottage, while I suggested some breakfast at the café in the village. She nodded.

Once at the café, on the deck overlooking the somewhat dark waters of a Mediterranean Sea covered in January clouds, sipping espresso demitasses warming us both, she told more of the details of her background. Any questions I had would soon be answered

I gazed at her soft face and her hands that held the espresso cup so delicately. She explained that the tribe's benefactors eventually united and formed a Swiss bank account, along with the creation of a formal brotherhood to help fellow European members of the cult become able to make the journey, no matter what their financial condition. The tribe remained healthy and fed from this brotherhood, and the brothers were able to make the treacherous journey under cover to encounter the stone. Some had already lived well past their life expectancies and were considered by many back in their homeland to be the picture of youth, vim, and vigor.

"You were away at school in Switzerland during part of this time then."

"Yes, I was. In the end, the instructors all said I was an exceptionally bright student but it was a slow start at first, though that would not be unusual considering my background. My benefactor provided the schools with a false identity for me. I also attended finishing school, so customs and etiquette are part of my training as well."

That accounted for her ability to be a chameleon in different social settings. Another clue unlocked.

While she talked about the past, I thought about the future during her periods of silence. I wondered about Bruno, where he could be. I also wondered about why I seemed to be so suddenly obsessed with this woman and why it took so long for me to realize it. Maybe my head injury knocked some sense into my skull, or maybe out of it, depending on the point of view.

After the visit to the café we strolled along the beach back to the house, holding hands, with silence our companion.

Nothing more was shared during the rest of the evening even while Nonna served another huge meal on the porch. This time it was a wonderful dish of shellfish and pasta. After the meal, the usual guests and friends of our host and hostess retired inside to the kitchen to smoke and drink. I, for once, preferred to lay on my cot on the porch. I lay there on my back, the light shining from the kitchen table inside the house to end up over the ceiling of the porch. Noise, conversations I didn't understand, movements of the shadows of people under the lights, all played out across the ceiling above my bed.

Like a great silent film I watched the distorted images move with the sound and laughter that they made. The sound and images on the ceiling created an abstract dreamlike story to me, and I watched in complete fascination, guided and curated by the several glasses of wine that I had had during dinner.

I lost several hours due to sleep. I awoke, who knows when, in the night by a voice. It was Tika. "Come lay next to me. I need to talk to you."

There was no hesitation on my part. We lay and faced each other and caressed under the glow of the moon that flowed from outside of her window to cover her bed. We didn't look at each other, we just held on. She did indeed have more to say.

She took up where she had left off at the café.

"I returned after my schooling only to find the Old Woman slowly dying from a jungle infection. She took me into ritual very quickly, transferring the rest of her spiritual knowledge telepathically by a joining of our third eyes. It was sudden knowing of the mysticism involved with the stone."

I didn't say anything. I only listened and took it all in.

She continued her tale, and the darkness of the room, coupled with the warmth of her body, caused me to enter that twilight zone between sleep and wakefulness, that grey area, that almost dreamlike state, where my own mental visions of her past were being narrated by her voice.

When the Old Woman died soon after, Tika, with her new found knowledge and contacts from the outer world and financial benefactors, began to set up a series of night clubs and modern businesses in order to create a hidden empire of wealth and power. Along with appropriate money laundering, she would often make journeys to check on her holdings in other countries, going under the auspices of General Advisor to the clubs under the corporate structure. But she would always return like a moth to the flame, back to the tribe and bask in the glow of the green idol. Here she would stay, sometimes for weeks, strengthening the cult through ritual. Her wealthy backers would return periodically to go native, as well to take part in the secret ritual and regain youth and strength under the stone's influence.

It was at one of these life strengthening rituals that Bruno Durst broke in.

Once the stone had been stolen from Tika, she had her contacts and protectors try their best to track the stone down. The contact in Singapore failed. Other attempts were made. Without the stone to place in the eye of the idol periodically, the idol would weaken even more, eventually losing its power altogether – hence, the importance of returning the stone back to the cult. If Tika cannot regain it, then the struggle shifts to others to reclaim the stone and take the power contained within back to the statue. The stone, once placed back in the eye of the idol, would give the guardian instant knowledge of the ancient keepers, and would make the holder a new queen of the cult, as only women can have this effect, as only women are the life givers.

I had to admit, in my dreamlike state, that this was as fantastic as anything I had ever heard. Whether I believed all of this hocus pocus business didn't matter. I only knew that she believed it, as did everyone involved.

This is what made the journey so dangerous.

CHAPTER 33--HOSPITAL

Bruno awoke to the sounds of strange tongues wagging in the distance. Female tongues mixed with chirping birds and the distant sound of the sea. He tried to focus, but all he could make out was white everywhere. He knew he was laying on his back, or was he? Disoriented, he tried to rise only to fall back, to rise again, fall back again, keeping a rhythmic beat with the distant waves he heard.

"I need to turn my head." Instant pain shot through his neck and spine. He was just now noticing an intense burning on the right side of his face. His legs were held down, trapped, his right arm was positioned above him held by a pulley contraption. He couldn't help himself at this point. He cried softly, but his tears didn't roll down his cheeks. They were trapped, encased in tight goggles that held his head and eyes in place. All the while, there was a constant burning on the right side of his body, a low level steady sensation that slowly ate away at his sanity.

Feeling boxed and imprisoned, he tried to shriek and fight against his confines. He couldn't make any sound beyond a gurgle, and every movement brought waves of pain, forcing him to try to close his eyes.

Nothing showed anything but white. Feeling less pain with the slowness of movement, he turned his head toward the sound of the sea. Everything remained white, but for a sliver of hazy blue. The sound of the birds was coming from that sliver. Slowly as his focus grew stronger he realized he was looking out an open window to the sea.

The sea called to him, wanting him to join with it, to sink and die, but not to die. Instead to stop breathing and float in a gossamer existence, a jellyfish, letting the tides determine his fate. The tides did his breathing for him and he let his lungs obey their frothy timing.

A sweet serenity overcame Bruno. He was beginning to feel at peace finally. Sweet sleep offered sweet surrender.

Or so he imagined.

A clang of metal on metal, a sharp breaking of glass shredding its deadly talons on the ground.

Bruno turned his head towards the intrusion. A white figure with wings on her head had a tray of something that looked like food while another similar figure bent to the floor with a white washcloth wiping and scrubbing. A slight splash of color interrupted the winged creature's scrubbing, but quickly dissolved until the entire scene was white again.

The primary winged creature spoke something Bruno didn't understand but that didn't stop the creature from trying to shove something into his mouth. Before he could bite or spit, another winged creature grabbed his free arm and shoved a needle into it. The quick jab brought him to awareness.

A quick focus gave him realization that these creatures were some sort of religious order of nuns and he was trapped in a hospital.

"Oh great religious fools who worship an invisible lover," he murmured.

A reflexive scowl at his benefactors brought a quick jolt of pain.

A rancid sounding sort of German emerged from the larger older head winged woman. "You are in Sicily. You are badly hurt and burned. We love and will take care of you in our holy father's name."

"Holy hell, what father would let his son burn? What father would let his son be beaten cruelly by those that didn't understand his importance and what he had to offer to the world? Jesus and I have a lot in common so it seems," Bruno thought to himself.

Cleansing and a return to civility and order. What is wrong with that? And that is what I need and crave.

Time dissolved for Bruno. A darkening pierced by pins of light seemed to appear. "This must be night."

He could feel whatever medicine he had been injected with start to take over his sensibilities and whatever consciousness he had for the moment. Throughout the following days he would feel gentle hands begin turn him on his side, bathe him with sponges and touch him caressingly, sometimes giving him warm pleasure. Other times he would become lucid enough to think to himself how these whores for Jesus must enjoy touching a man and then bask in their own redemption, pleading forgiveness but never forgetting.

Day into night, night into day.

Bruno awoke.

The long dream was over. He sat up but not without discomfort. That didn't matter. He smiled against his pain as he was able to use his good arm to raise himself long enough to swing his legs to the floor. His right arm was free now, wrapped in loose bandages, his legs were movable and strong enough to stand. His balance was off and he slid a bit as he managed to finally get up and brace himself against the hospital bed and slowly walk towards the door to his room.

Pausing at the foot of the bed to catch his breath, he took in his surroundings. The dream was now real. There was the window to the right of his bed where he could hear the sea and birds, and see the sky. The rest of the room was all washed white, blanketed by the incoming light of a warm sun.

A sink and full length mirror were in the corner by the door. He slowly made his way towards the mirror. He stood, looked at his reflection then shrieked and collapsed.

He awoke again some time later.

He seemed to remember standing and walking only to see a grotesque vision of himself. Half of a bandaged face, a shriveled arm, something from a horror film greeted his vision.

He was in bed again and as he started to move once more, the winged women came back in grumbling and speaking their wagging tongues.

He spoke in German since they seemed familiar with his language.

"What has happened to me?"

"You were pulled from the terrible shipwreck and explosion. You were brought here along with other patients. Most have gone. You are one of the last to leave. You are also lucky to be alive."

"Was I conscious?"

"Barely, but enough to tell us to send a message by wire saying you would contact a certain person when you were able. They were also informed that you had been injured"

Bruno gave out a small sigh of relief. "How long have I been here?"

"A month, sir." Bruno scowled slightly. A month! At least his message had gotten through.

"May I see my chart please. I want to know my injuries."

The big winged head woman had the face of a clam left to shrivel on hot pavement but appeared dutiful enough, with a supposedly compassionate well practiced grin. "Here it is." She grabbed the chart from the end of the bed and handed it to Bruno. "I know your case quite well."

Bruno studied the chart and listened. The nurse began to tell what he could slightly remember, and then only to remember it as she spoke.

An explosion, fire, smoke, hitting the water, being buoyed by the floating debris, fire on the water burning spilled oil from the ship, intense heat from the burning oils buoyed by icy waters. Apparently he had been pulled free by someone and placed in a lifeboat, his skin turning dark and charred against the oily flare from the fires. No memories beyond pain except for the otherworldly feeling of being transported to a higher place then poked with needles and losing all contact with reality

As he focused against the flood of images coming back he also focused on the chart he was handed. He rose again, this time helped by the old Sister, and demanded she go over his injuries on the chart while he stared at himself naked in the mirror. He looked himself over while the great winged headed sister, Jesus concubine, whore, queen dyke of this lesbos community, whatever the hell this woman was, filled in the blanks of his misery.

Bruno became a bit dazed as he was read his injuries as interpreted by the stocky wing headed woman. The chart and explanations included loss of all toes on his right foot, his arm burned and malformed creating a lobster hand, the right side of his face melted and spotted like an old dead sun grilled Dalmatian left to die in a desert. His hair was sparse and a bit wiry, what was left of it. What he did have left of his beautiful blonde thick mane of hair resembled something one would find on a balding hedgehog. His right eye had been boiled away like an overdone poached egg replaced with a crusty film, eyesight gone.

Bruno became sick and overwhelmed, retching into the sink in front of the mirror, barely able to stand. Large chunks of his ego, along with bile filled the sink. It was then in the realization of his loss of vanity that he realized he had just become angrier and more than deadly. "Anger is an energy," he repeated to himself again and again. "I will use my loss to prevent my enemies' gain." He felt as if his head would explode.

He made his way back to his bed and was helped by the nun to swallow a handful of pills. He slept once more, sensing day turn into night and back again, more than once, occasionally broken up by more pills and feeding, but never becoming truly awake.

One day he finally awoke still hurting with a sensation of cool fire, but coherent.

He became aware of the head nun taking his pulse.

"Can you remove my bandages yet?" His throat groaned against non-use.

"Yes."

"Then do so and take me to the mirror," he demanded of the head nurse. Her smile cracked for a second but his voice was commanding enough for her to obey.

"It would be a good idea to leave the bandages on a bit longer, plus you should have some ministry and counseling first. The shock could be damaging to you mentally. I need to pray for your soul"

"Too late," Bruno laughed so loud the head sister stepped back.

"Unwrap me now!"

She slowly unwrapped Bruno's bandages, mumbling in what he thought was Latin and leaving his scarred flesh free and exposed. He felt a sharp burning and discomfort once the flesh was open to the air, but the pain quickly subsided to the point where he felt he could feed from the sensation, feed his anger, give that anger direction and focus.

She gingerly undressed and unwrapped him where he stood, and as his robe fell he admired his new form, although in a revulsive manner. "Very good my stern nun. I look as horrible as you described I would. Gimpy foot, claw like arm, partly spotted forehead and scalp, cyclops eye." He began to laugh. At first a small chuckle then that chuckle gave birth to a torrent of wild tumultuous laughter. The nun recoiled from this outburst at first, but then came forward to hold him while his body still trembled in the aftermath of his vision.

As he steadied himself once more, the nun stepped back again. He stared at his mutilated body and he felt renewed. "It took a bit of doing," he said to himself. "But I have succeeded as usual. The explosion left me jarred but not confused. My injuries that would be tragic by normal human understanding have given me power and the strength of will. I have become different than other men physically, but then I have always been different than other men in every other way. And always for the better. There is no change."

Bruno moved slightly and wobbled a bit, and continued "The loss of my right foot's toes gives me a slight hobble to my walk now. Damn. Gimpy Boy, they would call me back in school if I were there again. I will fool all my enemies like I fooled those idiot schoolboys. I will stick paper into my shoe to take the place of my toes. I will keep my right hand in my pocket while my left hand becomes stronger. I will wear an eyepatch which should give me the look of sophistication I require. As for the rest…"

Bruno gave a slight pause in his reverie as he realized that his injuries had transformed his face in becoming a close resemblance to his masquerade mask of the skulled faced red death. "Nurse, I require facial makeup, eyeliner, concealer, mascara, facial powder."

She became stern. "We have nothing from the devil's paint box."

"I suppose for now I am gifted with what I have." Bruno paused for a second while he covered himself and sat down in the lone chair by the bed.

"Tell me about what you found when you found me."

The nurse stood in front of him and gazed upward to recount the events that had been told to her by the rescuers. "The people that brought you here brought many others, plus many bags and suitcases. Many of those that were rescued with you have passed on to glory with our father and savior Jesus Christ."

Bruno smiled inwardly laughing at this foolish nonsense.

She told him that with the rescue of so many wearing costumes, it was difficult to tell the identities of them all.

"Saints preserved, you were brought here wearing a Satan cloth. Because you had the swastika on the front of the costume you wore, we gave you special priority." She looked downward as if not wanting rebuke. Clearly the Nationalists had succeeded in controlling this outpost.

"We were lucky with you. You had several items in what was left of your costume that we could salvage and save. You had enough identification on you to tell us what your identity was, along with what other items you had on you at the time."

Bruno's eyebrows lifted.

"We found a curious green stone that you were carrying. It was so carefully wrapped that we knew you must treasure it."

Bruno's throat started to swell up.

"We saved it and will return it to you along with other personals that we found on you."

Tears began to appear in Bruno's eyes. If he had believed in a god he would have given thanks. He got up slowly and returned to his bed in thought.

The head nun noticed his gratitude and wanting to take advantage of it, left the room only to return with a much younger nun holding a large container.

"Vas is los?" Bruno thought to himself while looking over the soft form of the young nun. "We hope you are pleased with what we have done." The young nun smiled shyly at Bruno and turned away from the slightly disapproving frown of the older nun.

The young nun then opened the box and presented the contents to Bruno. It was a complete SS officer's uniform, complete with his stolen identity. "We were able to find a cap to match."

"I supposed you will tell me that some beautiful boots were found as well."

"No sir."

"Aw, that is too bad, mein little flower."

She quickly responded "You were still wearing your boots when you were brought here. We have repaired and polished them for you. Mother Superior has also supplied an eyepatch and hand glove to hide your injuries."

Bruno grinned, and was genuinely pleased with this little virgin. As he grinned, she turned bright red, turned her head down, but her eyes came up to look at him. He suddenly realized what he must look like to her. "I am not so much to gaze upon right now."

"Oh, but I am not concerned with outwardly appearances. I can tell you have great strength and courage."

"This little girl has a great insight, and so pretty as well," Bruno thought.

"I can also tell you have a great hurt." she said

Bruno's smile turned cold and froze.

The old nun frowned. "Sister, you have displeased our patient. Leave at once."

Bruno stared the young nun's form up and down as she quickly left the room.

He thought for a second and turned to the head nun. "Don't be so hard on her, she is still young and so inexperienced. You must tell me wise nun. How were you able to get my uniform so pristine? How did this come about? Are you all sorceresses here?"

The head nun laughed, then gave a direct look at Bruno. "I understand you, just as my younger Sister did. Only I know you are not so innocent. I also know that if I do not please you, there is a chance that we will be visited upon by forces greater than we can stand. So, I give you the wealth of our crafts. The sisters here are expert weavers. The wreck produced many items to give our fellow sisters much material to use to recreate what would be needed by our patients."

Bruno began to admire this whore for god for her ingenuity.

"Wreckage washed up hourly on our shores. Village fishermen and local divers contributed shipwrecked items and materials towards our monastery, as all good Christians do with items they no longer have use for. Among those items were many German uniforms in various stages of condition, along with many personal items. I realized you as a person of importance, due to your identification papers on you."

"You are truly miracle workers." Bruno hesitated at saying the word "sister." This was no sister of his. "You have done a quite an amazing job; only may I give you some suggestions about this uniform of mine? It is already well done but a few slight touches are missing to make it perfect."

"Of course."

"I see you had my identification papers to place my name properly, but my insignia is not quite right. I was recently promoted to a much higher rank that has yet to show up on any papers I have. It was all so sudden, I received the news just before I boarded, so there was no time to make the transfer of upgrades. I was but a captain, but I had a field commission given to me, that of a colonel. Well deserved I might add."

The nun smiled patiently. "Of course it shall be done. As I said, we have resources. Now here, you need to take this for your pain." The head nun set up the fix for Bruno to take his meds. He smiled as he gladly offered up his left arm to sacrifice.

As Bruno took the injection he closed his eyes and listened to the seabirds from his bedside window. How peaceful it was to plan with this gentle sound of surf and birds. They seemed to be whispering ideas to him. Ideas that told him what to do next, how to do it, and when to do it. He smiled as he slept.

He woke up cheerfully, more than he had been in quite a long time, no dreams to haunt him. After a tranquil hour a breakfast was served by the young sister with both parties exchanging smiles. Just as Bruno was relaxing, confident in his next few moves, the morning sun began to get obscured by incoming clouds moving across the horizon from the sea, and chilly winds started to blow in. This slight discomfort actually pleased him. Bruno soaked in his unease. "This is what I need, this is best for me to plan. Comfort makes me weak, I need the jags and rough edges of life to keep me alive."

He glanced at the uniform hanging neatly on the hook on the white wall of his room. "Such a good job." Bruno smiled and wafted into sleep once again.

In his dreams, he realized what his plans needed to be in order to get the job done. Once he got the stone back to his ancestral home, there would be quite a sizable fortune waiting for him.

How proud his father would be if his father was witness. His father. His very strict cruel father. The bullies may have beat him on the schoolyard and his father would beat him at home, but there was a difference. While he hated the bullies, he wanted his father to love him.

He grew angry as he fought with this past realization.

At that moment the young sister entered his room to remove his breakfast tray and bring him his pain pills. Bruno's anger ceased as he stared at this beautiful penguin.

"Good morning my dear." He smiled as a lover would the morning after.

"Good morning, sir." The young nun turned beet red. She lowered her eyes, only to lift them again, to stare with a hint of lustful urgency into his eyes.

"Do you get lonely here? You are so young and seem so passionate."

"You embarrass me sir. I save my passion for the Lord."

"Excuse me then. You must pardon me. You seem so vibrant, so full of this passion. I admire you for the strength of your will."

"It is not so easy. Sometimes…sometimes…I have want for the warmth that only a man might bring."

She quickly turned and placed the breakfast tray on a cart. Bruno just as quickly grabbed her hand and sat up.

He pulled her to him. She started to protest but that was only in reflex, and reflex quickly dissolved into want. There was pain as Bruno took her in his arms as he sat up and she fell into his embrace. The heat of the moment eased his discomfort and the nun became as a young girl begging to be taken for the first time.

He was able to stand with his injuries not stopping her from grappling him. "Clumsy thing," he thought. She groped him uneasily as he lifted her dress only to find no undergarments beneath. "Religious trollop, hypocritical tart," Bruno exclaimed, pulling away. "I imagine with that crucifix around your neck you have Jesus every night."

The young nun pulled and tried to pull away in shock but not before Bruno twisted the chain that held her crucifix around her neck and held her tightly to him.

He was standing now, towering over this scared young dove of mercy, pulling the chain of her crucifix tighter and tighter. She didn't seem to know what to do at first, should she try to free herself or strike him? Her teachings were against violence, so she only tried to break from the choking chain that Bruno only pulled tighter.

She fell to her knees, turning blue. "Colorful young girl, aren't you?" She could make no noise, except for a loud panting of fear mixed with lust, ending with only a slight gargle as spittle and her tongue were forced from her mouth by the crushing of her larynx. She went limp, let out a gurgle, her eyes bulged for mercy.

Bruno, standing above her in his white hospital gown reflected the irony of the situation and realized this painted quite a scene. The young dead nun seemed to bow before him pleading for mercy while he stood above her dressed in white and offering her a passage to eternal afterlife. As if to accent this artistic pose, the morning sun streamed in muted light, casting rays from the window to descend over his shoulder down on the dead repentant nun. Michelangelo would be filled with envy.

After taking a moment to pleasure in the scene, Bruno dropped the girl, stepped over her to hobble to the uniform teasing him from its lone hook. He dressed himself slowly, taking care to keep the greenstone securely in his breast pocket though there was great pain with every movement. Finally he was done completing his uniform to regulations. He took one last look in the mirror. "Poor face, such beautiful features it once had. Now it is a mess." He adjusted the eyepatch the head nun had given him earlier and fiddled with the glove on his right hand until it covered his deformity properly.

He raided the young nun's pockets, finding the bottle of pain pills, then took her shroud that was crumpled beside her on the floor and looked out of the hospital room window. Excellent, he was on the ground floor, with only a small but steep incline to deal with for his escape. Using the shroud, he tied one end to some plumbing just below his window, and carefully went over the window ledge, lowering himself as much as he could towards the ground. The shroud ripped suddenly, leaving him with a short drop of a foot or so and he was free. Gritting his teeth from the pain incurred by the drop and still holding what was left of the shroud, he limped his way stealthily into some bushes by the corner of the nunnery and soon found himself on a coastal road, the nunnery fading in the distance through the trees behind him.

He limped for a while and found an old broken bare tree limb that he was able to fashion as a walking cane, enabling him to move quicker and more naturally. As he continued to walk he wrapped the torn shroud around his still healing skull. The road he traveled was bordered on his left by a steep cliff, dropping several hundred feet to a rocky beach, with a bit of an angry surf crashing against large stones. There were clouds moving in that quickly covered the sun. and not knowing where he was, he sensed that if he kept to this road he would either encounter another traveler or a village.

He did not have to wait long. Up the dirt road a figure emerged. The entire sky was dark now with all objects turning grey, and with an annoying drizzle in the air. The figure approached, and as it did, it separated into different objects and clarified itself into the form of a rather gaunt old man and a young boy of about eight riding in an overstuffed buckboard full of hay, pulled by a slightly swaybacked horse. There were some tools attached to the side of the wagon, including a shovel and a pitchfork. Bruno took all of this information in and smiled, made sure he had covered the wounded portion of his face with what was left of the shroud.

The old man approached on the dirt road to the left of Bruno. The old man pulled in the reins and the horse came to a halt.

"Hello sir," he smiled in German, obviously noticing the details of Bruno's uniform. Bruno returned the smile. "What might bring a high-ranking official such as you out in this damp weather?"

"I have been spending time at the wonderful monastery up the road. I was injured very badly, but now I have been released."

"Please be careful sir, the winds on this cliff can be very strong this time of year. Take care!"

"Thank you, I shall take care."

"I am sorry to bother you with small talk, sir, but my grandson and I live alone and don't get a chance to visit with new people."

Bruno continued to smile as he strode to the side of the wagon. "I admire your selection of tools."

The old man turned his head towards Bruno. "I may be a poor shepherd, but I do pride myself on my tools."

"May I look at this?"

"Of course, sir! It would be my pleasure!"

Bruno unlatched the pitchfork, held it close to him and tested the prongs with his fingers. "Most sharp. This will be suitable, quite suitable." The sudden cold wind blew his words away from the shepherd's ears.

The shepherd suddenly spoke. "Good sir, my curiosity has overtaken me. Why is such a personage as yourself wandering the high cliff roads?"

Bruno walked back to the front of the shepherd's buckboard, the pitchfork still in his hands. He waited a second or two, leaned the pitchfork against the side of the wagon, tucked his cap under his arm then removed the torn shroud from his face.

The young grandson instinctively gave a loud gasp and nestled into his grandfather's side at the site of Bruno's partially melted features.

"To steal your clothes and the wagon."

Without warning or waiting for an expression from the old man, Bruno grabbed the pitchfork and struck him with the blunt handled end knocking the old man out of his seat and onto his back on the ground, as Bruno jabbed at the shepherd's face and eyes with the prongs from the pitchfork. The young boy recoiled in horror, covering his face and crying moanfully.

Bruno ordered the old man. "You will remove all of your clothing and give it to me or I will throw the boy off the cliff." Bruno let his bleeding victim up as the old man did as he was told.

Standing naked in the brisk air beside the buckboard, the old man shivered, his grandson continuing to cry.

Bruno quickly moved, skewered the old man fatally through the gut with the pitchfork, lifted him up like a bale of hay and shoved him over to the cliff and over the side, the old man groaning all the while in pain and terror as he was flipped from the cliffside towards the rocks below.

The boy stopped crying, and anger prompted him to leap out of the buckboard into Bruno's side as Bruno watched the old shepherd hit the rocks below. Without hesitation Bruno kicked the boy in the stomach, caught him as he bent over and lifted the boy like a football over the edge to join his grandfather on the surf bleached rocks below.

Without wasting a second, Bruno stripped, put the old shepherd's clothes on and complained that the clothes were too tight. He pulled the shepherd's hat down over his face to hide his wounds. He took the greenstone from his former clothes and put it in his pocket. Never will he not have it on his person he thought to himself. He took a saddlebag from the carriage of the buggy and while placing his uniform in it neatly, he discovered a good wad of cash. "Guess the old boy was going to do some trading. Too bad." He unhitched the horse and its bindings, released the cart, and pushed it over the edge of the cliff to spread its contents over the broken bodies below.

Taking the horse by the reins, Bruno gingerly lifted himself onto the back of the beast. "Now I look like a typical inhabitant of this island."

He turned the horse around and headed back the way the old man and the boy had come. At the first intersection in the dirt road, he turned inward towards the center of the island.

"I know enough of this island to realize that the Germans are covertly setting up communications here. Perhaps I will be lucky enough to come across a small town that will serve my needs for contacting the outside world."

By mid-afternoon he came to the edge of a settlement consisting of a half a dozen of small structures centered around a square. In it were a few shops without much activity. At the center of the village he noticed what he had been looking for. "Ah, perfect," he thought.

There was a small park at the center of the village, surrounded on one side by what looked like an official building of some sort, while on the other side, on a corner adjacent to the park was a friendly looking drinking house and inn. "Perfect."

There were vehicles outside of the inn, and by their clothing, a couple of workmen wandered out, grabbed some wire, and wandered back inside. "This is exactly right."

Bruno got off of his horse and tied it to the waiting rail outside, grabbed the saddlebag and strolled inside the inn. He was greeted by a long wooden bar, with a bevy of happy looking bottles behind a rather unhappy looking shriveled woman. The rest of the room consisted of well used wooden tables and chairs, with some well used old gentlemen scattered about quietly playing cards, smoking enough to look as if something was afire and with full glasses containing various liquids. There was a dark pallor to the place except for one area to the right of the bar. A couple of workmen were working on what seemed were telephone lines. Bruno continued to smile at this as he enquired of the old woman behind the bar as to what was going on.

"Germans," she grunted in Italian. "Germans want to talk." That was all that Bruno needed. "I would like to book a room upstairs," Bruno demanded in Italian.

"So sorry sir," she replied as she took a good look for the first time at what showed of his face and noticing his slight limp, almost looked sympathetic, though Bruno thought it might crack her face to do so. He gave her the money and said he would return later for a meal. He surveyed the bar and purchased a pint of ale to take up to his room. She gave him the key and he ambled up the steep stairs behind the bar to his room.

Once inside, he let out his breath, and sipping the ale, slowly relaxed himself on the bed. The room was tiny, quaint, but quite enough for his needs, with a small chair and writing table by a lone window. It had been a busy day. He slept.

It must have been only a short while, for the grim grey sun was still looming through the window of his room.

He arose, washed up and changed from his peasant clothes back into his SS officer's uniform, and felt the better for it. He looked in the mirror and reluctantly admired his face again while adjusting his eyepatch and glove. It hurt to smile but he did anyway. He felt so good to be back in uniform, even if it was a hobbled together replica. At least he had a higher rank, a rank he deserved.

Straightening himself up in front of the mirror, he did a clipped about face and stumbled a bit towards the doorway to his room then descended the stairs with an authoritative air. All eyes turned in his direction as he banged on the corner of the bar.

"Brandy!" this time he demanded in German. The old woman behind the bar moved quickly.

"I didn't realize you were…" She stammered as she fumbled for a bottle and glass.

"That is fine. I didn't expect you to realize what I was, dressed so shabbily and out of uniform as I was before. This is to be a surprise visit"

She handed the snifter of brandy to Bruno. He raised it, sniffed delightedly, winked at the old woman and walked towards the workmen who were still installing the phone line, working now from the side of the bar down through a hatch that led to the wine cellar.

"I am to assume everything is going well?"

"Yes sir," one of the workmen said. The two other workmen looked up at Bruno, while he just smiled back. "We weren't expecting anyone from the high command so soon," One of the workmen said. "Not to worry, the reformation of the present lines will be completed in a few hours."

"I am sure they will. You look like a very efficient crew. Might I inspect the cellar?"

"Why of course, sir!" the workmen moved aside quickly as the Bruno descended the stairs to the cellar. The cellar was dank and dark, not surprisingly so, and the workmen's temporary lights cast a greenish hue where the single bulb light shone through the different bottles stacked in various racks. "You there." Bruno smiled friendly but firmly at a worker. "You will show me how this works."

"Of course," the worker sheepishly moved over to a big black box with dials and knobs and a large antenna jutting out that was held fast to a wire that ran up the ceiling of the cellar and disappeared out through a small crevice and presumably angled its way to the roof.

"This is still a new set up, but should work easily and efficiently." The workman instructed Bruno on the basic operation of the radio, describing its use and range. "It has quite a powerful signal."

"Can its signal reach, perhaps another relay station on the southern coast of Italy?"

"Quite so sir." The workman instructed Bruno on how to reach a relay station that would boost his signal and send that signal further down the line to where he wanted it to go. He also told Bruno the better times to transmit his message, owing to atmospheric and weather conditions. Night was the best, so he was advised. Bruno soaked this quick course in radio communications quite easily.

"I know that you gentlemen were not informed of my coming and I am sure I have put added pressure on your good work by being here."

"Oh, no, sir, we are quite glad that you are pleased with what we have done thus far." The lead workman's face showed a strained smile.

"Your work is better than I was expected." As Bruno said this there was a general exhalation from the crew. "I shall be happy to have access to this equipment tonight to test a transmission and show my gratitude for your labors to the high command. You have done quite wonderfully with my surprise inspection."

The workers smiled at this. "I will be happy to reward you personally and with my recommendation that you be paid double for your efforts." The workers smiles began to make them look like Cheshire Cats at this mention.

Bruno knew that the workers, being local people, would be happy to get any extra money they could.

The foreman of the wiring project held his cap in hand and spoke with a bit of nervousness to Bruno. "Sir, on behalf of my workmen we are simple people, happy with what we have. This war does us no good. We live from day to day, season to season, no matter who is in charge, so why should we not help whom we can for whatever might profit us the most?"

Bruno stopped tinkering with the radio device and slowly turned to the head workman. The head workman took a step back, not knowing what Bruno might say.

Bruno only smiled. "I admire your ethics." Bruno reached in his pocket for some of the cash that he had procured from the saddlebag of the long dead old farmer. "This is just a sample of my generosity. Buy your crew a round at the bar upstairs."

A general ease cascaded across the room. "Alright, let's get this place organized for our visiting officer!" the head foreman barked. A quick shuffling had the wiring and set up of the transmitter finished in moments time, accompanied with whistling and happy humming.

Bruno thought over what the head foreman had just told him. "They will work at their jobs no matter who is in charge, as the war does them no good. These Sicilians figure this is a good way to test the system with me handling it, so of course they let me use it. Any questions over who I am has been quickly resolved by my uniform. Gullible greedy peasants. They do serve their purpose on occasion."

By the time the workmen had bought a few rounds of beer upstairs, and were happily slurring their words in song, Bruno had already contacted his destined radio connections.

Laying out his needs and further instructions via radio and telegraph, he rewarded himself by meandering upstairs to the main pub to join his somewhat drunken ignorant conspirators for a few pints, then toddled off to his upstairs room.

He sat at the small table by the window in his otherwise sparse room. Procuring a pencil and some paper from the drawer in the table, he began to make notes.

Bruno schemed on what he would do upon his return to the family castle. He must do it stealthily, for the castle grounds are surely being watched by the Nazis seeking their deserted renegade brother in the SS, or by anyone else seeking favor and a possible reward for his capture.

He thought of his family servants. Those amazingly loyal servants. They will set him up in the garden's nursery green house, where he will pose as a gardener. Under the nursery greenhouse is a root cellar, where he used to like to hide and read as a child in the warm summer months. It is a big enough space to set up radio communications. If anyone decides to visit the house, he will be in disguise, easy enough since his features have changed, and the servants will say he has not returned. And though he will be disguised as a gardener, he will be giving the orders.

He paused and quietly gave thanks to his amazingly loyal servants. The estate and the castle grounds had been in his distinguished and respected family for centuries. The family servants and groundskeepers were multigenerational and owed their livelihoods to the House of Durst, having served his family without questions for generations. Their loyalty is true. Bruno smiled confidently at this thought.

Heavy drops of rain began to beat rhythmically against his window as if keeping time to some swing tune swung by Satan's All-Demon Orchestra. The occasional flash of lightning followed by a thundering cymbal crash startled Bruno, but just as quickly his thoughts turned to his uncle. The income of the estate was presently being generated by the war profits of the family factory, and that was being run by his father's brother. Again Bruno smiled. Though his uncle knew of Bruno's plans, he could be trusted as well. His uncle and father, though they were brothers, detested each other, and only agreed on carrying on the family name with efficiency.

Everything seemed in place for the next step.

He got up slowly, turned out the lamp on the desk and made his way towards the bed. He fell on his back on the mattress and began to drift into the satisfactory sleep that only a few pints of beer can bring.

As he slowly went under, his mind wandered from his easily won communications from earlier that evening. The chorus of drunken Sicilians grew louder from downstairs and along with the storm outside, provided a Hellenistic soundtrack to his thoughts of accomplishment that evening.

Bruno was thinking in a half haze now. "Money will indeed be wired to me through the nearby bank, I will be able to settle up with the locals to help keep them quiet, and then I can hire a boat to take me to the mainland."

As Bruno passed out slowly, his thoughts and ideas passed with him. He thought about his future operation with meeting the plane on the train through the Italian Alps. Bruno chuckled, half asleep, knowing he can't afford to go through any German borders with any questionable identification, it would be too risky, for his stolen papers would surely be noticed by this time. The plane was formerly his father's, and would be flown by his family's private pilot, another faithful family servant, bless his heart. Bruno would be flown to the estate without worry of passing through any customs or demand for his papers. Lovely.

"They can steal my body but they can't steal my spirit." Bruno whispered to himself in the darkness. "I will survive. I need to go home, to eat, to replenish, to survive, to question, to find strength. Thanks that I have support from those who worked for my father. Loyalty from the few remaining slaves, the bastards. Saved by bastards. What an epitaph. The plane should meet me in the longest stretch of the train's ascent into the Alps. Perfect. A simple climb from the roof of the train and I'm gone."

The harsh wind brought another window rattling gust of rain against the lone window of his room. One last smile found him mumbling through the visions of his dreams. "I did it! The sacred stone is mine!"

CHAPTER 34--THE NEXT MOVE

I stood looking at the sky, so open and free with its clouds barely resting, then looked at the water and felt a bit anxious when I spied a dead creature belched from the froth of the life liquid. I felt a bit beached myself. I had had the happiest most carefree days that I can remember since I was a kid wanting to join the carnival. If I wasn't so damned restless, I would have wanted to stay here forever.

I had an itchy feeling that I needed to be somewhere but fast. Walking along the beach kicking the sand, I made my way over to the village to check on any communications for me. I made my way up from the shore with my eyes squinting against the glare of the sun and slipped on a rock. The sudden jolt on my spine gave rise to my old back injury again, which in turn gave rise to old nagging anxieties. What hell has happened to my career? I had tried more than once to contact the studio with no response. Even Ha-Nee won't answer to let me know how things are at the house or if I even have a house anymore. I just can't escape the feeling that I have been cut off from my former life.

At least I have Tika, though even with so much bonding that we have done lately, even she is beginning to worry me a bit. Something about her is beginning to change, she is acting more, well, girly. Normally that would be nice, but this change is different. Her thoughts aren't as focused or as sure as they were. I haven't quite been able to figure it out, but it is as if she is reverting somehow, but to what?

These thoughts occupied my mind as I entered the café and made my way to the telegraph room. The next few minutes knocked my melancholy away. There was a wire! I had not only some money being wired to me, but a somewhat lengthy though oddly cryptic message was waiting as well.

I made my way excitedly back to the seaside cabin of our hosts where I met the wide grin of Akbar. "I see we are both most jubilant!"

"Yes, I am for sure. Where is Tika?"

"She is at the ocean playing with seashells and staring at the sea."

I immediately made for the beach, Akbar trailing.

I called her name as I saw her sitting on the beach, and she turned her head towards me, the wind catching her hair and playing with it, framing her beautiful face. She smiled as she saw me. She looked so young, so fragile for a moment. Then she seemed to straighten a bit, become mature, but still sweetly open to me.

Akbar was not far behind, and caught up to us in seconds. "My friends most glorious, what excitement is to be had?" I explained to both what I had learned.

I told them that it was time to move. I had finally gotten instructions on what I had to do. Suddenly everything seemed alright. Akbar just grinned that silly grin of his, Tika smiled a bit vacantly. I had heard from both the Colonel and Thickwilly almost back to back. They had wired some serious money to the local bank and told me what to do next. I was double dipping for profit, and at this point I didn't care what I had to do. I was just happy to have a plan of action. Tika turned to stare at the sea again, her eyes lost on the horizon, her face blank of emotion.

"Wonderful news for you! I, too, have news. I will tell you over lunch and wine!" Akbar sang. He danced merrily in the sand on the way to the cabin, singing some odd tune. Tika and I began to laugh at his antics as we followed. It brought me happiness to hear her laugh.

Once inside Nonna had a spread ready for us, with grapes, pasta and wine, while Akbar took a deep breath and announced "I am going to Lisbon, Portugal!" he grabbed a piece of bread and stuffed it in his cavernous mouth. A bit surprised, I raised my glass to toast him and asked why Lisbon.

Chunks of bread fell from his mouth as he spoke. "I have a cousin that owns a little vaudeville theater there. He says I can work as a performer with magic and miracles for six weeks. This job will me the money I need to go to the wonderful, most beautiful, I mean the really swinging United States that are in America."

"You seem to have a lot of cousins everywhere you go. Just how many cousins do you have anyway?"

"Like sands through the hourglass, so are the cousins of my life!"

Not only did I begin to believe that, but I was also beginning to think he couldn't make any kind of a statement without getting excited about it at a loud volume.

"Congratulations. Seems we both are embarking on a new adventure. When do you leave?"

"Straight away, no stopping to mess around boy, as you American hepsters say. I leave in the morning on a ferry to mainland Italy, from there I catch a ride on a freighter bound for Lisbon"

"Great. Tika and I have a bit of business to take care of on a certain train bound for Alps."

"I can only imagine what that might be," he said with a knowing smile. "I know of your quest."

A moment of seconds' silence for reflection was broken by Akbar.

"Oh, yes, when you are finished we can meet in Lisbon for celebration!"

He leaned over conspiratorially towards me. "When you are done with your mission, we can meet at the theater. I will produce exit visas and passports for all of us. We will all three be able to board the next ship to New York!"

"How the hell can you be so sure? It is not going to be easy to do what you say."

"I am a magician!" he said this with a grand flourishing of his arms towards the heavens. I must admit, I was beginning to almost believe him. If it worked out, this would be his greatest trick of all.

We all had a great laugh, downed a good bottle of vino, and stumbled off to hit the rack with smiles on our faces. Tika was wrapped in my arms all night.

When I woke up the next morning Akbar was gone. Scratching randomly, and with Tika still sleeping, I stumbled into the main dining area. Nonna and Babbo were already there having a breakfast of eggs, fruit, and coffee.

I said good morning, but it came out "g'sh maun." After a few gulps of coffee to clear my throat I related the news I had received the previous day, and that I was a bit disturbed about how to get to the rendezvous with a certain train on the mainland. They both smiled as Nonna exclaimed "Akbar is not only one magician!" They mentioned their underground connections, and promised they would be able to get what ever travelling papers we needed in time.

Letting Tika continue to sleep, I took one last long walk on the beach. I stopped off at the bank to make a connection to withdraw some money that I had had wired. Walking back, the balmy breeze in my hair, I realized how worried I was about Tika. Her childish little girl behavior was becoming more distinct, but still hard to pin down exactly. She was just sitting and staring into nothing more and more, and when she was lucid, she would joke and giggle, and be somewhat out of character with the Tika I knew before the connection to the stone was broken.

When I entered the house again from my walk, Nonna smiled and told me not to worry. "Babbo has gone to get what you need-a for the next day. We have much famiglia here."

Sure enough, that afternoon, Babbo showed up with travelling papers for both of us, and produced a box camera. Tika was sitting and staring at nothing on the table by this time.

"What is the soul-stealing camera for Babbo?" I kidded. Anything to distract me from wondering about Tika's condition.

"Dis is-a for the pass-a-ports."

"Great! Babbo and Nonna you are both amazing – I will repay your kindness someday, not to worry." Tika looked up and smiled sweetly.

"OK," Babbo shouted. "Say formaggio!" I had barely enough time to slick back my hair as the camera went off.

"Hokay sweet stuff, now you." Babbo pointed the camera at Tika, but now all she could muster was a moon faced expression, devoid of emotion. The camera clicked again.

He happily trotted off with a slam of the screen door to wherever his underground connection might be.

That evening he showed back up with passports and everything we needed for the next leg of this journey.

It was a journey into consequences unknown.

CHAPTER 35--ALPINE SPRING

Click clack, click clack. Two railroad tracks. One going forward, the other one coming back, trains passing me going back as I move forward giving me a dizzier feeling than I already had. Tika was asleep with a slight stirring as she snuggled closer to me. The papers for Tika and me had worked perfectly through customs. There was a tense moment or two, but nothing serious. Tika was quiet as usual. I reached in my pocket and felt my white knight chess piece wrapped in a cloth that Nonna had given me. This small object was giving me strength, reminding me to focus on what had to be done. Get the greenstone, not just for the compensation from the Colonel and Thickwilly, but for Tika's safety. If a woman ever cast a spell over a man, she had one on me.

    We both sat together in the coach of the train, resting from a rather exhausting trip so far. I was dressed in an average looking but ill fitted suit, while Tika was doing her best to look conservative in a light blue jacket and skirt. She could have worn a potato sack and she would still be stunning. We had made a connection in Salo, an amazingly beautiful resort by a large lake and were heading up into the Italian Alps, which was also a headquarters for Mussolini and his thugs. As nice as the setting was, I couldn't stand to be distracted. I knew who I was looking for. He was on this train. The Colonel had told me where to find him. He hadn't have told me much, given all the run ins I had with this character before. He was a certain Bruno Durst, and was wearing a Nazi SS officer's uniform. There were several Nazi and Italian soldiers on this train, as it carried both them and civilians through the slightly melting northern Alps of Italy. The sun shone brightly through whatever windows did not have their shades drawn down. Even so, the sun's rays reflected like an array of spotlights bouncing from snowbank to mountainside to hanging ice crystals across the countryside.

    I continued to reflect on the odd communication that I had with my two benefactors. I recalled the Colonel's wire about "get stone", and strangely Marion sent another telegram with two words. "Kill Tika." I felt as if I had too much to think.

    The German soldiers scattered through the car were of a lower rank and I could only guess that the higher-ranking officers were in the staterooms. Bruno had to be in one of them naturally. All I had to do was haunt the passageway of the staterooms and hope Bruno would exit.

    I knew I would need some sort of leverage. I certainly couldn't just walk up to him, offer him a cigarette, then ask if he would be so good as to hand a certain trinket over. I would need a gun and some sort of opportunity to get him alone without distractions or disturbances that would alert this train of soldiers that I was attacking someone who was supposedly one of their own.

Soon fate played into my hands.

A couple of very drunk Nazis, both looking barely eighteen stumbled into our car and collapsed in the open seats in front us. Tika quickly formulated an idea.

Whispering, she told me what she wanted to do, and I rejoined in what I would do. Tika was genuinely smiling for the first time in a while. The Nazis were slumbering slightly when Tika stood up and moved forward down the aisle towards the rear of the train. Stopping next to the seats with the drunken Nazis, she pretended to stumble and slipped onto the lap of the one nearest the aisle. He quickly awoke.

She smiled, excused herself in German, he smiled and grabbed her tightly, slurring at her. His companion just snorted moodily and turned towards the window, ignoring this intrusion on his nap. From what I could make out in my rotten German, he was mumbling something about how she reminded him of his fraulein back in Munich.

They both giggled. He said something to the effect that he wanted to hold her while he slept. There was a bit of a high pitch to his voice that made him sound like a young innocent boy as he closed his eyes with a smile.

Tika kissed his cheek and his smile widened as he tilted his blonde head back and opened one blue eye.

Tika, still sitting in his lap, cooed in his ear, whilst I stood and went past her. I was ready. I went to the coupling area between cars.

Standing midcar, I had to admit I enjoyed the rustling icy air and penetrating sunlight illuminating all my surroundings. I felt alive, more refreshed than I had in a while. I felt strong. Strong enough to pull off what I envisioned. I took the few moments I had to rest my senses for what was to come.

Looking through the hazy window that separated one car from another, with only the coupling and shoddy platform barely connecting the cars, I grabbed a piece of metal outing jutting from the side of the doorway, and held on so I could observe what was going on in the car with Tika.

I stared with great interest as I watched Tika and the soldier. The scene played like a silent film, only this one was in color. I felt a bite at my heart as I watched Tika sit in the soldier's lap and try to seduce him. I had to pull my gaze away as the Nazi would lean his head in my direction, then inch my gaze back hoping he would not notice. It didn't take a lip reader to figure out what was going on.

Quiet smiles, his arm around her as she sat on his lap, his left hand on her knee playing just inside her skirt that was moving up a bit, a silly sloppy smile on his face, she kissing him around his ears, her lips moving, his smile getting wider. A slight nod of her head towards the exit of the car to where I was waiting and I could tell she was offering him a tryst in the loo just as we had talked about. He nodded in appreciation of her thoughtful cleveration.

She stood up, helping him to his somewhat wobbly knees, and led him down the aisle. I pressed myself flat as I could against the outside wall of their car as they approached, hoping to remain unseen.

As soon as I did the train made a slight curve and I saw into the next car where the conductor was making his way towards the door and me leading to the next car, with me in between. The conductor stopped to talk to a passenger when I heard a mechanical opening of the hatch to my car let loose girlish giggles and drunken Germanic guttural noises. The cars straightened back and I lost sight of the conductor. Tika and her new boyfriend entered between the cars where I was, she holding him so his back was to me.

  I moved fast, grabbing him around his neck with my arm and simultaneously relieving him of his Luger sidearm. Tika neatly squeezed his groin with a firm grip of her hand, causing the young soldier to give a forward bow to her just as she brought her knee up to his face breaking his nose with an audible snap. I struggled to hold on to the Nazi and as he flinched, the train made another slight curve, causing us both to give a slight spin, giving me the glance that showed the conductor moving ever closer to the end of the car.

  Tika noticed the conductor as well. "He is stopping again to chat," was all she said as I bashed the soldier's head into the metal grab bar attached to the steps leading from the coupling area between cars to the rushing cold bright embankment of stone and ice waiting railside.

  I let go of the soldier and Tika and I both kicked him free of the train as he emitted a surprised shout of pain as he left. He managed to hold on to a lower step and a piece of the forward car, and I watched as his feet went under one of the grinding metal wheels, neatly severing them and causing him to lose his grip, only to disappear completely under the car. The last vision I had of his face was a bloody pained mess crying up to me with eyes closed but again very childlike. He was just a young kid after all.

  "The conductor!" Tika grabbed me quick and forced me up against the bulkhead of our car, pressing her body, her lips onto mine, and grabbing my ass just as the conductor entered our space.

He laughed as he saw us and said something I didn't understand, and then went into the next car.

Tika pulled away from me slightly. "Not to worry. He only told us to be careful between cars. Someone could slip and get hurt." She smiled coquettishly as she said this. I had just beaten a kid up and kicked him under the wheels of a train. My hands were shaking, my knees felt weak, I had trouble standing on my own two feet, but I had a slight smile as well.

I escorted Tika to a seat farther back from where the other young Nazi was snoozing and drooling. Once that was done I explained to her that I needed a drink to calm my nerves for the next step. Badly. I had it figured that if Bruno came out of a stateroom, the only place he would head would be the observation lounge car at the rear of the train, so that is where I headed.

I went forward through the other cars, passed through the stateroom cars and the dining car hoping for a glimpse of my antagonist, but no luck. Entering the lounge car I did a beeline to the bar that was to the right of me, ordered a double whisky using my best sign language so I wouldn't give myself away as an American. I lit up a Lucky, and did a quick visual take of my surroundings.

The bar was a small but well stocked affair. At the far tail end of the car was a sliding door for those customers that didn't mind the cold to go out and sit on a small platform and enjoy the brisk mountain air and see and reflect on where they had been.

The observation lounge was overall a very warm inviting place with many windows wrapped around on all sides of the car offering spectacular views of the Italian alps. I glanced around checking out what people were in the car with me. There were quite a few people, civilians and both Italian and German soldiers, mostly keeping in their own groups, and speaking in low tones, being careful not to antagonize anyone. At the same time the impressive scenery reflexively made people speak in quiet voices so as to appreciate the beauty of the landscape. The room itself was filled with quarter moon shaped couches and low tables, with a waist high solid cloud of tobacco smoke drifting hazily throughout the car.

 Bright sunlight streamed blindingly occasionally, the sun peeping and hiding between the mountain peaks, then blasting its brilliance into the car.

 Some "oohs" and "aahs" could be heard, as outside the passengers could see large chunks of ice slipping and breaking free from the high slopes as the warming sun glared down at the slow melting peaks, the falling snow and ice shooting off occasional rainbows as they broke free to descend to the valley below.

 The whiskey warmed my belly, giving my head a gentle feeling of contrast against the bitter cold bright outside scene. I downed my drink and ordered another double, hoping the booze would steady my nerves a bit more. if Bruno doesn't show up in this car I was not sure what I would do.

 Gulping my drink and pantomiming an order for another, I stubbed out my Lucky in a rather clumsy fashion. Taking my fresh drink, I began to wander a bit around the car. I was feeling rather toasty at this point and noticeably weaving a tad like a bobble-headed cat when not knowing if it wants to go out a door or stay inside. I finally noticed one fellow sitting by himself at the far end of the car by the rear door to the observation platform. He was alone and apart from all others. He was wearing an SS uniform, facing away from everyone, sitting solo and nursing a bottle of Riesling, while staring out portside windows to the open expanse of labyrinthine chasms leading down to the valley below and the mountains beyond. The rest of the car was busy watching the melting iceworks of the mountain peaks on the starboard side of the train.

Moving somewhat to the side of this character to observe him better, I knew this could not be Bruno. Not the Bruno I had run into before. That Bruno was a fairly dashing sort, and if he hadn't been such a bastard and under different circumstances, he could have been in moving pictures himself.

This officer had a different name tag and a different face. A cruel withered burned face. A broken hooked nose. A mean looking scar ran down the center of his forehead to join the top of his eye socket, that eye socket covered by a small eyepatch. His scalp that was half hidden under his cap was a deep pink and black discoloration that ran over most of his mottled head, giving him a slightly Dalmatian like appearance. Leather gloves on both hands as if to hide scars. An obvious burn victim, his other injuries only accented his disfigurement. I couldn't help but to compare him to a wax soldier doll that a small child had left too close to the fireplace.

Puzzled, frustrated, and a bit wobbly, I sat in an empty seat next to his small personal table with the bottle of wine between us.

"Sterling."

I snapped to. He had spoken to me, but continued to stare at the passing view outside. I had to stare at him. His head didn't move, just his mouth.

"I noticed you the minute you entered the car. I don't have to turn my head to notice someone's presence. Especially yours."

I shifted uneasily, slopping a bit of my drink in my lap. This man had changed. He seemed so different, so much worse than before, and that was already bad.

"You have something I want and I am going to take it from you." I said this with not quite the bravado I was looking to achieve.

Something resembling a half-cocked smile hit his face. "So you think."

Silence reigned for the next few minutes. I was sitting rather uneasily, feeling the wet spot from my spilled drink slowly dry in my crotch.

"I have a gun pointed at you," I declared quietly, while shifting my hand into my pocket to direct the Luger at him through my pants

"Ah yes, I was just hoping you were glad to see me," Bruno whispered.

A waiter speaking in German interrupted our repartee and seemed to be inquiring if we were alright and if I needed a drink. Bruno answered him.

Bruno then turned his head towards me with a smirk. "Not to worry, you have another drink coming, my jungle movie friend. I must say, I find it surprising how you keep popping up. How are your films coming these days?"

I began to get distracted and to boil a bit at the same time. Right now my concern was not film, mine or anyone else's, I had to stay focused, this man was trying to throw me off the point. He knew it and so did I.

"I wouldn't know, I haven't checked in with my studio in a while."

"Tell me. If you could compare this with one of those wonderful jungle adventures you used to make, what would this adventure be most like?"

He continued to needle, and I would be a liar if I said it wasn't working. "Maybe Chapter Nine of Secret Death Squadron." My trigger finger was getting sweaty in my pants.

Bruno continued to face away from me, looking out to the valley scene below. "Do you not realize that I have a weapon as well?" His hand started to move slowly to his hip.

"Stop it. I can shoot you before you even have a chance to reach it."

He just smiled and turned his wound riddled face towards me. "Of course you would. It seems we are at an impasse. What do you suggest?"

"I suggest you hand over the stone."

"Oh, you are quite ridiculous. This is not a movie where we follow a script, and what you demand I must do as it says in the script. Should we have a shoot out? Right here in front of these wonderful people and loyal soldiers?"

"Sorry for the regular folks, but loyal soldiers? To your ideal of leadership? People everywhere just want to be free"

"Oh, please spare me your time worn clichés learned at your mother's knee." He smirked at me with his chin lifted up in a condescending manner, while blinking his good eye.

"Look down your nose all you want. What is left of it, anyway."

"Oh, aren't we clever. Now we resort to physical insults, like schoolboys on the playground. I have had plenty of your type. Catcalling, insulting, bullying, aggressive idiots. I was always smarter than the entire lot.

"But then, that didn't really matter did it? I was smaller, they certainly considered me more fragile, so I was an easy target."

Bruno was starting to make me a bit more nervous than I already was, as he became more demonstrative in his memory dump into the situation.

"How I would love to meet those lads again, with the power I have now."

"Hey, growing up is all about besting the bullies along the way it seems." I was almost philosophical sounding.

"Hmmmmm…" Bruno gazed out the window and into the past for a moment. "I fell in love one day"

OK, that threw me a loop. The best I could do was to go along. He was obviously nuts at this point.

"I had seen her on an outing with my father in a park. Some boys from the school saw me talking to her. I was ten and showing her how I could hang upside down in a tree. Those boys came along. They laughed and jeered at me as I was hanging."

I stayed silent, waiting to see where this was going to go.

"They yanked me out of the tree. They insulted me. I called a challenge to the lead boy, while another came behind me and pulled my pants down in front of the girl. Everyone laughed"

"I thought your father was there." I played along as our waiter delivered our drinks and I tried to think of a way to end this as best I could.

"OF COURSE!" Bruno shouted, then smiled and composed himself, turning his head towards me. "He laughed the loudest."

"So you had a tough childhood, so what, a lot of us have. All I am concerned about is that stone. I suppose you are going to contribute it to the great occultists in the glorious Third Reich to handle."

He smiled and gave a small laugh. "You certainly don't understand my mission. When I mean 'my mission,' I mean for me and no one else."

I must have looked confused.

"Have you ever collected anything?"

"Paychecks and dames."

"I am afraid you still don't understand. My father was a serious collector. I am a serious collector because I want to make the memory of my father proud. Serious collectors will stop at nothing to possess what they want. Nothing. Rarity only reinforces our desire. We don't try to make sense of what we do. Collectors acquire art only to hide it, they collect coins but don't spend them, they collect stamps but not use them. Ask anyone who collects great works of art or antiquities why they do it. There is only one answer."

"Alright then, what is it you plan on doing with this?"

"I plan on possessing it. That is all the reason I need."

I didn't expect to reason with this Nazi goofball, don't know why I thought I ever could. Some people gave a loud shout of astonishment at some falling ice from the mountain into the canyon rifts, causing me to turn my head for a second and that was all it took.

Bruno's smile turned grim quickly as he suddenly stood with his hand inside his jacket. I rose slowly, keeping my aim true as well from inside my pants. We stood and faced each other now, ignoring the continued sounds of amazement from the other passengers at the melting mountainsides.

A slow dance began to evolve as the we faced each other, Bruno moving left, me moving right. Neither of us dared take a shot for obvious reasons.

Bruno smiled to me as he would an old friend. "We will act as best of friends enjoying a drink together on the observation platform."

"A little cold there, isn't it? What is your point? Gonna make a leap for it? You won't make it."

"To tell you the truth, I am about to meet someone."

"The only one you're going to meet is the guy that hands out wings and halos if I get a chance."

"I am going to meet a man in a flying vehicle."

"A plane through these mountains with all their curves?"

"It will be in a new German bit of airborne technology called a helicopter. A Focke-Wulfe Fw 61 to be exact, ironically and partially developed by my family's company."

"I have heard of those contraptions. Not quite workable yet."

"This one is."

I wasn't quite sure to believe this clown or not. He was nuts, but he had the power to make being nuts OK.

We formed a sort of standoff and slowly went to the door that opened onto the observation platform.

A cold blast of wind and noise greeted us as we made our way outside, with a slamming of the door. With the way we were staring at each other so intently, it must have looked like we were queer lovers looking for some privacy. I noticed from my periphery vision that a couple of heads turned towards us then quickly turned away in disgust.

Once outside we could openly talk, although it was closer to yelling, what with the wind and noise. We both moved closer together in order to carry on conversation, and to make sure we both had a bead on each other.

"I know you and that Tika want the stone, but you shan't have it. Neither will the others."

"Others?" I knew there had to be others. This stone was at the center of a very large, very secret and influential organization, from savages living in trees to the mighty industrial barons of Europe, so there were plenty of "others".

"There are two in particular," Bruno smiled all-knowingly. "I have been given information about you from persons already familiar."

I was beginning to feel a bit helpless. I also heard an odd sound over the noise of the train.

"Here he comes," Bruno said as I reluctantly joined him in looking at the source of the discordant sound. It was indeed an odd looking contraption, like a big dragonfly made out of paper mache. Flimsy covering, three gigantic blades the length of the craft supporting the whole flimsy affair at a definite angle. The damn thing was flying, moving up and down in a way that no regular aircraft could move. Heading toward us quite rapidly in comparison to the speed of the train.

"Before I leave you I must deliver one last caveat." Bruno almost laughed as he delivered this line. "You and I have been working for the same master. I have been receiving assistance from a certain Colonel, same as you."

I was glad I had been drinking quite a bit, otherwise my knees would have given way. At present they only wobbled.

"You seem so surprised. The Colonel and my father were great friends, both sharing a great competition for collecting rare items. When my father died, the Colonel and I would still correspond occasionally. When I was assigned to the detail of going after the stone by the High Command, I let the Colonel know. He happily convinced me of the power and rarity of this stone, and offered to finance me to retrieve it for him. I took advantage of his generous offer. I forsook my duty to the Reich."

"All for the Colonel."

"Nein. All for me."

The flying contraption was gaining on the train, and I was gaining the knowledge that I had been had. "It looks like the Colonel was playing us both against the middle."

"That is what he thought. I was only playing for me." His smile became more twisted.

A sudden roar of the approaching helicopter and it suddenly rose up and away, giving us both a start. Bruno lost his cap to the sharp winds, showing his brutally pockmarked and scarred head, probably from the terrible bashing he received under the plane when we all flew over the jungle.

Then everything turned black as the train lurched to the left. Enveloped in darkness, the grinding noise of the train's wheels and metal frame became almost overwhelming. A shot rang out, I fired back and grappled Bruno. We wrestled, trying to keep hold of our guns, and not slipping off of the platform. Then with a flash we were in daylight again.

We had just gone through a tunnel.

Still wrestling, my hand on Bruno's throat this time, my other hand gripping the wrist that held his luger, we struggled to disarm each other, his shot fired in the dark had missed me, but mine had struck his left leg, now bleeding quite a bit in those few seconds.

As we strained against each other in a constant lock, his wounded leg started to slowly give out, and he gradually lost part of his balance, slipping to the deck of the platform. I heard the sound of the return of the helicopter and I raised my head. It was very close now, having flown over the mountain ridge where the tunnel was carved through the rock. The mechanical beast had descended again and was now hovering twenty feet above the platform.

This moment's distraction brought Bruno's knee from his good leg into my lower groin, causing me to lose hold, but at the same time causing him to lose his luger, only to have it go clattering on the rocks by the side of the tracks. I lay in an agonizing fetal position, trying to adjust my personality, while he grabbed the metal ladder on the corner of the car that led to the roof and ascended quite rapidly.

After a few seconds, I was able to stand. Drunk and pissed off by this point, I didn't care what happened to me, I was going to get him. I clambered onto the roof and got a face full of arctic air and sun. This only made me angrier.

Bruno stood awkwardly on the roof of the car, arms outstretched like a messiah on a cross as something strange dropped from the sky. It was waving back and forth and Bruno smiled. It was a rope ladder to heaven and the helicopter. I made a lunge the few feet towards him, and with a swift kick to my face, Bruno happily grabbed onto the ladder with both hands and began to climb.

I struggled to stand and tried to reach him, but I slipped and dropped my gun and ended up eating the metal railing on the car's rooftop platform, giving my hip a good crack.

Running on alcohol as my power source, I pushed up with one leg and reaching up, managed a hand grip on the rope ladder as it constantly moved up and down. Drunk, dizzy, but damned determined, I felt the scene turn black and white, and suddenly I was in Chapter Six of Nazis on Dress Parade. I knew what I had to do, having worked it all out in rehearsal on the set months ago. Damned stunt directors knew their stuff. Or so I thought.

Grabbing a solid hold of the rope ladder, I went up after Bruno, who was three feet ahead of me. The blood from his bleeding leg was causing him to slip slightly and was spraying me crimson. The helicopter veered up, then down suddenly, as the mountain drafts switched their directions. I felt like a mouse tied to the tail of a kite on a windy day.

The cold blast of Alpine air was relentlessly hitting my face as the helicopter moved upward and over the train. No longer blocked by the train itself, the freezing wind blasted me awake, still drunk, but now everything was all in color. Bruno moved higher towards the waiting copter.

Amazingly, I could still use the moves I had been trained in, though I felt the snot, slobber and tears on my face begin to freeze as I faced towards the sun and the rushing wind. The copter and the train moved northward almost in unison. On the right, mountain crags of melting ice and snow, and on the left the blinding sun from the West showed no mercy.

I was gaining on Bruno as he wiggled the rope ladder to try to lose me. My arms ached as I inched closer to his feet. He deliberately stepped on my hand, crushing my finger and causing me to give way. I instinctively locked my legs around a rung on the rope ladder. I dangled below him, flipping about upside down in the air, but that was no matter, I had enough booze in me at this point to do what I would never have thought of otherwise.

I was proud of my prowess as I hooked my hand up over to the rung that my legs had grasped. I became stuck. I needed an extra push to lift myself up to the next level to grab Bruno. The copter gave me that push.

A turn of the train and a sudden veering of the aircraft caused it to descend, giving me the impetus to reach and finally grab Bruno's pant leg. The shift in weight made the copter swerve to the left unexpectedly creating a whiplash effect on the rope ladder. I held tight but unfortunately swung my feet free from the rope ladder. Still holding Bruno's pant leg with both hands, the copter then came down far enough for me put my now running feet on top of the train for a second, allowing me to jump higher up and again lock my legs in the rungs. I wasn't going anywhere now, or so I thought.

Another swift kick to my face made me appreciate the fine workmanship of Nazi boots. I broke free of my hand grip and dangled upside down again. Good thing my legs were still locked. Pain in my head, no vision except for the usual five pointed stars and little Saturns revolving around my head, mixed with the suddenly deafening sound of the train combined with the copter. At least I didn't feel the biting wind for a few seconds.

Bruno had climbed higher and was now snaking his way farther up the ladder. My snotcicles were running red with warm blood from a smashed nose, my head starting feel puffed. Pain made me stronger, and soon I resumed my hold on his pantleg much better with both hands this time. The copter tried to pull away now, but was hindered by the extra weight, plus the fact he was a pilot trying to operate a rather untested vehicle against the sharp drafts of the Alps.

The copter was attempting to remain at a steady clip so Bruno could climb aboard in comparative ease, but that was not to be. I had worked upward a bit and I now secured both hands on Bruno's trousers as he attempted to climb. I saw him try to prevent his slipping from my extra weight by securely twisting part of the rope ladder around his left wrist.

The copter hit an air pocket as if the massive mountains inhaled and blew out again. The copter was forced down and then up quickly against its will, causing the rope ladder to suddenly tighten. I was lucky enough to unlock my legs and slide out of the rope before the big tight yanking of the rope came. Bruno wasn't. The sudden down and upward movement trapped his hand in a loop, and the knotted rope cut into flesh and bone in a second of crushing fastidiousness.

Sharp sound of a scream, like a small boy, as I knew his wrist was crushed and broken. We all turned a ridge into the blazing sun. Bruno was stunned, stayed still while he tried to assess the pain enough to move upwards, so close to his goal. This was the point where I was able to climb high enough towards him to finally grab the opening of his pants pocket, and using that leverage quickly grab the back of his belt, then the top of the back of his pants.

His useless left wrist was the main concern of his. He tried to move his legs to continue the now ten foot climb to comfort, crying all the while in a high hurt strange mumbling whine.

Looking up, finally satisfied with both my hands now on the back of his pants, I saw the pilot frantically trying to maneuver the copter while aiming a pistol at me. We were now flitting all over the place, riding air currents, ups and downs, avoiding collisions with mountainsides.

He fired. He missed. He shot again. He hit. Not me. He creased the back of Bruno's head, creating a pink rip, that slowly swelled with blood.

Bruno was stunned and cried again in a high child-like voice.

The pilot couldn't bother to try to shoot anymore, he had larger duties. The copter was starting to lose its balance against the alpine winds. A quick forward lean of the copter brought it to about midrange of the train and the swinging ladder towards a craggy output.

I had time to brace my legs against the hit of the crag, but Bruno was too enveloped in his own misery and pain. We swung against the rocky mountainside and I relaxed my legs then pushed away as I hit the crag, the same as a swimmer turns against a wall, springing and pushing away just after point of contact. Bruno didn't fare so well, bashing the back of his injured head directly in the crag's sharp rocky point. From what I could observe, the back of his skull was now open and exposed a dark pink portion of his bleeding brain. His body was now completely held fast twisted up in the rope ladder.

I heard a loud snap of a belt, and noticed a loosening of my locked hands on the back of Bruno's pants. I carefully but quickly moved my handgrip on his pants to a wider angle on the side of his hips. I was beginning to slowly lower down anyway.

As we continued our erratic meandering against the hard bright mountains, I noticed I was slowly pulling Bruno's pants down, revealing his neatly pressed military green buttoned Nazi boxers. I had to tighten my own leg's grip against the waving of the ladder as I realized I had just pantsed Bruno in the same humiliating fashion he had endured when he was a youth. I could have sworn that his pasty legs under his mooning military boxers became even whiter against the frosty air.

Our transport through frosty freeze land became more delirious when the copter hit an unexpected bit of snow and rock falling from the upper alps down upon the train and us as well. We were still above the train when the copter made a wild move to the left to avoid a rather large rock tumbling towards us. The copter didn't make it.

Bruno's legs flew free of the rope ladder, with my grip on his pants, which were now shredded and ripped apart in my hands from the centrifugal force of the copter's tug.

A crash against the rotor blades finished the flight. I was forced to let go of the rope from the impact of the boulder hitting the blades of the copter, but not the shred of Bruno's pants. Luckily I fell only several feet and managed to end up on top of the forward part of the train's second car roof.

As I was gasping for breath, laying on top of the car, holding a major part of Bruno's pants in my grasp, I saw the copter, now out of control, heading on a collision course with the train. I almost felt sorry as I watched Bruno, broken and bleeding, what was left of his pants draped down around his ankles, screaming in a little girl's voice "Mein Papa, mein Papa!"

I didn't feel sorry for long, as a smile crossed my lips when the copter swerved and dashed against the rocky hillside, burst into flames, and took Bruno, crying for daddy, naked and abused down to the depths of a bottomless alpine pit.

I continued to try to get my breath and felt my sweat starting to freeze. Slowly, carefully, but doggedly, I made my way to the coupling between the second and third car of the train as it passed through another tunnel, giving me a share of darkness in order to slip between the cars and make my way to the latrine in the third car towards Tika.

Once inside, I washed my face and looked in the mirror. What it showed me was a man who had been in a serious fight. Dirty with bruises making their dark mark, and my clothes ripped and soiled I washed up gingerly as best I could. I stared for a second at Bruno's shredded pants.

I rifled through what was left. What I found gave me a thankful smile, and made me not mind my aching body. Inside the front pocket was his wallet, some folded papers and a pouch containing a hard object. Opening the fur lined pouch, the greenstone revealed itself to me.

Replacing the stone in its pouch, I stuck it in my own pants' left front pocket. I slowly pulled out the other object I had almost forgotten that was there as well. I pulled it out and looked at it. A bit banged up itself, but nevertheless having its hold on me was the chess piece, the white knight. I placed it back in my pocket and made my way out of the latrine and back to the car where I had left Tika. As disheveled as I was, no one seemed to notice or care, with the car all a-twitter in conversation and noses pressed to windows. Between the falling kaleidoscopic colors of snow and rock tumbling from the upper regions of the mountains and the disastrous spectacle of a mad helicopter with a human dope on a rope crashing into glorious fire before descending out of sight, I might as well have been invisible.

I spied Tika sitting alone and watching the view. I had to stop for a second and think about what to tell her. Should I tell her I finally recovered her stone? If I did so, she might revert back to her priestess role and I would have a strong chance of losing her again to the power of the stone.

I sat down next to her and gave her a bit of a start as she faced me. "Sorry, darling," I said.

She gazed sweetly at me. "Oh dear, you have been hurt." She took out a small cloth from the seat pocket and started to clean me up a bit.

"Did you see anything?" I asked.

"Very little. The mountains blocked most of what happened."

I was glad of that.

"Anything, anything at all on where the greenstone could be?"

She asked this with such wonder and longing in her eyes that I had to swallow before answering.

"No. the stone is gone and has died with Bruno." Her eyes welled to tears and her face turned red as she assumed a child like fetal position in her seat. She believed me. She knows I would never lie to her.

CHAPTER 36--DEATH SHIP

We waited until the train was getting ready to pull in the station before deciding that we should jump. The conductor had let it slip that the station had been alerted that there was some disturbance on the train and that police would be waiting. We went between cars and stood there holding hands, finally managing to escape by bailing out onto a snow bank and rolling out of sight as the train decreased its speed on a narrow bend in the mountains near a small village.

After realizing that we made it safely, we had a good giggle and held on tightly to each other for a minute. We walked to the village inn, and we were able to hire a driver to take us to a tourist lodge by the Swiss border where I was able to wire from the local telegraph office and obtain money from the Colonel's Swiss bank account. Tika stepped over to the café to get us a couple of warm coffees. While she did that I also wired the Colonel that I had his object and needed to get to Lisbon in Portugal so I could catch a ship home. Luckily Tika was next door in the café waiting for me and didn't know the contents of my wire.

I retired next door to join Tika. I felt bad for lying to her about the stone, but then I also knew that this was the way it had to be if I was going to keep her with me. Once I got the stone to the Colonel, she and I could do what we wanted together.

I entered the café and returned her sweet smile. As I sat down I made a sudden grimace.

She looked concerned and asked "You alright?"

"Just another flare up of my old back injury from years ago. I guess with all this jumping and banging around, it is letting me know how it doesn't approve."

We both smiled at each other. The coffee was good, warming, and melted the snowflakes out of my head. I was thinking clearly, and planning for the future.

After about an hour of coffee and pastries, I wandered back to the telegraph counter alone. Waiting for me was the answer I needed. A payment with a message. The Colonel told me this was his final payment, generous, with more when I arrive at his home. I smiled again, noticing that this must be my record for smiling in one day.

When I told Tika my plans she melted into my arms, making my neck and shoulder soggy with her tears of happiness. We were to travel to Lisbon to meet Akbar if we can, then sail for the states and whatever awaited us there.

Our travels went easily enough, almost too easily. Maybe I was just getting paranoid after all that had happened. Maybe I should just learn that sometimes things actually do go easy. Maybe.

We hit our connections right and got into Lisbon. The final train dropped us off near the main pier, where a large sea liner waited. I once again left Tika at an outside café on the corner of a busy sun filled street to go secure our tickets at the Pan-American offices pier side. Refugees from all over Europe crowded the offices, babbling away in a variety of tongues. While I couldn't understand them, their meaning was clear. I wondered how the poor besieged ticket masters could take it. It almost seemed as if half of Europe wanted to get out while they could.

After an untold amount of time, I appeared before a rather young fellow, looking a little worse for wear, but actually very kind and understanding. My hands trembled as I was handed the tickets. The states and home.

I must have skipped out, fairly knocking people over as I left the place and bounced my way to where I had left Tika. She was still sitting there, but was now talking to a rather robust animated person of questionable heritage, dressed in fine European style except for a white towel wrapped and secured over his head, standing in front of her and rambling in a loud voice.

He must have sensed me approaching, for he turned towards me as I did.

I saw the big, broad, wide hook nosed face of Akbar Fatui, grinning wide enough for me to distinguish bits of tobacco between his teeth.

"Amazing to see you, my honored and noble friend!' He shouted in his enthusiasm. I must say, I was surprised to see that he had made his promise good about our meeting.

"How did you manage to arrange this? You do have some incredible timing." I told him this while vigorously shaking his hand. We pulled a couple of chairs to the table with Tika and we all sat down as the hostess brought our steaming cups of coffee.

Akbar began to explain in his usual excited loud voice how he had worked as a magician at a small theater that was, of course, not up to his expectations, but it was enough to provide him with certain connections for him to get all the arrangements for the trip to the states set up. Though all was arranged, it was not quite honestly done. He felt he had to pull "one more feat of miracleness" on the personage of someone of the ruling class and was escorted off to jail for a month.

"But now all is happy as we are able to meet as we planned."

"I really didn't expect to see you again. We said we would meet here in Lisbon at the port, but how could you know what day or time?" I had to ask.

"I am truly a magician. I also have much family that lets me know where you might be along the journey you have taken. I knew where you were going of course, I knew with those special papers you had, that you should be showing up around this date. Once you arrived, I was given word that I would be able to meet you here at the pier."

I started to respond but he interrupted in a plaintive voice. "Oh, how I wish I could join you now. The three of us traveling as adventurers going to the most glorious exalted of land, that of Hollywood!"

"Yea, it is sure exalted alright, if you like cardboard and glitter." He ignored or didn't hear me. "So what is stopping you from joining us?"

"I have more time in wonderful prison where I am to spend my time for cleverness. You see the rather disquieting gentleman by the gate?" I turned my head to see something that looked like a local cop. He waved towards us. "He is graciously taking me away, but gave me this moment with you."

"Look, no worries, contact me in America when you get out. I will do what I can to get you out of here and over to Hollywood."

I swear a tear welled up in his eye as he stood. "You are of heaven's generosity. I shall leave you with one joke I have perfected. Why does a fireman wear red suspenders?"

We all paused for a quarter second.

"To get to the other side! Now I must go with one last kiss and hug!" We both stood, Tika and me, and group hugged while Akbar planted juicy fowl tobacco flavored kisses on our cheeks. "Goodbye my friends!" He walked over to where the waiting cop was, and graciously walked away, interlocked with the cop's cuffs.

A loud blow of the ship's whistle grabbed our attention and we focused on getting to the ship. Already having gotten our way through the boarding process, it was easy for us to make our way up the plank.

All still went as expected. We made our way to a small but efficient stateroom, clean, bright, a small dagger of sun streaming its way through the porthole, giving a cheery glee of the whole room. After putting away our meager belongings, I opened a bottle of port and some small chocolate pastries I had secured earlier, and Tika and I settled in to look forward to a romantic voyage on our way to New York.

After the barrage of annoying ship's announcements and whistle blowing, things calmed down after about an hour out to sea. The ship was giving a gentle rocking back and forth, and the effects of the bottle of shared port mixed with the smoke from a couple of Luckies played with our senses. The light in our room grew less as the sun told us she was getting ready to go to sleep under the sea. We lay together in the bunk, enjoying this moment of peace and togetherness and solitude. We said nothing. We didn't need to. We slept.

The room was filled with orange when I woke up, not sure of the time, if it was day or night, or where I was. A small moan beside me returned my memory. Tika. Lovely Tika. I have her now. The orange glow of the last departing rays of the sun only accented her beauty. I must have stared at her for ten minutes before I made up my mind.

I smiled a bit at my own lunacy. I needed another cigarette for this. I guess I must be nuts. I wanted to go to the ship's captain and ask him to perform ceremony, a most life changing ceremony.

I knew there would be a tip involved, so I slithered out of our bunk as the cabin's light dimmed. I searched my jacket pocket, found some cash, putting it in my pocket along with the dingy dirty chess piece and that damned greenstone that had caused all this trouble.

On my way to search out the captain, I strolled along one of the starboard outer decks. I passed the observation lounge, with merriment frothing within, sounding like the waves rhythmically beating the side of the ship, though soon the babbling and loud laughter from the lounge drowned all else out as I approached.

I stopped to scratch my chin. This is a big decision after all. I turned and went in the lounge. I needed to lubricate my brain so my thoughts would come together quicker. Four bourbons, a couple of Luckies later, and a good stare down at the oaken bar in front of me, and I was ready.

I was able to track down the location of Captain Carnecarocao in the officers lounge. He was a big portly fellow, broad but tall, with a scruffy goatee, and a deep loud explosive laugh. He sat at a table near the back of the bar, drinking from a bottle of what looked whiskey or rye, and was regaling anyone in earshot in somewhat fractured English about travels in his wild youth. I stood towards the side of the bar and listened politely while he happily sung about his adventures with women that had ebony skin and snapping black eyes, run-ins with a high hat beaver moustache man and his pirate friend, and he surely would have gone on if my patience hadn't started to run out. I stumbled over to his table and sat down. He eyed me warily at first, then chuckled as I introduced myself. I told him my plan that made him grin even more so. He asked me in his mild Portuguese accent if I knew what the hell I was doing, and shouldn't I take a cold shower first and rethink this just to be sure?

"Nope, thish ish it," I clumsily replied, a slight bit of drool escaping the side of my mouth..

He lowered his voice and grabbed me by the arm. "Alright son, if you insist. If you want to stay in that barrel for the rest of your life that is your decision."

I wasn't quite sure what he meant by that, but I was happy anyway. I thanked him, stood up warily and awkwardly, and started back to the civilian lounge to celebrate, but was grabbed by a couple of officers on my way out that were standing at the bar.

"Perdon, we shall toast to your announcement," one told me. Of course I joined them.

Suddenly a sailor rushed in, leaned over to the captain, offering him a word. The captain looked wide eyed and startled, stood up clumsily and stormed out.

Before the sailor could leave, the officer on my left grabbed ahold him and asked "Que tal?" the sailor looked confused and a bit scared. "The Nazis have a U-boat in this area. We must run in darkness tonight."

The officer smiled, "Run as a ghost ship with all lights out? Fine, we have done that before. What else was told the captain?" the officer increased his grip on the seaman.

"There is a very good chance we hit a severe thunderstorm. The clouds and wind are gathering now. That means much lightning, exposing us and our position to attack."

The poor sailor looked thirsty, so the officers with me shared a shot with him, and not just to calm his nerves, but ours as well.

After another one or three I excused myself gratefully to the friendly crew and headed out to the main deck. It was getting dark as I returned outside and the wind was definitely picking up. High intensity flashes almost concealed by the roiling clouds muffled the sound of thunder while the breaking of the waves clapped against the side of the ship.

I descended back inside as the captain made the announcement in several languages for a shipwide blackout. The overhead lights went out in the passageways and every ten feet dull yellowish lights close to the deck slowly flicked on. Not too concerned, I wobbled my way to my stateroom, not sure if my wobble was from the booze or the rising and tossing of the ship. I realized that if I skipped, I could gain my bearings better. So that is what I did, skipping to the delight of those that saw me, including one guy that tried wink at me.

Once in my familiar passageway, I turned a corner and banged into the cleaning cart belonging to one of the housekeeping crew that was outside the open door to our room. She was a little dark woman clothed in a blue cleaning woman's outfit that stood in the open doorway. I said "Shcuse me," as I fairly burst through the open cabin door calling out "Tika, M'darling!" No answer. I looked at the empty bunk and all around. The room was neatly made up, but no sign of Tika. I cleverly deduced she was not there. Smiling to myself for being so smart, I wandered over to the small desk where a low level light was shining. There a was small piece of paper on the desk. I picked it up and read what she had written. "Gone topside for a stroll," I read aloud. "The little scamp!" I chuckled to myself and lit another Lucky from the pack on the desk, and puffed merrily.

Placing the Lucky firmly in one side of my yap, I tossed the paper in the waste basket and headed topside, again banging into the housekeeping cart on my way out. I was glad that the chambermaid had quickly left and was not there anymore to see me once again be a stupid buffoon as I gently bounced from bulkhead to bulkhead on my way to the upper hatch.

Topside, the open deck passageway was black as King Kong's armpit. Out on deck the ship was running without lights per the captain's orders. I stood for a moment to let my eyes adjust to the difference in what light there was. No moon was in the sky to help me see and no passengers were about for an evening stroll, and I don't blame them. The ship was now tossing about quite a bit, so much so, that where once I staggered, now I walked perfectly straight while the ship staggered. There was nothing to see in the darkness except my glowing butt of the Lucky that was becoming an ember. I saw no Tika. An occasional flash of light in the sky from a good sized lightning storm going on in the upper clouds gave an eerie otherworldly black and white look to my surroundings of secured deck chairs. Rain and flashing light gave the strange impression that I was in a grainy old silent film that was badly damaged, only the fifth film cell revealing the scratchy blurring lopsided scene in front of me tilting back and forth.

    Through the deafening sounds of the storm and wailing winds I heard a movement, a scuffle, a clanging of the deck chairs mixed with animal sounds that got my attention, causing me to run towards the dark conglomeration of noise. As I did, the wind suddenly shifted, and a near horizontal torrent of rain began smashing the deck as well as it did me. Thankfully I was boozed up enough to perform as a surfer on a wild ocean ride, staying level where others would have most likely slipped and been washed over the side.

    Strobe effects of the lightning storm flashed the image of Tika on the deck ahead of me struggling with the dark woman that had just been cleaning our stateroom. They were in what seemed a deadly struggle. I tossed aside my Lucky and yelled out for help as I leapt into the fray.

    My hands gripped Tika's attacker by the hair, who was by now on top of Tika gripping her throat in a vicelike hold as Tika lay helpless on her front, her face getting smashed in to the wood of the deck, arms helplessly flaying against the dark woman's ribs. I placed my knee against the attacker's spine and yanked her hair again with one hand while beating her head with my other, but I might as well have tried to seduce a jungle cat into submission. The dark woman's hold was a deathgrip, and Tika face down, was quickly suffocating.

Though I yelled for help, my voice was drowned out by the wind and excitement of the waves beating against the ship. With the fury and sound of the storm, I began to realize that no response might be had. Tika's screams were getting more distant, and I could tell she was going under from this woman's grip. I let go of the female hellion's hair and slipped my right hand underneath her throat to lock with my left arm up by my left shoulder. Placing my left hand behind the woman's head, I was able to lock her in my embrace, and continuing to use my left hand, pushed her head forward, effectively cutting off her windpipe and jugular. In a few seconds, she began to loosen her grip and pass out.

"What do you want? Why are you attacking her?" I screamed loosening my grip somewhat, but still holding her tight. The dark woman answered me in a throaty accented voice that was hard to understand at first.

"She was the queen, the holder of the greenstone, but now she has forgotten it and its powers, so she must die so others may protect its sacred gifts."

I looked at Tika, and she seemed so little and helpless against this woman's abnormally strong attack. Others appeared on deck, illuminated by lightning flashes and in the form of a couple of deckhands that struggled in the darkness to reach us, but between the storm and crashing waves sweeping across the deck keeping them off balance, nothing seemed to help.

I tightened my grip once more, shaking the woman, demanding she loosen her grip on Tika. The struggling deck hands were useless at this point, unable to reach us because of the tilting and diving of the ship and torrential hammering of the sea and waves sweeping across the deck. I was the one in control.

Tika was barely breathing and turning blue. She had stopped resisting. "What the hell must I do that will make you quit!" I demanded tearfully of her tormentor.

"I want the greenstone! It is not gone, it is near her right now! I can feel its power!"

A sudden lurch of the ship tossed all three of us sliding to the outer railing, thankfully where we got caught up in some tackle without plummeting over the edge. Tika, though not gripped as hard, seemed out of it, loose, unfeeling, unconcerned about breaking free. With the continuing flashes of light I could see her face turning blue in the black and white storm.

I did what I had to do. I still had the greenstone in my pocket next to the knight. I let my grip go and grabbed it without thought. I waved it in front of the attacker's face. "Is this it? Is this what you want? Take it then but let her go! Let her go NOW!" I yelled in the she-demon's ear.

The nasty drooling she-witch turned her hideous hair matted sea monkey face towards me just as a lightning flash burst. Her spittle dripped silver as she hissed "You have the stone? Now it shall be mine, and with it, I shall be the new queen!"

Tika seemed comatose as this new queen-bitch let go of her and grabbed the stone away from me just as the two deckhands finally made their way to her. In their effort, while they were able to finally grab the crazed wench that would be queen, she let out a yowl of victory equaling that of the roar of the storm itself, holding the stone aloft towards the heavens, clutching it greedily in her grasp, she cried out.

"I did it! The sacred stone is mine!" She seemed to glow in the triumph of this statement, holding it aloft in final glory, but taking just a little too long in victory.

Neptune claimed his own at that point. A huge wave descended upon the deck, sweeping clean. Tika and I were shoved violently against a rail, stopping our movement, while one of the deckhands held fast to his buddy that was slipping over the side. The crazed and supposed new queen didn't fare so luckily, laughing, shrieking, cackling loudly and holding the stone up high, she was violently washed by the pounding water over the side, her wild laughter drifting up and getting softer before finally disappearing into the roar of the sea and storm.

The two deckhands righted themselves and we all fought as best we could to get Tika safely inside the ship.

Once inside, we were quickly escorted to the sick bay. I went to Tika and held her gently as I could. It was there that once I was able to catch my breath and thank the two deckhands, that the medic informed me Tika was critical.

"What do you mean? OK, she might have taken a few bangs, but she has had worse."

"She seems to have been poisoned."

I froze in a quick moment of time as I held her in my arms as close as possible. "How?" was all I could get out.

The ship's doctor explained it to me, about how a little puncture wound hidden behind the scalp was the point of entry. This doctor was able to figure the method of poisoning better and quicker than those quacks in Mexico. The parallel to my son's death struck me like a blow to the gut. Tika had told me she was in danger, and I didn't take her seriously enough. Now she lay dying.

A mumble from Tika caught my attention. Her eyes streamed hate at me. Hate and betrayal as she weakly tried to push me away. "You lied to me when I trusted you the most," she whispered. That whisper could have been shouted from the mountains and it wouldn't have been louder than what she had just said to me. She muttered other utterings then stopped. She was gone.

I stared at the ceiling of our stateroom the rest of the night. The ship's tossing meant nothing. Eventually the cradling effect of the ship's movement let me slip into in to a bittersweet unconsciousness. My last words I spoke as I drifted that night were a slight remembrance of a bible verse I had once heard.

"Yea, though I walk through the valley of death, I fear nothing, because I am the dumbest son of a bitch in the valley."

CHAPTER 37--TRAIN TO NOWHERE

    Once the ship reached New York, I spent a rather grueling and humiliating time with the authorities. Captain Carnecorazon was quite forthcoming with his sympathies, and the two deckhands and ship's doctor were all generous with their time, enabling me to get through the ordeal much easier than it otherwise would have been. Then there was the matter of getting through the press.
    The press has always been a bunch of bloodsucking jerks and this time they continued to prove it. At least there were only a few of them to contend with. They reminded me of how long I had been gone, disappeared from public view. At one level I was sort of surprised anybody still cared. Their questions were brief, wanting to know how I felt being mixed up in some murder, and did it have anything to do with my lengthy departure from the movie business. I lied as I tried to fend them off by letting them know I had not contacted my studio yet, when one of the loudmouthed jackals rudely opened his trap to let me know I didn't have a studio anymore. I instinctively swung a punch and of course the others popped their bulbs for a grand shot,

even though I missed the sorry bastard by an inch. Great. At this point in what was left of a career, these idiots had turned into the vultures I always knew they were.

They quickly flew away, haven gotten their scoop of dirty meat from a dead star for the weekend edition.

I made my way into a cab and headed for Grand Central to catch the Santa Fe Super Chief to Los Angeles. While there was a bit of a wait, I used that sweet time to contact the studio myself to talk to them and let them know that I was back. Good luck. After getting through half a dozen gatekeepers I finally reached a voice that I didn't know, only to be informed that no one I knew from before was there anymore and that I was not to bother the studio again or harassment charges would be filed. If there were any questions, I should contact their lawyer division. A quick hang up from her side. So much for my contract.

I called the number for my house in the Hollywood Hills that had been purchased for me by the studio, knowing full well that it was probably gone. Instead of that sweet piece of pot sticker joy, Ha-Nee, I got the steady buzz and an operator kicking in with the suggestion that even though that was not a working number with no forwarding contact, was there someone else I wanted to contact. I did the hanging up this time.

OK, I tried to steady myself and lit the ongoing stream of Luckies from the pack in my pocket in the slightly stained and soiled suit jacket as desperation was starting to grab at me with its tentacles. I needed to call the Colonel anyway, so with the time I had, I did just that.

This went worse than I expected. "Hello?" Marian answered. I was caught off guard, but not entirely surprised, and in a strange odd way I was glad to hear her voice. Maybe she could give me some reassurance, though about what I couldn't place. Trying to jolly myself up to the occasion, I replied "Hi honey," with a bit of forced enthusiasm that seemed fairly obvious.

Before I could proceed she blurted "Is she really dead?" Her voice gave me chills like a blast of the last north wind in March. I hardened my attitude. "Yea."

My heart became numb in an instant. Fumbling, some mumbling in the background, and the Colonel grabbed the receiver with a curse towards anyone that might hear.

I didn't say much, in fact I didn't say anything beyond a grunt. He rambled angrily at me as I drifted into a haze of memory about these past several months, and all the clues I had been given about what really was going on right under my own dumb face.

He made a remark about how finding the greenstone was all important, that boy was a connection that had to be met, and what did I think he was really paying me for? Was I really that stupid. Well, I guess I was.

I managed to jump in when he took a breath "I thought you at least would like to know why the boy was killed," I told him. He raged back. "Of course I know why the hell the boy was killed. Because of that greenstone, you dolt! It was all part of the set up. I didn't give a damn about that sissy boy, I wanted that stone!"

Then a bit of obvious revelation

"That damned sweltering tub of guts Thickwilly, I almost had him!"

All part of the set up, the slimy bastards. I should have guessed. He continued to rage about his losses, condemning me, all I could do was think of mine. I hung up on him in mid rant.

The outside dimming light signaled the setting of the sun as I boarded the train like someone in a dream. I still had enough money I had gained from the Colonel to get me back to Los Angeles and that was it. What I did from there was up to me alone.

After checking into my cabin, trying to nap with only a thousand demons prodding me with their little pitchforks into a sea of eternal wakefulness, I finally quit trying to rest and just stared at the ceiling as evening brought darkness to my room. I slept, not knowing how long, only thinking it was very late. It was black inside the cabin when I finally got up. I opened the window shade, only to reveal passing bits of light from the outside, street lamps, occasional neon from small structures, window lamps from homes, all hiding their secrets, all the while giving me the twisted sensation of what it would be like on some starship, flying by moons, Saturns, and stars, losing myself far away from this world.

I flicked on a light and finally ended up staring at myself in the unforgiving mirror in my cabin for a timeless moment. I washed my face, cleaned up sparingly and headed aft. I had somehow skipped dinner but ended up at the bar in the observation car.

The bar was very dark, with lights down to almost nothingness due to the late hour. I placed myself at the bar, feeling the comfortable rumble and slight jostle of the train as it rounded the occasional bend.

"Yassuh?"

A voice out of the darkness of the car addressed itself to me. Behind the bar stood a large black man of the porter trade. He blended into the dark surroundings with only the whites of his eyes gleaming. He seemed very big, and had a black uniform on, the only standout was his name tag that was black on white printing that said "Rinso."

I guess I stalled for a second before he spoke once more.

"Yassuh? What bese yo delight dis ebenin' boss?" His bright toothy smile seemed as wide as the Mississippi. I couldn't help but smile back.

I guess I must have given one of those upside down smiles that gave my worries away.

"Ah knows," Rinso said. "Yes, Ah sho knows what you needs." He began to mix and shake a drink with a master chemist's precision. He poured it large and proudly in an icy cold martini glass.

"Now why don't you jus' tell ol'Rinso whus on yo mind? It is jus' us and it is a quarter to three, ain't no one hyea but you and me. Sounds like a song! Hyuck Hyuck Hyuck!" He couldn't help but make me smile as he tried to hide his guffawing at his own cleverness, blubbering his cheeks and snorting and snuffling at his own self.

He wiped his eyes with the bar rag after laughing so heartily. I glanced around the car and he was right. The only light was over the bar, the rest of the car was in dark quiet solitude, no one there except an obvious honeymoon couple grappling each other as if one of them had state secrets hidden in far places inside their clothing.

"Sure, Rinso, I have something to tell." I sat there while Rinso fed me a liquid dinner.

My mouth did the talking as I rambled, thinking, drinking, until I was stinking, the sucking of the never ending Luckies giving the place a hazy shade of a London fog at midnight.

Rinso seemed to genuinely feign interest as I gave him the Readers Digest condensed version of my most obvious travails.

I talked about the conspiracies that I knew nothing about. Rinso had no idea what the hell I was talking about, but he gave the true seasoned bartender's conversation of "Yuh," "Uh-Huh!", "Well, dat ain't right," without once trying to interject anything that could interrupt the flow of my confessional.

Around the sixth martini, the entire affair took on a Daliesque effect. As I stared into the icy cocktail glass, faces loomed, floating in and out, all wanting to argue with the image of the dancing greenstone, which had now resumed the countenance of the olive in my martini. Inside the olive, instead of a pimento was an eyeball, staring and flickering to the faces that bubbled up from the bottom of my glass.

The faces that bubbled up began to resemble jig saw puzzle pieces, slowly fitting together.

Bodiless puzzle images of everyone I had encountered shouted at the martini greenstone, the voice of Rinso occasionally speaking with a reassuring "Dey sho do," and setting me up with another gin fueled insight.

I felt like a twelve year kid in a confessional booth blurting out guilt about wanking off, and making the listening priest get hot. Rinso just exuded safe comfort and booze, refilling my glass when I wavered.

I was thinking loudly to myself, some things I might have said out loud, while other thoughts were internalized. I couldn't tell.

I talked about my new freshly baked conspiracy theories about the Colonel and Thickwilly, how they were only concerned about the greenstone, not love or life. As I talked I had more than one revelation, flashes of moments as I figured one thing out and ended up realizing another connection.

That slimy Colonel didn't even care about that supposed son of his. The Colonel and Bruno had a lot in common. They were the worst kind of sleaze. I had a hard time understanding that Marian would not care about her own son and would continue to slide under the covers with the Colonel every night.

As I yammered with the visual clarity of veins pumped with alcohol in my neck, I realized that I was a just a pawn for others' doings and others' ambitions. Lord Thickwilly had been in competition with the Colonel for the power of the stone from the beginning. It was all part of this obsession for the extended life that was a gift from the sky, only to be given to such a guarded few.

I had originally thought Bruno's want of the stone was to secure his place in his father's dead eyes as a supposedly good son, but now it seemed that Bruno's father was just another collector of this valuable commodity, and possibly in competition with the Colonel and Thickwilly. I remembered that the Colonel had old ties with Bruno's father. Bruno had spilled some clues as to why the stone needed to be with him and his family alone, though Bruno had seemed to have been originally part of the Nazi crew to steal it for Hitler. Bruno's father must have had ties with Hitler himself through the family's military purchasing.

This patchwork grew more complex as I wove it. I grew more blue as I realized what I had lost.

I had my thoughts in a whirlpool. I sank slightly in my barstool looking around the car and noticing the honeymooners were gone. "Gimmee anudder." At least when I bury myself in booze, I don't have to feel the pain just then. I can kick that hurt on down the road until another day.

The darkness was now all encompassing around me like a blanket, except for the light from the bar accompanied by the Cheshire cat brilliance of Rinso's smile, flicked with the reflection of a gold tooth from his satchel mouth.

I thought of Tika. Her death made me tired, so tired the marrow in my bones hurt. I wanted to collapse in a jelly fish puddle of self pity.

The doctor had said she died from poison introduced by two slight puncture wounds in her scalp. Just like my son. The revenge of the cult had struck. I couldn't count the times Tika had said she would be killed if she didn't recover the stone in time.

I had lied to her. I guess I hadn't really realized that her superstition might have some truth to it.

Akbar. He must have been behind Tika's attack somehow. He always bragged about his many cousins that all seemed to work in the housekeeping business. The banshee that attacked Tika was a housemaid, could have been one of Akbar's supposed cousins. Maybe Akbar was a cult unto himself. I didn't know at this point. I felt as a lost child in the wilderness.

The darkness of the car was a cocoon, only I was not going to emerge as something greater. I gave myself a self congratulatorily chuckle for nothing in particular.

The booze had silenced me for once. Rinso just ignored me with great courtesy.

I took a drink for everyone I cared for and a drink for those who were still alive and cared for me. The odds weren't good for me. So I took another drink for me from me. Not because I especially liked me, but because that was supposed to be who I was. So, I looked in the mirror behind the bar and let Dick Hardwing of the Jungle Patrol buy me my final drink for the evening. As I reached in my pocket for the money to pay for the drinks, my hand fell across Harry's knight.

I got up, handed the barkeep a large tip
"But sir, is you sho, dis be quite a lot."
"Keep it. It's done its job."
I slugged back my last drink.
I pulled the dirty and banged knight from my pocket. I left the knight on the bar with the tip.
Goodnight, Dick Hardwing.

Made in the USA
Middletown, DE
08 May 2021